TILL SHILOH
COMES

BOOKS BY GILBERT MORRIS

THE HOUSE OF WINSLOW SERIES

1. *The Honorable Imposter*
2. *The Captive Bride*
3. *The Indentured Heart*
4. *The Gentle Rebel*
5. *The Saintly Buccaneer*
6. *The Holy Warrior*
7. *The Reluctant Bridegroom*
8. *The Last Confederate*
9. *The Dixie Widow*
10. *The Wounded Yankee*
11. *The Union Belle*
12. *The Final Adversary*
13. *The Crossed Sabres*
14. *The Valiant Gunman*
15. *The Gallant Outlaw*
16. *The Jeweled Spur*
17. *The Yukon Queen*
18. *The Rough Rider*
19. *The Iron Lady*
20. *The Silver Star*
21. *The Shadow Portrait*
22. *The White Hunter*
23. *The Flying Cavalier*
24. *The Glorious Prodigal*
25. *The Amazon Quest*
26. *The Golden Angel*
27. *The Heavenly Fugitive*
28. *The Fiery Ring*
29. *The Pilgrim Song*
30. *The Beloved Enemy*
31. *The Shining Badge*
32. *The Royal Handmaid*
33. *The Silent Harp*
34. *The Virtuous Woman*

CHENEY DUVALL, M.D.[1]

1. *The Stars for a Light*
2. *Shadow of the Mountains*
3. *A City Not Forsaken*
4. *Toward the Sunrising*
5. *Secret Place of Thunder*
6. *In the Twilight, in the Evening*
7. *Island of the Innocent*
8. *Driven With the Wind*

CHENEY AND SHILOH: THE INHERITANCE[1]

1. *Where Two Seas Met*
2. *The Moon by Night*

THE SPIRIT OF APPALACHIA[2]

1. *Over the Misty Mountains*
2. *Beyond the Quiet Hills*
3. *Among the King's Soldiers*
4. *Beneath the Mockingbird's Wings*
5. *Around the River's Bend*

LIONS OF JUDAH

1. *Heart of a Lion*
2. *No Woman So Fair*
3. *The Gate of Heaven*
4. *Till Shiloh Comes*

[1]with Lynn Morris   [2]with Aaron McCarver

GILBERT MORRIS

LIONS OF JUDAH

TILL SHILOH COMES

BETHANYHOUSE
MINNEAPOLIS, MINNESOTA

Published by Bethany House Publishers
11400 Hampshire Avenue South
Bloomington, Minnesota 55438

Bethany House Publishers is a division of
Baker Publishing Group, Grand Rapids, Michigan.

Printed in the United States of America

Library of Congress Cataloging-in-Publication Data

Morris, Gilbert.
    Till Shiloh comes / by Gilbert Morris.
        p.   cm. —(Lions of Judah ; bk. 4)
    ISBN 0-7642-2919-2 (pbk.)
    1. Joseph (Son of Jacob)—Fiction. 2. Jacob (Biblical patriarch)—Fiction. 3. Bible. O.T.
Genesis—History of Biblical events—Fiction. I. Title II. Series: Morris, Gilbert. Lions of Judah ;
bk. 4.
    PS3563.O8742T53   2005
    813'.54—dc22   2004020610

To Alan and Dixie
You two are gifts from God to us—
both miracles of God's grace!

GILBERT MORRIS spent ten years as a pastor before becoming Professor of English at Ouachita Baptist University in Arkansas and earning a Ph.D. at the University of Arkansas. During the summers of 1984 and 1985, he did postgraduate work at the University of London. A prolific writer, he has had over 25 scholarly articles and 200 poems published in various periodicals, and over the past years he has had more than 180 books published. His family includes three grown children, and he and his wife live in Alabama.

PART ONE

THE PIT

CHAPTER

I

On a flat grassy slope in the midst of blue haze-covered mountains, a woman held a crying baby as she watched over a herd of goats. A little girl skipped alongside her, picking the crimson and white wild flowers that dotted the hillside. Colorful tents lay scattered on the hillside below them, adding splashes of cinnamon, light green, and bright yellow to the surroundings. In front of one of the tents, another woman steadily rocked a leather bag set in a wooden tripod, churning milk into butter. The tent flap was open behind her, revealing three men seated on a carpet, intently discussing a matter of importance to the tribe of Jacob, son of Isaac, grandson of Abraham.

While they talked, the men watched an older girl amble freely through a flock of sheep, singing and calling the animals by name. She was the subject of their conversation, for at fourteen, Abigail was being considered as a wife by the men of Jacob's tribe. She was tall, strong, and graceful, with long black hair that gleamed in the sunlight. Her beautiful dark eyes had caught the attention of many of the young Hebrew men.

Now Abigail's eyes sparkled and danced as she spotted a young man who was leaning on his staff in the midst of some woolly sheep. She grinned as an idea occurred to her. Moving stealthily across the open space so as not to make a sound, she came up behind him and tickled his ribs with her strong fingers.

The young man yelled and dropped his staff, then whirled around with a scowl. "Abigail! I've *told* you not to do that! It's unseemly behavior for a girl."

"Why, Joseph, if I didn't know better, I would think you were afraid of me." She smiled up at him coyly.

The second youngest son of Jacob was three years older than Abigail and a head taller. He was not yet filled out with a man's body, and his skin was as smooth as a girl's, but he had rugged good looks, large expressive eyes, and hair as black as Abigail's.

"I'm only afraid of bears and lions."

With a flirtatious gaze, Abigail touched his chest with her hand and leaned closer. "I know you're not afraid of bears, but I do think you're afraid of girls. You never chase after any that I can see."

Joseph's dark eyes turned warm as he laughed and caught her hand. "Girls are much more dangerous than bears."

"How can you say such a thing!"

"Because it's true. Think about poor Lomeer. He killed a bear last year with nothing but a spear, but then got mixed up with that awful Hittite girl—and now he's the most miserable man in the world!"

"That was his own fault. He didn't have any business marrying a Hittite woman." Abigail freed her hand from his grasp and stepped back a little.

Joseph winked. "Oh, I think all girls are pretty much alike whether they're Hebrew or Hittite."

Abigail flushed. "What an awful thing to say! I'm going to tell your father on you."

"He won't believe you," Joseph said.

"Why not?"

"Because he always believes me."

Abigail laughed. "That's right. You're his pet, aren't you? I wish my father spoiled me like Jacob spoils you."

"I guess you're not as sweet as I am," Joseph said airily.

"How would you know?" Abigail leaned close against him again and murmured, "You've never tried to find out if I'm sweet or not."

"You're just a child, Abigail," Joseph said, playfully pushing her away.

"I'm fourteen! I'm practically ready to be married."

Annoyed that Joseph was getting the best of this teasing match, Abigail tried to think of a way to even the score. With a glint in her eye, she reached up and ran her hand along his jawline. "Besides, you're no man! You don't even have a beard."

"Why, Abigail, it's not a beard that makes a man!" Joseph reached out and began to tickle her. She squealed and struggled to free herself, but he was too strong for her.

The two were raising the dust in their scuffle when a short, broad man appeared and grabbed Joseph by the arm. "Turn that girl loose!" he said roughly. "You've got to learn to treat people with more respect."

Surprised, Joseph released his hold on Abigail, and she stepped back as Joseph's brother Dan stood between them.

She did not particularly like Dan, who was the shortest and least attractive of Jacob's twelve sons. Not only was he homely, he showed little affection toward anyone, even his own mother, Bilhah, and he was bitterly jealous of Joseph.

"I wasn't hurting her," Joseph protested. "We were just having a little fun."

"You're too old to be putting your hands on girls," Dan snapped. When Joseph tried to pull away, Dan cuffed him roughly. The blow caught Joseph more on the neck than on the face, but it angered him.

"Turn me loose, Dan!"

"You deserve a good beating!"

"Father will give me any beatings I need," Joseph said loftily. He struggled, but Dan's grip was too strong. "If you don't turn me loose, I'll tell Father about the way you treated me."

Dan glared at him, his lips twisting in a snarl. "I know you run to him with every lie you can think of. You always do."

A shadow fell across the two, and Dan and Joseph turned to see Reuben towering over them. Jacob's firstborn was head and shoulders taller than any man in the tribe and bulky as well. His usually pleasant expression was now clouded with anger. "Turn him loose, Dan!"

"He's threatened to go to Father again to tell on me."

"I said turn him loose. Are you hard of hearing?"

Seeing the look on Reuben's face, Dan dropped his grasp on Joseph's arm. "He was hurting Abigail. I just tried to stop him."

"He wasn't hurting me, Reuben!" Abigail spoke up. "We were just having fun."

"That's right." Joseph nodded. "There was no harm in it at all."

"You're too hard on Joseph, Dan," Reuben said. "He's still growing up. You need to be more thoughtful."

"Of all people, you're the one who ought to be rough on him, Reuben. After all, he——"

"That's enough!" Reuben snapped before Dan could blurt out the story in front of Abigail. Joseph had once caught Reuben with their father's concubine Bilhah and had revealed the outrage to Jacob. Reuben had since suffered much guilt over his behavior and was certain his father had never forgiven him for it. "You've got work to do, Dan," Reuben said gruffly. "I suggest you get to it."

Dan flashed him a defiant look, but turned and left, muttering.

"You run along too, Abigail," Reuben said.

"But we weren't doing anything wrong."

"I know you weren't. Dan's just got a bad temper."

"I'll see you later, Joseph." Abigail smiled demurely, then turned and made her way back toward her tent.

Joseph watched her go, then leaned over and picked up his staff with a sigh. "Dan is always giving me grief, Reuben. Why can't he be more pleasant?"

"You bring a lot of it on yourself, Joseph."

The younger brother looked surprised. Despite his sweet temper and gentle ways, Joseph was in truth a spoiled young man. His father favored him and his younger brother, Benjamin, because they were the sons of Rachel, the one whom Jacob called his "True Wife." Naturally the six sons of Leah and the four sons of the concubines Bilhah and Zilpah had grown to resent Joseph. Benjamin was too young to draw their ire, but Joseph was guilty of constantly showing off before his brothers and bearing tales about them to their father.

Reuben stood for a moment contemplating his half brother. He had a genuine affection for Joseph, in spite of the fact that he was spoiled. Reuben sensed that the young man shared his father's spiritual gifts, for he had a quality about him he and his brothers lacked.

"If you'd just try a little harder to be more pleasant to our brothers, they wouldn't despise you, Joseph."

Once again Joseph was surprised. He had no idea how much his brothers resented him, and now he protested, "But I don't do anything to them."

"Sometimes it's what you don't do that matters."

Joseph looked puzzled.

"For instance, you don't do your work as you should because you know Father's not going to punish you for it. He lets you take off whenever you want to just sit by the stream or watch the clouds go by. How do you think that makes the rest of us feel?"

Reuben's remark stung Joseph, and he whined, "We're not all perfect, Reuben. We all have our faults."

Reuben flushed a dusky red as he realized Joseph was reminding him of the sin he had committed with Bilhah. This happened every time

Reuben tried to correct the young man. Joseph found some way to throw up to him that he had sinned terribly and had forfeited his birthright.

Reuben shook his head and turned away without a word.

"Thanks for getting Dan off my back," Jacob called out. Not particularly concerned about having insulted his brother, he turned lightly away, walking among the sheep and thinking about what he would have for supper that night.

———————

The older sons of Jacob often ate their evening meal together. As they gathered late that afternoon to share a pot of stew, even a casual observer would have seen one characteristic that several of the brothers shared: they had red-rimmed eyes like their mother, Leah. Leah had been cursed with an eye infection that had made her eyelids red, and she had passed this affliction on to all six of her sons, giving them odd-looking red eyes. It did not affect their vision, but it enabled outsiders to easily recognize that Reuben, Simeon, Levi, Judah, Issachar, and Zebulun were sons of Leah. The four sons of Jacob's concubines, Bilhah and Zilpah, were referred to by many as the "Sons of the Maids." Jacob's youngest two sons, Joseph and Benjamin, whose mother, Rachel, he considered his True Wife, were not welcome in these gatherings of the other ten brothers.

Since Reuben had not joined them this evening, Dan, a son of Bilhah, launched into the story of how Reuben had once again defended their half brother Joseph. Dan's eyes glared as he spoke vociferously and punched the air to make his points. "The pup was entirely improper, putting his hands on that young daughter of Eliza! When I tried to stop him, he gave me nothing but what he thought were clever answers. He needs a good whipping."

Naphtali, the other son of Bilhah, was dipping a ladle into the stew that was bubbling on the fire. He was a lean, stoop-shouldered man and spoke softly. He tasted the stew, then shook his head and gave Dan a disdainful look. "You should have known better than to say anything to him. He never listens to any of us."

"I would have thrashed him with my staff if Reuben hadn't come up and stopped me," Dan grunted.

"If you had, he would have gone straight to Father like he always does," said Levi, a short, muscular individual with dark eyes and a quick temper.

"I don't know why Reuben defends him," added Simeon, the second oldest of the brothers. He was sitting with his arms locked around his knees, staring at the others. He was lean and quiet, and his close-set sharp eyes revealed a cruel streak. "After the Bilhah incident, you'd think he would hate him."

"Sometimes," Dan said, "I think Reuben's not very bright."

"Oh, he's bright, all right," Judah argued. "And you're lucky that he stopped you from beating Joseph. If Father had heard about it, he would have had you whipped raw." Of all the brothers, Judah was the most insightful. He was a proud man but sensitive, quick to weep or laugh, and he knew his father well.

The brothers were still talking about Joseph when they were joined by Gad and Asher, the two sons of Zilpah. When they heard the story, they became incensed. "Joseph thinks he can get away with anything," Gad grumbled.

Asher agreed. "I say Reuben's just too dumb to know that he lost his birthright because Joseph told Father about his affair with Bilhah." A sturdy fellow with red, sinewy arms, Asher was forthright and honest as a rule, but, like the others, he was jealous of Joseph.

"It wasn't an affair," Judah defended Reuben. "He was only with her once."

"Once is enough!" Gad snapped. "It was a terrible thing to do."

"Nobody knows that better than Reuben," Judah said. He looked around and said quietly, "All of us had better learn one thing. Our two little brothers are the sons of the True Wife. Jacob loved Rachel better than any of our mothers. It's just something we have to live with."

The brothers decided to talk to Leah about Joseph, so two of them went to her tent to ask her to join them for supper. While eating a bowl of stew, she patiently listened to Judah explain what had happened. She glanced around at their sullen faces and realized that her oldest son was not there. "Where's Reuben?" she demanded.

"I think he's gone off to check the sheep in the lower pasture," Judah replied.

Simeon turned to his mother and said, "It's a shame the way Father favors Joseph over the rest of us."

Leah agreed. She was still bitter over Jacob's preference for her sister, even though Rachel was gone now, having died giving birth to Benjamin.

She stared out into the gathering darkness and shook her head. "It's always been that way. From the time Joseph was born, he was the favorite."

"Couldn't you talk to him, Mother?" Levi pleaded. "I don't think Father understands how spoiled Joseph is."

"He doesn't realize it, and he never will."

"He favors those two sons of Rachel more than he should," Judah remarked.

"Not so much Benjamin," Simeon countered. "I think Father blames him for causing his mother's death."

"You're right about that," Leah said with a thoughtful nod.

Just then the two youngest of Leah's sons spoke up, having kept to themselves throughout this conversation. Issachar and Zebulun were the closest in age to Joseph. Together with their little sister, Dinah, they had often played with Joseph and Benjamin when they were growing up, and now they halfheartedly tried to defend the sons of Rachel.

Leah dismissed their efforts. "You're both fools if you think anything good is ever going to come to any of you except Joseph. All Jacob thinks about is his True Wife and her offspring." Her lips twisted into a grimace. "He never loved anyone but her, yet I bore him six sons and a daughter."

"One of *us* ought to get the blessing from Father," Levi insisted.

"Yes, and it should be the firstborn," Zebulun said.

Simeon snapped, "But Reuben forfeited that when he slept with Bilhah! I'm the second-born. I should get the blessing!"

Judah faced Simeon and said, "You and Levi ruined your chances when you butchered the men of Shechem."

Simeon stared at Judah fiercely. Both he and Levi were men of violent tempers, and when a young prince of Shechem had defiled their sister, Dinah, the two of them had taken revenge by setting a trap for the Shechemites and slaying all their men. They captured all the women and children and plundered their goods, bringing great trouble to their father among the people of the land. Levi knew that Judah was right, although Jacob had never actually said he would withdraw his blessing as a result. Levi was irritated and snapped, "I guess you think *you* should get the blessing, Judah!"

"No, I don't," Judah said calmly. "And you can stop thinking about it. Father will see to it somehow that Joseph gets the blessing of the firstborn."

Judah's words enraged all of the brothers. "It's not fair!" Simeon shouted. "It's just not fair!"

"Life isn't fair." Judah shrugged. "Don't forget that our father stole his own blessing from his brother, Esau, with help from his mother. They tricked the old man. I love my father, but he's a crafty man. He knows how to get his own way, and you can depend on this: Joseph will get the birthright and rule over us all."

There was grumbling and complaining about this until Leah finally snapped, "All of you hush and eat!"

Judah drew close to his mother and said quietly, "Why do they have to quarrel like that?"

Leah looked surprised. "Don't *you* resent that Jacob loves Joseph best?"

"I have to live with it. We all do. I find the best way is just to ignore it."

Leah's red-rimmed eyes flared. "I will never ignore it, and neither will your brothers—and neither should *you!*"

CHAPTER

2

Early one morning Joseph said to his little brother, "Naphtali told me that a caravan of traders has stopped at a village north of here. Let's go buy ourselves some fine presents."

Benjamin was delighted at the prospect of a day with his big brother but asked a little anxiously, "Will Father let us go?"

"Oh, we don't need to bother asking him," Joseph replied with a shrug. "We'll just bring him a present too."

"But he might not like it if we go without telling."

Joseph laughed at the boy and tousled his hair. "Don't worry. I'll make him think the trip was his idea."

Soon the brothers were well on their way, and the sun was reaching its zenith as they walked along the rough pathway. From time to time Joseph would smile down at his younger brother, for there was no one on earth he loved more. He and Benjamin were all that were left of their mother. Since she had died at Benjamin's birth, Joseph often talked to his little brother about her, sharing all the details he could remember. The younger boy loved to hear the stories over and over.

Benjamin was a chubby-cheeked eight-year-old with a sunny disposition. He had unusual smoky gray eyes, and thick, shiny auburn hair, which was molded to his head like a metal helmet. He walked along happily clinging to Joseph's hand, wearing a short-sleeved, knee-length garment of rust red with a blue embroidered hem.

Although Benjamin was usually cheerful and friendly, at times a painful sadness would overtake him. The child bore the weight of his mother's death like a tragic burden, knowing intuitively that his father, Jacob, somehow blamed him for it. His father would often act in a reserved manner toward Benjamin, not meeting his gaze; yet at other times he would hold him tightly and tell him tales of his mother. The confusing alienation Benjamin felt with his father had brought him closer to his big brother Joseph, whom he idolized completely.

As the pair walked hand in hand past an olive orchard that clung precariously to a steep hillside, Benjamin looked up and saw the Sons of the Maids picking olives and putting them in baskets. He did not call to them, for he knew that these four older brothers did not much like him or his brother Joseph.

Joseph had been whistling one of Benjamin's favorite tunes, but he stopped as they passed the orchard and went on in silence. Once they were out of earshot of their unfriendly half brothers, Joseph looked down and asked, "Are you tired?"

"No, not even a little."

"Are you sure this isn't too long a trip for your short legs?"

"No," Benjamin said with a quick smile. "I promise I won't be a burden to you."

"All right. But if you get tired, tell me and I'll carry you."

Benjamin merely shook his head and smiled up brilliantly at Joseph.

"Please tell me a story, Joseph," Benjamin begged. "The one about Noah and the animals." Joseph had an endless supply of stories—either ones he made up or stories of their ancestors. The story of Noah was one of Benjamin's favorites, and now as they strolled northward, Joseph told the story of their ancient ancestor who had gathered two each of all the animals of the world and put them on a huge boat to save them from the flood.

After two hours of walking and several stories later, Joseph insisted they sit down to rest at a tiny spring. He slung a leather bag off his shoulder and opened it, pulling out two chunks of bread and strips of dried mutton for their lunch, which they ate along with sips of water from a flask. There were also succulent dates, and Joseph made Benjamin open his mouth and stand away while he tossed them in. Benjamin managed to catch most of them, and even those that fell to the ground he retrieved and ate anyway, brushing off the dust first.

As they rested Benjamin asked, "Joseph, why do the Sons of the Maids and the sons of Leah dislike us so much?"

Joseph was surprised. "I think you know the answer to that one."

"But I try to be as nice to them as I can."

"You can never be nice enough to make them like you, Benji. They're jealous of us because we're the sons of the True Wife."

The little boy knew this well but could not understand it. "We all have the same father."

"Yes, but not the same mother. Our father loved our mother more than anything in this world. You've heard him say so himself."

"Doesn't he love Leah and Bilhah and Zilpah at all?"

"Yes, he is fond of them, but he does not love them like he loved his True Wife. Haven't you ever heard how our father worked for his uncle Laban for seven years to get Rachel for his wife, then on the wedding day he was tricked into marrying his older daughter, Leah, because they hid her face with a veil to deceive our father?"

"That was a wicked thing to do, wasn't it?"

"Very wicked."

"But Father did marry Leah."

"Yes, but he never loved her like he did our mother." Joseph regarded Benjamin curiously. "Haven't you noticed how much better looking we are than any of our brothers?"

"No. Are we?"

"You foolish boy! Just look at yourself sometime—see your reflection in the water or in that bronze mirror Leah has. Then look at those red-eyed sons of Leah and the rough Sons of the Maids. Then look at you. What a beautiful, handsome boy you are!"

"And you too, Joseph. You're the best looking of all of our father's sons."

"Oh, I don't know about that." Joseph shrugged modestly, though in fact he could not deny Benjamin's statement. "And we're smarter than they are too," he went on. "They know this and it makes them dislike us."

Benjamin struggled with this for a time, then said, "Father is unhappy with me because my mother died giving me life."

Tears sprang to Joseph's eyes and his heart swelled, knowing that his brother spoke the truth. He bent down beside the boy and put his arms around him, holding him to his breast. "I love you enough to make up for our father and all of our half brothers."

"Do you really, Joseph?"

"Never doubt it, Benjamin. You and I are all that's left of our mother, and no matter whether the earth stands or falls or if the sun stays in heaven, you and I are brothers. True brothers."

Joseph saw the tears in Benjamin's eyes and jumped to change the subject. "You've got to stop asking so many questions or I'll have to put a bug in your mouth."

"No, don't do that!" Benjamin said, but he only laughed because he knew Joseph would never do any such wicked thing. "Tell me more about the dream you had last night."

"Well, like I said, it was quite beautiful. . . ."

———

Jacob limped back and forth in front of his tent, his infirmity not so much a matter of age as a result of his encounter with an angel years earlier on the way back from Laban's country. They had wrestled all night, and he had received a new name—Israel. It was a name he and others in the tribe spoke with great pride because it meant "prince of God," whereas the name Jacob had the rather unsavory meanings of "deceiver" or "usurper." Nonetheless, he was usually called by his given name on an everyday basis.

The head of the tribe wore a cotton garment woven with narrow pale-colored stripes. He was of medium height and stooped with age. His beard joined with the hair on his temples and fell from his cheeks to his breast in sparse strands. His eyes were still sharp, with pouches of soft skin beneath them, but his face was etched with worry. He finally stepped inside the tent where Leah was busy with the evening meal. "I'm worried about Joseph and Benjamin."

Leah struggled to keep her anger from showing in her face as she looked up. "They'll be all right," she said curtly.

"But where are they?"

"They're out playing somewhere. You know how careless Joseph is. He's headstrong, and Benjamin thinks his brother is the Almighty himself! He'd stick his head in the fire if Joseph told him to."

"I suppose that's true enough, but I can't help worrying about them."

Leah replied sharply, "When Simeon and Levi were lost last month for two days in the wilderness over by Bethel, you never even said a word."

"That's different," Jacob said defensively. "They're grown men. Joseph and Benjamin are just children."

"Joseph is seventeen years old. He's old enough to get married or get into trouble or do anything else a man can do."

Jacob gave her a startled look but knew she had spoken the truth. He also knew that he favored Joseph, and to a lesser degree Benjamin, but he went to great lengths to conceal the fact. He did so now as he tried to cover up his anxiety.

Then he heard a voice call out, "Father!" and his expression grew relieved. "Oh, good—there's Reuben," he said. "I sent him off to find them." He ducked out of the tent to find Reuben alone. "Where are they?" Jacob demanded. "I told you to bring them back with you."

Reuben's massive shoulders drooped with fatigue. "I've looked everywhere," he muttered, "but I can't find any trace of them."

"Well, go look some more. Don't you care that your brothers are lost?"

"Yes, I care, Father," Reuben groaned, "but they could have gone in any direction. Which way should I look?"

"How should I know! Make yourself useful for a change and go!"

Reuben could never look his father full in the eye and could not face him now. Having disgraced himself with Bilhah, he knew he had forever lost the position a firstborn son should have. Not only had he lost his father's respect, he knew Jacob would never give him the blessing—the most important sanction among the wandering tribespeople of the region. It was a special privilege given to the firstborn son and included a double portion of the family inheritance, along with the honor of one day being the family leader. Although it was a birthright to which the firstborn son was entitled, it was not actually his until the blessing was pronounced. Before such time, the father could take away the birthright from the oldest son and give it to someone more deserving.

Reuben trudged away with a heavy heart. He had no idea which way to look for Joseph and Benjamin, but he determined to stay up all night if necessary.

Jacob watched him go, then limped back into the tent. "He didn't find him," he grunted to Leah.

"Yes, I heard, but you can't blame Reuben for Joseph's wrongdoing."

"I'm sure the boy didn't mean any wrong."

"He never means any wrong because you always let him off the hook," Leah said. Her eyes narrowed, showing their red, irritated lids as she stared at her husband. She had deeply loved him once, but she no longer had any illusions about his feelings for her, even though she had borne him six children. Her blind jealousy still reared angrily when she saw Jacob spoiling Rachel's son.

Jacob barely tasted the food Leah put before him, mostly just pushing it around in the dish, with shoulders slumped. When Leah left him alone, his mind drifted back to the difficult time when he had left his father-in-law's house, worried sick about having cheated his brother out of his birthright. His strength had been drained that night as he waited for morning with the certainty that he would suffer his brother's vengeance. Then he had wrestled all night with a man whose noble visage was indescribable, demanding that the stranger tell him his name. But the man had refused to do so.

He remembered that when dawn came, he had struggled with his last bit of strength to overthrow his visitor, whom he knew was more than human, and his thigh had been thrown out of joint. The pain had never completely gone away. The stranger had asked him, "What is your name?" Jacob had finally admitted who he was and also confessed that he had cheated his brother. Before the stranger left, he said to Jacob, "Your name will now be Israel."

He thought then of Rachel, and he felt his grief as fresh as the day he had buried her at the place where she had died giving birth to Benjamin. Tears came to his eyes and he began to pray: "Oh, El Shaddai, let no harm come to my boys! You have been faithful to provide for me as you promised when I left my father and mother's house. You met me on the way and gave me a dream of a great ladder reaching up to heaven, and you promised to bless me, and you have."

Jacob concentrated fully on God. He had heard his father and grandfather speak of their encounters with the Strong One, the almighty and everlasting Lord. Both of them had been men of great faith, especially his grandfather, and now as Jacob prayed, he sought to summon up the faith of Abraham.

Jacob had been praying a long while when he heard voices coming, and his heart leaped with joy to hear Joseph! He got to his feet and hobbled out the tent door, ignoring his discomfort. He could see by the light of the torch Dan carried that Benjamin was sound asleep on Naphtali's shoulder.

"Well, we found them," Naphtali said. "You ought to thrash them until they can't stand up, Father."

Jacob was angry enough to do so and demanded of his favorite son, "Joseph, where have you been?"

"We went to the village where the Midianite traders were passing through. We wanted to buy you a present."

"You went alone through the wilderness with your brother? Shame on you, son!"

Dan and Naphtali gave each other a look. Dan shrugged, leaned over, and whispered, "He'll bluster and shout at Joseph, but in the end he'll wind up giving him honey cakes."

Such almost proved true. Benjamin could hardly stand up he was so tired, and Jacob said, "Bring him into the tent. Joseph, I'm not through with you yet."

Dan and Naphtali waited for their father to thank them, but he ignored them completely as he gathered his "two lambs," as he called them, into the tent.

"We should've let the wolves get 'em!" Dan snarled.

"You're right. Father will wind up making heroes out of them, and not give a word of thanks to us for wearing our legs out looking for them!"

Leah brought the boys food and Joseph ate ravenously, but Benjamin was so sleepy he wound up slumping over his dish. "Take him and put him to bed, Leah," Jacob said, pulling Benjamin to his feet. "I'll speak to you tomorrow, young man."

"Yes, Father. I'm sorry. We should have told you we were going."

"Indeed you should." Jacob tried to sound angry, but the woebegone, tearstained face of the lad was too much. He put his arms around him, held him close, then kissed him and whispered, "Go on to bed, little lamb. Go to bed."

As soon as Leah had taken Benjamin to the tent he shared with Joseph, Jacob turned and said, "Joseph, I continually think you have reached the height of foolishness, but this is the worst!"

Joseph fell to his knees. "Father, I deserve your just punishment. I was indeed wrong. Get out the rawhide and beat me until my back is bleeding."

"Don't think I won't do it!"

"I deserve it, Father. I was thoughtless and had no more sense than one of the lambs that wanders away from the herd."

Jacob had been frightened at the possible loss of his two favorite sons, and now he was filled with indignation that Joseph had been foolish enough to risk both his own life and his brother's.

Seeing his father's face, Joseph sought to assuage his anger by pulling a bag out of his woven sack. "We really went to buy you a present, Father, and here it is—sugared dates all the way from Damascus. Your favorite!"

"You shouldn't have done that," Jacob said. Nonetheless, he took the bag and sampled one of the dates. "They are very good, but you were still wrong."

Joseph embraced his father and said, "If only our beloved mother were alive, I wouldn't have done such a thing. I miss her so much, and Benjamin wants to hear about her all the time. I'm such a wicked lamb because she's not here to correct me."

To this day, Jacob could not speak of Rachel without weeping, and now the tears ran down his cheek. "Yes, my beloved Rachel. She would have been the ideal mother. You will never know how I miss her, son."

"So do I, Father. Except for you, I have no one, and little Benji has only you and me. We're all that's left of our beloved mother."

And so it was that, instead of beating Joseph with a strap as he richly deserved, Jacob found himself holding the boy, weeping, and whispering, "Oh, my dear lamb, if I had lost you, I would have lost the last I have on this earth of her, the True Wife. You must never, never take such risks again!"

"I promise I won't, Father."

With the danger of his father's punishment over, Joseph felt a quick surge of relief, though he had never been in doubt about how the thing would turn out.

Jacob dried his eyes and cleared his throat. "My son," he said, "you must thank your older brothers for searching for you. They have worn themselves out."

"Oh, I will, Father, I will. How I dearly wished that they loved me more."

"It is within your power, my lamb, to make them love you more. I must say to you that you need to show more humility. They are your elders, and you need to show them the respect that older brothers deserve."

"You are right, and it was good of Dan to find me. He is a good man . . ." Joseph hesitated, then could not help adding, ". . . even if he does visit that Canaanite harlot over the hill." He clapped his hand over his mouth and said, "I didn't mean to say that!"

Jacob stared at his son grimly. "He's that kind of a man, Joseph, and you must never be like him. You must never be like any of your brothers."

"But Reuben is a good man, Father, even if he—"

Joseph broke his words off, and Jacob stared at him sadly. "I wish you had never told me about the sin he committed with Bilhah."

"I wish I hadn't told you either, Father. It just came out. I love Reuben."

Jacob stood still, staring at Joseph as though something was preying on his mind. Suddenly he reached into his tunic and drew out an object suspended on a leather thong.

Joseph had seen it before, but he was always fascinated by it. "Can I see the medallion, Father?"

Jacob nodded, and Joseph inspected the gold piece shining in the light of the lamp. On one side was a lifelike lion and on the other a lamb.

"I love to hear the story of the medallion," Joseph said. "Tell me again, Father."

Then Jacob began to tell the story of how the medallion had been given to men so far in the dim past that no one could remember it. "It was handed down to those of the line of Seth, to Noah, and continued through the generations all the way to Abraham, and he gave it to me."

"And one day it will belong to me, won't it, Father?" Joseph said eagerly as he stared hypnotically at the medal.

Jacob stared at his tall young son, longing to give it to him, but he shook his head. "No one can say who receives this medallion but El Shaddai, the Strong One. When it is time, the Lord himself will tell me who will wear this medal and from whom will come the line of Shiloh."

"Shiloh. Who is that?"

"It's the name I've given to the One who will redeem the world. In a dream years ago I began to imagine this coming one, whom my fathers waited for, as having that name. It is simply the name of a village and it means 'peace.' Perhaps it is a foolish fancy of mine. I don't know."

Joseph held the medallion between his fingers. He rubbed it lovingly and said, "I hope I will be the one to receive this."

"I hope so too, my son, but no man can know. Now, get to bed. It's late."

"Good night, Father." Joseph embraced his father, kissed him, and left.

As Jacob stood alone in the semidarkness, he realized a terrible truth. "I'm glad that Reuben sinned with Bilhah!" As he spoke the words aloud he felt shame for thinking such a thing about his firstborn. A father should always uphold his firstborn in honor, but he had never felt that way toward Reuben. Nor had he felt that any of Leah's sons deserved honor, although he loved them all. They were difficult boys, some of them having Leah's fiery temper and several having the devious behavior of their grandfather Laban.

But to be glad that his firstborn had committed such a sin! Shame washed through Jacob, and he fell on his knees and cried out, "Oh, forgive me, God, for such a wicked, awful thought! Cleanse me, I beg of you." The old man knelt there for a long time, holding the medallion between his trembling fingers. Finally he bowed over completely, his head against the carpet that formed the floor of his tent, and cried out again, "Let me be Israel and not Jacob!"

When he rose, he still felt a heavy burden of guilt. He realized that, despite his prayers, his fondest hope was that Joseph—not Reuben, nor Simeon, nor Levi, nor any of the other brothers, but Joseph, the beloved son of the True Wife—would be the one through whom would come Shiloh, the Bringer of Peace, the Redeemer.

CHAPTER

3

As Jacob lay underneath a light covering, he was conscious of the night sounds drifting in from the outside world. Wild dogs howled in the distance, disturbing his peace of mind. He had always hated wild dogs. There was something primitive and terrifying in their cries. He loved most animals, especially his flocks of goats and sheep and cattle. But the wild dogs were different. He had fought them off after they had scattered the remains of one of his sheep or cows, and many times in his long life he had seen them in packs, pulling down a helpless lamb or sheep, tearing it to pieces and devouring it while it yet lived.

A shudder went over Jacob at the memories. He was blessed—or cursed!—with an accurate memory and could recall events from when he was a mere boy as if they had just occurred. It was a blessing that he could remember so clearly the face of Rachel, his beloved True Wife. He often took refuge in the silences of the desert, thinking of her smile, her touch, or her beautiful eyes.

But his good memory was a curse when he could also vividly remember how he and his mother, Rebekah, had robbed Esau of his birthright. As if he were watching a scene painted on parchment in living, dynamic colors, he saw himself and his mother fastening animal skins to his forearms to make the blind, unsuspecting Isaac think he was blessing Esau.

And so Jacob lived on his memories and his hopes. His memories of Rachel and his hopes for the future centered on her child Joseph, the lamb that Jacob loved with every bit of his strength.

The harsh symphony of the wild dogs ceased, and silence reigned over the desert. Jacob listened intently. His hearing was good, despite his age, and he began to distinguish the hum of night insects. Their tiny voices were comforting to him. They were a sound to which he was accustomed, and he liked things to remain the same, though he knew they never would. The memory of the recent days came trooping in. He trembled, even as he had when he discovered that Joseph and Benjamin were missing. It was as though a mighty hand had reached into his breast and closed around his heart with the coldness and finality of death. For in these two, especially the older, his hopes and love were imprisoned.

"Joseph must be more careful. I would die if I lost him!" Jacob whispered the words aloud, thinking of Joseph's face, smooth and carefree, with happiness in his dark eyes, so much like those of his True Wife. The memory comforted him, but then he thought of the animosity of the six red-eyed sons of Leah and the four Sons of the Maids. Oh, how they despised Joseph. The thought troubled the old man, and he struggled to find anything he could do to undo what the years of his favoritism had woven into the fabric of his family's life, but he could think of none.

He began to drift toward sleep, but he was troubled by the thought of Joseph's dreams. He himself was a man who dreamed and put great stock into them, as had his fathers before him. Joseph, however, relied so much on his dreams for guidance that he seemed to Jacob to be like one of the so-called oracles, men or women who went about babbling wildly of dreams and visions and shouting their findings. Most of them were mad, "touched by God," as the people of the desert called it, doing terrible things like mutilating themselves by walking about with sharp stones in their sandals, or going filthy and naked, creating fear among the people.

Jacob made a sharp distinction between such fanatics and the dreams that sometimes came to him. He had heard enough of the tales of his forefathers and their encounters with God that he was convinced his own dreams were a legitimate word from God.

And of all things in his life the old man longed for most, it was to hear from God. He was convinced that God wanted to communicate to human beings, and at one time or another he had tried to find God's will by studying the entrails of birds or by observing the direction of the smoke from a burnt offering. All this was right in Jacob's opinion, but he was troubled by Joseph's foolish ecstasies, in which the lad shook and trembled, his eyes rolling back. As Jacob finally dropped into a deep sleep, his last thought was a cry: *Elohim—help me, O almighty Lord. . . !*

Under a gray sky, an old man plodded alongside a younger man who led a donkey piled high with sticks and dry wood. Jacob had had this particular dream many times before, and as always, the images frightened him. He was always a silent spectator, trying to avoid seeing what was about to happen, but he could not escape the image of the old man's stern face, the grimness of his expression modified by the pain and sorrow in his eyes.

Jacob knew the old man was Abraham, and the lad beside him was Isaac, Jacob's own father. He could not help but stare fascinated at the young man, who looked startlingly like his son Joseph. He had the same well-shaped eyes and round face, the same youthful innocence and loveliness. This was Jacob's own father and grandfather on their way to a faithful rendezvous.

The dream was so real Jacob inadvertently cried out in a babbling moan of fear. He saw the young man bound and placed on a rude wooden altar. The sticks from the donkey had been placed under him and around him and were ready for the fire. He saw the flash of the knife in the old man's hand. But most of all he saw the agony in the old man's face as he stared down at this son. Jacob was aware of the miracle that had produced his father, Isaac. Abraham and Sarah had aged beyond their natural ability to conceive and bear children, but by a miracle God had touched the old man and restored to him the vigor of his youth. He had touched the dead womb of Sarah and made it blossom, and out of these miracles came a child born purely by the will and power of the almighty Lord of heaven and earth.

Jacob watched helplessly as the raised knife caught the last rays of the sun. Beneath the hand of Abraham lay the helpless lad, his eyes closed, his face ashen with fear, but obedient to his father's command. The knife was ready to plunge into the young boy's heart—

Then Jacob heard himself crying out, "No, no, do not kill him—"

Suddenly the dream changed. Before it had always been the same. The voice of God had come crying out to Abraham before the final thrust of the knife: *"Do not harm the lad."* The old man had dropped the knife and fallen with tears upon his son as God had commended him for his faith: *"You have not withheld your only son from me."*

But now the dream was different. The images swirled and twisted in Jacob's mind until it was no longer Isaac who lay on the altar but Joseph, the lamb of the old man Jacob! And it was not Abraham who raised the knife but he himself, Jacob the son of Isaac. He felt the cold sharpness of the blade as he found himself looking into the face of his beloved Joseph, the son he loved more than life itself. And he heard God saying, *"Strike and make your son a sacrifice to me."*

In crazed fear Jacob cried out, "No, I can't give him up! You can't have him! You can't have my only son. . . !"

And then the dream was gone, and Jacob was being held by strong hands. With eyes wide open he looked wildly about and there kneeling over him was Joseph. The young man's face was highlighted by the flame of an oil lamp Jacob kept burning at night to ward off his dreams and night terrors, and he reached out and grabbed at Joseph, holding on to him and crying, "No, I can't do it—I can't do it, God!"

"Father, you're having a bad dream!"

Jacob clung to the boy who bent over him, his hands frantically feeling the warm flesh of the boy's body as if to assure himself that he was alive. He began to weep, and Joseph leaned closer so that his face loomed before Jacob's tear-filled eyes.

"What is it, Father? What's wrong?"

Reality came slowly back to Jacob as he lay there, holding on to the son of the True Wife. "My lamb," he whispered, "my little lamb, my child!" He muttered these endearments over and over again, then took a deep breath and struggled to sit up. He clung to Joseph as a drowning man holds on to a floating board that might keep him from sinking. "A dream," he muttered, his voice a thin, trembling sigh. "I had a horrible dream."

"What was it?" Joseph asked anxiously, for he loved dreams and wanted to know what they meant.

"I dreamed of my grandfather putting Isaac, my father, on an altar and lifting the knife to slay him."

"But you've had that dream many times. You've told me so."

"I know, but this time it was different."

"Different how, Father? Tell me about it." Joseph's eyes gleamed, and his hands pulled at the old man, urging him to talk. "How was it different?"

Jacob trembled from head to foot. His strength had been drained by the terror of the dream, and he knew he could never speak of this to anyone. "It was nothing, my son. As you say, I have dreamed it before."

"God was cruel to ask your grandfather Abraham to kill his only son," Joseph said. "I've always disliked Him for that."

"No, no, you must not say that, my child!" Jacob grabbed Joseph's hands and clung to him. "You must never say that."

"Don't you think it was cruel?"

"I used to think so, but now I know better. God is good. We are the ones who are evil."

"You are not evil, my father."

"Yes, I am. There is evil in me as there is in all men."

Joseph shook his head firmly. "No, that isn't so. You are good. I will not hear you talk like this."

Jacob could say no more, and he released his hold on Joseph. "Go back to sleep, my son. I'm all right now."

"I will sit with you if you wish, Father."

"No, you need your sleep. Go to bed."

Joseph leaned forward and kissed his father. Jacob was tempted to cling to him again, but he forced himself to lie back down, and Joseph left the tent.

The dream had left Jacob drenched with sweat. He threw back his cover and allowed the night air to cool his body. As sleep returned, he relived the dream against his will. He wanted it to go away, but he knew God was speaking, and he could not ignore the Almighty. He could not drown out the sound of God's voice commanding him: *"Sacrifice your only son. . . ."*

Jacob had twelve sons, but in one sense he had only one. Joseph was the beloved son, and Jacob knew that God was saying, *"You must choose whom you will love the best, me or your son."* It was the same test Abraham had physically been forced to take, and even though Jacob knew God had rescued Isaac, he could not be sure that God would do the same for Joseph. Rebelliousness rose up in his heart. "God," he whispered, "you can't ask me to give up Joseph. Take any one of the others, even Benjamin, but not my precious lamb—not the son of the True Wife."

The silence of the desert grew oppressive, pressing in upon the old man, whose breath became labored. In spirit he was clutching Joseph to his breast and crying out, *No, God, not my only son. Not him. Take any of the others, but not Joseph!*

———————

Old Zimra raked his fingers through his beard, and his eyes glowed with admiration. "It is well, my boy. You have done well."

Joseph leaned back and smiled benevolently at the old man. Zimra had been his teacher since his early childhood. The old man had wandered into

Jacob's camp one day shortly after Jacob had brought his family back from the house of Laban. He had been half starved and was babbling incoherently, but Jacob showed him mercy and fed him. When the old man had recovered his right mind, Jacob had discovered, to his delight, that he was a scholar. He immediately made Zimra part of his retinue and assigned him the task of first educating Joseph, then Benjamin. The older sons had no desire to receive such education, their hearts having been given over to meat, drink, women, and work.

And so old Zimra had taught Joseph many things. He had instructed the young man in the nature of the universe, teaching him that it was composed of the upper heaven, the heavenly earth of the zodiac, and the southern oceans of the heavens. He had taught him well that the earthly universe was divided into three parts, the heavens, the kingdom of the earth, and the earthly ocean. Joseph had absorbed the teachings concerning the sun and the moon, together with the five other moving stars, and as Zimra had pointed to the gleaming white heights of Mount Hermon in the distance and spoken of the Tree of Enlightenment, Joseph had learned of the wonder and the mystery of numbers. He had found order and harmony in numbers and received his training from old Zimra with delight.

He learned that the world the Almighty had made consisted of cycles of years, each year having its own summer and winter. Joseph found all of this a most majestic knowledge, and he hung on Zimra's words as the old man shared what he knew of the larger world outside of Canaan. Joseph learned about the Babylonian methods of measuring the length of a pendulum, which made sixty double oscillations in a double minute. He learned to measure length and distances both from his own pace and from the course of the sun. Joseph learned the weights and money values of gold and silver according to Phoenician measurements. He learned how to exchange different forms of money for animals, oil, wine, and grain. Joseph was so quick-witted that even Jacob, who often sat in on the lessons, would marvel at the cleverness of the boy's mind.

Jacob had little knowledge of the geography of the larger world and was pleased beyond measure at how quickly Joseph took in old Zimra's teachings. He listened as the old man told of wild savages who dwelt in the far northern land of Magog, and how Tarsus, far off to the west, was a frightful place. Zimra spoke of these places from personal experience, for he was widely traveled. He spoke often of the peoples of Egypt, which Jacob knew more about from the tales of his forefathers than other exotic far-off places.

For the lessons Joseph would squat with his knees apart, holding in his lap the writing tools of the day: a clay tablet on which he made wedge-shaped signs with a carved instrument, or he would write on papyrus sheets made of reeds pressed together. Sometimes he wrote on a smooth piece of sheepskin or goatskin, using a reed sharpened to a point and dipped in red or black pigment on his paint saucer.

Joseph's education had its downside, unfortunately, for the lad was not modest about his attainments. He let it be known to his older brothers what a great scholar he had become and would often swagger in front of them. He would even ridicule them at times, though to him it was done in a playful spirit. He would cry out to Zebulun, "My brother, have you not seen how beautiful my writing is? What a scholar I have become!"

Zebulun would glare at him and shoot back with a curse. "All of that doesn't feed the sheep or shear the wool. Get away from me, you dreamer of dreams and writer of books."

Only two of Joseph's older brothers admired his achievements, Reuben and Judah. Although they said little about it to their other brothers, they often spoke about it to each other. "He's got something in him that most young men don't have," Judah said once. He was an introspective man himself, who had some measure of discernment. However, he always seemed to carry a weight on his shoulders. He talked to no one about what it was that burdened him, but Reuben had come to believe that it had something to do with Judah's early marriage to Abra, a young Canaanite woman, the daughter of Shua. She was a strange and sullen woman, and the three sons she'd borne to Judah were much the same.

To a lesser extent than Joseph, but more so than his brothers, Judah also had dreams. They were frightful dreams, which he hated, but he spoke to no one about them, for he did not understand them. Now he and Reuben were speaking of Joseph's dreams.

"If Joseph would only keep quiet about his dreams," Reuben said moodily. "One of these days Levi or Simeon are going to strangle him."

"They won't do that," Judah answered quietly. "But they do hate him for it."

———

Most of Joseph's education was received in Jacob's tent, where Jacob could listen in as Zimra guided Joseph through the intricacies of mathematics or foreign languages. The tent was made of woven black goat's hair, stretched over nine stout poles and fastened by strong ropes to pegs driven into the ground. It was by far the most impressive and beautiful tent of any of the tribe, fitting for the head of the tribe to dwell in. Jacob now dwelt in it alone, having nothing anymore to do with Leah or his concubines. He was past all of that now and was content to spend much of his time alone in his beautiful tent. It was divided from front to back by curtains, and the floor was covered with beautifully worked carpets purchased from traveling merchants from Damascus and other faraway places. One of the rooms served as a general storehouse and supply chamber and was filled with camel saddles and traveling gear.

The other half was the main dwelling place for Jacob and his guests, which were not many as a rule. The tent was open in front to the height of a man, and earthen lamps with ornamental bases and shallow bowls with short snouts for the wick were kept burning day and night. To one side was a tall-legged coffer with a vaulted lid, carved with intricate designs and filled with Jacob's treasures. In the middle of the room a glowing brazier kept the tent warm when the temperatures dropped. Samples of gold-covered Syrian and Canaanite carvings decorated the interior.

It was in this room that Joseph sat one morning listening to Zimra speak of the wonders of foreign places. But when he began to speak of Egypt, Jacob interrupted. "Speak not of Egypt, Zimra," he said, "for it is an evil place."

"Evil, my lord?" Zimra said with feigned surprise, for he actually knew well the old leader's thoughts on Egypt. "It is a place of men and women like any other."

"It is not," Jacob said stubbornly. "It is a place where they go about clothed in garments made of air. You can see right through them."

"But, my lord—"

"Speak no more of it. Did you know that they have no word for 'sin' in their language?" Jacob demanded. "What place could be more evil than that?"

Zimra had learned long ago not to argue with the old man, and he at once changed the subject. After the teacher left, Jacob turned to Joseph and gave him a hard look. "Zimra knows much, but pay no attention to his teachings of Egypt. It is an evil place."

"As you say, Father," Joseph said, although he was sure that his father knew no more about Egypt than he knew about the surface of the moon. Joseph had learned to agree with Jacob in all things, no matter what he himself thought.

"You have done well. I have a present for you, my lamb."

"A present! How wonderful. Your lamb is grateful. What is it, Father?"

Jacob got to his feet and limped over to the carved chest containing his treasures, opened the lid, and took out a large box. "I have made something special . . . something I've worked on for years. I am waiting until you are old enough to take care of it." Coming back to Joseph, he opened the box and pulled out a garment. It was an outer robe designed to be worn over one's normal dress for special occasions. Jacob held the garment high, and Joseph caught his breath at the interwoven gold threads and colorful embroidery glittering in the lamplight. Reds, blues, olive green, and rose colors formed the background on which were depicted trees, animals, and angels.

"How beautiful!" Joseph cried, and he reached out and took the garment, clutching it to himself. "Is it really for me?"

"Yes, and you will have it soon, but you must be very careful with it."

"Be careful not to spoil it or get it dirty?"

"No, be careful not to boast of it before your brothers. You must wear it only for very special occasions, my son."

"But it's so beautiful! Look—here is an embroidery of the face of a woman. Is that my blessed mother?"

"Yes. That is the image of my beloved Rachel."

The two went on admiring the coat, and Jacob allowed the boy to try it on. Joseph strutted back and forth, his eyes flashing, thrilled with the garment, as he was with anything new.

"Father, let me have it now."

"No, not yet." Deep down in his heart, Jacob knew he was making a mistake. "Such a gift should really go to the firstborn, but I am not yet sure who will receive the blessing. Your brother Reuben fell away, and I had to take the rights of the firstborn away from him. Then Simeon and Levi became bloody men—I do not know yet."

"Oh, but it must be mine! Surely they would not appreciate it.

Especially not with this image of my blessed mother. Surely you intended it for me from the very beginning."

Jacob leaned back and watched his beloved lamb move back and forth with the beautiful coat as it caught the reflection of the lamps and thought of his beloved Rachel. *It must be his*, he thought. *It must be Joseph's!*

CHAPTER

4

Of the six red-eyed sons of Leah, Judah and Reuben were the closest. There was more in their features of Jacob than the other brothers, who strongly favored their mother. Although Reuben was the firstborn and Judah was the fourth, they often drew together to talk over the problems of the tribe and especially of their own part of the six.

They met late one afternoon out in the fields while they watched over the flocks. Reuben was aware that Judah had said almost nothing for several days. He had been especially moody, so Reuben asked him, "What's wrong with you, Judah?"

"Nothing."

"I don't believe you. I can see that something is wrong. What is it?"

Judah looked up with misery in his eyes. "I married the wrong woman, Reuben."

"Why would you say that? You have three fine sons."

It was true that Abra had given Judah three sons, and when he had married, Judah had fancied himself in love with her. He had been surprised indeed when Jacob had given his permission for him to marry a Canaanite woman. But now he worried about his boys. For some reason they displeased him, though he was at a loss to explain why he felt that way. For the first time he expressed his fears to Reuben. "I'm worried about my boys."

"Why? What's wrong with them? They're healthy enough."

"I shouldn't have married a Canaanite woman, Reuben. They're a bad breed. They worship Baal and Molech and all sorts of terrible idols." Looking distressed, he moaned, "I wish I had never married at all. It's Father's fault. He should have forbidden me to marry a Canaanite."

Reuben stared at his brother, unable to form an answer. He was powerful in body but not known for his deep thoughts. He had a dumb loyalty to his own wife and children, but the guilt of his behavior with Bilhah was such a continual burden he could never look people directly in the eye. "They'll be all right. They'll marry and give you grandsons," he said gruffly, trying to comfort Judah.

Judah shook his head, then changed the subject as if it were painful. "Have you talked yet with Joseph about that coat of his?"

"Not yet, but I will."

"You have to. He's making a show of it before all of us."

"Father said he can only wear it on special occasions."

"Special occasions!" Judah spat bitterly. "For him a special occasion is any occasion he wants. He's wearing it all the time now, and you know what that coat means."

"You mean it's a sign that Joseph is our father's favorite, the one to whom he may give the blessing of the firstborn?"

"Yes. Oh, brother, I've never spoken of it, but what a terrible thing it was that you had to sin with Bilhah. Why didn't you go off and find a prostitute instead?"

Reuben bowed his head and ground his teeth together. "I was insane," he said. "I don't know what came over me. It was just the one time."

"The one time was enough. If you hadn't done that, you would have received the blessing of the firstborn. But now it's obvious that Father thinks only of Joseph."

"I'll talk to him about wearing that coat."

"Do it now. There he is. Go on. Do it now!"

Reuben turned and walked away, his back straight as he approached Joseph, who was indeed strutting around in his colorful coat. The sunlight caught it, and as beautiful as it was, Reuben thought, *I wish Father had never given him such a thing. He should've known what Joseph would do with it.* "Joseph, come here."

Joseph turned with surprise, and a smile crossed his face. He was actually fond of Reuben, even though he thought him slow of mind, and when he came over to him, he had to lean his head backward and look up. "What is it, my brother?"

"I must speak with you about that coat."

"It's so beautiful! Don't you think so, Reuben?"

"You should not wear it. Didn't Father command you to only wear it on special occasions?"

Joseph did not want to be reminded of this. He had decided to wear the coat every day, regardless of his father's wishes. "What does it matter whether I wear it today or not? Father gave it to me, so I can decide when I wear it."

"I don't care who gave it to you. Can't you see that you're offending all of your brothers?"

"I'm offending you? Why should it offend you because I wear a beautiful coat?"

Joseph had little difficulty beating Reuben at the game of words. Words flowed from Joseph in an endless stream without need for thought. He was intelligent and witty, and it was child's play for him to speak circles around his big brother until Reuben could only stand there tongue-tied. "So don't worry about it, my brother," Joseph went on. "You are making this a bigger issue than it should be."

Reuben could not answer. He knew something was wrong with what Joseph was doing, but to put the matter into words was beyond him. Joseph had mastered the magic of words, whether spoken or written, and Reuben could only say in a brokenhearted tone, "Joseph ... Joseph, can you not see that by wearing that coat you insult all of your brothers? I beg you to put it away before it becomes a snare. It has lifted your heart up with pride." Without another word, Reuben turned and walked away.

Joseph watched him go, troubled for a moment, but it was only fleeting. He finally turned away, laughing and saying to himself, "Reuben worries too much."

———

Jacob had not known at first what to make of the young woman named Tamar. She had joined his tribe when she was only twelve, an orphan with no one to care for her. She was half-starved at the time and either would have died or been forced to become an immoral woman in order to survive. But Jacob had felt pity for the child and had commanded his people to care for her. Levi's wife had taken her in, and Tamar had proved to be a hard worker, never shirking any task.

She was also clever and affectionate and soon grew attached to Jacob. She enjoyed cooking special foods for him, and the old man was pleased with her attention. She in turn loved to sit at his feet and listen to his stories of the history of his people and of his God. She hung on to his words with such attention that Jacob often said, "I wish my sons paid as much attention to our history as you do, my child!"

Early one afternoon Tamar brought Jacob a dish of tender-roasted kid and fresh dates covered in honey. The old man blessed her, and she sat at his feet as he ate, begging for more stories of El Shaddai and of the tribe. She was eighteen years old now and had blossomed into a womanly, dusky beauty. Jacob smiled and shook his head. "Daughter, you know all of my stories."

"Please tell me again about the ladder reaching up to heaven, master."

Jacob was always willing to tell of his encounters with the Lord, and he spoke for a long time, then finally reached over and touched the young woman's crown of lustrous black hair. "Why do you love to hear about these things, Tamar?"

"Because they're so wonderful, master!" Tamar's eyes glowed, and her lips were parted in wonder. "To think that El Shaddai has chosen your family to bring a Redeemer into the world! Is this not so?"

"Yes, it is so. I call the One who is to come Shiloh."

"When will He come? In our lifetime?"

"Only God knows that, child."

Tamar was silent for a moment; then she asked, "Will it be through your firstborn that Shiloh will come?"

The question troubled Jacob, and he hesitated before answering, "I do not know that either. But I do not think so."

Tamar knew very well that Reuben was not Jacob's choice to receive the blessing, even though he was the firstborn. She also knew that the old man had never forgiven Simeon and Levi for their murderous attack on the men of Shechem. For a long time she had considered the sons of Jacob, trying to understand which son would be chosen to bring Shiloh into the world.

During the years she had lived with Jacob's tribe, Tamar had slowly developed a desire to be an instrument in the family of Abraham, the man of faith. She had soaked up the history of his family, and as the years passed, she had developed a longing to be a part of the history of the Redeemer. How she came by this, not even Tamar herself could tell, but it was now the strongest force in her life.

By a process of elimination, she had come to believe that the fourth son, Judah, would receive the birthright and the blessing from his father. She had pondered on this for many months now, and as she sat at Jacob's feet, she decided to make a bold request.

"Master, I am old enough to be a wife, am I not?"

"Why, so you are, my child." Jacob smiled. "Which young man has been looking on you with desire?"

"I wish to be the wife of one of your people, for I have come to feel myself as one of them in spirit."

Jacob was pleased that she would identify so closely with his people. "Has one of the men spoken to you of marriage?"

"I would like to be the wife of Er, the son of your fourth-born, Judah."

Now Jacob was indeed amazed! "Er? But why him, daughter?" He wanted to demand, *"Why would any young woman desire such a weakling for a husband?"* Both of Judah's older sons, Er and Onan, were weak men. Even worse, they were immoral men, who could not be controlled either by Jacob or by their father.

As for Tamar, she would have tried to have Judah for a husband, for she was convinced that he was the son through which the Redeemer would come. But Judah was already married, so Er, his oldest son, would carry the seed of the Promised One—at least so Tamar had come to firmly believe.

"I will be a good wife to him," Tamar said, her eyes brilliant as she faced Jacob. "Will you ask Judah to command his son Er to have me for his wife?"

Jacob was reluctant to fulfill such a request, but at the same time, he knew that Er would not find a better wife than this young woman. And she would have children with the blood of Abraham, Isaac, and Jacob!

"I will speak with Judah—if you are certain this is what you wish."

Tamar smiled triumphantly. "Yes, master! It is what I want most of all things."

———

At first the engagement of Er to Tamar was the subject of much discussion, but after a few days the novelty of the union passed away. Er himself had no desire to marry, but his father had ordered him to agree. Er had said to his brother Onan, "Father can force me to marry her, but he can't make me be faithful to her!"

Two weeks after Tamar had spoken with Jacob, the time of harvest arrived. The late rains had been plenteous, and a fine wheat crop was thick in the fields. The harvesting always began with the reaping of the barley, a task most of the sons of Jacob enjoyed. Joseph was the exception, for he was not particularly given to hard labor. He had learned to get by with as little of it as possible, but at harvest time he joined in with his brothers. They all cut the bearded grain with a sickle, then gathered the stalks together and bound the sheaves with straw. Joseph was in one of his happy moods and did not notice his brothers' sullen looks toward him. He had laid aside his coat of many colors, it not being suitable for working in the fields. He also stripped off his tunic, working only in a loincloth, and the sun gleamed against his smooth olive skin. On one level Joseph actually enjoyed working with his brothers on the harvest because it brought him into contact with them. It was strange that a young man so intelligent in so many ways could be so blind to the fact that he had alienated himself from his older brothers by all of his boasting. For his part, he loved them and counted on their love in return, but a veil had fallen over his understanding, and he could not see what had happened to their relationships.

They worked for several days at the harvest, their bronzed bodies tanned even darker by the blazing sun. Patches of stubble were all that was left now of the barley, and on top of a small hill, Jacob's servants used pitchforks to separate the stalks as they threshed out the grain, then tossed the stalks down before the oxen.

By early afternoon Joseph was tired, having worked hard in his opinion, and he lay down in the shade of a terebinth tree.

As the brothers made their way to the next field, they eyed Joseph with disgust. Dan looked over at him and muttered, "Well, the son of the True Wife has quit on us, I see."

Issachar laughed. "I'd do the same if I could get by with it, wouldn't you?"

"We could never get by with it," Dan grunted. "Only the dreamer there can take off anytime he pleases."

Ignorant of their complaints, Joseph slept for several hours, and Reuben noticed more than once that the boy was twitching and his lips were moving. "Another one of his dreams, I'll be bound," he muttered, then went on with his work.

Late in the afternoon when the work was done for the day, the men were sitting around talking about new methods of harvesting the barley. Levi had seen a new implement called a threshing table. It was drawn by oxen and had pointed stones on the underside that tore the ears open.

"It'll never work," Reuben said. He hated changes and was against all of them.

"Why wouldn't it work?" Dan insisted. "Don't be so stubborn, Reuben."

They argued back and forth peaceably enough until Joseph suddenly sat up. He looked around wildly for a moment; then a smile crossed his face. He got up and interrupted Issachar, who was putting in his views about new methods of harvesting.

"Listen, my brothers, I must tell you something important. I've had a dream."

"Surprise—surprise! The dreamer has had a dream!" Simeon laughed harshly. "Away with you, dreamer! We want none of them here."

"But it's such a beautiful dream." Joseph was quiet only for a moment; then he interrupted again. "My brothers, listen. You must hear this."

"Let him tell us his silly dream," Levi grunted, "or we'll never have any peace. What is it, dreamer?"

"I dreamed that all of us were together," Joseph said, moving his hands to illustrate his words, "and we were harvesting grain."

"Oh, that's a marvelous, wonderful dream!" Naphtali cried out. "Wonderful! That was no dream. That's what we're actually *doing*."

"No, but it was a different field in my dream. We were working together to bind the sheaves after cutting the stalks."

Gad scoffed, "That's what we do, boy. Have you gone stupid? There's no wonder in this dream."

"But this was so real," Joseph said. If he had looked around and seen the frowns and sneers on the faces of his brothers, he would have held back, but his eyes were still dreamy and he said excitedly, "We were in a field, and all of us were binding sheaves."

"Even little Benjamin?" Judah asked moodily.

"Yes, even Benjamin. So there were twelve sheaves."

"Twelve brothers and twelve sheaves. What's so wonderful about that?" Zebulun cried out. "Away, dreamer!"

But Joseph ignored them and went on. "Suddenly my sheaf rose up in the middle and the others gathered around in a circle. And you know what?" Joseph cried, his eyes flashing. "All of the eleven sheaves were bowing down to my sheaf, which was still upright in the center!"

A cry of anger went up from the brothers. "Don't you see how offensive this is?" Judah said roughly. "Are all your brothers to bow down to you?"

"That is the worst dream I ever heard," Gad shouted.

Simeon jumped up and ran over to Joseph, along with several of the other brothers. They shouted at him, their faces red with anger. "So we're to bow down to you! We're your servants now, are we?" Simeon took Joseph's arm and began to shake it while Zebulun grabbed the other arm, tossing Joseph in the air and hurling him to the ground. "We've heard enough of you, and we've seen enough of your coat!" Simeon shouted. "I'll teach you what happens to little brothers with big heads!"

Reuben suddenly appeared, pushing Simeon, Levi, and Gad back. "Leave him alone."

"You always defend him, Reuben!" Naphtali shouted. "Why do you do that?"

"Never mind. Just leave him alone."

Reuben walked Joseph out of the circle, protecting him from any further attack.

As the two disappeared, Levi snarled, "Reuben always takes up for that puppy, but I hate him."

"So do I," Gad said. "Something's going to happen to him someday that'll take that pride right out of him."

Joseph was shaken by what had happened, and as Reuben dragged him away, he said, "What have I done? Why are they so angry?"

Reuben waited until they were out of earshot of the others, then turned Joseph around and held him by the upper arm, his hands like vises. "You fool," he said. "You're so smart and so stupid at the same time. Can't you see what an insult you've offered to all of us? You're so much better than we are that our sheaves have to bow down to yours?"

Joseph stood there dumbfounded, his eyes wide, for indeed he'd had no thought of how insulting his comments would be. When Reuben dropped his hands, Joseph said, "I'm sorry, Reuben. I didn't mean to offend anyone."

"Joseph . . . Joseph, don't you see? You're filled up with pride, and for all your knowledge of numbers and stars and geography, you don't know how offensive you are to your own brothers. Wake up out of your dreams and put them away from you."

Joseph tried to think as he watched Reuben walk away. He thought over the dream and finally murmured to himself, "But it was a real dream. Why are they so angry?" He shook his head and went away, knowing that the rest of the harvest would not be quite so pleasant for him.

As Reuben related the incident of Joseph's dream of the sheaves, Jacob's heart seemed to shrink, and he could say nothing in response.

After a moment of silence, Reuben said, "You should beat the boy, Father. I know you love him, and he's the son of the True Wife, but you're letting him ruin himself."

"He means no harm by retelling his dreams."

"He doesn't know any better because you have never brought him up short. You had no trouble caning the rest of us when we misbehaved. Can't you see that you've spoiled Joseph to the point where he has no sense of wrongdoing where the rest of us are concerned?"

Jacob had no defense, but he persisted feebly. "The boy will grow out of these things."

"Do you believe in that dream? It can mean only one thing, Father— that he's to be elevated among all your sons."

"Not all dreams are from God, Reuben."

"Do you think this one is?" Reuben demanded.

"I can't say. I will speak to the boy about it."

Reuben stared at his father hopelessly. "One day you will regret letting him run wild," he said harshly, then turned and walked away.

Jacob called after him, "Wait!" But Reuben did not even look around.

Jacob held his hands together, his heart troubled, for he knew Reuben was right. He was an intelligent man and could see how Joseph had alienated his brothers. It was now the ten of them against the two sons of the True Wife, and the thought of where that might lead frightened him.

It was logical that Joseph could not see what was happening, for he had grown up as the favorite of his old father, given his way at all times. Being born so much more intelligent than the rest of his brothers, perhaps it was inevitable that he would think of himself as a very special person. His education had reinforced this opinion, and Jacob's favoritism had so saturated him that Joseph accepted it as his God-given right.

It was only four days after the dream of the sheaves that Jacob came to watch his sons and servants work. He arrived in the morning and was greeted first by Joseph.

"Good morning, Father. Does all go well with you?"

"Yes, my son. How goes it with the crop?"

"You see it is well. The best crop in years."

"Little thanks to you," Gad muttered under his breath, barely loud enough for Jacob to catch it.

Jacob ignored the comment, however, and allowed himself to be shown the harvest. He spent the morning with his sons, and at noon they stopped to have a meal. For once things seemed to be going well. Jacob was pleased with the crop and said so. He had found a way to get around to each of the six red-eyed sons of Leah and the four Sons of the Maids and commend them, something he had never done before.

Joseph watched with some impatience and finally piped up, "My father, I have had another dream you must hear."

"No, not now, my son," Jacob said hastily.

"But you must hear it," Joseph cried. "It concerns all of you."

"Father, must we listen to this puppy and his interminable dreams?" Judah complained. "We're sick of them!"

"It would be better if you did not tell any more of your dreams," Jacob warned.

But Joseph was beyond correction. This dream was so like that of the sheaves he knew it must be of God. He began to move and twist in the peculiar way he had when he spoke of his dreams. "I dreamed," he said, "that the sun and moon and eleven stars were around me in a circle, bowing down before me! It's true."

Jacob could not move except for his eyes. He shifted his gaze around and saw the anger burning in the ten sons, Benjamin not being there. With all his heart he wished Joseph had not told such a thing. He could not blame his sons for being angry, for in truth it angered him as well. He could hear the gnashing of teeth, and finally he knew he had to say something. There was no defense against this sort of insolence, even for the son of the True Wife.

"Boy, have you lost your mind? Your parents and your brothers are to bow down and worship you! I am shamed by such a dream! I will have no more of it!" It was the culmination of Joseph's arrogance. Jacob's anger woke him up to the realization of Joseph's pride, and he felt terrible fear at the deadly hatred he saw in the faces of his sons. He knew that Levi and Simeon had butchered the Prince of Shechem without a moment's thought. They were men of blood. Dan also had a fierce and ungovernable temper. There was no telling what these men would do to his lamb if he did not stop them.

"Come, you shall be punished for this. I vow it!" He started away, grabbed Joseph by the arm, and pulled him after him.

As the two left, Gad laughed harshly. "Punishment! He'll never punish *him*. He never does."

"He'll probably give him a stiff lecture and Joseph will laugh at it," Simeon said. "Are we to put up with this, my brothers?"

"We'll have to put up with it no matter what," Judah said, "because that's just the way things are."

"Not if we do something to stop it," Simeon said, his eyes redder than flame with his anger.

The brothers stood there raving and shouting, some of them so angry they threw stones at trees and took sticks and broke them. Simeon and Levi seemed the most volatile, and finally Reuben tried to quiet them. "Don't trouble yourselves," he shouted over them, trying to calm them down. "This will pass away."

"Pass away! Why would it pass away?" Simeon screamed. "It'll pass away when Joseph is dead, that's when it will pass away!"

"Don't speak like that," Reuben said, horrified because he feared the wrath of these brothers was being kindled to the point where murder was a very possible outcome. "Remember, he is our brother!"

"He's no brother of mine," Issachar said bitterly. "He gets everything and we get nothing. I hate him!"

A murmur went around, and Reuben's eyes met Judah's. Judah shook his head as if to say, *There's nothing we can do about it.* Reuben's shoulders drooped, for he knew Judah was right. He had a premonition of a terrible future. He was not a man of much imagination, but it did not require much to know that things could not go on like this without tragic consequences. He turned sadly and said, "Well, let's get the rest of the crop harvested."

The men went to work, but they were sullen. Some of them continued to cry out against Joseph's insolence, and their threats were more dire than ever.

CHAPTER
5

Benjamin tripped along happily beside Joseph, holding his hand, as usual, when they went out to the fields together. The sun was bright, and the desert flowers blooming. Although the heat was oppressive, Benjamin did not care, for he was with his beloved brother, Joseph.

"Tell me about the dream again, brother."

Joseph looked down at Benjamin and smiled. His heart was always filled with love for his little brother. "Why, Benji, you're the only one who wants to hear them."

"Oh, I can't believe that."

"It's true." Joseph shrugged. "Our father has forbidden me to speak any more of my dreams."

"But why, Joseph?"

"I can't imagine. I know Father himself has dreams, and he has great faith in them. But he says it is bad for me to tell them to others, especially to my brothers."

"Even to me?"

Joseph laughed and ruffled Benjamin's hair. "Not you, Benji. I'll tell you all of my dreams."

"Tell me of the ones again about the sheaves and the moon and the stars."

"I've told you a hundred times. You know them yourself."

"But it's different when you tell them!"

Not unwillingly, Joseph told the dreams again. He had nourished them, knowing somehow deep in his heart these dreams were central to his life. He could not press the interpretation too much, but he could see very well that it would take only one act on his father's part to make them come true. He had said many times to himself, though never publicly, *If my father would declare that the blessing of the firstborn would be given to me instead of to Reuben, then all my brothers would have to be obedient to me. They would bow down just as the sheaves did to my sheaf, and just as their stars did to me.* He never voiced this, however, for he was beginning to understand how much danger there was in saying such things.

Benjamin listened again, his face beaming, as Joseph related the dream; then he said, "I will bow down to you, my brother."

Joseph laughed, picked up the boy, and swung him around, holding him tightly in his arms. He kissed him and said, "I know you would. You are my true brother. Indeed you are."

Benjamin clung tightly to Joseph's neck. Joseph had indeed become the center of his world. Young as he was, he was aware that there was a barrier between him and his father because his mother had lost her life bringing him into the world, and he felt great guilt for that.

"Come along. Let's hurry," Joseph said. "We don't want to get into trouble with Father again."

"No indeed! We must obey Father," Benjamin said eagerly.

The two spent a delightful afternoon wandering in the fields, and now the sun was approaching the horizon. Joseph suddenly stopped and pointed. "Look. There's a caravan—traders, I see."

"Let's go look at their goods," Benjamin said, excited.

"All right," Joseph said. "We have no money, but we can look."

When the two brothers were about a hundred paces from the caravan, Benjamin said, "Look, there's Levi."

Joseph stopped. "Yes, and there's Simeon."

"Maybe we'd better not go there. They'll tell Father."

"I'm not afraid of what Simeon and Levi would say. Father knows we're spending the day together." Nevertheless, despite these brave words, Joseph nodded. "Maybe you're right, Benjamin. We'd better not continue."

"But let's stay here and watch them awhile."

"All right," Joseph said, and the two lingered at a distance. The caravan had obviously stopped for the day, and cooking fires sent smoke into the air in tall spirals. The smell of cooked meat made the boys hungry. They could hear singing and see some women dancing.

"Look at those women. I've never seen dancing like that," Benjamin said. "What is it, Joseph?"

"It's not a good thing for you to see."

"Why not?"

"Because those women are harlots."

"What's a harlot?"

"A bad woman that makes men do bad things."

"Oh, I know what that means. Like Elspeth did when she was gotten with child with Lomenie of Lomar?"

"Yes. Like that."

Joseph watched, seemingly riveted to the scene. He saw the women dancing in their scanty costumes, and then he saw that Levi and Simeon were drinking heavily. "They need to get away from those women," he said. "They're bad for them."

Benjamin was struck silent by the scene and did not answer.

Finally the two boys watched two of the women grab Simeon and Levi and pull them to their feet. They took them to two separate tents, and Joseph said abruptly, "Come along, Benjamin, we need to get away from here."

"All right, Joseph. This is a bad thing."

As they made their way back, Joseph was silent, and Benjamin looked up and asked, "Are you going to tell Father?"

Joseph was lost in thought. "I think I'd better. He needs to know such things."

"They'll get mad if we tell."

"You're not going to tell. I am," Joseph said. "It's for their own good!"

———

Leah was giving her sons Simeon and Levi a tongue-lashing that had all the bite of a scorpion. She was a woman with a sharp tongue anyway, and now as her sons stood before her, both married heads of households, they stood humbled like two boys caught stealing sugared dates.

"You defile yourself with those harlots!" Leah screamed, her voice carrying over the entire camp. "Have you no shame! Both of you have good wives, and you defile yourselves. I'm the mother of fools!" Their mother struck them both and sent them out of her tent.

Simeon turned to Levi and said, "It was that talebearer Joseph. He's the one who brought the report to Father."

"We were fools," Levi said heavily.

"Maybe we were. I've learned one thing, though. If you're going to sin, don't do it in public."

The public shame of the two men was painful, and they blamed Joseph for telling on them. All ten of the brothers were absolutely furious at Joseph.

Even Reuben could make no defense for Joseph. After all, he had also carried the evil report to Jacob of Reuben's misbehavior with Bilhah, which was much worse. But still he kept silent as his brothers raved and shouted, angry to the core. He knew that the Sons of the Maids were just as angry, and he whispered to Judah, "Try to quiet them down. They're crazy."

"Don't they have reason?" Judah said bitterly. "Does that pampered brother of ours have the right to carry tales?"

"Simeon and Levi were wrong."

"It makes no difference. Talebearing is wrong, especially against your own brothers! That is a sin against God himself! Family is important, Reuben."

Reuben could not argue, for he felt the same. He thought of going to Joseph and trying to talk him into apologizing, but he knew he did not have the words or the skill to speak to his quick-tongued younger brother. He sighed heavily and shook his head. He had no one to share his burden with except Judah, and even Judah was fed up with Joseph's behavior.

Two days after Jacob had received Joseph's reports of Simeon and Levi's behavior with the Canaanite harlots, Levi came to him, saying bitterly, "We're going over to Shechem. Not only the six of us but also the four Sons of the Maids."

"All ten of you?"

"Yes," Levi said defiantly. He waited for his father to protest, but Jacob seemed crushed.

"Why don't you wait awhile, my son?" he pleaded.

"We're not waiting for anything." Levi had never spoken to his father like this.

Jacob knew well of the anger that burned in the hearts of his ten sons. "All right," he soberly agreed. "The grazing is better at Shechem, and it will be good for the flocks. Be careful."

Levi did not even say good-bye but turned on his heel and walked out. Jacob bowed his head, knowing that things were completely out of his control. He tried to pray but could not. He slept a troubled sleep, for he could not help thinking of his dream in which he had held a knife over Joseph. It was not difficult to interpret such a dream, and he had struggled inwardly, trying to give up Joseph to God as Abraham had given up his son Isaac. He knew, however, that he was weaker than Abraham and could not find the faith to do it. He had wept over this silently in the darkness of his tent, but somehow he felt better that the ten would now be absent. "At least," he whispered to himself, "they can't harm their brother as long as they're in Shechem."

Since the brothers had left, the weather had grown hotter, and the earth had become parched and dry. Jacob's spirit was no better. The heat was oppressive, and he was troubled by his own inadequacies. He knew he should give Joseph and Benjamin up to God, but they were all he had left of Rachel. No matter what he said to God in his prayers, in the secret chambers of his heart, he knew he would give up the ten in order to save the two.

The days passed, and Jacob's emotional struggles did not lessen. It affected his health to the point where he was now in poor condition. Tamar, now married to Er, often brought him tasty food and wanted to listen to his stories. A few times Jacob asked her about her marriage, but she avoided speaking about her husband's behavior. It was common knowledge that Er was a violent man and beat Tamar and that he was unfaithful to her, but she refused to complain.

As for Jacob's problems with his sons, it was not that he did not love his ten sons. He saw their shortcomings, but his own history was unsavory enough that he could forgive them.

There were times when Jacob feared for his own sanity, and he was often plagued by the frightening thought, *I'm possessed by some evil spirit that makes me disobey my God.* Like all of his people he had a deep fear of madness and would run quicker from an insane person than he would from a bear or a lion. Day after day he struggled, and slowly he began to be filled with a desire to bring peace to his family.

"I've got to make my ten sons understand that I love them," he said to himself, but could think of no way to do this. Finally he began to formulate a plan that perhaps Joseph was the key to bringing peace to Jacob's heart and pacifying his brothers.

He called Joseph to his tent, and when the young man was inside, Jacob said, "Sit down, my child."

"Yes, Father. What is it?"

"I am very worried about this problem you have with your brothers."

"So am I, Father. It grieves me that they do not love me."

Jacob resisted the impulse to deliver a sharp and bitter sermon about how Joseph had brought his brothers' anger on himself. He did not say a word about this, however, but spoke of his own responsibilities. "I have twelve sons," he said, "and I have spoiled you."

"Not so, Father," Joseph protested.

"You know it is true, Joseph. Do not pretend."

Jacob's eyes grew flinty, and Joseph could not bear the sight of them, so he dropped his head. His father had a strength that he himself lacked. "I am sorry, Father."

"I hope you are, for I have decided to send you to your brothers."

A flare of joy leaped into Joseph's breast, though he kept it carefully hidden. He had never been sent out alone on such a journey, and excitement burned in his spirit. "To go see my brothers?"

"Yes. I have decided you are to take them some good provisions, but mainly I want you to use the time to make peace with your brothers."

"How shall I do that, Father? They hate me."

"I must tell you the truth, my son. Your brothers hate you because you think you are better than they are."

"No, Father, that's not—"

"Do not interrupt me. You know it is so." Jacob's eyes again bored into Joseph, and the young man could only drop his head. "It is largely my fault," Jacob admitted, "for you *are* gifted above any of your brothers. You are better looking and more intelligent. You have far more imagination than any of them. These things are good, but you have let pride in them lift you up. The dreams you've had about their sheaves bowing down to yours!" Jacob's voice grew bitter. "What a fool thing to tell them of this. Stupid! Unthinkable! I cannot see how you can hold your head up after speaking of such a thing."

Joseph kept his head lowered as Jacob droned on and on about incidents where Joseph had let his brothers know his feelings of superiority. Finally Jacob said, "Do you not see, my son, how wrong you have been?"

"Yes, Father, I understand."

"I hope so," Jacob said fervently. "You are clever with words. You have imagination. So when I send you to your brothers, I want you to humble yourself. Try to win back their confidence. I know this can't be done in a day," he said sadly, "but it *can* be done over a period of time. Take them gifts. Offer to help them with their work—and above all say *nothing* of your dreams. Do you understand me, Joseph?"

"Yes, Father."

"And will you try your best to keep your dreams to yourself and to keep your pride under cover? I know it's there, but at least don't let them see it."

Joseph, in all truth, was only listening to half of what his father was saying. Instead he was thinking of the delights of the journey, but he was a fine actor, and he played the part of a penitent to perfection. In short, he managed to convince his father that he'd had a change in heart, but even as he listened, all he saw was himself going forth on a delicious adventure.

"You will leave in the morning," Jacob said. "You will take three beasts loaded with the finest food we have. It is time to be generous. They will be your gifts to your brothers. Make that plain. And partake of them little yourself."

"Oh yes, Father, I understand."

"And above all do *not* wear your coat of many colors! Do not even take it with you. It is an affront to your brothers, and I erred greatly in giving it to you."

"It shall be as you say, Father," Joseph said, but his thoughts were not on the coat. It was on the adventure that lay ahead of him. He pretended to listen to Jacob's careful instructions, then ran to tell Benjamin that he would be gone for some time.

"Take me with you, Joseph," Benjamin pleaded.

"No, Father would never let us both go. But when I come back, I will tell you everything that happened."

"Be sure you forget none of it. When will you come back?"

"I will probably not stay with my brothers more than two or three days. Then I'll return and tell you everything."

Benjamin looked up with awe in his eyes. This brother of his could do anything. "I wish I could go with you," he said.

Joseph laughed, his mind not on his little brother but on his journey. What a fine thing it would be to wear his coat as he traveled! He would not wear it in front of Jacob, of course, but it would be good to wear it on his journey. People would know that a prince was passing through their midst!

CHAPTER
6

"I wish I could go with you, Joseph!"

Joseph knelt and put his arms around Benjamin. "I wish you could too, my dear little brother. When I come back, you and I will make a shorter journey. I promise."

"Really! You mean it?"

"Of course I mean it."

Joseph kissed Benjamin's tearstained face, and his heart gave a tug. He had asked his father halfheartedly if Benjamin could accompany him, but Jacob had almost exploded. "Both of you at once! No, never!" It had been as Joseph had expected, but at least he had tried.

He gave the boy one final hug, then stood up and looked to where the three donkeys were waiting. Two of them were loaded down with cheese, dates, baked bread, and all the delicacies Joseph and Jacob could find. Jacob was standing to one side of the donkeys, his eyes filled with apprehension. Joseph went to him and said, "Promise you will not worry about me, my father."

"How can I help it?" Jacob said, his voice breaking. "It is in my heart now to change my mind."

"Oh no, don't say that," Joseph said quickly, and his mind raced to explain why he should go. "It is our one chance to restore my relationship with my brothers. Please do not rob me of this, Father." It took some pleading, for Jacob was indeed capable of stubbornly calling the entire journey off. Joseph spoke quickly and glowingly about what a glorious success the trip was going to be. Finally, when Jacob began to relent, Joseph quickly said, "I must go before the sun gets any higher. I'll be back in just a few days."

Jacob opened his arms, and the tall young man embraced him. Joseph was shocked at how his father clung to him, almost as a small child clings to his father. He knew his father loved him dearly, but being seventeen years old, he had no fears for the future. When Jacob finally released him, he leaped on the donkey, waved to the two concubines and Leah, who stood watching silently. They did not look happy, but then they seldom did.

"I'll give your sons all your good wishes, good mothers," he called and kicked the donkey in the side. The animal started forward, and Joseph waved until the village faded behind him. He took one last look at his father, who seemed at that moment more pitiful and vulnerable than Joseph had ever seen him. The sight shocked him, but with the exuberance of youth, he said, "I will bring him back a good report and make him happy."

Jacob trembled as he watched his beloved son and the donkeys fade from view. He felt a touch on his hand and looked down to see Benjamin by his side. He took the boy's hand and squeezed it, then knelt down and put his arm around him.

Benjamin said, "Everything will be all right, Father. He'll be home in just a few days."

"Yes. Just a few days, and I will see my son again—and you will see your brother."

"Joseph said he would take me on a journey, a very short one. Will that be all right, Father?"

"Yes. That will be fine. I promise."

The two stood watching the empty horizon, where only a thin puff of dust marked Joseph's trail. Benjamin went away to play, but the old man stood there staring, his heart filled with such dread and turbulence he could not bear it.

Joseph was excited to be journeying to Shechem alone. As soon as he was out of sight of his father, he stopped the donkeys, rummaged through the bag of his things, and got out the coat of many colors. He shook it out and was delighted with the flashing rainbow of light it made. He slipped into it, then mounted the donkey, and kicked the animal forward.

He encountered several travelers throughout the day, and all of them turned their eyes to stare at the young prince who wore such a beautiful coat that glimmered in the sun like golden fire.

Joseph was pleased with the impression he made and thought more about that than about the mission he was on. His conscience bothered him slightly for not obeying his father's order to leave the coat at home. But, as always, young Joseph in all his glory found a way of rationalizing his decision to go his own way, and as he watched the admiring stares of others, he decided his father had been wrong to deny him this pleasure.

"My father would be proud of me," he said as he caught the admiring glance of a passing family. He greeted them cheerfully and smiled regally as they all stopped to watch him pass by.

He would be pleased to see how the coat draws such admiration even from strangers, he thought, utterly convinced that he had been wise to wear it.

Thus Joseph made his way across the country. He traveled steadily that morning with a light wind caressing his face. He stopped at noon for a meal, then went on his way along roads and mountain paths. From time to time he would pass through a small village and draw the admiration of all, especially the women.

That night he chose to stay in a village where he could stable his donkeys safely. He paid to have them fed out of the money his father had given him, and afterward he had dinner with the chief of the village, who was very impressed with Joseph's finery.

The oldest daughter of the house, a lively brown-eyed girl with a womanly form and a sensuous mouth, made herself conspicuous to Joseph. After he went to bed, she slipped into the room reserved for guests. Seeing her enter, Joseph sat up at once. She wore a dress of fine-spun material that clung to her enticingly. "I came to see if there was anything you wished, master."

Joseph took a deep breath, for the words could have many meanings. The girl did not drop her head and hide her eyes as many young women would do. There was a boldness in her looks as she stood waiting, and Joseph struggled with the temptation being put before him.

"Th-there is nothing," he finally managed to say. "Thank you, mistress."

She stepped closer to Joseph, and his head spun as he smelled her pungent perfume. "If there's anything at all you'd like, I am here to serve you."

The words seemed innocent enough, but the curve of the full lips, the sultry look around the eyes, the heady scent said something else entirely.

Joseph was a spoiled and headstrong young man, but when it came to women, he had kept himself pure. There had been countless opportunities for misbehavior with the younger girls of the tribe, all who thought him quite the handsomest man they had ever seen. But Joseph had a strong sense of his calling from God to someday be in a place of authority, and he knew this was one line he could not cross without losing his father's approval. He remembered Jacob's reaction to the transgressions of his brothers in this area, and his head argued against the urges this young woman was arousing in him. She stared at him with an open invitation in her eyes, and everything in him cried out to take her up on her offer. *Father would never know,* he reasoned. *Who would tell him?*

One word from him, and she would be his. But he could not speak that word. Instead he curtly muttered, "Thank you," and lay back down. He winced at the scornful glare the girl gave him as she whirled and left the room. A mocking voice in his head kept saying, *You fool! You could have had her. What's wrong with you?*

Joseph closed his eyes and breathed deeply, forcing himself to think instead of the pleasure of the journey and the excitement of meeting his brothers. It was not an easy thing to do, but he controlled the urges of his flesh and drifted off into sleep.

———

After three days of hard travel Jacob reached his goal, the narrow Valley of Shechem. But he quickly discovered that his brothers were no longer there, and he began to ask the inhabitants of the place about their whereabouts.

"Yes, there were ten men here with large herds and flocks." The speaker was a short, squatty man with one eye missing and gaps in his teeth. He was chewing on some tough meat as he sat in the shade of a tree.

"Where have they gone? Do you know?"

"As it happens I do, but information comes with a price," the man said. He was eyeing Joseph's expensive coat, and there was admiration mixed with greed in his remaining eye.

Joseph laughed. He reached down into his pouch, pulled out a coin, and held it up. "I'm willing to pay."

"Give it to me."

"First, where did they go?"

"Over to Dothan."

Joseph stared at him. "Why would they go there?"

"I have no idea, but I heard them say that's where they were going. Now give me the money."

Joseph handed over the coin and turned and remounted his donkey. As he rode off, the man held up the coin, admiring it. "Should have asked for two of these," he grunted. "That young lord would never miss 'em."

———————

The ten brothers quit early for the day, leaving the flocks in the hands of several servants. As they cooked their midday meal Reuben glanced around at their faces, feeling a little relieved. *They're not as angry as they were when we left Father,* he thought. *They'll get over Joseph's foolishness.*

But in truth the other nine brothers were still angry at Joseph, though for the time they kept their feelings to themselves. Like a fire that had settled down, there was no longer any visible flame, but the coals underneath were hot!

While the brothers ate, Reuben chose to sit by himself and think about his life. It seemed to be nothing but a series of mistakes. He was troubled about the future and about the meaning of Joseph's dreams, for he alone, with the possible exception of Judah, felt there was some truth to them that he could not understand. Somehow Joseph was different from the rest of them. It was more than the fact he was the son of Jacob's True Wife. Indeed, that seemed to be the least of it.

Reuben had always seen qualities in Joseph that made him stand out from the other brothers. It was not so much that he was better looking or more intelligent than the others; it was the spirit in him that Reuben could not grasp. It flashed out at times, overshadowing his foolish youthful pride, and there was definitely something to his dreams. Of that Reuben was certain.

Having finished his stew, Reuben got up and said, "I'm going to check the flock to see if the servants are staying alert." He left without another word, and the nine paid him little attention. He had not been gone long, however, when the subject they had tried to keep hidden whenever Reuben was around now bubbled to the surfaced.

Gad was the first to speak. "I can never forgive Joseph for being a bearer of tales. It's bitter when we honest men have to kowtow to a puppy like that."

All at once they began talking. Simeon and Levi were the loudest, their faces flushed with anger as they went over and over the many times Joseph had insulted them. It infuriated them that their father showed such favoritism, and they began to speak wildly.

This had gone on for at least half an hour when Asher, who had the keenest eyesight of the brothers, suddenly stood up and said, "What's that?"

The other brothers looked about casually, and Judah said, "I don't see anything."

But Asher insisted. "There's something flashing over there. It's like silver."

This caught Gad's attention, and he got up and stood beside Asher. They both stared into the distance while Asher insisted that something unusual was coming. Then they all got up to look.

"There's something there all right," Judah said with a frown. "But I can't make it out."

"It's not a man. It's only a boy."

Asher exploded with indignation. "Why, it's that dreamer coming," he shouted bitterly, "and he's wearing that accursed coat!"

Perhaps if Reuben had been there, things would have gone differently. The brothers were all afraid of his prodigious strength, and none of them would have stood up to him. But Reuben was not there, and the angry talk ran through the brothers like lightning.

"Look at him in that stinking coat!" Simeon raved.

Levi was quick to put in his angry remark. "I'd like to break his fool neck! That's what I'd like to do!"

A murmur of assent went around, and it was Dan, perhaps the quickest thinker of them all, who said, "You know why he's come, don't you?"

"What do you mean?" Judah demanded.

"He's come to lord it over us by wearing that coat. It's as if our father has said right out that Joseph has the blessing and the birthright."

The angry murmuring and cursing rose louder until the rage that had been festering among them for years spewed over. They had come here to get away from Joseph and his nonsense about their bowing down to him—and here he came wearing that coat, the very symbol of their father's favoritism!

By the time Joseph had gotten close, the nine brothers were in a murderous rage. Like flood waters that have built up behind a dam over time, finally causing it to burst, so had the brothers' anger so built up over the years that nothing could have held it back.

Joseph was totally unprepared for the ambush that awaited him. He had come ready to do his father's bidding, to be humble, to give his brothers the food, and try to mend the breach between them. His spirits were high as he rode into camp and slipped off his donkey. "Greetings, brothers! I bring you greetings from Father, and I bring you——"

But Joseph never finished his speech. With a roar of rage Levi stepped forward and struck him in the face with his powerful fist. The blow cut off Joseph's words and drove him backward.

Dan cried out, "Beat him!"

And another cried out, "Kill him! That's what he deserves!"

Seven of the nine rushed forward—only Judah and Issachar held back—but the others fought each other to get at Joseph. Their shrieking voices rent the air with their suddenly released hatred.

A pack of hungry wolves could not have fallen on an innocent lamb with any more vicious action. The fact that there were so many of them saved Joseph some blows because they got in each other's way. Nevertheless, their fists struck out at Joseph and their hands ripped like claws at his beautiful coat. He cried out, "Brothers——" But his words were strangled by the blood filling his mouth and throat.

Though he could not understand it, Joseph knew he was doomed to die at the hands of this maddened pack when Reuben suddenly appeared, knocking the brothers aside and screaming, "Let him alone! What's wrong with you?" He struck them on either side, like a ship slicing through stormy waves, until he came to stand over Joseph, who lay bloodied and broken on the ground. "Have you lost your minds?" Reuben bellowed.

"Lost our minds! Have you lost *yours*?" Levi yelled back. "You're not going to save him this time, Reuben."

"Yes, I am."

"You can't whip all of us," Dan screamed. "Come on, brothers, this is one time that little rat's going to get what he deserves!"

Operating on pack instinct, the brothers, who had been resentful of Reuben for some time, saw here a chance to overcome him. Reuben had ruled them all by his physical strength, but together they were stronger, and they began screaming, "Get out of the way, Reuben!"

Reuben was not quick of mind, but there was little to think about here. He glanced down at the beaten form of Joseph, blood running down his face, his beautiful coat and tunic torn to shreds, revealing the bruises swelling on his naked side where he had taken fearful blows and kicks. Reuben shifted his gaze to the brothers, who now circled him exactly like a pack of wolves would circle a dying animal. He knew he could defeat any one or two or even three of them, but they were all grown men, strong and hearty, and he stood no chance against all of them together.

If Reuben had possessed the persuasive ability of Dan or the quickness of Judah, he might have talked them out of their rage, but he had no such gift. He could only stand there and beg—something he had never done in his life. "Please, my brothers, you must not—"

"Shut up, Reuben," Simeon yelled. "We're going to kill him!"

The brothers had not begun with murder in their hearts, but their humiliation and resentment had festered over the years, finally driving them to this frenzied state of rage. Reuben then had the only imaginative thought in his life. He saw that Joseph was a doomed man. The brothers had gone too far. Even if Joseph went back home now, bruised and bleeding, the wrath of Jacob would fall upon them all.

"We must not kill him," Reuben said. "We can't have our brother's blood on our hands." And then the idea came as if from someone else. "We can throw him into the pit," he shouted, "and leave him to die. That way his blood won't be on our hands."

"Yes!" Levi shouted. "Throw him into the pit!"

The pit was an ancient well that had long ago dried up and had partially filled in with the drifting desert sands. It was still some twenty feet deep, however, and the brothers knew there was nothing at the bottom but stones and sand that had caved in from the top. Nobody could climb out of it.

The brothers were relieved at Reuben's plan. None of them really wanted to bear the burden of actually killing their brother with their own hands, but in their minds leaving him to die would be different.

"Yes!" they shouted together. "Throw him into the pit."

All of them knew they had gone too far, but they could not back down now. Even Judah agreed. A plan had formed in his mind, and he carried the day by saying, "Look, we'll throw him into the pit, and when we come back to our father and he asks for him, we'll say he is no more. He was lost along the way. Who will know the difference?"

"Yes," Levi shouted. "That's what we'll do."

Simeon reached down and jerked Joseph to his feet.

"Have pity on me, brothers. Do not harm me!" Joseph cried.

Reuben knew there was no way he could save his brother from his fate. He did not protest as his brothers dragged Joseph to the pit, ignoring his wailing pleas for mercy.

When they reached the ancient well, it was Dan who grabbed Joseph, saying, "Now dream your dreams in that pit!" and shoved Joseph in.

CHAPTER
7

As Joseph disappeared into the black abyss, a silence fell on all the brothers. They stood staring at the ominous hole in the ground, then quickly looked up, each searching the face of the other and seeing guilt, anger, and fear all reflecting from their eyes and in the twists of their mouths.

The feeble voice of Joseph came up out of the darkness with a pitiful quality that tore at Reuben's heart. "Oh, please, my brothers, do not do this thing! I am bleeding and will die if you leave me in this pit. Please hear me and pull me from this terrible place! Reuben—Judah! Oh, my brothers Levi and Simeon, I am sorry for all the pride that was in my heart. Forgive me and take me out of the pit so that I may not die here. I am your brother!"

The cries struck Reuben like a blow. He straightened up to his full height, then growled, "Come away from this place." He whirled, and the others could not follow quickly enough. As they left, the voice of Joseph came floating to them, and they broke into a run as if to get away from some fearful monster.

When they had stumbled and run for at least a mile, Reuben glanced at the others and said, "We cannot run away and leave our flocks."

"The servants will tend to them," Judah said. His face was pale, and his lips trembled. He was about to say more, but Simeon broke in. "What's done is done. We must leave him in the pit."

"It would have been kinder to kill him," Judah said, slumping to the ground as if his legs had no strength to support him.

Gad stared at him. "What's wrong, Judah?"

"You know what's wrong. We will never be able to face our father again."

The words echoed in the heart and mind of every one of the ten brothers, for they knew Judah had spoken the truth. They began making excuses, one blaming the other, until finally Reuben said, "You gather the sheep. I'm going to that village and see if we can hire more men."

"Why do you want to do that?" Asher demanded.

"We have to go to our father and tell him what has happened."

"No," Gad exclaimed, "we can't! Just let the boy be missing."

Reuben shook his head. "We'll have to go back home, but in the meantime I'll hire more servants to take care of our flocks." He turned and walked rapidly away.

Reuben had formulated a plan in his mind to help Joseph. He would find a long length of rope and return after dark to pull him out of the pit and get him far from this place, where his brothers could not find him. He quickly made his way to the closest village and located a farmer who sold him a long rope. He started back toward the pit, taking a roundabout way so his brothers would not see him. He was surprised at how easily the plan had come to his slow mind. He hurried on, thinking of nothing but how terrible it would be to tell Jacob that his beloved Joseph was gone.

***

Meanwhile, the other brothers were not sure what to do with themselves. They were talking and arguing together as to what they would say to their father when Simeon cried out, "Look, a caravan." They all stood up to see a long line of camels plodding in their direction.

"I think they're Midianites," Levi said. "Traders, by the look of them."

Dan spoke up. "Brothers, I know what we must do." They all looked at him, and his eyes were wide. "We must sell Joseph to these traders as a slave. That way we have not killed him—yet it will be as if he were dead."

"Yes," Levi agreed eagerly. "We can take that coat of his and put animal blood on it and have someone take it back to our father. That way he will think a wild animal has slain him."

The idea seized them all like fire, and they immediately turned and headed back for the pit. Naphtali thought of finding a rope to pull Joseph up. "We'll have to throw it down to him. He can tie it around himself and we'll pull him up. Dan, you go talk to the traders about buying him."

"I'll do that, and I'll get a good price too." Dan grinned wolfishly and set off at a run while Naphtali went the other direction to locate a rope.

"Be quick," Levi called after him. "We need to get him out before Reuben comes back."

Joseph lay in the fearful darkness of the pit, aching and bruised and bleeding, and his thoughts raced wildly in his mind. His own brothers! Why had they done such a thing to him? He whispered to himself, "I know I have not been too kind to them, but who would have thought they would throw me in a pit to die? How their eyes glowed like coals and their teeth were like fangs as they struck me!"

Joseph's mouth was parched. He felt beetles and crawling things beneath him, and his teeth chattered as he huddled in the blackness, rolled into a tight ball.

As time passed, young Joseph lay there like a stunned beast. The beatings he had received had at first dulled his feelings, but then the pain began to flood through his poor, tortured limbs like waves. He cried in agony as he thought back over his life, remembering now the many times he had carried evil reports of his brothers to his father. He thought of how he had laughed at the stupidity of Zebulun and Naphtali and how he had made fun of Reuben, who had shown such concern for him. He thought about how often he had deceived his father, lying to him and taking advantage of the old man's love for him.

He had led such a pampered life that he'd always been able to brush things off, not ever carefully examining his behavior. But now that death lay waiting for him, Joseph became honest with himself for the first time in his life. He wept with the realization that he had been filled with pride and had no real love for his brothers, other than Benjamin.

He even found himself weeping over his father, knowing that with his death the old man would, in a sense, die too. In the darkness of the pit these thoughts overwhelmed him with grief, and he could do nothing but cry out to the God of his fathers. But his cries were feeble, and he had little faith that they would be answered.

Then he heard the voices of his brothers returning. . . .

Reuben was gasping for breath by the time he got back to the pit with the rope. His circuitous route had enabled him to avoid any of his brothers. He dropped the rope and fell to his hands and knees, calling down into the darkness, "Joseph...? Joseph!" He waited and listened hard, but not a single sound. He cried again louder, "Joseph, are you all right? Speak to me, my brother."

But there was only silence. The awful thought came to him that Joseph had already died, although it had been but a few hours. Reuben continued to call down, but there was no answer. Only silence.

He had to climb down into the pit himself. Tying one end of the rope around his waist, he secured the other end to a nearby rock outcropping, then lowered himself into the pit. His feet scrambled against the wall of the well, sending stones and sand downward. Fearing that he was further injuring his brother, he kept calling into the darkness. When he reached the dry dirt and rocks at the bottom, he felt all around and found no one. Joseph was not there!

"He's gone! Where could he be?" Reuben moaned. As quickly as he could, he grabbed the rope and pulled his huge bulk back up the top, then scrambled out and looked around frantically. "Joseph," he called out. "Where are you?"

He began to run around crying loudly, but it was all in vain. Finally he stopped and bowed his head. "What has happened to him?"

Finally a hopeful thought occurred to him. *Maybe my brothers came and took him out. They must have thought better of what we had done!*

Clinging to that hope, he ran stumbling toward the place where he had left them. When he got in sight of his brothers, he began to call out their names. "Levi . . . Simeon," he gasped. He saw them all turn to look at him and knew they were surprised to see him coming from the south. "Joseph—you took Joseph out of the pit, didn't you?"

Dan spoke for the others. "Yes, we took him out."

"Where is he?" Reuben cried out, looking wildly around. "What have you done with him?"

"He's gone forever," Dan said.

"What do you mean *gone*?" Reuben demanded. He looked from face to face and saw a stubbornness, lips tightly sealed and eyes half closed against his gaze. "What have you done with my brother?" he cried out. "Judah, where is he?"

"We didn't want to . . . kill him," Judah said in a halting fashion, "so we . . . sold him to a group of Midianite traders."

"You sold our brother into slavery?" Anguish was in Reuben's voice, and he began to tremble.

"We thought it all out," Levi said loudly. "We put blood on that colored coat of his, and we had a man take it back to Father. He'll identify it and think an animal tore him."

Reuben looked around at the faces and saw determination, cruelty, and guilt in every face. He begged them to go after the traders, but Levi said, "It's too late for that. Even if we did get him back, he would tell our father what we did. You know what would happen then."

Reuben bowed his head and began to sob. It was strange to see such a huge man crying like an infant. He stretched out on the ground and put his face on his arms, and sobs racked his huge body. "Joseph, my brother! My little brother a slave!" he cried.

The others watched him, and then Levi said, "We must never let our father know what we have done. We will vow never to tell."

"Yes," Judah said, his face pale as he licked his lips. "We will all swear the oath."

―――――――――

Jacob looked down at the remnants of a once-beautiful coat, nothing but rags now, stiff with dried blood. His hands trembled as he touched it. The two men who had brought the coat stared at him. They had been well paid to deliver the coat to Jacob, telling him they had found it and thought perhaps he could identify it.

Leah was standing behind Jacob and saw the old man begin to sway. She leaped to his side and cried out in a high-pitched voice, "Jacob, husband!"

Jacob appeared not to hear her. He pressed his face against the tattered remnant of the coat that he had presented to the son he loved most of all. "My lamb is dead," he cried, his voice muffled as he pressed it into the tattered garment. "It is the hand of God upon me." He thought of his dream and how he had refused to sacrifice his son, and now God had struck, and the son was gone. He suddenly stiffened, and his legs refused to hold him. Leah cried and threw her arms around him as he slumped to the ground. The two men stared, turned, and walked quickly away.

Benjamin and Bilhah came into the tent when they saw the strangers leave and stood staring speechless at the scene before them. Jacob was slumped sobbing over the bloodied coat, and Leah held him, moaning and crying, "My poor husband. . . . He loved him more than anything."

Jacob lifted his head and tore his own garments, baring his thin chest and skinny arms. He began to claw at his chest with his fingernails, uttering a wild, almost inhuman, cry of grief. "My son is lost. My child!"

Benjamin was sobbing too as he watched the scene in grief and fear. "My brother," he whispered. "Oh, my brother Joseph, gone! Killed by the wild beasts!"

The old man and the young man continued to weep, each consumed by their own sorrow, and as Leah watched, she said under her breath, "It will kill him. He cannot live without Joseph."

PART TWO

THE ACCUSATION

CHAPTER
8

A sudden blow to the small of Joseph's back brought fresh waves of pain surging through his body. He cried out and remained in a fetal position, throwing his hands up to protect his head. Bracing himself for another blow, he clamped his teeth together and shut his eyes tightly—but the next cry of pain came not from him but from one of his captors. Opening his eyes, he rolled over and saw the burly, sunburned Midianite wallowing on the ground, with Ahmed the slave trader standing over him.

"You spawn of the Evil One!" Ahmed raged. "Did I not tell you this one must not be harmed!" He aimed a vicious kick to the fallen man's thigh, which brought another cry of pain. "Get up—and if you lay another hand on this slave, I'll tear your tongue out by the roots! I'm tired of listening to you anyway."

Ahmed turned to look at Joseph. The slave trader made a rather terrifying sight, with one eye white as milk, and the other black as obsidian. A scar wound down the left side of his face, drawing his mouth into a permanent sneer, and he was tall and thin as a tree.

"Get up, boy," he said, but his voice was not rough. "Come now. You're not that badly hurt."

Joseph scrambled to his feet and stood there trembling in the fresh morning breeze. His coat of many colors and tunic had been stripped from him, and he wore only a loincloth. He had shivered all through the night, and someone had thrown a thin blanket over him at some point. "Thank you, master," he said. His tongue was thick, and his lips were dry, for the previous day they had been short of water.

Ahmed stared at the boy. "You look like a plucked bird," he said. "How old are you?"

"Seventeen, master."

"You don't look like much now, but I expect if you were cleaned up and didn't have all those bruises, you'd look like a prince."

Joseph swallowed and nodded. "I am a prince, sir, of sorts. My father is chief of a band."

"Oh, well, is that so? And those ruffians I bought you from are desert bandits, I suppose."

Joseph swallowed hard and looked down at the ground. His feet were bare and torn by briars. "No, sir," he mumbled. "They're my brothers."

Ahmed's one good eye opened wide in surprise. "Well, a fine lot they are! They didn't tell me that. Why did they sell you?" Ahmed watched the young man but got no answer. He studied Joseph, taking in the fine bridge of his nose, the thin nostrils, the wide center of his mouth, and the smooth skin, where it wasn't skinned or battered by vicious attacks. He was a man of great discernment where slaves were concerned, and he had driven a hard bargain. "I believe I could have got you for nothing," Ahmed said. "They were anxious to get rid of you." He waited for Joseph to speak, but again Joseph remained silent. "Come, boy, talk!"

"They . . . don't care for me."

"From the looks of those bruises I'd agree. The one I talked to, the shifty-looking one . . . What's his name—Dan? Yes, that's it. He said you were a scholar."

"Among my own people I passed for one, sire."

"You are able to calculate figures?"

"Yes, I can do that, sir."

"You can measure distances accurately?"

"Yes, I can do that too."

"What about languages?"

"I speak some Babylonian and Egyptian."

"Egyptian! How did you learn that?" Ahmed asked sharply.

"We found a lost man some years ago who knew the Egyptian language, and we took him in. My father said he was probably a criminal. Perhaps he was, but he was very intelligent."

Ahmed suddenly laughed. "Not all criminals are stupid. So you learned the Egyptian tongue from him."

"Yes—and about the stars. He was very learned, it turned out, and he taught me many things. Including how to write by several different methods."

Ahmed stroked his beard carefully and studied the boy. "You understand that in my business there's no room for mercy."

Joseph looked up and met the single eye of Ahmed. "I don't expect any, sir. If I couldn't get it from my own brothers, why should I expect it from anyone else?"

Ahmed laughed shortly. "A wise answer. However, your education will not be wasted. I have a potential buyer for you who will treat you well." He waited for Joseph to ask questions, but when the young man remained silent, he said, "Don't you care?"

"No, sire. I don't care."

There was such hopelessness in Joseph's voice that, despite his business and innate hardness, the slave trader felt a tiny surge of pity. "What's your name, boy?"

"Joseph."

"Well, Joseph, we'll have to dress you out a little better than what you've got there, and I have some ointments that may take some of the bruises out. The cuts will take a while to heal. Come along. You are a valuable property. I'll take care of you very well, you may be sure!"

Though he was a hard man, Ahmed viewed Joseph as extremely valuable property and would not allow any of his men to abuse him. He was also gifted in the art of healing, and by the time his caravan reached the borders of Egypt, Joseph was at least free from his aching bones, and the large purplish bruises had mostly disappeared. The cuts and gashes were also healing, but he would be left with some nasty-looking scars.

The scars on his body, however, were nothing compared to the deep inner pain he suffered. As he trudged southward day after day, his past haunted him, causing such pain and sorrow he could not endure it. He had many times in his life purposed in his heart to be a better son and brother, but such promises, even to himself, had always been short-lived. He wished he could turn back time and fulfill those promises now, but it was too late. He could not escape God's judgment and now had to endure a fiery trial in which his very soul, it seemed, would be consumed.

At times Joseph tried to excuse his behavior as the natural result of his father's having spoiled him from before he could walk. As a child he accepted all the gifts he received as his right, and he took it for granted that he would be allowed his own way and deserved the special privileges afforded him that his brothers never received.

Often at night, lying awake when his captors and the other slaves were asleep, he now wondered why he had never seen himself as he really was, but he never arrived at an answer. Examining his life was now a painful thing to Joseph, and he had no hope whatsoever for the future, no hope for an escape from a lifetime of slavery. His heart was heavier than the sands of the desert as he trudged deeper into a foreign land, each step taking him farther and farther from all he had known and loved.

Despite the pitiful state into which he had sunk, a change began in his spirit he could not account for. All of his life Joseph had believed that God had a special purpose for him, but he had never pursued a deeper relationship with the only One who could direct him toward that purpose. It had been too easy listening to his own voice and pursuing his own heedless ways. Now, however, since all this was lost to him, he could put his active imagination and keen analytical mind to work.

God can do all things, he thought as he trudged along beside a tall, motley-colored camel. *He knows where every person in this world is and what they're doing. He knew when I was born, what I would be, and what I would do. I can look back and see what I've been, but only the Lord knows what's in the future. It must be that something awaits me besides being a slave.*

Such thinking led to genuine repentance, and a tiny flame of faith began to grow in Joseph as they made their way deeper into Egypt. When they reached Thebes, the sight of the magnificent buildings and the busy commerce of the large thoroughfares captured his full attention. He was able to think of the here and now, and somehow the future did not seem as dark and miserable as it had when he had begun this journey.

———————

"There's Potiphar's house. That's where you will be living if I can make a sale," Ahmed said, pointing with his whip toward a fine home that rose several stories. Its polished white-stone facade glowed in the afternoon sunlight, and it was delightfully surrounded by flowers and trees, giving the house a cool, inviting appearance.

"Your master's name will be Potiphar. He's a very important man. A shrewd dealer too. It will be quite a struggle between us to settle this deal. He will want you for nothing, but I will not accept less than what you're worth. We will try to get each other so drunk that one of us can cheat the other!" Ahmed said with a hearty laugh. Then with a crafty wink at Joseph, he went on, "Ah, but I can hold my liquor better than Master Potiphar. Come along, now."

The caravan had been left behind at the entrance to the city, and Ahmed led Joseph up to the gated entrance of the house. They were met by an extremely fat man with eyes that almost disappeared into the folds of his face. His mouth was enormous and had a fishlike appearance. He was a pasty color but wore an expensive garment and gold rings in his ears.

"It's you, Ahmed. What have you got for us this time?"

"The bargain of a lifetime, Ufa."

"They always are. We don't need any more slaves."

Ahmed grinned wickedly, his twisted face looking even more sinister. "Oh, I didn't know you had taken over Potiphar's business dealings. I assume you make all the decisions now?"

Ufa cursed and turned away. "I'll see if he'll even want to admit you."

"Surly fellow. Mean-spirited. Mistreats the slaves. Probably will mistreat you, but don't ever react, Joseph, no matter what they do to you. Don't ever strike back. Do you understand?"

"Yes, sire, I understand."

"They'll whip you if you do, and if that doesn't do the trick, they'll throw you to the crocodiles!"

Joseph patiently listened as Ahmed spoke of Potiphar and his wealth. In ten minutes the fat man came back and said grudgingly, "The master will see you now."

"Why, thank you, Ufa. Your manners are exquisite."

The two men followed Ufa into the house and into a high-ceilinged room with a sunken marble pool. A man rested in the water who was as large, tall, and fat as his servant Ufa. His head was shaved, and under the rolls of fat on his face, he showed signs of having once been handsome. "What sort of awful merchandise have you brought me this time, Ahmed?"

"Oh, sir, you must always have your joke," Ahmed bantered, but he bowed low and touched Joseph, who knelt at once and touched his forehead to the ground. "I am in somewhat of a hurry, master. Couldn't we just eliminate all the bargaining? Each of us knows the ways of the other, and your time is so much more valuable than mine."

Without even glancing at Joseph, Potiphar studied Ahmed carefully.

A black servant girl, dressed only in a tiny bead costume, was fanning him, her large eyes fixed on Joseph.

"That thing?" Potiphar laughed, and his eyes almost disappeared. "Why would I want a scrawny fledgling like that? He wouldn't last a week in the fields."

"You are exactly right, master. That is why he would not go to the fields."

"Oh? What would he do, then?"

"He can do your accounts. He can write in four different scripts. He knows languages like no one I've ever seen. As far as the ability to figure, you have no one like him. In short, he is the perfect scribe and a fine-looking young slave too, when he gets some meat on his bones."

Interest flickered in Potiphar's eyes, and he said bluntly, "How much?" He listened as Ahmed named a price and shrugged. "You may leave, Ahmed. Obviously you have no intention of selling the slave. No one would pay such a price. I'll pay half."

Joseph remained perfectly still as he watched the two men argue. Eventually Potiphar crawled out of the pool and was toweled down by a male servant, who was fully as tall as Potiphar but thin as a rail. He was also lighter skinned than an Egyptian and had an intelligent face. He wrapped a robe around the master as Potiphar continued to dicker with Ahmed. Finally the servant leaned over and whispered something into his master's ear. Joseph saw Potiphar look in his direction with greater interest, and Joseph knew that whoever the tall slave was, he had great influence.

"I'm too busy to argue. Shave your price and we'll agree."

"You always win, sire. Very well." And he named what he insisted was his final price.

"It's twice what he's worth. Ufa, pay this thief the money. Now get out of here, Ahmed. I am used to dealing with crooked thieves in the government, but you put them all to shame."

Ahmed bowed and touched his forehead with his hand. "Thank you, sire. I think you'll find you got the best of the bargain." He turned to Joseph and said, "Joseph, I have done you a favor."

"And I thank you, sir."

"You see," Ahmed glanced back. "The boy already has manners."

"We'll see about manners. Now get out."

Ahmed went away with Ufa, and Joseph was still on his knees. "Get up, get up!" Potiphar said irritably. He slumped down on a chair and glanced up at the thin servant. "This is Masud. He thinks you look like a bargain, but we shall see. Masud, put him to work in the fields."

"But, master—" Masud objected.

"You heard me!" Potiphar bellowed. "I won't have a slave that can't work."

"Yes, my master." Masud mumbled something, and Potiphar looked at him quickly.

"What did you say?" he demanded.

"Nothing, sire."

"Turn him over to Ufa."

"Yes, sire. Come along, Joseph."

"Yes, sir."

Masud and Joseph left, and when they were far away from Potiphar, Masud said, "It's foolish putting you to work in the fields, but Potiphar has to show his authority. Work hard. Be obedient. I think you will not be there long."

"Thank you, sir."

"Be careful of Ufa. He likes to show authority too—with a whip!"

———

Joseph quickly discovered that Ufa was a cruel taskmaster. He put Joseph to work in the fields with the other slaves from sunup until sundown. There were days when Joseph nearly fainted, for he had led an easy life physically. He gritted his teeth and stuck with it, however, doing his work so well that Ufa had to find fault with him about other things.

Some days he put him to the task of emptying the slops and dealing with the garbage that came out of the large kitchen, sometimes having him help the kitchen maids wash the dishes. He was out to break Joseph's spirit, and he tried every trick in his book.

If it had not been for Masud's ongoing advice and encouragement, Joseph would probably not have made it. The tall scribe was not only intelligent, he was shrewd and did all he could to ease Joseph's burden.

Two weeks after Joseph arrived, Masud appeared and said, "Come with me." Joseph had been working hard in the fields and was dirty and covered with dried sweat. His limbs trembled, for the work was terribly hard. He followed Masud outside to a large marble pool used to wash clothes. It was full now with clear water, and Masud said, "Jump in there and wash yourself off, Joseph."

Gratefully Joseph peeled off his clothes and submerged himself in the water. It was comfortably tepid, and as he scrubbed himself with the sponge Masud provided, he began to grow very tired. Finally he laid his head back against the side of the pool and allowed his body to float. He was nearly asleep when Masud poked him. "Things will be better from now on."

Joseph jumped and opened his eyes, alert again to his superior. "What do you mean, Masud?"

"I finally convinced Potiphar that it was a waste of talent for you to be working in the fields. He knew it himself, but he's stubborn."

"What's he like, Masud? He's married, isn't he. . . ? So I've heard the slaves speak."

"Yes. But his wife is not around much. She stays at a town called On much of the time. She has a good friend there, the daughter of the priest of On. The two are inseparable."

Joseph ducked his head under the water, then rose up and let it drain off his hair. "What does the master do for Pharaoh?"

"Whatever Pharaoh says. He's not in the very upper rungs of government, you understand. I would say maybe in the fourth rung, but Pharaoh knows his name and has shown favor to him."

"Do he and his wife have children?"

"No. Never will have."

Joseph looked quickly at Masud, whose face was blank. "You mean she's barren?"

"No. *He* is the problem." Seeing Joseph's look of surprise, he said, "Shortly after they got married, we began one of those pesky wars with the Hittites. Potiphar was sent out with the army, and he was wounded."

"Seriously?"

"Very seriously for a man who wants children. He lost a very important piece of equipment. He is a eunuch now, for all practical purposes—an accidental one."

Joseph thought hard about that and then shook his head. "That must be very difficult."

"Difficult for his wife. She's doomed to a life of chastity, and . . ."

"And what?" Joseph asked.

"Well, she is a young woman, and women have their desires the same as men. As you say, a tragedy. Well, come. Get out of there, and we'll get you some fitting clothes. You're to be my assistant, and I'll be as hard a taskmaster as Ufa."

"I doubt that"—Joseph grinned—"and you won't be half as ugly."

He scrambled out, and Masud looked over to where two of the Nubian slave girls, wearing scanty beaded costumes, were watching Joseph and giggling. "I wouldn't advise you to have ... relationships, shall we put it? with the female slaves. It could lead to difficulty."

"I believe you and it shall be as you say."

Masud looked at the two sleek, shining young woman and shook his head. "It won't be easy. Those girls have no more morals than a cobra. Come along, boy. We'll get you started on your new profession."

CHAPTER

9

Kesi-el-Mutan, whose name meant "Woman of the Lilies," had been beautiful since childhood. But now that she had reached the age of twenty-two, she was carefully dressed and pampered by her maids until her full figure and striking features were enhanced by the well-developed Egyptian cosmetic arts. Her face, with its high forehead and shadowy hollows in the cheeks, would not have been considered classically beautiful by the artistic elite, but any man who looked on her visage was so taken by her enormous eyes and sensuous mouth that he had no thought for comparisons with other women. As head of Potiphar's household, she was inevitably a spoiled darling, and her every command was as though from the master's lips.

And yet for all her attractiveness, there was something missing from her countenance. Her expression revealed a deep dissatisfaction with her life, despite all her pampering. Masud, who studied her as he did every member of the house of Potiphar, understood the source of her discontent: *She needs a man in her bed.*

Some women are careful to keep company with women less beautiful than themselves to elevate their own attractiveness, but Lady Kesi had no problems with the beauty of her best friend, Asenath, who was closer to her than any sister of blood. Asenath had a classic beauty—honey-colored skin, large well-shaped green eyes, beautifully shaped lips, and a way of moving that was enough to stir the heart of any man who watched her. Both of these two women were secure enough that each did not fear any competition from the other.

The two of them had been in the court of Pharaoh for some time, waiting to be summoned into his presence. Late one afternoon they were given the summons, and they arose and went immediately into the throne room of his majesty Pharaoh Abadmon. The two women bowed continuously as they were ushered before the pharaoh and his wife, prostrating themselves before the royal couple until ordered to rise. As they stood up, they saw the afternoon sun streaming through the high arches of the throne room and flowing down over the faces of the pharaoh and his wife, Isiri. The couple they faced, seated on gold thrones above them, represented the formidable might of the royal household of Egypt.

Pharaoh Abadmon was not an attractive man. He was undersized with a protruding belly and a frog face with small eyes and a pinched mouth. But his wife was one of the most beautiful women in the kingdom. Isiri's beauty was such that she felt no jealousy over the beauty of the two young women standing before her. She smiled and said, "You two are like sisters."

"More than that, Majesty," Asenath said quickly with a slight bow. "Many sisters do not care for each other, but Lady Kesi and I were brought up together and love each other very much."

"Indeed." Kesi smiled and turned to look fondly at the woman beside her. "We seldom passed a day in our entire lives when we did not see each other."

Pharaoh Abadmon nodded. "It is good to have close friends." Then he sighed heavily and shook his head. "The pharaoh, unfortunately, cannot have such a friend."

"Indeed not!" Lady Kesi exclaimed. "For friends must be equals, and who could be equal to the god-king of Egypt?"

"Very true," Isiri said, "but it means a lonely life for my husband."

Pharaoh Abadmon proceeded to talk at length about his difficult life as the god-king and how he was more important than all the gods put together. His wife nodded politely, agreeing that the weight of responsibility of ruling Egypt was far too great for any mere mortal to bear, and that only a god such as he could possibly live up to the task. Lady Kesi and Asenath nodded their heads too, taking their cues from Isiri to agree with every word the pharaoh uttered. The polite talk continued until the pharaoh addressed Lady Kesi directly. "Tell your husband I expect him to come to court soon. We have missed his presence."

"He will be overjoyed, Your Majesty," Lady Kesi said, bowing low.

The pharaoh clapped his hands, signaling that the audience with Lady Kesi and Asenath was over. Two guards approached at once to escort the ladies from the throne room.

Leaving the pharaoh's presence was a challenge. One could not simply turn around and walk away. It was necessary to back up and at the same time bend over, making obeisance, but the two women had developed a choreography that made even this difficult and ungainly exercise look graceful.

When they were outside the throne room and the two guards left them alone, Kesi stood up straight and put her hands over her ears. "It is so difficult," she uttered quietly, "to listen to the pharaoh. All he wants to talk about are the gods and how he is the highest of them all!" She leaned close to her friend and whispered, "Just to look at the man, you know he cannot be higher than the gods ... but I would lose my head if he heard me say that."

Asenath laughed. "Well, you had better watch your mouth, then, Kesi. It is not worth losing your pretty head over such a man! You must learn to be thankful that you are even allowed into his presence."

"Bah! I have enough else to do in my life to keep me occupied."

Asenath looked around to make sure that no one else could hear their conversation. "You and I had better not let the god-king hear such heretical comments!" she said under her breath. "And the next time he calls for us, you know as well as I that you will come bowing and fawning before him just as you did today."

Lady Kesi smiled at her friend. "Of course you're right, Asenath. You and I are not going to change the way things are." As they walked toward the litters that were waiting to take them back to Potiphar's house, she shook her head. "You would think the gods could at least produce a handsome offspring, instead of that potbellied frog face!"

The two laughed, and Asenath agreed. "The gods should indeed be handsome. There's enough ugliness in this world among humans and animals."

The two women entered Potiphar's house and passed through the western hall, which looked out on an orchard. Asenath remarked, "That's a beautiful sight, isn't it?—where the sunset lights up the columns and fills the rooms."

Lady Kesi glanced at the scene and said, "You notice everything, Asenath. I suppose I thought it was pretty at one time, but anything you see every day loses its beauty."

"Not at all," Asenath argued. "I never tire of the beauty of this home." She stopped to look at the colorful murals covering the walls and ceiling, with their exuberant nature scenes—wild bulls running; so lifelike you could almost hear them snorting, crocodiles with their mouths wide open about to engulf a woman who was carelessly bathing on the banks of the Nile, white birds with long wings and long beaks flying across the ceiling's painted sky.

The elegant doors leading outside were framed in glazed tiles, which were covered with hieroglyphics in blue, red, and green. The house was a marvel that could only be achieved by a very rich man.

Lady Kesi became impatient with her friend's attention to the surroundings she herself had taken for granted for years now. "Come along. My husband is usually sitting outside in the garden at dusk."

As she predicted, the two women found Potiphar in the garden, wearing a simple white robe draped over his bulky body. He was alone, and he glanced up at the two women with an expression that neither of them could decipher.

"Well, how was the royal court?" he greeted them.

"Boring—as usual," Lady Kesi said. She made no move to kiss her husband, for their intimate life together was over, except for public ceremonial caresses.

Potiphar looked at Asenath and said, "You've kept my wife company a long time. I'm afraid you spoil her."

"Oh no, sir, on the contrary. She spoils me."

Potiphar listened as the two women chatted, and finally when he'd heard all about their one-sided conversation with the pharaoh, he stroked his jowls and said, "I think the man's insane."

Both women were startled.

"You surely don't believe that!" Kesi said, shocked. "After all, he *is* a god."

"Who says that a god can't be insane?" Potiphar shrugged. "Some of the things we worship are downright stupid."

The two women stared at Potiphar. They did not really believe in the pharaoh's divinity themselves, but they would never have uttered such bold blasphemy out loud.

"He's a self-absorbed child, but I don't think he's insane," Asenath said with a shrug. "If he believes he is more powerful than all the gods, so be it. In the end, it'll come to nothing."

"I think you're right—in the end all gods come to nothing!"

"What a terrible thing to say, husband!" Lady Kesi exclaimed, yet her eyes were laughing. "You shock me."

"I would like to, but I fear it would take more than my heretical comments to shock you, my dear wife."

The two women enjoyed Potiphar's company. He was witty, knowledgeable, and knew intimately the inner workings of the court of Pharaoh and the vast hierarchy that spread throughout the kingdom.

Finally Kesi rose and said, "Come along, Asenath. We're not going to get any sense out of him."

"I must agree." Asenath smiled. "Excuse us, my lord. We are both weary after listening to so much wisdom from the pharaoh."

"I'm sure you are."

The two women went back inside, giggling as they walked down the hall. Kesi was laughing at something Asenath had said, and just as they reached an intersection where one hallway crossed another, Asenath had her head turned toward Kesi and did not see the man who came from the other direction. She ran right into the large pottery vase he was holding, knocking it loose from the man's grip so that it hit the marble floor and shattered into a thousand pieces. Even worse, the garbage and night soil it had contained splashed on the feet of the two women and on the lower portions of the man's legs.

Kesi screamed and Asenath jumped back, both of them wrinkling their noses at the rank odor. Kesi whirled and screamed, "You clumsy fool!"

"I wouldn't have a slave that clumsy in my house!" Asenath snapped, her eyes flashing. "Who is this?"

Kesi realized she did not know the man. "Who are you?"

"I am Joseph, Lady Kesi."

Joseph still had to perform disagreeable tasks assigned by Ufa, such as carrying out the night soil jars.

"Where did you come from?" Kesi demanded. "Never mind!" she quickly added as she saw Ufa staring at them. He appeared to be hiding a smile, and Lady Kesi shouted at him, "I ought to have you whipped!"

"Yes, my lady." Ufa was stupefied. "But I—"

"Anyone who would have such a worthless, clumsy oaf of a slave needs a whipping."

"It is not I who bought him but your husband, my lady."

"Then I will speak to Lord Potiphar. In the meantime I hold you responsible."

Lady Kesi looked then at Joseph, and her eyes narrowed. "You're not Egyptian."

"No, my lady, I am a Hebrew."

"A savage from Canaan, I suppose."

"Yes, my lady," Joseph said simply, then stood quietly as both women stared at him.

Asenath snapped, "I would have him whipped if he were mine."

"You are right," Lady Kesi said sharply. "Ufa, have him severely whipped."

Ufa grinned sadistically. "I can assure you he will feel the blows."

"Don't spare him," Asenath said cruelly. "Savages like that need to be tamed."

"I don't trust you to do the job properly, Ufa," Lady Kesi put in. "We will watch you whip the slave."

"Of course, Lady Kesi."

Ufa grabbed Joseph by the arm and said, "Come with me. I'll teach you what happens when you are clumsy."

The two women, their noses still wrinkled at the terrible odor, followed Ufa to the outer court, where he dragged Joseph. He went over to the ornamental trees lining the courtyard wall and broke off a sturdy stick, the thickness of a man's thumb but strong and hard. "On your knees and bow down, slave."

Joseph obediently knelt, leaned over, and crossed his arms over his chest. Both women watched as Ufa lifted the stick and brought it down full force on Joseph's back. His thin garment tore, and as the blows resounded again, it was completely ripped away. The flesh began to be crisscrossed with welts and bleeding wounds, and finally Lady Kesi called out, "That's enough, Ufa."

"I will be happy to continue, my lady," Ufa wheezed, breathless with the effort.

"No, that's enough. Now have him clean up that mess in the hallway."

The two women turned, and Kesi said, "Come. We must bathe." She began calling for her maids, who were not far away. As they left the courtyard, Kesi said, "He was clumsy, but that was an awful beating."

"He deserved it," Asenath said with a shrug.

"You know he's better looking than most slaves."

Asenath laughed. "I didn't notice," she said, and her eyes sparkled. She knew as well as Masud that the wife of the impotent Potiphar was hopelessly attracted to men, but there was no outlet for her desires. Other women in society had affairs, but Lady Kesi had little opportunity for any indiscretions, for Potiphar's servants kept close watch over her.

"I hope Ufa hasn't scarred his back."

"He's only a slave, Kesi. Don't worry about him. They don't feel things like we do."

———————

Masud made Joseph stretch facedown on a bench and cleansed his lacerated back. The whipping stick had broken the skin in many places, and Masud used a special ointment with a secret formula to numb Joseph's entire back.

"You are a great physician, Masud," Joseph said gratefully.

"Yes. I could have pursued that profession, but I didn't." He continued to cleanse and anoint Joseph's back with the numbing ointment and finally said, "Those two women are dangerous. Both are spoiled to the bone." He paused and thought, his brow furrowed. "Stay away from them, Joseph—especially the mistress."

"It's hard to stay away from someone when I'm tied to this house. Maybe she'll go away again. I hope so."

———————

Potiphar listened as his wife told him what had happened. "He's such a clumsy fool," she said. "I'd like for you to get rid of him."

Potiphar usually gave heed to Lady Kesi's requests when they did not interfere with his own comfort or his own plans. This time, however, he simply said, "No, that can't be."

Kesi blinked with surprise. "Why not?" she demanded. "He's only a slave."

"A slave, yes, but not only a slave. Once in a while one finds a jewel among these people. Joseph is one. He's smarter than half the people in Pharaoh's upper circle. Maybe smarter than any of them. I can use that. The Hebrew is a brilliant scholar. I may have to have Ufa beaten for his stupidity in harming such a valuable slave."

"But I told him to do it."

Potiphar smiled. "Well then, perhaps I should beat you, my dear."

Lady Kesi stared at her husband, then saw that he was speaking in jest. Still, she was upset. "He's only a slave, Potiphar."

"Nevertheless, I intend to get my money's worth out of him."

"I hate the look of him."

"Then don't look." Potiphar was tired of the argument and turned and walked away.

Kesi stared at him, her nostrils flaring in irritation. "He's only a slave," she muttered angrily, making up her mind that Joseph the Hebrew would get no consideration from her!

CHAPTER

10

"And so, my lord, by doubling the fields under cultivation with the new methods I have implemented, we have more than quadrupled our crop yield."

Potiphar sat on a high stool on his verandah, bent over the papyrus charts Joseph had laid out on a table before him, listening to his young servant explain his new farming methods. The master wore only a fine linen apron, his upper body bare in the glaring Egyptian sunshine. His enormous body seemed even larger without many clothes on. His eyes were narrowed to slits, and he did not move as Joseph continued with his report on the progress made over the year and a half since he had taken over Ufa's responsibilities.

Potiphar had become fond of Joseph in his own way, but he was not given to outward expressions of affection even with his own family, let alone any of his servants. Having been robbed of the natural means a man has to share intimacy with the woman he loves, Potiphar had thrown himself into other interests. He had become a collector of fine art and had spent an enormous amount of money on the golden objects he kept in a special room. The quest to enlarge his holdings was a game with him, and with Joseph at work on his accounts during the past months, his treasure had been almost doubled.

But it was not simply the fact that Joseph had been financially profitable that endeared him to Potiphar; it was something else he could not exactly name. He knew it had to do with the god Joseph worshiped. Potiphar was not a religious man, except to declare publicly that Pharaoh was a god. No Egyptian had any choice about this, whether or not they truly believed it. Joseph, however, had an inner strength Potiphar could not understand, and this troubled him, for he was a man who liked to analyze things and assign meaning to them.

Potiphar interrupted Joseph's report by saying, "So your father and grandfather spoke face-to-face with this god you mention?"

Joseph was not completely taken off guard, for Potiphar had expressed an interest in his God before. Joseph smiled and turned to face his master. In the last year and a half he had changed physically. The hard work had helped develop his build, and with his growing responsibilities he now exuded an air of confidence that had been lacking before.

He rolled up the papyrus he was reading from and bowed slightly. "No, sire. They did not exactly speak with God face-to-face, for God has no body. He is not a man. If He were, who would want to serve Him?"

"But Pharaoh is a god."

"That is the accepted truth in Egypt," Joseph said blandly.

Potiphar could not help but smile. "You are as much a cynic about the godship of Pharaoh as I am."

"Yes, my lord. I think we are exactly the same in that."

"Pharaoh himself worships other gods. That's why I do not believe he is a god."

"Again I would agree with that," said Joseph. "A god does not need to worship anyone or anything."

Potiphar nodded his head and stroked his chin in thought. "But this god of yours—you say he cannot be seen ... he has no body. I do not understand how a man can worship something he cannot see. If I were to worship one god, I would rather worship the sun. *That* I can see, and I know it gives us warmth and helps our crops to grow for food. Without the sun we would all die, would we not?"

"Yes, that is true," said Joseph. "But the sun is just an object. Someone made it, and whoever made the sun is the true God—and the giver of life—not the sun itself."

Potiphar squinted his eyes in concentration as he considered this novel idea. "So you believe your god, whom we can't see, made the sun, which we see every day."

"Yes, He made the sun, the moon, and all the stars as well. That is the religion of my father and his father before him. After all, my lord, *someone* had to make them. They couldn't make themselves."

"I have no answer for that—nor has anyone else that I know of. But do you think your god is ... what's his name?"

"He has many names, sire. One is El Shaddai, which means 'The Strong One.'"

"Then if he is strong, do you believe he takes a role in the affairs of men like me and you?"

"Most definitely, my lord."

Potiphar sat up straight. "But if that is true, he must be vindictive, for he allowed you, certainly a religious man, to become a slave. If your god were strong, Joseph, he could have kept you from slavery."

Joseph himself had been over this thought many times, but now he simply said, "God knows all things, my lord. He makes no mistakes. If He wanted me to become a slave, it was for His own reasons. It's not for me to question."

"I find that difficult to accept," Potiphar said, shaking his head. "What good is a god that makes a man suffer?"

———————

As Joseph was explaining his God to Potiphar, the Lady Kesi was going through her daily cosmetic ritual with her maids. Like other fine ladies of the nobility, Kesi was worked upon for hours each day to achieve the height of beauty. The maids had given her a perfumed bath and had carefully removed every single hair on her arms and legs, for none was allowed to grow on the bodies of noble ladies. They carefully polished her fingernails and toenails until they glistened. They flitted about, applying fragrant ointments to her skin and dramatic color to her eyes. They brought out elegant wigs for her to choose from for the day, some with plaited tresses, others with pearl-decorated fringes, all gleaming with gold dust.

Two of the maids, Pili and Rabiah, led Lady Kesi to her couch to lie down when all the preparations were finished. Ordinarily, the noble lady paid no more attention to their conversations than she would to the jabbering of the birds outside, but on this occasion she overheard Pili cooing, "Joseph is the handsomest man in the whole land of Egypt."

Rabiah clearly sighed and said with intense longing, "Yes. His eyes are enough to make a woman melt!"

"Eyes! It's the rest of him that's beautiful. Those long lean muscles, not a spare ounce of flesh. So strong and smooth."

Lady Kesi held her breath to better hear Rabiah's words. "He's shy, though, or else he has a woman somewhere else. None of us have been able to get anywhere with him."

"I'm going to, though," Pili boasted. "If a woman knows what she's about, she can have any man she wants. I'll have that Hebrew in my bed before the month is out."

Kesi closed her eyes and sucked in a deep breath, trying to control the sensations that flooded through her. Her first encounter with Joseph had been a year and a half ago when she ordered him whipped for dropping waste in the hallway and soiling her and Asenath. But that incident was almost forgotten now. As the months had passed, she had begun to pay more attention to Joseph, although she had been sly about it. She had made it her business to be in whatever part of the house he was working, and the sight of his lean, sinewy body gave her such pleasure, she struggled to hide her delight. Now as she listened to her maids speak of his attractiveness, she grew angry and thought, *What business do those two have with him! I could have him anytime I want!*

The two maids came in shortly to ask their mistress, "What's all that noise outside?"

Kesi opened her eyes wide. "Don't you remember? This is the day of celebration for the entire house."

"Oh, I'd forgotten that," Pili said and Rabiah nodded.

Three times a year, Potiphar declared a holiday for the house. There was food and delicacies of every sort, and all the servants and slaves were allowed to eat and drink their fill and spend time relaxing with games and merriment.

"Could we go outside and watch the contests, my lady?" Rabiah pleaded.

"Oh, I suppose so. I may go myself."

Lady Kesi rose from her couch and walked gracefully outside. She stopped short of joining the servants, who were crowded around the food tables, but her eyes went at once to Joseph. He was surrounded by a crowd of men and women, which certainly did not surprise her. She was well aware of how much every servant and slave in the house admired the man. He was laughing and smiling with an air of assurance that no slave in her knowledge had ever possessed.

A few minutes later there were shouts as all the men formed lines for the traditional race. Potiphar offered a prize to the fastest of them, and as the younger men stripped off their outer garments, leaving only their loincloths and aprons that covered them from the waist to just above the knees, Kesi caught her breath. Joseph was a perfect specimen of a man! He was not heavily muscled as some of the slaves, but his body was smooth, and his muscles were long and flexible. His body gleamed with perspiration, and as they lined up and crouched for the start, Kesi's eyes were fixed on him.

The signal was given, and the men bounded off. Joseph easily took the lead. He loped like a deer with long smooth strides, his head held up and his arms moving rhythmically at his side. As Kesi watched him, she felt within her the pain of having a husband who was no man to her. A desperate yearning seized her to have more of life, more than what her present circumstances could ever offer.

Kesi could not even remember when she first began to notice Joseph. At first she had treated him like any lowly servant, being sure to frown often at him with her displeasure. But that time had long since passed, and now whenever she looked at him, it was with a strong womanly desire to reach out and touch him. In fact, Kesi was thoroughly infatuated with Joseph, though she tried hard to keep such feelings hidden and barely admitted them even to herself. It made no difference to her that she was several years older than he, for a woman in love knows no such bounds.

The race ended with Joseph having easily taken the prize. Potiphar motioned to his young servant, who went forward and knelt before him. Potiphar handed him a small leather bag, and he took it with a smile, his teeth gleaming white against his golden skin, his hair black and glossy. When he rose and turned, his eyes went to Kesi.

His were large, expressive eyes that seemed to burn at times, and as Kesi felt his gaze, she took in a sharp breath, then turned and left, ashamed of her thoughts.

———————

That night was especially warm, and as was his custom at the end of each day, Joseph stood under the stars, letting the quietness soak in. It was a time when he was freed of all his duties, and he would spend it alone, thinking often about his father and brothers with a longing he could not allow himself during his working hours.

When he thought of Benjamin, he could not keep the tears from his eyes. He missed his father greatly, but he missed his younger brother even more.

He had been there for several minutes when he was startled by a voice behind him calling his name. He whirled to see Lady Kesi approaching him, her elegant sheer gown shimmering and floating on the night breeze. She walked up close to him, and he could smell her perfume and see her fresh makeup, the black eyeliner and dark blue powder on the eyelids, giving her eyes a sensuous look. "I didn't mean to disturb you, Joseph."

"You have not, my lady," Joseph said quickly, hiding the discomfort he always felt around her. He was aware that she often watched him, and Masud had warned him to never allow himself to be alone with her. He had not worried much about that over the last year and half, however, for he was usually surrounded by other servants, and this was the first time the mistress had interrupted his quiet nighttime ritual.

"Why do you come out alone like this at night, Joseph? What do you think about?"

"Oh, I think mostly about my youth."

"Were you very happy?"

"Very happy indeed, my lady."

Kesi moved closer to him, so that she was almost touching him, and looked up into his face. She had learned that to look up at a man gives a woman an advantage, making her seem smaller, more vulnerable.

"I've been wanting to talk to you about the business of the house."

"Yes, my lady? Is there something wrong?"

"No, indeed. The estate has never been run so well. My husband says he does nothing but rest while you take care of everything."

"Oh, there are others who do more than I."

"Now, Joseph, you know that isn't true. And that's what I want to talk to you about. There are things I would like to do to the estate."

"You have but to name them, my lady."

Joseph was highly disturbed now at the closeness of his mistress, but he did not wish to offend her by trying to move away. Her perfume was rich and heady, and the expression on her face gave him pause. He tried to keep his voice steady and his manner polite. "I will meet with you at any time, Lady Kesi."

"Now is good enough. Let us talk."

Joseph nodded and asked her some questions about her concerns but found it impossible to talk sensibly, for she knew little about the actual running of the estate.

It was Kesi who changed the subject suddenly, saying, "Joseph, I've been meaning to tell you something that's been on my heart for some time." She placed her hand over her heart and held it there. "I have felt badly about having you whipped the first time I saw you."

"It is not worth mentioning, my lady."

"Yes, it is." Suddenly Kesi reached out, took Joseph's hand, and held it. "It was wrong of me, and I wish I could do something to make it up to you."

Joseph would have withdrawn his hand, but she was holding it firmly. She was also leaning toward him, her lips parted slightly. "Isn't there something I could do to make it right?"

Joseph could not speak for a moment. This woman was making advances! He had to get away, and he said quickly, "My lady, it is forgotten, and now if you will excuse me, there are a few things I must do before I go to bed. My duties, you know."

Kesi released his hand reluctantly. She watched as he bowed, then walked quickly away. Her eyes narrowed, and her lips parted in a smile. She did not speak, but something had passed between the two of them. He had been aware of her as a woman ... and he would become more so. She would see to that!

CHAPTER

11

Masud had developed a protective armor over the years and had come to believe that a man's first duty was to take care of himself. Almost a lifetime of slavery had produced this attitude, and during his mature years he had protected his position in the house of Potiphar and honed his skills until now he felt secure. He had no true friends, for a man must give up part of himself in order to form a friendship. It was not that he had a cold, scheming heart, for under other circumstances Masud would have been quite a different person. Slavery, however, is not the proper soil for warm, trustful feelings to develop in an individual. So Masud did his job, and having mastered the politics of the household and knowing Potiphar and his wife better than they knew him, he spent his days enjoying the favors that had fallen to him.

Those favors were not new, for Potiphar despised the mechanics of running a large estate. Perhaps he had once been interested, but he had passed beyond that. Unable to be a true husband to his wife, he spent his days collecting valuable objects of art and reading what interested him—mostly the politics of empire. He had risen in the three years since Joseph had come into his house from the fourth tier of Pharaoh's favorites to the third, a magnificent rise, for the men under Pharaoh fought like wolves for their positions. Most of them spent a great deal of their time devising schemes to cut the ground from under their rivals. Potiphar was as deadly and fierce at this game as he had been as a soldier and was determined not to be maimed as he had been on the actual battlefield.

Masud had long ago learned the weaknesses of the members of Potiphar's house, and how to play on them. Masud himself was challenged only by one individual—Ufa, the steward. The two men distrusted each other intensely and for years had been struggling for the master's favor. So far Masud had won the battle, but he always knew Ufa was watching for a single mistake he might use to take him down in Potiphar's eyes. The two men had one thing in common—neither of them had other friends. They had silently declared a shaky truce years ago and had learned to work closely together to make the household run smoothly.

The two men often played the game of Jackals and Hounds. This had become a symbolic rivalry, the game mirroring the more serious business of gaining the favor of Potiphar. The game was sophisticated and required considerable reasoning powers, imagination playing more of a part than luck.

The two of them were playing one evening and the score was tied. They sat at a table leaning over, their eyes intent on the sticks that rested in holes on the board. Half of the sticks had the head of a hound while the others had the head of the jackal god. Ufa had managed to win the last game, and he leaned back and smiled with satisfaction. "You are not yourself tonight, Masud. I won that game rather easily."

Masud shrugged. "The game is like life itself. The gods will decide who will win."

Ufa laughed, then reached down and picked up a goblet of wine. He downed it, smacked his lips, wiped his mouth with the back of his hand, and shook his head. "You don't believe that any more than I do."

"Why, of course I do. One must give the gods credit."

"Nonsense," Ufa scuffed. "A man makes his own life."

Masud argued, for he was careful to follow a ritualistic form of religion. It cost him a little to pay the priests, but one had to cover oneself. The priests were powerful in Egypt—second, perhaps, only to the king. Even Pharaoh had to think twice before reaching out to strike down a priest, for the whole land was organized in a network of religious rules and rituals so that the priests controlled a large part of the power. "My religion is probably about the same as yours, Ufa. Neither of us has a great deal of use for it, but we must be careful."

Ufa had drunk enough wine that he was careless. "It's all rot," he scoffed. "A priest gets to the top of his profession exactly as a soldier or a politician does. They trample everybody in their path, and they spend their days fighting for supremacy."

This was Masud's opinion too, so he did not argue. "It's getting late," he said. "I'm going to bed."

"One more game," Ufa insisted.

"No. I've had enough. Tomorrow we'll have to begin thinking about next year's crops."

Ufa scowled. "If Joseph will allow us to be of some help," he sneered. "He thinks nothing can be done without his approval."

A smile tugged Masud's mouth upward at the corners. He knew that Ufa hated Joseph with a deadly, cold passion and would love to find some way to undercut him. "Joseph is probably no better at running the estate than you, Ufa, but he has one quality that neither you nor I will ever have."

"What's that?"

"He has the ability to draw people. Have you noticed how all the freeborn servants and all of the slaves love him?"

"They're trying to use him," Ufa snapped. "They're all fools!"

"You're wrong about that. They really care for him, and he doesn't have to work at it. Whatever it is in a man that draws people to make them trust him, this young man has it."

Ufa's face grew crimson, and he blurted out, "Well, the mistress cares for him. That's plain enough to see."

Masud fixed his eyes on Ufa's face. "What is that supposed to mean?" he asked quietly.

Ufa stuttered, knowing he had gone too far to back out. "You've seen it as well as I have. She's dying to get him into her bed."

"A dangerous statement! If Potiphar were to hear such a thing, it would be perilous for the bearer of the tale."

"I make no charges," Ufa said and finished off his goblet of wine. "But one day something will come of it. You see if it doesn't." He lurched to his feet, nearly overturning the game board, and staggered off to bed, much the worse for wine.

Masud sat quietly at the table, not moving. He stared unseeingly at the board before him, his mind working rapidly. *So Ufa has seen what is clearly evident. He's a fool in some ways, but Joseph is in danger from this man.* Rising to his feet, he started for his room and murmured, "I must talk to and warn Joseph."

The years of service under Potiphar had changed Joseph from a boy into a man. He had grown even more attractive than he had been as a youth, for now he had not only the physical features that were pleasing to all, but he had also developed the confident bearing of a man who is self-possessed and powerful, impressive to all who met him.

Had others been able to see the inner changes in Joseph, they would have been even more impressed. After an early life in which he was entirely dependent on family relationships, he had been cut off from his own blood ties. Now isolated in an alien land, he had so mastered his duties as steward that he could perform them to perfection, without conscious thought, leaving his inner life free to go where it would. His memory of his family had not grown dimmer, for he had a flawless memory. He could go back in time to his early childhood and remember insignificant details of going to a village market with his father, holding his hand, and he spent part of every day thinking of his brothers.

The memory of their treachery was real, but just as real were the earlier days when he was a selfish and prideful young man. That part had been stilled now, and he had arrived at a state of repentance. He had thoroughly grieved over his early failings, and his attitude had completely changed.

Joseph's youthful selfishness had been burned away by his brothers' betrayal and the loss of all things he held dear. It was this that drew the servants of Potiphar to Joseph. At times he had to be stern with them, but it was the sternness of a father with a mischievous child. Though his expression might be severe, his eyes were kind and his lips never hardened into a sneer. He ruled the house of Potiphar with gentleness and kindness, something that Ufa would never understand.

During these years Masud had been the one individual with whom Joseph felt free to speak freely. Joseph was as close to having a friendship as was possible with a man like Masud, who built a wall around himself and was incapable of giving the innermost part of his heart to anyone. Still, he had an affection of sorts for Joseph, and occasionally that affection would override his natural caution and the two men would spend time together in a more intimate fashion.

It was on one of these occasions one evening that Masud decided to try to warn Joseph of the pitfall that lay ahead of him. The two men had worked hard all day and were now sitting on a bench in the garden. The air was fragrant with the blossoms of the flowers so carefully culti-vated under Joseph's direction, and overhead the stars were glittering like diamonds against the black velvet sky. The two men talked awhile of inconsequential things, but finally Masud said, "I must speak with you, Joseph."

Joseph turned and was able to trace Masud's features by the faint light of the moon. "We *have* been speaking. Is something troubling you?"

"I've been thinking of how well you have done here."

"God has favored me—although I'm sure you don't believe that."

"I would like to," Masud said simply, "but I have no faith in any god. Listen, Joseph, I must warn you that Ufa would do anything to see you cut down, to have you disgraced in Potiphar's eyes."

"Of course he would. I've known that ever since I came to this house."

"So far," Masud said, "you've been able to avoid him, but there's one area in which he may be finding a handle to hurt you."

"What area is that?"

Masud hesitated, finding it hard to put his warning into words. Even before Ufa had let it slip that he was watching the behavior of Lady Kesi, Masud had noticed her interaction with Joseph. It had been more than a year ago that Masud had first noticed the mistress going out of her way to spend time with the handsome young steward. But it had been a stealthy sort of behavior, nothing a man could really put his finger on.

"I must warn you about our mistress."

"Lady Kesi? What about her?"

"Joseph, you're not a fool," Masud said half angrily, for he knew Joseph could not have missed the attention the woman had paid him. "She has eyes for you."

Joseph shook his head. "That's impossible. She has only the normal affection that a mistress of a great house will have for a slave."

"Now you talk like a fool! You know she doesn't care for anyone but herself."

Joseph knew this was true and said quickly, "Well, I can't answer your accusation."

Masud stared at the young man and said, "I know your heart is good, but hers is not. She is a woman who should have a husband who can satisfy her. Since her husband cannot, I have been waiting to see whom she would try to entice into her bed, and I am convinced you are the man. You are young and strong, good-looking. You're intelligent and witty, but you're a slave. She is certain you will do her bidding no matter what it is."

"Never!" Joseph said quickly. "That would be a sin against God."

"It would be a mistake that would get you thrown to the crocodiles, that's what it would be," Masud said testily. "Wake up, Joseph! All your wisdom won't save you if you let this woman have her way with you."

Joseph sat there silently. He could not answer Masud because he had noticed the same thing himself. Yet he shook his head. "I will be faithful to the master," he promised.

"You need to get out of this house, Joseph. Spend more time in the fields. Don't *ever* let that woman get you alone without witnesses nearby."

"I'll do the best I can," Joseph said. Then he smiled, reached over, and squeezed Masud's shoulder. "You're watching out for me, aren't you?"

"Well ... I'd have to go to all the trouble of breaking in a new steward if the crocodiles ate you." Masud roughly covered his affection for the young man, and Joseph understood that he had received the only warning from Masud he would ever get.

Joseph spent a great deal of energy and most of his time seeing to Potiphar's estate. As head steward he was essentially the master of the house. Potiphar had his own pursuits, and from time to time would call Joseph in to give him a report. But as often happens with a trusted servant, all he wanted was a general overview, and he left the details up to Joseph. By some means not quite understood by Potiphar himself, he had put all the other servants under Joseph's authority, for he found this convenient.

During this time Kesi and Asenath had suffered some breach in their friendship. At first Asenath could not understand it fully, but she knew there was a change in Kesi. Being an intuitive woman, she put her mind to the problem, and it was at a religious festival that she began to figure it out.

The two women had gone into Memphis on one of their outings, and, as always, the religious part of the festival occupied them but little. They spent the rest of the time meeting with their friends, gathering the gossip of Pharaoh's court, and wandering the streets of the great city under guard and protection of faithful servants.

Late one afternoon they walked by the temple of the moon goddess. Asenath paid little attention to the temple prostitutes who were part of the goddess worship, but Kesi stopped with such a strange look on her face that Asenath said, "What's wrong?"

"Look at those women."

Asenath, accustomed to the sight, said, "Why, they're just the temple prostitutes. What about them?"

"I wonder what their lives are like."

Asenath had never wondered such a thing. She gave little thought to the masses of people, and was even less concerned about any woman who gave herself to men for the sake of a goddess. It was beneath her. "Why would you think about such a thing?"

But Kesi was staring at the temple steps as a man came up to one of the prostitutes. The woman was no longer young and attractive, but she spoke to him in a sultry, enticing tone. "Come. Make your offering, and we will love together to worship the goddess."

Kesi seemed to be fascinated and said with some irritation, "Come on. Let's go. We'll be late."

They began to walk on when Kesi suddenly turned and said, "Asenath, have you ever known a man?"

Asenath stared at her. "Why in the world would you ask me such a question. You know I have not."

Kesi's eyes were hooded, and she said, "I have known a man. My husband was strong when we were first married, and he knew how to please a woman."

Asenath was shocked and astonished. It was the first time her friend had ever referred to the physical side of marriage she had experienced before her husband had been rendered impotent. "It's not proper to speak of such things."

"Don't you ever feel desire for a man, Asenath?"

Asenath reared her head back because Kesi had touched on a sore spot. She had indeed had thoughts of what love would be like, but being a proud young woman, she had not yet found a man who would satisfy her ideas of an ideal husband. "I'm leaving if you're going to talk like that." Asenath waited for Kesi to respond, but when she saw that her friend's eyes were still taking in the scene on the temple steps, she turned and angrily walked away. She could not tell if her anger was for Kesi's insolence or for the passion that suddenly had been stirred in her own breast. Such emotion was unusual for Asenath, for she was a woman who knew her place, and Kesi's question had suddenly made her life more complicated.

———————

A while after Kesi's dispute with her friend Asenath, the noble-woman began to admit that something drastic had occurred within her. She could not pinpoint when it had begun, but it was clear now that she was besotted with desire for the young steward Joseph. Since his refusal of her advances in the garden, she had struggled against these feelings, but they had only become worse. She had literally become intoxicated, entranced, by the thought of possessing him.

Lady Kesi became oblivious to everything except the feelings that stirred within her. More and more she put herself in Joseph's way and made it impossible for him to be away from her presence. When he tried to go into the fields, she commanded him directly to stay and take care of the household affairs. And she always saw to it that she was there to "help" him with such things.

She began drinking more wine, spending her days intoxicated with alcohol—but also with the desires that raged within her. When she could no longer bear the struggle, she gave in to the desires, and they became one with her own will. Without any guilt, she began to make overt approaches to Joseph.

She hunted him down late one afternoon when the sun was falling. Joseph had gone out to view the gardens, and when she found him, he at once bowed and said, "I was just going in, Lady Kesi. I will leave you to your privacy."

"No. Stay. I need to talk to you, Joseph."

Joseph could not disobey a direct command, and he stood there while she began to speak. Her comments made little sense to him, and he saw that she had been drinking rather heavily.

"Come and sit by me. I'm tired." She stopped, took his arm, and drew him down on one of the benches. Joseph tried to withdraw his arm, but she clung to him. She turned to face him, and as the scent of her perfume alerted his senses, he saw the strangeness in her eyes. She leaned against him, and there was no way he could avoid the soft curves of her body pressed against his side. "Joseph, I am unhappy."

"Unhappy, my lady? But why? You have everything a woman could want."

"No, I do not. You must know as everyone else that I have no sol-ace." She pressed closer against him, and her lips were soft and parted with desire. "I have no husband, and I get so lonely."

Joseph could not speak, for her meaning was unmistakable. He longed to get up and flee, but to refuse her advances could mean death.

"I get so lonely," she said, reaching up and touching his cheek. "Don't you get lonely, Joseph?"

"All people get lonely, my lady."

"But there is no need for it." And then Lady Kesi put her arms around Joseph and drew his head down. She kissed him full on the lips, and her voice was thick as she said, "We need each other, Joseph. Come, lie with me. Let us take our fill of love!"

Joseph stood on the brink of disaster. He had the normal desires of a man, but suddenly the memories of his father's warnings about the Egyptians, who had no word for "sin," and about the women who wore dresses as thin as air, came to him. He rose, disengaged her hands, and said, "My lady, this would be unfitting. You are not yourself. I will leave you." He rose and moved away quickly, his heart pounding, for he knew that death was only a step away.

As for Lady Kesi, she sat there rebuffed and angry. "I will have him!" she whispered with fierce determination. "I will have him! He's a slave, and I will find a way to win his love."

CHAPTER
12

Joseph knew he was dreaming, yet it seemed so real he felt as if he were awake. Against the vivid color of the sky and the gritty sand of the earth, he watched a pure-white fleecy lamb move away from the protection of the flock. The lamb bent his head from time to time and nibbled at the rich foliage, moving farther and farther away until he was finally out of sight of the flock and the shepherd. He lifted his head when he heard the shepherd calling him, but with a shake of his head, the lamb moved on, looking for more delicacies.

Joseph wanted to call out to add his voice to that of the shepherd, but he could not speak, and he saw the lamb frolic around closer to an outcropping of sharp rocks.

Then suddenly a wolf appeared, his eyes green with fury and his fangs sharp as knives! The lamb looked up and panic took him. He tried to turn and flee, but the wolf was on him, his sharp fangs digging into his neck while the lamb bleated piteously—

Joseph woke up wet with sweat. He lay there for a while, his body stiff, for he could not interpret this dream. Who was the lamb? Who was the shepherd? What did the wolf stand for?

Finally he got up and went outside. He stared up at the stars. Many Chaldeans believed that the stars controlled the fate of men, but Joseph had no such belief. He knew in his heart that it was the great El Shaddai who had made the stars and the earth and the men and women who inhabited it. He was the one who controlled everything. Joseph cried out, "O great strong and mighty God, show me the meaning of this dream!" He stood in the night air, the cool breeze drying the sweat on his body, but no answer came. He turned to go back inside, but he could not shake the sense of danger surrounding him.

———————

For a week Joseph had worried about the dream and what it could mean. He had other things on his mind too, for he had been receiving valuable presents from Lady Kesi. He sensed that she was giving him these gifts as a means of possessing him, and he had the awful feeling that if he accepted her gifts, she would believe he had become *hers* in some mysterious way. He tried to refuse them, but she insisted and there was little he could do.

Her latest gift was a very expensive gold ring with a precious red ruby in it. When he tried to turn down her offer, she said, "Don't be silly. It's just a little something to show my appreciation for your good work."

But at the end of the week following Joseph's dream, he was brought a note by Kesi's maid Pili. She giggled and rolled her eyes as she handed it to him, and he waited until she left before he opened it. He saw it consisted of a series of Egyptian symbols, the meaning of which was vague, but what leaped to his mind as he read them was the phrase, *Come sleep with me.*

Feeling weak, Joseph quickly folded the note. He picked up a burning lamp and set fire to the note, holding it until it disintegrated into blackened ash. As he stared at the ash, thoughts raced through his mind. He knew he could not give her an answer she would accept. And if anyone had said, *Why don't you give in to the woman's invitation?* he would have said that he was dedicated to the God of his fathers. Even if the Egyptians saw nothing wrong with such an act, he knew it would be an abomination to God.

But there were other reasons, and Joseph was intelligent and sensitive enough to know that something was wrong with the fact that Kesi pursued him. He had become the object of a woman's bold invitation, and he felt it would be degrading to give in because she merely wanted to use him like one of the temple prostitutes.

Joseph was also kept from surrendering to the desires of his mistress because he held to a tradition of racial purity that warned him not to mingle his blood with hers. This teaching had been handed down to him by Jacob, and he had heard the stories of how Abraham had sent his servant to find a bride for his son Isaac among their own people so he would not have his blood tainted with a Canaanite heritage.

Over all of this, however, he also sensed that this was a test of whether he would be faithful to El Shaddai. He had heard the story so many times about how Abraham had been asked to slay his only son Isaac and had found victory of faith. He had heard how God had rewarded Abraham's faith, and now he was determined that since everything else had been stripped away from him, he would maintain his integrity no matter what the cost.

Ever since Joseph had received the love note from Lady Kesi, he had worked diligently never to be alone with her by keeping a servant by his side at all times. Now the household was busily preparing for a special festival Pharaoh had called for to give worship to the sun god. It was to be a momentous event, and the entire household of Potiphar was involved in one way or another.

Lady Kesi waited until it was time to leave for the celebration at the palace and then sent word to her husband by one of her maids that she would be unable to go. This brought a quick response from Potiphar, who came immediately to her quarters. His face was taut with irritation as he said, "What's this? We both must go. Pharaoh will be offended if we do not."

"I cannot go, husband. I am in the manner of woman and so weak I cannot rise from my bed."

Potiphar glared at her and argued stringently, but in the end he had to give up. He left her room, and when he encountered Ufa, he said, "The Lady Kesi will not be going to the celebration. I want you to stay with her, since all the other servants will be taking part."

"Of course, master," Ufa said. He smiled and thoughts began to occur in his mind. He knew it was not Kesi's time of the month, for he kept track of such things. *She's planning something*, he thought. An oily smile moved across his lips. *We will see what the dear lady is up to. . . .*

Joseph was so busy with the preparations for the sun festival that he put Lady Kesi out of his mind. He would be making an appearance, and he dressed in a rather modest garment. This was the tenth year since he had been snatched from the pit, and now at age twenty-seven he had been thoroughly immersed in the Egyptian way of life. With certain reservations, he participated in the feast and shared in some of the outlandish customs of the people. As the head steward of an important man in Pharaoh's government, this was necessary.

He had left for the festival before the others and was not aware that Kesi was staying home. He spent all afternoon coaching the servants in their responses to the rather complicated ceremony Pharaoh had devised.

In the middle of the festivities, he received a note from one of the house servants. He opened it and saw Lady Kesi's handwriting: *Come at once. I am in danger.*

Joseph questioned the servant, who was a rather stupid old man and could not tell him much. He had strong misgivings about going back home, but he knew he could do nothing but obey his mistress. He rushed away concerned, although he could not imagine what danger could have come to the lady or why she had remained at home. When he entered the house he was greeted at once by Kesi.

Lady Kesi's eyes looked unnaturally large and bright. She had applied quantities of black antimony to her brows and lashes with her pencil, and her mouth was painted and sensuous. She wore a garment of the thinnest royal linen, which revealed her contours, and from her hair came the odor of cypress. There was nothing subtle about her intentions as she put her arms around his neck and pressed herself against him. "I have been waiting for you. Come, you will lie with me, Joseph. I am dying with love for you!"

Joseph panicked as he realized he'd been ambushed. Instead of seeing the loveliness of the woman who clung to him, he searched frantically for a means of escape. With a short, sharp cry of distress he whirled, and as he did, Kesi's hands caught at his tunic. The garment ripped from his shoulders as he fled the room.

As the object of Kesi's unquenchable desire fled, she began to scream. She ripped the upper garment into shreds, and wrath flowed out of her in place of the lust that had been there. "Help me! Will nobody help me! I've been attacked!"

Almost at once Ufa appeared. He had lurked in the shadows, watching and listening, and knew exactly what the truth was, but he now rushed to her side, feigning concern. "Mistress, are you harmed?"

"Yes! I have been attacked by that vile Hebrew! Go, Ufa, stop him! Beat him! Tie him up! He will die for this outrage!"

Ufa cried out, "The beast! I will see to it, mistress." He rushed from the room and called to the two men he had kept back from the festival. "Joseph has attacked the mistress. We must seize him." Ufa grabbed a heavy beating stick, and the three of them ran straight to Joseph's quarters, where he had gone to put on another garment. They hurried in and grabbed him. Ufa lifted the stick and brought it down on Joseph, intending to smash his skull. Joseph managed to twist so that it struck him on the shoulder instead.

"Stop this, Ufa!" he cried. But he had no chance to do other than cry, for the two servants were on him, beating him to the ground. He heard Ufa's orders: "Seize him! Tie him up!" And as his hands were bound behind him, he realized with utter clarity that *he* was the lamb in his dream who had wandered into the jaws of a wild beast.

Asenath came immediately when she heard of the outrage her friend had suffered. She comforted Kesi, who wept and ripped her own garments, embellishing her story with each retelling.

Asenath held her and eventually found the courage to ask the question she had difficulty putting into words. "Did he actually have his way with you?"

Lady Kesi's eyes were swollen with weeping. "He would have, but I screamed and fought him like a beast. I clawed him with my fingernails and tried to bite him, but if Ufa had not come, he would have possessed me."

"I knew he was an evil man!" Asenath cried vehemently. "Now we will see justice done."

Justice was indeed meted out that very day. The household of Potiphar gathered together in the courtyard to observe Joseph's sentence. Asenath sat next to Lady Kesi, holding her friend's hand.

It was a strange group, for all of the servants trusted and loved Joseph and despised Ufa. Most of them also knew that it was Lady Kesi herself who had burned with desire for Joseph. The household gossip system kept them all informed, and they were well aware of the gifts she had poured on Joseph and of the melting looks she gave him.

Potiphar stood and cried out, "Bring in this man Joseph!"

Asenath was staring avidly, as was everyone else. Joseph came in with his hands bound and wearing only a loincloth and an apron. His body was terribly wounded and bruised by the beating he had taken. She kept her eyes on him; then he turned suddenly and their gazes met. Asenath could not fathom what was going on in his mind. She had formed a bad opinion of the man from the very beginning, but could not define why she disliked him so much. Now she tried to find some satisfaction in his downfall, but to her dismay she felt pity creeping into her heart instead. She could not breathe a word of this to Kesi, of course, who was calling out, "My lord, give me justice!"

Potiphar lifted his hand for silence and spoke. "I have brought you here for judgment, Joseph," he said sternly. "You have betrayed my trust in the most terrible way. What went through your mind to do such a thing?" But then he shook his head. "Do not answer. We know the truth. The mistress has told me of your attack on her, and now I shall pronounce your sentence."

Lady Kesi was staring. Her lips were opened, and her eyes wild. "Death! It must be death!" she cried.

Potiphar ignored her, and at that moment Joseph, who had purposed to say nothing in his own defense, saw something in his master's eyes. *He's known about his wife all this time!*

As Joseph's eyes locked with Potiphar's, he knew he had found the truth. *How could Potiphar have not known what was going on in his house?*

Potiphar let the silence run on. Nobody spoke or moved. Then he addressed Joseph. "You are fortunate that your attack on my wife did not come to the uttermost end. If it had, you would have been thrown to the crocodiles. But I do pronounce this sentence on you. You will be taken to the prison at Khari-de-Sun, where you will no longer belong to me but to Pharaoh."

Kesi's voice broke out in a wild cry. "You call this justice, my husband?"

Potiphar turned and moved toward his wife. She flinched at the frightening look in his eyes, then closed her mouth and dropped her head, not making another sound.

Asenath did not understand what was happening, for she had fully expected Joseph to be staked out to the crocodiles, a most horrible death. Earlier, she would have welcomed this, but now she thought there might be more to this story than anyone supposed. She turned and faced Joseph, who was watching Potiphar and his wife. His eyes lifted and his gaze met hers. Neither of them spoke, and then Potiphar said, "Take him away. I no longer want him in my house." Joseph was seized and marched out of the room, and the door closed behind them. Then Potiphar said in a low voice, "Wife, you will never speak of this again. Do you understand me?"

Kesi was trembling, and her voice was a mere whisper. "Yes, my lord, I will obey."

And so the drama was over, but Asenath remained disturbed by it all. She could not understand how this slave had aroused such strong feelings in her. She tried to put them away and purposed to herself, *I will never think of him. I thank the gods he's out of my life forever!*

PART THREE

THE PRISON

CHAPTER
13

The prison where Joseph was sent was called Khari-de-Sun, meaning "Place of the Doomed Ones." Prisoners at Khari had no political power or money to buy their way to freedom, so most of them were there for life.

The acacia-wood burden boat that ferried Joseph upriver to Khari was designed mainly for transporting goods up and down the Nile. Ufa had been put in charge of Joseph, and he spent the long journey doing everything in his power to make the time as unpleasant as possible for the prisoner. Joseph tried to distract himself by watching the boat's crew. Four oarsmen stood on a raised platform on the forward deck, two crewmen worked the ropes and sails, and a steersman attended the tiller.

One afternoon Joseph was sitting with his back against the forward mast, his arms bound tightly to it. The ship was going past Memphis, and he knew from overhearing the talk of the boatsmen that they would reach the prison that evening.

As the ship sailed on, he studied the life of the Nile, observing the hippopotamus herds in the water and crocodiles swarming the banks. White ibises sailed gracefully overhead. The Nile made a green, twisting ribbon down through the arid desert of Egypt. On both sides the floods had deposited thick, black alluvial soil for a distance of several miles. These sections were carefully cultivated and controlled with canals and irrigation ditches that had to be dug again each year. The engineers figured out exactly who would get how much water from the Nile. Woe be it to any man who displeased them and consequently did not get his share, for it meant starvation for him and his family.

Joseph sat listlessly thinking of the other boat trip he had made ten years earlier when the Midianite trader had brought him to Egypt and sold him to Potiphar. That journey had seemed like an eternity ago to him! He had been without hope then, but his life in the house of Potiphar had become tolerable as he rose to a level of respect and authority among the servants. Even though he still mourned the loss of his family, he had been living a reasonably comfortable life in Egypt. But now that life had been destroyed, and here he was heading toward a future that seemed even more hopeless than a life of slavery. He was weak with hunger and thirst. The dry tissues of his mouth craved water, which Ufa doled out to him sparingly. He tried not to imagine what his life at the prison was going to be like, for it only caused him to despair. He was well aware of the prison's evil reputation for devouring its inmates.

He thought of his youth when he had been the spoiled darling and pet of his father. And he thought often of his prideful behavior toward his father and brothers. Though he had often cried out to God for mercy and forgiveness, he had never ceased to regret his sins against his family.

He looked down at his slave's hip apron, the same the crew wore, and he thought with sadness of all the finery he had worn in Potiphar's house. He thought of the curled wig, the enamel collar, the armbands and necklace of red and gold, and the fine linen tunic Lady Kesi had ripped from him as he fled her embraces. The memory was bitter.

Ufa's ugly face suddenly appeared before him. "Well, I see you are asleep! Good that you are asleep, prisoner, for you will get little of that in Khari-de-Sun! I have a letter here from the master with orders for the prison to work you until you are merely bones crumbling under the sands."

Ufa squatted down in front of Joseph, his eyes burning with hatred. He had hated Joseph from the time the young Hebrew had first gained favor in Potiphar's house. The keenest joy of his life had come on the day when Joseph's dark hour of judgment had fallen. The only thing that would have given Ufa more pleasure in seeing Joseph punished for the lies about his behavior with the mistress would have been if he himself had engineered it. As it was, he had informed Potiphar that he was suspicious of the pair but had been unable to get sufficient evidence to prove it to the master.

"Ah, you're not so high now. Not so mighty, eh?" Ufa gloated. "Where is all your pomp and ceremony now? You had all the servants fooled, but you never fooled me. I knew you were an evil man from the first time you came to our house."

Joseph sat quietly staring into Ufa's face, making no reply. He had not spoken one word to him on the entire journey. It enraged Ufa that Joseph never cried out or begged for mercy when he was mistreated, and now he said roughly, "Unfortunately, I have to feed you. I am not allowed to let you starve."

Joseph did not move as Ufa reached into a bag and pulled out a coarse chunk of bread and tried to stuff it into Joseph's mouth. His mouth was so dry he could not swallow it, however, and with a curse, Ufa got a water bag and squirted a small stream into Joseph's mouth, which only made Joseph choke.

"It gives me great pleasure to know that you will die in this place," Ufa spat. "I am sick of you. This gives me even greater pleasure than if you had been staked out for the crocodiles—although it would have been fun to watch those black monsters devour you alive! But never fear, Khari will make you pay for your crime much more slowly."

Joseph finally managed to swallow the bread without responding to Ufa's taunts in the least. In frustration, Ufa slapped Joseph three times on both cheeks. "I'd like to take a cane to you—and I may yet. Why don't you try to escape and give me an excuse?" When Joseph remained silent, Ufa got up with a curse of disgust, walked to the aft, and began speaking with the steersman.

Joseph breathed a sigh of relief for the momentary reprieve. He closed his eyes and thought of his little brother, Benjamin. He would be a young man now. Of all his memories, Joseph's memory of Benjamin was the sweetest. So he put his head back against the mast, swaying with the craft as it sliced through the water, and thought of his lost brother.

The prison had been designed for misery. It consisted of a collection of mud buildings, irregular in shape, thrown together on a peninsula on the eastern shore of the Nile. The buildings included barracks, stables, and storehouses clustered around a tower that served as the residence of the governor of the prison. All of this was enclosed by a high wall of unbaked bricks from which jutted out bastions and platforms. The landing bridge and the fortified gate admitted the boat, and Ufa shouted that he was bringing a prisoner with him.

A squad of tough-looking soldiers came to meet the boat. Ufa stepped onto the wharf, addressed himself to the soldier in charge, and gave an evil report of the prisoner.

"He's a crafty one and not to be trusted," he spat out, motioning toward Joseph. "It would be well if you beat him now while I'm here. Just give him a taste of what he's going to get from now on."

The officer gave Ufa a sour look. "We don't take our orders from anyone except the governor. Now, be off with you."

Ufa turned and marched back to the boat disgusted, accompanied by two of the soldiers. As they untied Joseph's bonds, Ufa cried out, "Better keep him tied. He's vicious."

One of the soldiers grinned crookedly, exposing a mouthful of broken teeth. "Where is he going to run to, fellow? Now, on with you."

Joseph stepped out of the boat onto the wharf, each arm grasped by a soldier. He never looked back but heard Ufa cursing him, praying for his death.

The officer in charge said roughly to Joseph, "Well, come along. The governor wants to meet all new prisoners. What's your name?"

"Joseph."

"What are you, a Hittite?"

"No, a Hebrew."

"All the same," the officer grunted. "The rest of you go back on duty. I'll take this violent criminal." He wore a bronze sword at his side and laughed as he added, "He won't be escaping from this place, will he?"

The officer led Joseph through the busy prison yard where many prisoners were working and a smaller group of soldiers were watching them. As they crossed the open space, Joseph prayed silently, *O God, I am in your hands. I know you have made me for a purpose, and I await, O mighty everlasting God, to see what it is.*

————

Joseph accompanied the soldier inside the tower and walked down a corridor into a large room where a stocky figure seated at a table waited for them. He wore a brown wig and had dark eyes that he fixed on Joseph. His beard was thick, and he appeared totally uninterested in this new prisoner. "Who is this, Captain?"

"He comes from the house of Potiphar. Here is the letter that accompanied him. His name is Joseph."

"The house of Potiphar, eh?" A flicker of interest came to the governor's eyes as he took the letter. He then addressed the prisoner. "I am

Governor Rashidi. You will please me, or things will go badly for you."
He waited for Joseph to answer, and when Joseph merely bowed, he
grunted and opened the letter. He read it and then laughed.

The captain who had brought Joseph in asked, "Is it amusing, sir?"

"It is rather." Rashidi turned to look at Joseph, his eyes closing
slightly as he studied him. Grinning, he turned and said, "Well, Captain,
we get mostly murderers here—revolutionaries, robbers, defilers of the
gods—but this fellow is ingenious. He has committed a new crime."

"A new crime? I didn't think there were any," said the captain with a
smile.

"Well, Joseph here has found one. He is guilty of endeavoring to
plow in his master's field. I refer to Potiphar's wife, the Lady Kesi."

The captain laughed shortly. "And Potiphar did not have his flesh
stripped from his bones?"

"Apparently the prisoner was not particularly successful. He merely
attempted to force himself on the lady. Is that right, prisoner?"

"It is what the letter says, Governor," Joseph replied.

"Rather a raw sentence, don't you think? Life for something you
never did."

The captain prodded Joseph in the ribs with his thumb. "You should
have had the wench. At least you would have gotten something out of
it."

"I doubt he'd still be alive if he had accomplished his evil purpose.
That's enough, Captain. I'll call you after I've interrogated the prisoner."

Joseph watched as the captain left, then gave his full attention to
Rashidi. There was something unmilitary about the man, but then he
was not a soldier but an official of some type. The keepers of most
prisons grew ugly along with their ugly trade, but there was a geniality
about Rashidi that encouraged Joseph. The mildness of his expression,
the gentleness in his eyes, belied the man's reputation.

"Tell me about yourself," Rashidi said and, without waiting, turned
back and sat down in a padded chair. He poured himself a cup of wine
and stared at Joseph. He listened as Joseph gave him a brief account of
his life, and when he was through, he said, "So you have been educated.
Tell me this," he said, "how many beasts of burden would it take to carry
food to five hundred workers along with all of their officers and overseers?"

"I would think about fifteen oxen and thirty asses might be about
right."

Interest flickered in Rashidi's eyes. "And how many men would you order to drag a block of stone three feet square for five miles to the river?"

"At least a hundred," Joseph said, "depending upon the territory they would have to cross."

"Would you use men or beasts for such a task?"

"You would want to use men because men are cheaper than oxen."

For some time Rashidi questioned Joseph, and finally he said, "You have a fine education, but we're not here for your benefit. You will work in the fields and at hard labor. Some think that the prisoners brought here are kept in cells. None of that loafing will do! The pharaoh has many projects that require much labor. Someday, perhaps, your education may come in handy." He hesitated, then said, "You read also?"

"Yes, sir."

"Do you enjoy poetry?"

"Very much."

Rashidi stared at him. "I am a poet," he announced. "If you do well, I may allow you to read some of my work."

Joseph smiled for the first time. "That would be a blessing indeed, master."

Rashidi studied Joseph, wondering about the smile. "We will see if you survive the fields. If you live, we may find better use for you." Getting up from his chair, he walked over to the door and called out, "Captain, put this man to work."

"I'll put him under Yafeu," the soldier said with a curt nod.

"A rough one indeed, but he will tell us whether there's anything of use in this wife stealer. Go along, wife stealer. Let me hear no evil reports about you."

Joseph bowed to the governor, turned, and walked away with the captain. When they were out in the open air, the captain said, "You will get a little break. No work today. Just a meal. Tomorrow you can start with Yafeu. Let me give you a bit of advice. Don't aggravate him. He's got a temper like a cobra."

"Thank you, Captain," Joseph said. "I will do my best to please him."

"You won't do that. Just don't get his temper stirred," the captain warned. "More than one man who did wound up as food for the crocodiles. Now, come along."

Joseph's overseer, Yafeu, was indeed a hard man. He demanded that every prisoner under his care arrive at his sleeping mat at night absolutely drained of energy. Anyone who did not haul with his full strength on the rope or did not dig fast enough to exhaust himself found the taste of Yafeu's whip on his back.

Joseph was stronger than many of the criminals who came to the prison. When he was delivered into his hands, Yafeu walked around him, carefully observing him. He prodded Joseph's muscles, squeezed his arms, and nodded. "You're the kind I like, wife stealer. You belong to Pharaoh now, and you owe him all of your sweat. If I don't get it out of you one way, I will another. You understand?"

"Yes, sir, I do."

"What fine manners," Yafeu said with a sneer. "They won't do you much good here."

Joseph went to work that day, and by the time he got back to the prison he was trembling in every nerve. Though barely able to stay awake long enough to eat the bowl of thin gruel and the chunk of rock-hard bread that was provided for the evening meal, he was pleased to know he had satisfied Yafeu. He slept until he was roused before daylight, ate an equally unappetizing meal, and went to the quarry for another full day of work.

During the days that followed he knew only work, gobbling down the meager fare, and sleep. He saw other men lashed, but he himself was spared, for he never failed to give his best. Yafeu, who knew the strength of men and their weaknesses, was not one to waste his lash on a man who was already giving all he had.

From time to time the governor would ask about the wife stealer Joseph, and Yafeu would shrug. "I wish they were all as strong as he is and worked as hard."

"He works hard, does he?"

"I am surprised at how hard," Yafeu said. "He was some kind of aristocrat, wasn't he?"

"Yes, he was the head steward in the house of Potiphar."

"You'd never know it. Most of the times when scribes and weaklings like that come here they collapse the first day. But he's a strong man. The pharaoh will get his money's worth out of him."

And so the sun rose and set each day and the weeks rolled by until three long months had passed. Joseph was so exhausted he had no time to dream or think of his family back in Hebron. His struggle to survive the rigors of Khari took every bit of strength he had.

———————

"Come along, Joseph."

Joseph had just eaten his morning meal, a thin, tasteless fish soup. He had discovered a large fish eye in his bowl, which was a great delicacy to him, and he was careful not to let anyone else see that he had it. Now he looked up to see Yafeu standing beside the captain who had first escorted Joseph to the governor. Joseph stood up quickly and waited.

The captain said, "Come along, Joseph. The governor wants to see you."

"Bring him back when you're through with him. I need him on this job," Yafeu called out as the two left.

"That's up to the governor," the captain called back. As the two walked toward the governor's tower, the captain studied Joseph. "You've lost a little weight."

"I was probably too fat anyway," Joseph said.

Amused, the captain grinned. "Well, there's an idea. We can bring all the people who can't lose weight to work for Yafeu."

"That will do it," Joseph murmured.

When they reached the governor's tower, the captain said, "Aren't you going to ask why you're being sent for?"

"I assume that if you knew, you would tell me, Captain."

"You're right. The governor hasn't said. But as far as I know, you're in no trouble."

When they entered Rashidi's large office, he was seated in the same chair and seemed to have the same cup before him he'd had three months earlier. "All right, Captain, you may go."

"What about the prisoner, sire?"

"Don't worry about him. If he tries to escape, I'll kill him myself."

The captain laughed and left the room. Rashidi poured himself another glass of wine, and then to Joseph's surprise, he reached over, got another cup, and poured it full. "Have a glass of wine, Joseph."

Joseph did not let any surprise show on his face as he accepted the wine. "Thank you, sir," he murmured and sipped it.

Rashidi drained his own cup and then used it to point to a chair. "Sit down, Joseph. We have things to talk about."

Joseph sat down and studied Rashidi. He had no idea why he was here, but he knew somehow that God was behind it. Whenever he had strength to think, he remembered that the God of Abraham, Isaac, and Jacob did not change. Somehow he was to be used in this place.

Rashidi asked, "Do you believe our pharaoh is a god, as he claims?"

Joseph could not help smiling. "Is every new pharaoh a new god? Aren't there enough gods already?"

Rashidi laughed and sipped more wine. "I would think so. I'm writing a poem about them, which no one will ever see because it would get me thrown to the crocodiles if anyone read it. It's very atheistic. But you are not an atheist, are you?"

"No, master, I am not."

"Yes, I understand that you believe in a god that has no form, no body that we can see."

"Yes, that is true, sire."

"I like that. Most of the gods I see are artistically rude. You would think if a man would make a god, he would make him beautiful. And the pharaoh himself is much too ugly to be a god in my opinion."

"If a man creates a god, or says he himself is a god," Joseph said, "then the so-called god is no more powerful than the man who made him, is he not?"

"I would agree with that," Rashidi said, taking another sip of wine. "That would seem like common sense, but the people have no common sense and they believe Pharaoh when he says he is more powerful than all the gods! Pshaw! I would as soon worship the sun myself. That at least makes some sense." Rashidi narrowed his eyes and gave Joseph a long, hard look. "Now, tell me about your god, Hebrew. How can a man know that your god is as powerful as you say?"

Joseph took a deep breath and swallowed hard. He had no idea if this invitation to speak of his faith would mean a one-way trip to the crocodile pit. But it was also possible that he was witnessing a miracle in being allowed this opportunity to honor the God of his fathers. Whatever the outcome, he had no choice but to speak about El Shaddai. He related his grandfather's meeting with God, the miracle of the birth of a son when Abraham was a hundred years old and his wife nearly so. He even told of his own father's experience on the way back from Laban's house when he saw a ladder reaching up to the heavens.

"You say it reached to the heavens, eh?" Rashidi said. "Now, that's a poetic way of saying it. I think I'll put that in my poem. You don't think it would be stealing, would you?"

"Certainly not. My father would be honored, sir."

Rashidi leaned back and said suddenly, "From now on, Joseph, you will not be working in the quarry. You will be a foreman in charge of men." Rashidi waited for Joseph to show some surprise. When he did not, he leaned forward, his eyes bright with interest. "You don't seem impressed. Most men would be turning handsprings for joy."

"I am happy, sir, to be out of the quarry—but not surprised."

"Why is that?"

"Because God has more for me to do than to haul pieces of rock out of the ground for another pyramid or another temple to a god who doesn't exist."

"That's bold talk. You could be filleted alive for that."

"But you feel the same way, that God has put something in you that you will not achieve except by using it."

Rashidi's eyes flew open. "That's exactly right. I have no idea, but I know that I won't be in this accursed prison forever. I'll be a poet."

"I think you will be, and I will look forward to looking at your work someday, that is, if you allow me to, Governor."

Rashidi stared at the man before him. "You'll have to get cleaned up. We'll get you some more clothes. If you're going to be an overseer, you're going to have to look the part."

Joseph smiled. "That would be most kind of you, sir."

"Go get dressed up, then come back. We'll have a meal together and talk about your duties. And, also, I will allow you to read my poem. If you don't like it," he said frowning terribly, "I may have you back in the quarry."

"You will hear nothing but good from me about your poetry."

Rashidi laughed. "Ha! I will never get an honest opinion out of you now."

"Yes you will," Joseph said with a smile. "I am not afraid of going back to the quarry, and although I am not a poet myself, I will give you my true judgment."

"Good. Now, go and take this order. You will have your own room and your own uniform. Hurry. I am anxious for you to hear my poem. It's by far the best thing that's ever been written!"

CHAPTER

14

Rashidi threw his writing materials across the room and grabbed his hair in frustration. He appeared to be trying to lift himself out of his chair when Yafeu came into the room and stopped dead still. He grinned slightly, then said, "I take it the poem is not going well, Governor?"

"No, it's not going well!" Rashidi shouted. "It won't come out of me. I know it's inside somewhere, but it . . . it *hides!*"

"Perhaps it's hidden behind your liver," Yafeu said, trying to stifle his laughter.

"What do you want, Yafeu?"

"I hate to interrupt a genius at work, sir, and I know your poem is all important, but—"

"Never mind all that. What do you want? Out with it!"

"It's the bearing walls for the new temple, sire. One of them just collapsed, and I'm afraid the rest of them are going to do the same."

"It was designed by an idiot! What do you expect me to do about it? I'm not an engineer."

"I think the pharaoh expects you to do something, Governor," Yafeu said with a shrug, "and he thinks these buildings raise themselves up. It never once enters his mind that it takes sweat and blood and intelligence to put up a new temple."

"Exactly! And I will certainly tell him so the next time I see him!"

"I doubt that, sire. You have too easy a life here. If you told the pharaoh that, you would probably be out working in the quarry yourself."

Because Rashidi knew that his overseer was right, he could only mumble, "Well, *someone* needs to tell him."

"When you're a god, who can tell you things, sir? Only another god, I suppose."

Rashidi got up and began to pace the floor. He stopped long enough to pick up the sheet of papyrus he had been writing on and stared at the lines. "I can't make this come out right. I'm writing the greatest poem ever written, and you expect me to lay it aside to worry over a stupid bearing wall?"

"I think it might be wise, Governor."

"Well, I can't do anything about it. Go find Joseph. Take your problem to him."

Yafeu laughed aloud. "That wife stealer is running this prison now, not you."

"That's just the way I want it, and it's why I brought him out of the quarry so I would have time to devote to my work—my *real* work! Not this infamous, stinking prison I have to live in. Go find Joseph. He'll fix it."

"Go find Joseph" had been Rashidi's refrain for the past year and a half. He had at first put Joseph to overseeing one gang of men, but his efficiency had become so evident he had risen quickly to become head of any project Rashidi was commanded by the pharaoh to complete. Joseph was not an engineer, but he had found two engineers in prison whose expertise was being wasted. Joseph had taken them out of their work in the field, cleaned them up, fed them well, and promised them that one day they would have their freedom if they served well. They had done more than that, and now Rashidi was free to think up new lines for his poem. Whenever a problem came up, he simply waved his hands and said, "Go find Joseph."

It was an excellent solution for both Joseph and Rashidi. They often had their evening meal together after their day's work—Joseph's work consisting of building and agricultural projects while Rashidi sat and stared into space waiting for the inspiration to write down a new section of his poem.

"Joseph, you've got to do something about this new temple," Yafeu said. He had found Joseph speaking with several of the overseers who were supervising the building of some new canals. Joseph looked up from the diagram he was pointing at and said, "What is it, Yafeu?"

"It's the new temple, the pharaoh's pet project," Yafeu said with a shrug. "There's something wrong with the plan. The bearing walls aren't holding up. There was another collapse this morning. Killed three workers. Three good ones too, I might add. When these things happen, why can't the weaker ones die? But no, it's always the efficient ones. I don't know why the gods bring these things on me."

"What makes you think the gods are doing it, Yafeu?" Joseph smiled. "Maybe it was the fault of the engineers."

"Well, I don't care *whose* fault it was—it's got to be fixed!" Yafeu took the diagram from Joseph. "Look, I'll take over here. You go down to the new temple and see what's going on down there." Yafeu shrugged his burly shoulders. "It had better be fixed soon, whatever it is. The pharaoh thinks that the gods themselves are building this temple. He won't accept excuses."

"I'll go see what I can do, Yafeu." He started to walk away, then turned and said, "Aren't you going to send guards with me to see that I don't run away?"

"Oh, take a couple. It's a nice break for them, but I know you aren't going anywhere."

"That's right," Joseph said with a smile. "I won't run away."

"You still have the crazy idea that your god has put you in this place, haven't you?" Yafeu said with a sneer. He had gotten this information from the governor. "He must not be much of a god to put you in a prison like this."

"My God is in no hurry," Joseph said. "He's waiting for the proper moment to do something with me."

"Well, he can just wait while you go fix the pharaoh's new temple! Get on with you now, and let me know when you've fixed it."

———————

Joseph worked for three days with the engineers and workers who were laboring to erect the new temple Pharaoh had ordered. It was a difficult job, for the original engineer seemed to have done all he could to produce the wrong results. Joseph stayed on the site, sleeping on a cot furnished by one of the soldiers, and managed to solve the problem with the plan. Cleaning out the wall that had fallen and building a new one had been more difficult.

Joseph was the sort of man whom others trusted. They also liked him for ordering better food and shorter work hours for the men. Both Rashidi and Yafeu had been horrified at these changes, but Joseph had explained, "This is not like dragging a block of stone for ten miles. It's careful, exacting work, and the men can't do it if they are exhausted and starving." He had convinced them, and now every man in the crew was anxious to do his best to please the Hebrew who had once been called the wife stealer. That label seemed now to have faded from memory.

Joseph was working with a plumb line, making sure that the next wall would be exactly straight, when he became aware of muted voices behind him. "Where is the overseer?" one of them said.

It was a woman's voice, and Joseph turned, saying, "I am the overseer—" Then he stopped dead still.

The woman was Asenath, and Joseph knew that the tall, heavy man beside her was probably her father, the priest of On.

Asenath's eyes flew wide open, and she stared at Joseph in consternation. "It's you!" she cried. "What are you doing here?"

"Who is this, daughter?" The priest of On, one of the most powerful men in Egypt, was dressed in all the finery Egypt could provide, with gold rings circling his upper arms. "How could you know him? This man is a slave," he said roughly.

Asenath was breathing hard. She could not seem to find her voice, but she finally tore her eyes from Joseph and said, "This is the man who assaulted Lady Kesi."

"But I thought he was sent to prison."

"He was," Asenath said, "but there he stands, free to run away. Where's your master?"

Joseph had by now collected his thoughts. He saw that Asenath was as beautiful as ever. She had been almost a child when he had first seen her in Potiphar's house, but now she had grown to full stature as a lovely woman. She was tall, erect, and her honey-colored skin seemed as fresh as was possible. Her large, well-shaped green eyes were flashing, and her mobile lips were drawn into a frown. "What are you doing here? You're supposed to be in prison. Where's your master?"

"I *am* a prisoner. The governor sent me to correct a fault in the building of the temple."

"Where are your guards?" the priest demanded.

"I think they went to get something to eat, but there is no danger, sir, of my running away."

Asenath had thought much about Joseph, and now she said, "You should have been thrown to the crocodiles! If I'd had my way, you would have been."

"I'm sure that's true, mistress," Joseph said quietly. "My master was merciful indeed."

Asenath was staring at Joseph with a mixture of anger and wonder. "You have a way of rising up after you fall. You did that at Potiphar's house—rising from the lowliest of slaves to being overseer of his entire house—and now you've done it again!"

"God is merciful."

"Which god do you speak of?" the high priest demanded.

"I worship the God of my fathers."

"And which one is that?"

Joseph wanted to say, "The only God." But he knew such a statement would be fatal. "I am not Egyptian, master," he said, "so I do not worship any of your gods."

"So an infidel is allowed to build the new temple! I think the pharaoh would be furious if he knew this."

Asenath was trembling as she stood there. All her memories of this man Joseph were evil. The first time she had ever seen him, she had been instrumental in having him lashed. She had shown her displeasure to him many times since and had been horrified to learn that he had attacked her friend, the Lady Kesi. "You ruined Lady Kesi," she cried, pulling at him accusingly. "You should have been executed."

"It may not be too late for that," Asenath's father said sternly. "I think we should report to the pharaoh that an infidel slave guilty of assaulting a high-ranking member of his court is working on his new temple."

"Yes," Asenath said, "let's go tell him at once." She stared at Joseph, started to say something, then shook her head and walked away.

Joseph watched them go, expecting to feel fearful. He knew that the high priest of On had great power and authority. All he had to do was convince Pharaoh that Joseph should be sent back to prison and it would be done.

He did not, however, feel any fear; in fact, he was amazed at the peace that came into his heart. *It is your will, O almighty and everlasting God. You have kept me in the pit, you have kept me in the prison, and I ask only that you keep your hand on me and let me do the work you have prepared for me to do.*

For several days Joseph waited for word to come that he was to be sent back to the prison, but nothing happened. He could not know whether Asenath and her father had decided against going to the pharaoh after all, or whether they had and he had refused to accept their plea. In either case he was grateful that the encounter had not destroyed him, and as he went about his work, he found himself thinking often of Asenath. Physically, she was by far the most attractive woman he had ever seen. But her personality was not at all attractive, for she was proud and spoiled. More than once he had thought, *If her spirit were as beautiful as her outward appearance, she would be the perfect woman.*

Finally the fault with the temple was corrected, and Joseph went back to the prison and was greeted by his master.

"So ... you're back," Rashidi said. "It's a wonder. You know the priest of On went to the pharaoh and tried to get you sent back here."

"I'm surprised he didn't succeed," Joseph said quietly.

Rashidi laughed. "He would have, but I told the pharaoh you were a man with a powerful god, and that his temple would be built better by such a man. To my surprise, he listened to me."

"What is he really like, master, this pharaoh?"

"I've never met a less impressive man physically," Rashidi said, ruminating on the question, "but I've also never met a man so stubborn! All he thinks about are his building projects. He spends his life trying to impress the gods. Still, I can't believe in any of them."

"One day you will, Rashidi," Joseph said with a smile.

"No, I won't. I'll go to my grave disbelieving in any god."

Joseph did not argue. The two had become close friends, and now he said, "I saw the priest and his daughter, Asenath. I'm surprised that she hasn't married."

"Well, she's had chances enough, but nobody's good enough for her—at least that's what she thinks. Her father thinks the same."

"What work is there for me now?" Joseph asked.

"Take some time off. I've reached a point in my poem that I need to talk about the world and what it means."

"You're going to cover all of that in your poem, sire?"

"Of course," Rashidi said. "My poem will have everything in it that all poems before it should have included but didn't. Go get cleaned up. I want to read you the new parts."

C H A P T E R
15

Five of the red-eyed sons of Leah were busy shearing sheep. They kept at the job in the searing sun until Reuben suddenly realized that their brother Judah was missing.

"Where is Judah?" he asked. "He should be here helping with this job."

Simeon cut the last of the fleece from a bleating sheep, then released the animal. He stood up and arched his back. "He's probably drunk again—asleep behind some rock."

A murmur went around the rest of the brothers. All of them had complained that Judah had become worthless. Issachar went over to get a drink of water from a leather bag, washed his mouth out, and then spat it out before saying, "I know what's wrong with Judah—he's never gotten over what we did to Joseph."

Levi, who was standing next to Issachar, reached out and struck him in the chest, driving the smaller man back. "Keep your big mouth shut! We vowed never to mention that again."

Issachar stared at Levi sullenly. "Well, it's true. You know it is. We all do."

No one knew the truth more than Reuben, and except, perhaps, for Judah, no one had suffered more over what they had done to their brother. He did not want to listen to such things, and when he had finished the sheep he was working on, he said, "Keep at this job until it's done. I'll go bring Judah back to help."

As soon as Reuben saw Judah, he knew at once that he was indeed drunk. His brother's normally inflamed eyes were even redder, a sure sign of his inebriated state. In the last few years it had become a common occurrence for Judah to drink too much. He sat sullenly outside his tent, barely glancing up when Reuben approached him, sat down, and said, "You're supposed to be helping us shear the sheep today."

"I'm not coming."'

"Are you sick?"

"No, I'm not sick. I'm drunk. Can't you see?"

Reuben did not answer but felt a mixture of anger and compassion toward his brother. He was closer to Judah than to any of the others, and now he ignored the irritation that troubled him and said, "I've been worried about you, Judah."

"Find somebody else to worry about!"

"Judah, you can't keep going on like this. You're going to ruin your stomach."

"It's *my* stomach! I'll do what I want to with it."

Reuben leaned over and squeezed Judah's shoulder. "Brother, I hate to see you harming yourself. I know you're troubled. So am I, but we've got to keep going."

Judah turned his head away and sat silently for several moments. When he turned back, there were tears in his eyes. "What's the use, Reuben? I'm no good. You know it. I know it—everybody knows it!"

Reuben put his arm around Judah's shoulders and held him tightly. "You're still grieving over the tragedy of our brother, aren't you, Judah?"

"Of course I am! I don't see how any of us could ever put that out of our minds."

"It was my fault," Reuben said. "I was the oldest, and I should have fought for him."

Judah shook his head. "It wouldn't have done any good. We were crazy. We had lost our minds! We would have beaten you, all of us together."

The two brothers sat there silently, both of them suffering inwardly, and finally Reuben murmured, "It was the end of everything for our father. I don't think I've seen him smile since that day."

"He still has Benjamin."

"Yes, he does, but it's not the same thing. Joseph was his favorite."

"Even though now Benjamin's married with children, Father still treats him like a child—won't let him out of his sight."

"He's all Father has left of his beloved Rachel."

"He's never forgotten her. All one has to do is mention her name, and he starts crying."

The men watched as two women walked by on the way to the well, accompanied by several children. When they were past, Reuben asked, "Why do you drink so much, Judah? It won't bring Joseph back."

Judah struck his knee hard with his fist. "Why do I drink? Can't you see? I've lost my two sons—and my wife. Only Shelah is left."

Reuben couldn't think of anything to say. Judah's two sons, Er and Onan, had obviously been wicked men, and even Judah himself had once told Reuben, "God struck them dead. There's no other answer."

"Shelah will marry one day and give you grandsons."

"I don't think so. I think God has cursed me, brother."

"Don't say that."

"It's on my heart all the time. Not only have I lost my brother Joseph, but now also two of my sons and my wife. I wish I were dead myself!"

"No, you can't say that! God loves you."

"Loves me? Then why do I feel like this?"

Reuben tried to comfort Judah but to no avail. Judah's sorrow was so great that nothing could touch it. Finally Reuben rose up and said, "Don't worry about the sheep." He gently touched his brother's head, then turned and walked away.

Three days later Judah knew that his dark thoughts were going to wind up killing him. He had drunk himself into another stupor the night before, and when he awoke, his head was pounding as if someone were driving a stake through his temple. Nonetheless, he decided to help with the sheep shearing and forced himself to get up and get dressed. When he stepped out of the tent, he stopped short, for he saw Tamar standing nearby.

Judah had always felt uncomfortable around Tamar. Even though she had been married to each of his dead sons, he had never fully accepted her as a daughter-in-law. There was something strange about the woman. She was attractive enough, tall and well formed with beautifully shaped lips and large dark eyes. It was something else that troubled him. He knew she spent many hours with his father listening to the tales of their people and that she took more interest in the tribe than most of the brothers. Perhaps that was the problem.

He addressed her gruffly. "What do you want, Tamar?"

"I've come to remind you of your promise."

"Promise? What promise?"

"You know what promise, Judah. When Onan died, I asked you to marry me to your son Shelah."

"He was not old enough."

"That is true. You asked me to wait until he came of age. Now I've come to remind you of your promise."

Judah stared at her, disconcerted. "Woman," he said harshly, "two of my sons have died that you were married to. I cannot risk letting you marry my third son."

"It was not I but God who punished them."

Judah stared at her, and his heart grew hard, and his voice grew even rougher. "You are not going to marry Shelah, and that's all there is to it. Why don't you go away from here? We're not really your people."

"You gave me your word, Judah," Tamar said evenly. Her voice was cold, but her eyes were burning. "Are you a man of honor or not?"

"Get away from me! You're a witch, and you'll never have my last son!"

As Judah strode away, Tamar watched him go with a determination in her heart to have what she desired. Her goal to be in the line of the Redeemer had never faltered. She had made it her business to serve Jacob faithfully and had listened earnestly to his stories, soaking up his words about the Redeemer who was to come. It had become the focus of her life, and as Judah disappeared from her sight, she whispered, "I gave you every opportunity to keep your word, Judah. Now I will find another way!"

———

To Judah's relief, Tamar did not press her argument, nor did she remind him again of his promise. He felt badly about it, for he *was* a man of honor, but to give another son to this woman who seemed to devour his sons—this he could not do! He waited for three months, and gradually came to believe that she had put the foolish idea out of her head. She was too old for Shelah anyway.

For a time he thought that Tamar might go to Jacob to plead her case, for he also had given his word that Tamar would have Shelah as a husband. But Jacob never mentioned the matter, and Judah breathed a sigh of relief. "Well, she's gotten that wild idea out of her head. I'm sorry for her, but I can't let her have my last son."

———————

"Where are you going, Judah?" Reuben asked. The two had eaten an early meal together, and Reuben wondered at Judah's restlessness as he got up to leave.

"I'm going up to Timnah to work with the flocks there," Judah said.

"Maybe it'll be good for you to get away for a while."

"I think it will," Judah said with a nod, leaving at once.

Neither brother noticed that Tamar was nearby cooking over a fire. Her back was to them, but she was within hearing distance of their conversation. As soon as Judah left, she rose at once and went to her tent.

On arriving in Timnah, Judah sought out his friend Hirah, who was glad to see him. The two men were close friends, and all that day they enjoyed each other's company, and Hirah invited Judah to stay with him that night.

When Judah arose the next morning, he decided to go into the small village close by.

"Shall I go with you?" Hirah asked.

"No. I'm only going to buy a few things. I'll be back soon."

"All right. Tonight we'll fix a special feast for your welcome."

Judah went to the village and bought his items in the small market-place, including some special foods to share at the feast that night. On his way back, he had no more gotten to the outskirts of the village than his eyes caught sight of a woman sitting beside the road in front of a small tent. Her dress indicated she was a harlot, and her face was veiled. She called out to him. "Good morning, master."

Judah's wife had been dead for over a year, and during that time he had had nothing to do with women. Ordinarily he would not have touched a prostitute, but he found himself drawn to this woman and began to speak to her. He noticed her beautiful eyes peeking out from her veil, and could see that she was a shapely woman. For reasons he could not fully understand, he was overcome with desire for her.

The woman saw this desire and quickly said, "Come. We will take our fill of love."

Judah hesitated momentarily, but then said with a nod, "All right. So be it."

"What will you give me?" the woman asked.

"I will give you a goat from my flock."

"You have no goat that I can see."

"I have many. I promise you will have a goat."

"Men are generous before love, but afterward they forget. I must have a pledge."

"A pledge?" Judah asked. "What sort of pledge?"

"You must leave something with me. Later when you bring the goat, you can have it back."

"What do you want, woman?"

"I want your signet with its cord and the staff in your hand."

"All right," Judah said impatiently, taking the cord off from around his neck. "You shall have them."

He gave the woman the items and followed her into her tent.

———————

Judah sent his friend Hirah to take the goat to the prostitute, but he returned shortly. "I could not find any harlot on the road where you said she would be."

Judah looked up. "You must have gone to the wrong place, then."

"No, I asked several men of the area, and they all said there is no harlot in their village."

Judah rose and scratched his head. "You must be wrong, Hirah."

"I asked everybody I could find, and they all said the same thing. So I've brought the goat back."

"Well, she must have changed her mind and gone somewhere else. Perhaps she thought the signet ring was worth more than a goat."

Hirah stared at him strangely. "I've never known you to go to a harlot before, Judah."

"I never have," Judah said gloomily, shaking his head. "I thought I was a better man than that."

"Well, it's over now," Hirah said. "Forget it."

"I'll try, my friend, but when a man fails, it's hard to forget."

———————

As usual, it was Reuben who had to perform the unpleasant task. His shoulders were bowed, and his lips were turned down in a moody frown as he approached Judah's tent. "I'd give anything not to have to do this. Poor Judah's had enough to bear without this."

He found Judah butchering a goat, his hands bloody and the carcass before him in pieces. He looked up. "Why, hello, Reuben. Have some of this goat. It's a nice fat one."

"Judah, I've got something to tell you."

"You look like you've seen a ghost. What's wrong?"

"I hate to be the bearer of evil tidings."

Judah stood up and wiped his hands on a rag. "It would be best if you just told me."

"It's Tamar."

"What about her?"

Reuben gnawed his lip, but there was no way he could put it easily. "She is with child."

Judah stared at Reuben, and his face grew red. "She's with child by whom?"

"She will not say. I've talked to her myself. She won't say a word about the man."

"I've always known that woman had a streak of evil in her," Judah said slowly, his lips growing into a tight line.

"But she's had a hard life losing two husbands," Reuben said in her defense.

"That's no excuse!" Judah spat. "She'll have to pay the penalty."

Reuben was startled at Judah's harshness. "Surely you don't mean to have her stoned!"

"She will burn for her offense!"

Reuben was horrified. "You can't mean that, Judah!"

"It's the tradition of our people to put to death any woman caught in harlotry. You know that as well as I do. Remember the woman five years ago over in the camp next to ours? She was stoned for the same offense."

"She was nothing but a common woman, but Tamar is your daughter-in-law."

"My sons are dead," Judah said flatly. "She will die as she deserves."

Reuben pleaded with him, and when Judah would not listen, Reuben appealed to his brothers to dissuade him. But Judah remained firm in his resolve. He refused to see Tamar and insisted that the sentence be carried out at once.

When Jacob heard the news, he too was startled and went to Judah to try to persuade him to show mercy, but Judah would have none of it.

"You've always been one to keep strict rules, Father. If we allow women to behave like this, what will become of us?"

Jacob could not answer, and Judah left to carry out the punishment. He called his friend Hirah, who was visiting the camp of Jacob's tribe, and commanded him to go bring the woman to be executed. Hirah stared oddly at Judah but shrugged and went to carry out Judah's orders.

Judah waited, and when Hirah returned shortly, he straightened up. Hirah held a staff in one hand and a signet ring on a cord in the other. "What are those?" Judah demanded.

"The woman says that the father of the child is the owner of these." He extended them, but Judah drew back as if the man held deadly snakes in his hands. He stared at the items, unable to speak. Finally he reached out and took the signet ring and staff. "These are mine," he admitted.

"I know. I recognized them," Hirah said simply.

Judah stared at his friend and his legs went limp. He slumped to the ground, holding the items as tears began to flow. Judah's shoulders shook as he sobbed, and when he looked up, his red eyes were inflamed with grief. "She has been more righteous than I!" he cried. "Go and tell her that—" But then he stopped. "No. I will tell her myself."

He lumbered out of the tent and went at once to Tamar's tent on the edge of the camp. She was sitting in front of it, and when he stood before her, she looked up at him with an unreadable expression in her eyes.

"I have been evil, and I grieve over what kind of man I am." Judah waited for her to speak, but she did not. He nodded and said, "I will acknowledge your child as my own." Then he stumbled blindly away.

As Tamar watched him go she smiled with satisfaction, laying her hands on her abdomen. Her purpose had been accomplished.

———

Jacob ordered that Tamar's tent be moved back to the center of the camp to await the arrival of her child. Everyone there came to accept her condition, even though they all knew the child was Judah's. Judah in the meantime could not face the humiliation, and he left to stay in Timnah with his friend Hirah.

Jacob managed to ignore the unpleasantness by acting as if nothing unusual had happened.

When Tamar's time to deliver came, the midwives helped her. They knew she was delivering twins, and during the process, one of them cried out, "Look, there's the hand of one of the infants!"

The other midwife quickly pulled a scarlet thread from her pocket and tied it around the tiny wrist that had emerged to mark the firstborn. But then the two women watched as the hand disappeared, and they both felt something mysterious was happening.

Finally the two babies were born, but it was the second-born who had the scarlet thread around his wrist.

Tamar had not uttered a single cry during the birth of the two infants. She took the firstborn and held him to her breast. She looked into his face and said, "I will call you Perez, for you have broken forth." She stroked the red face of the infant and whispered to him, "You are the seed of Judah! God has touched you!"

CHAPTER

16

Joseph had made a place for himself in prison exactly as he had at Potiphar's house. He had risen to the point where Rashidi entrusted most of his work to Joseph, leaving the governor free to devote his time to writing his poem that was going to change the world. What time was not given to his creative endeavor, he spent in speaking with Joseph, for he had learned to prize the young Hebrew above measure. It did not trouble Rashidi in the least that Joseph did all of the work of the prison, and neither did it trouble Joseph. The more he worked, the less time he had to think about his grievous past.

Several new prisoners had arrived during the night, and Joseph went to interview them in the morning, as was customary. His policy of lenient treatment for prisoners was working out well. It made sense to him that men who were healthy could do more work than men who were half starved and beaten. The other prison officials had come to agree when they saw the huge increase in work accomplished by the prisoners under Joseph's care.

This time there were eight prisoners, and as Joseph spoke to each of them, he was able to gain some insight as to where they might best be used. He was always interested in finding prisoners with the intelligence to be trained as overseers.

He was only halfway through the interviews when he overheard one of the prisoners speak in the Canaanite language. Joseph immediately turned and walked over to the man. The prisoner, misunderstanding Joseph's interest, flinched and ducked his head.

"Don't be afraid," Joseph said in the man's own language. "I am Joseph, the overseer. What is your name?"

"I am Modach," the prisoner murmured, his eyes wide with surprise. He was of average height, with thin, sharp features and skin weathered to the texture of leather. "You speak my language," he whispered.

"Yes, Modach, I do. Which tribe do you descend from?"

"I am of the tribe of Shua."

Joseph interrogated him for some time, and finally he asked off-handedly, "I don't suppose you've ever heard of the Hebrew Jacob."

Modach's eyes brightened, and he nodded vigorously. "Oh yes, sir! I know the tribe of Jacob very well indeed."

Joseph gave a start, for in all his years of captivity he had never encountered anyone who had even been in his part of the world, much less had known of his family.

"How is it that you know of the Hebrew tribe?"

"I know because one of the sons of Jacob married a girl from our tribe."

"Which son?"

"His name is Judah, and he married the daughter of Shua."

Joseph blinked, for he had often thought of Judah and his ill-fated marriage. He had once even asked Judah why he married a woman who was not a Hebrew, but Judah had glared at him and told him to mind his own business.

"Did you meet this man?"

"Why, yes, master. Shua was very fond of his daughter, and twice I took gifts to her after she married. I became very well acquainted with many of the tribe of Jacob."

Joseph began to pepper Modach with questions and found that the man had a quick intelligence and a good memory.

Finally Modach shook his head. "It was a tragedy what happened to Judah."

"A tragedy?" Joseph said fearfully. "Is he dead?"

"No, not that I know of. He and the daughter of Shua had three sons. But it was a tragic thing. . . ." the prisoner said, shaking his head.

"What was tragic about it?" Joseph demanded impatiently, keeping his voice moderate despite the rapid beating of his heart. He had always had kind feelings for Judah and hated to hear that he had fallen on evil times.

"The man had three sons, and a woman named Tamar married the oldest son, a bad fellow indeed! He died very soon after their marriage. Then, as the tradition of that tribe dictates, his brother Onan took the woman as his wife to produce his brother's heir, but no children were conceived and he died too."

"That is indeed sad. Do you know what happened to Judah and his other son?"

Modach shifted and shook his head. "I only heard rumors."

"What sort of rumors?"

"It was said that the woman wanted to marry the youngest son, but Judah refused."

"What became of them?" Joseph asked.

"The woman became pregnant, and at first she was to die for her harlotry, but the sad truth came out."

"What sad truth?" Joseph demanded. "Tell me, man!"

"Rumor has it that the father was Judah himself."

Joseph's heart grew cold. "Then what happened?"

"The woman was spared, and she bore twins. I know no more, sir."

Joseph continued to question him, and since Modach was an intelligent man, Joseph promised him, "I will find a good place for you here. I am sorry for your trouble."

Modach bobbed his head and murmured his thanks, then asked, "Do you know the tribe of Jacob, sir?"

Joseph stood very still and dropped his head, then whispered, "Yes, I know the tribe of Jacob very well."

———

"Well, I hear we have some famous people in our little establishment."

Joseph looked up to see that Rashidi was smiling at him. The two of them had been going over the later verses of Rashidi's poem, and the governor was in a good mood. Joseph loved poetry, but he thought Rashidi had exalted ideas about his own work. The poem made little sense to Joseph, but he was careful about his critical comments, making sure to commend those parts that appeared to him to have some value. It was his opinion that the poem would never be finished, but that did not trouble Rashidi. It was the work itself rather than the end that seemed to please him.

"Famous guests? I haven't heard of them, sir," Joseph replied.

"They came while you were out yesterday."

"Who are they?"

"The servants of Pharaoh. One of them is Belsunu, Pharaoh's butler.

The other's name is Kamose, the baker, I believe. So we have the butler and the baker of the great pharaoh himself here in Khari. A most interesting development."

"Why are they here? What are their crimes?"

"They offended Pharaoh somehow. It doesn't take a great deal to offend the great ones. As far as I can make out, the baker cooked a meal that made the pharaoh ill."

"What about the butler?"

"Some minor infraction," Rashidi said carelessly. "I think he made a mistake about one of Pharaoh's appointments. I don't remember."

"How long is their sentence?"

"Indefinite."

Joseph smiled. "That's unusual."

"The Pharaoh *is* unusual. He may send for them today, or he may leave them here for fifty years. You know how the gods are." Rashidi grinned at Joseph, taunting the younger man's belief in God. "They are irrational."

Joseph smiled. "I think you believe more in God than you let on, Rashidi."

Rashidi attempted to look surprised. "Nonsense! I've told you ever since you came that I believe in no gods."

"So you say, but your poem leads me to believe that you aren't telling the truth."

"Ah, my poem! Well, that's art. That's different. A man may do things in art that he cannot do in real life."

"I'm not sure that's true," Joseph said. "I think art ought to imitate life as much as possible."

Rashidi was interested. "What do you mean by that?"

"Well, you've seen the pictures that our royal artists paint of Pharaoh and of others?"

"Certainly I have."

"What position are they in?"

"Why, they're always turned sideways and have one foot extended."

"Exactly. Tell me, Rashidi, is that the way people always are? Don't we ever see anyone's full face?"

"But it's the royal art. It's the tradition."

"Someday," Joseph said quietly, his eyes growing dreamy, "an artist will come along who will paint men and women as they *really* are. That will be true art."

"Oh, and a poet will come along who will tell things as they really are, I suppose," the governor said with a sardonic grin.

"That is what I would expect a great artist such as yourself to do, sir." Joseph smiled.

Rashidi suddenly laughed. "You're making fun of me. Get out of here and go see if you can put those two to work. Calm their nerves if you can," he added. "They're scared to death I'm going to cut off their heads—which I may be ordered to do."

———

Indeed both the butler and the baker were frightened men. Joseph discovered this as soon as he went into their cell. For political reasons, Rashidi had seen to it that they were given better quarters than the average prisoner. It was entirely possible that these two might go back to the court of Pharaoh, and Rashidi wanted no unfavorable reports of his work or of his prison going back to the palace.

Joseph stepped inside and instantly the two men rose. He thought wryly that it would be difficult to find two less similar individuals. One of them was fat and short, the other skinny and tall. "I am Joseph, the overseer. What are your names?"

"I am Belsunu, the butler of Pharaoh."

"The *former* butler," the skinny man said. "My name is Kamose."

"Well, I am sorry to see you here, but perhaps it will not be for long," Joseph said.

"It may be forever," Kamose grunted.

"You always look on the dark side of things, Kamose," the butler said with irritation. "Why can't you speak more cheerfully?" He turned to Joseph and bowed. "I am hopeful that our sentences will be short."

"I will hope the same for you. In the meantime, what can I get you to make your stay more comfortable?"

"You can let us out!" Kamose snapped.

"Why, I'm sorry, but that is beyond my ability. I am a prisoner like yourselves."

Both men stared at him, and Belsunu asked sharply, "I thought you were an overseer."

"So I am. The governor uses me in this capacity, but I can no more walk out of here than you can."

"How long have you been here?" Kamose demanded.

"Almost three years."

"Ah, me," Kamose moaned. He went over and sat down and put his head in his hands. "Why did this have to come upon me? The gods are angry with me."

"The gods aren't angry with you," Belsunu said, winking at Joseph. "Pharaoh is, because you baked him a bad cake. That's why you're here. Why didn't you bake a good one?"

"I didn't even bake that cake. My assistant did, but I get blamed for everything."

Joseph said to Kamose, "Perhaps you'd like to cook your own meals."

"No. I just want out of here."

"Well, I'll be sure that you both have good food."

"I heard the guards talking. They said we'd be put to work in the quarry." Belsunu shook his head. "That would kill me. I'm so fat and haven't done any real work in years."

"Nothing like that will happen," Joseph assured him. "We'll make your stay as pleasant as possible. Why don't you tell me something about yourselves?" He sat down and listened as the two told their stories. Belsunu, the butler, was full of cheerful words. He had had an easy life until now, and he was optimistic about getting out. Kamose was depressed and could say nothing good. He fully expected to remain in prison for the rest of his life.

Finally Joseph excused himself and went back to report to Rashidi.

"I calmed their nerves as best I could, sir. The baker is hard to encourage. He's a terrible pessimist."

"They'll be all right," Rashidi said with a shrug. "Now, sit down and listen to this new stanza I've written. . . ."

––––––––––––

For some reason the baker and the butler came to be much on Joseph's mind. He thought about them every day and did all he could for them, furnishing chairs and a table, as well as a good razor and a mirror so they could shave themselves. He even furnished enough water for bathing. He was following Rashidi's orders to make them comfortable, but he could not fully understand why he himself was so intent on carrying out these orders.

Not long after the arrival of the butler and baker, Joseph was sent away from the prison working on another building project in Thebes. He was responsible for overseeing the work on a new bridge in which slaves were used to haul the materials in from the quarry. On his third day on the job, he heard someone shout, "Make way—make way!" When he turned, he saw four bearers carrying between them a chair such as was used by the aristocracy.

As the chair drew nearer, the bearers had to walk carefully to avoid the broken stones. As they slowed their pace, Joseph suddenly found himself looking into Asenath's face. Her surprise was as great as his own, and she rose up slightly and twisted her neck to see him. She was wearing an emerald green gown interwoven with gold threads that flashed in the sunlight. Her hair was not bound but cascaded down her back in a wealth of blackness. Her eyes, made up to appear larger, were fixed intently on Joseph.

Joseph could not move. Though there was scorn on Asenath's face, he barely noticed it. Something about her drew him, and he felt a sense of frustration. The thought flashed through his mind, *Why am I staring at her? She can never be anything to me.* In that instant he knew for the first time, yet with a sharp pang, that he desired her and wanted to be a part of her life.

The thought startled and dismayed him, and when she turned her head away in a haughty gesture and called out to the bearers to move on, he stood disconsolately and watched the bearers carry the chair out of sight. The encounter troubled him. He had never been in love with a woman and did not want to believe that he was now.

She remained on his mind for days, and when he returned to the prison, he could only nibble at his food, he was so preoccupied with thoughts of her.

Rashidi noted this. "You're not eating," he said. "What's the matter?"

"I'm not very hungry."

Rashidi grinned. "When a man isn't hungry, he's either sick or in love. Which is it?"

"Don't be foolish!"

Rashidi popped a sugar-coated date into his mouth, sucked on it for a time, and considered his young friend. "Have you ever been in love?" he asked. "Have you ever made love to a woman?" he demanded.

Joseph found himself embarrassed but was honest. "No, I haven't."

"At your age! Why, you're nearly thirty, aren't you?"

"Yes."

"Thirty years old and never had a woman!" Rashidi shook his head. "I don't believe in miracles very much, but I would say you *are* one! Why have you avoided them, a good-looking fellow like you?"

"I don't want to talk about it."

"Ah, you are irritated. That means I have found the truth. Men are always irritated when they are found out. As a poet and knowing human nature, I long ago discovered that. Now, as for me, I had my first woman when I was fifteen. I haven't kept count since."

"I'm not interested in hearing about your amorous escapades."

Rashidi leaned forward on the table and put his chin in the heels of his hand. Propped thus, he stared at Joseph intently as if he were a difficult problem to be solved. "Thirty years old and never had a woman—and yet you're here because you tried to attack one."

"That was all a lie, Rashidi. I've told you the truth about that."

"Yes, yes . . . I've always believed you. And I've always thought you a fool. Potiphar's wife is a good-looking wench. She was available. Why didn't you just take her?"

Joseph gave Rashidi a look of intense irritation. "You wouldn't understand."

"I'm a poet. I understand *everything*."

"Don't you understand that it's wrong for a man to lie with a woman who is not his wife?"

"Who said so?"

Joseph was disgusted. "If you don't understand that, then I can't explain it to you."

Rashidi grinned sourly. "I wish you could. But I wish even more you'd tell me who the woman is that's got you all stirred up."

"I am *not* stirred up!"

"Ha! Joseph is angry with poor Rashidi because he's told the truth. Come on, now. Tell me. Who is she?"

Joseph rose to his feet and said shortly, "I'm going to bed."

"Maybe not. I'm the governor here. I may have you beaten until you tell me who your lover is."

"Go ahead," Joseph said defiantly, his eyes flashing. "I wouldn't put it past you."

Rashidi stopped smiling. He stroked his chin and then said softly, "Well, you are angry. I'm sorry, my boy, I was only teasing."

"It's all right, but I'm tired."

Joseph left abruptly, and Rashidi, the governor of the prison, sat there thinking for a long time. *Joseph is in love. It can't be an old love. It has to be someone he's met since coming here, which means it must be someone he has met out on a job. I'll get it out of him. He can't keep a secret like that from me!*

————

Joseph's conversation with Rashidi troubled him for the next week. He went about his duties, as usual, but found it hard to sleep at night for thoughts of Asenath. He often interrogated himself sternly as if he were a prisoner:

Have you lost your mind?

No, I haven't lost my mind. I'm in love.

In love, you fool? You can't be in love with a woman you can never have.

I'm sorry, but that's the way it is. I love her.

It's just that you're a man and you want her. After all, you've never had a woman.

It's nothing of the sort. It's a thing of the spirit.

Of the spirit! She's done nothing but insult you since you first saw her.

That doesn't matter.

You don't remember when you were whipped and she insisted on staying and watching it? Weren't you humiliated?

I'd forgotten that.

You liar.

Well, at least I put it away from me. She was very young then. What did she know?

She knew enough to be cruel.

She's changed.

Oh, you saw kindness in her then when she met you with her father? She spoke gently?

I don't want to talk about it.

And when you saw her pass by in her chair—she waved at you and told you how handsome you were?

She couldn't do that. It would be wrong.

I give up on you! You're impossible!

Conversations like this went on in Joseph's mind constantly, and he found it impossible to put the woman out of his mind.

He was thinking of Asenath late one evening when Rashidi sent for him. He went at once to the governor's quarters, and Rashidi said, "Well, I've got a job that you should relish."

"And what is that, sir?"

"They called you 'the dreamer' back when you were a boy—your brothers, I mean?"

"Yes, they did."

"And you even told me once that you interpreted dreams at times."

Joseph stared at Rashidi suspiciously. "What is all this about?"

"Our two star boarders, the butler and the baker—they've had dreams, and they are giving their keepers a hard time. They're not eating right. We want to keep them healthy so that if Pharaoh ever recalls them he can't blame us for their condition."

"What am I supposed to do about that?"

"You're supposed to go by and interpret their stupid dreams."

"I'm not an interpreter."

"Well, you are now. It's one of your duties. Just make up something."

"What did they dream about?"

Rashidi stared at him with astonishment. "You think I would leave my work to listen to foolish dreams of prisoners? Now, get out of here and settle the matter!" He waved his hand in the air with a final gesture. "I want to hear no more about it."

Joseph went immediately to the quarters where Belsunu and Kamose were kept. As soon as he entered, he saw that they were both in poor condition. Neither of them had shaved for days, and the food that had been brought for their supper lay untouched on the rough table. "What's wrong with you two?" he demanded.

"Joseph, I'm so glad you've come!" Belsunu cried. "I've had a dream and it troubles me greatly."

"You shouldn't let dreams trouble you. They usually mean nothing."

"I'm sure this one does," Belsunu insisted. His fat face was covered with perspiration, and he passed his hands in front of his eyes. "It was the most vivid thing in my life," he wailed. "It was as if I were seeing a painting by a great artist."

"The same thing happened to me," Kamose said gloomily. "I'm afraid of it."

Joseph tried to comfort them as best he could. "Dreams usually don't mean anything. You know that yourselves."

"I think it means something when both of us dream on the same night. There's a message from the gods in this," Kamose persisted.

"Will you listen to my dream and tell me what you think it means, Joseph?" Belsunu pleaded. He came over and tugged at Joseph's arm. "Please, sit down and at least listen."

Joseph shrugged and sat down on one of the chairs. "I'm no interpreter, but sometimes the meaning of dreams is obvious."

"Well, *my* dream's meaning isn't obvious," Belsunu said.

"Tell me about it, then, but I warn you—interpretations belong only to God."

Belsunu seemed relieved that Joseph had agreed to listen, and he began to speak rapidly. "It was a very short dream but so vivid! I dreamed that there was a vine in front of me, a very fruitful vine with three branches. The branches grew and blossomed before my eyes until the whole vine was covered with plump, ripe grapes. And then," he added breathlessly, "Pharaoh's cup was in my hand, the one he always drinks from. I took the grapes and pressed them into Pharaoh's cup, then put the cup into Pharaoh's hand."

"Is that all?" Joseph said, lifting his eyebrows.

"Yes. What does it mean?"

Joseph was surprised and delighted that the interpretation came to him at once. He smiled broadly and said, "Be comforted, my friend. God has given me the interpretation of your dream."

"What is it? Tell me!"

"Here's the meaning: The three branches are three days. Within three days Pharaoh will take you out of this prison and will put you back in your place, and you will fill Pharaoh's cup as you did before you came here."

Belsunu leaped up and began pacing around the cell. He lifted his hands, and his fat flesh shook as he cried out for joy. "Oh, thanks be unto the gods! Thanks be unto the gods!"

"I am happy for you, Belsunu," Joseph said. He then turned to Kamose, whose eyes were fixed on the butler. "And what was your dream, Kamose?"

"May my dream be as good as that of Belsunu," he said. He shook his shoulders in a strange gesture and said, "I dreamed that I had three white baskets on my head, and in the top basket were good foods for Pharaoh to eat. But the birds came and ate the foods out of the top basket. It was so real," he said. "What does it mean, Joseph?"

Joseph dropped his head, not wanting to face Kamose. As with Belsunu's dream, he was certain of the interpretation, but he dreaded to say it.

"What is it? Is it bad?" Kamose cried out.

Joseph lifted his head, and sorrow marked his features. "I am sorry to tell you this, but it is not a good dream."

"I knew it ... oh, I knew it!" Kamose moaned. He put his face in his hands. "Tell me. Do not spare me."

"I wish I could give you better news, but again the three baskets are three days. Within three days Pharaoh will have you executed and will hang your body on a wall, and the birds will eat the flesh of it."

Kamose gave a loud, hopeless cry and fell to the floor.

Joseph knelt down beside the weeping man and said, "Truly, I am sorry."

Belsunu came over and stood beside Joseph. He could not speak. His own good news had buoyed him up, but now the sight of the weeping man sobered him. "Is there no hope, Joseph?"

"The dreams are from God, and it will be as I have said."

Joseph shared the story with the governor, who was astonished.

"You actually told them those things were going to happen?" Rashidi said.

"Yes, I did."

"But if they don't, you'll look like a fool!"

"They will happen," Joseph said calmly.

Rashidi said nothing—only shook his head. But the next day he came rushing to Joseph, his face pale. "Word has come from the pharaoh."

"What word?"

"About the prisoners, and it was as you said, Joseph. Belsunu is to be returned to his position as butler."

"And Kamose?"

"He is to be executed. We are to carry it out here at the prison."

Joseph's eyes met Rashidi's. "That is sad indeed."

"How did you know? How did you know this?" Rashidi cried.

"God gave me the interpretation," Joseph said, putting his hand on the governor's shoulder. "You are wrong about God, Rashidi. There is a God in heaven, and I pray that one day you will find him."

The execution was performed on that same day. Joseph had stayed with Kamose and tried to comfort him, but there was little comfort to give to a man under sentence of death.

Afterward he went to stand beside Belsunu, who was sobered by the death of the baker but exuberant over his own good fortune as he stood waiting to get onto the boat that would return him to the palace.

"I am happy for you, Belsunu," Joseph said.

"Oh, I am grieved over my friend, but I am so happy that it was as you said for me."

Joseph put his hand on the shoulder of the smaller man. "Hear me, my friend. I rejoice that I could give you a good meaning to your dream, and I pray that you will do me a kind service in return."

"Anything! Anything you say, Joseph!"

"You know my history—that I have committed no crime for which I should be here. I know you have been too full of your own misfortune to think of me, but I pray that when you go back into Pharaoh's service, you will not forget me, nor my kindness to you."

"Forget? I could never forget you, Joseph!" Belsunu cried out. He grabbed Joseph's hand and kissed it, his eyes aglow. "I promise I will not ever forget you."

"I will take you at your word, Belsunu. Please speak to the pharaoh on my behalf—how I was sold into slavery and how I was innocent of any crime in the house of Potiphar. Will you do this for me, my friend?"

"Do it? Of course I will do it!" Belsunu said, embracing Joseph. "You may depend on it."

Joseph smiled. "I do depend on you, but I tell you this. You mean well now, my friend, but you will forget me when you get back in Pharaoh's court."

"Never! I will never forget you!"

The man continued his promises as he got onto the boat. When it moved into the middle of the river, he cried again, "I will never forget you! You will see, my friend!"

Joseph watched the boat disappear downriver, and then he turned away. He was happy for the man's release, but somehow he knew Belsunu would soon forget.

For many weeks, and then months afterward, Joseph waited for something to come of Belsunu's promises, but nothing did. Joseph filed them away as he had filed other memories and went about his work.

CHAPTER
17

The boat that fairly flew upriver manned by five oarsmen was a beautiful piece of work. It had a curving prow, a billowing purple sail, and bore the royal emblem. The prison guard stared at it in wonder, for rarely did royalty land at the prison. They watched as it came sailing neatly in, and a man leaped up onto the wharf, not even waiting until the craft was tied up, shouting, "Take me to the governor!"

Yafeu was standing to one side and nodded. "I'll do it, sir." He turned at once and led the visitor through the prison yard to the tower and into the governor's quarters. He knocked for admission, and when he heard Rashidi's voice, he entered and said, "A visitor from the court, sir."

Rashidi looked up from his desk, where he had been busily scribbling on his poem. "What is it?" he said, not even getting to his feet.

"I come from the court of the god," the visitor said. "My name is Menho. I have an urgent summons for one of your prisoners."

Rashidi sat up straighter. "One of the prisoners? Which one?"

"The prisoner named Joseph."

"What does the pharaoh want with Joseph, Menho?" Rashidi said, slowly rising to his feet.

"The pharaoh does not explain himself to mere mortals. Here is an order for you to release the prisoner into my hand at once."

Rashidi took the parchment and read it, then said to Yafeu, "Bring Joseph in."

"Yes, sir."

While Yafeu was off on his mission, Rashidi did his best to worm out of Menho the reason for Joseph's summons. Menho either did not know or refused to tell.

Joseph came in quickly. He had been outside working in the garden, cultivating his flowers, and was a rather muddy sight.

"Is this the man?" Menho asked.

"Yes, this is the prisoner named Joseph," Rashidi said.

"I can't take him like that. Have him cleaned up."

"Cleaned up for what?" Joseph asked, startled.

"The pharaoh demands your presence," Menho said. "Oh, never mind the cleaning up. We'll clean him up when we get into the palace. Come. We must go at once. The pharaoh demands speed."

"When will you have him back, Menho?" Rashidi asked hurriedly as the messenger almost ran out of the room.

"That is for the pharaoh to say."

Joseph had time only to call back, "We will meet again soon, I think, Rashidi."

Rashidi followed them out and watched as Joseph was shuffled into the boat.

Menho shouted his orders. "Quickly, back to the palace!"

The oarsmen plied their oars furiously, and Rashidi stood on the wharf, staring in astonishment. When the boat had disappeared from view, he turned to Yafeu, who was standing by his side. "What am I to make of that?"

Yafeu grinned and pulled on his one ear, having lost the other in a battle years ago. "I always said Joseph was a strange fellow. Now we shall see how strange he is."

———

Pharaoh did not look a great deal like a god as he paced back and forth in the throne room. He was small with spindly legs and a potbelly, and his face was wizened almost like a monkey's. He had been an unattractive child, and as he grew older, he grew more and more homely. Not even the expensive clothing or ministrations of those who applied his makeup and fixed his hair could do much about that.

His wife, on the other hand, was attractive beyond description. She was, in fact, as beautiful as her husband was homely. She was a clever woman, a little cruel at times, but she was always very careful when she dealt with her husband. He was insignificant in appearance, but there was a stubborn streak in him that she could not control. Once he set his mind on something, there was no changing it.

"My husband," she said gently, "do not disturb yourself. After all, it was only a dream."

"No, it was *two* dreams!" Pharaoh insisted. He shook his head and continued to pace. "I have not been unable to sleep since they came."

His wife had been the first to hear of the pharaoh's dreams. She put no stock whatsoever in dreams but knew that her husband was terrifically superstitious, or religious as he would call it. She was very careful not to ridicule him, however, for that would be fatal. She had insisted that he call in his scholars and listened as Pharaoh had told them his dream. It all seemed like foolishness to her, and the interpretations put forth by the scholars seemed even more foolish.

Pharaoh had listened to them for a time, then shouted, "Get out, all of you! You're all fakes!"

Since then the pharaoh had grown more and more impatient and hard to live with. Isiri was beside herself until the chief butler came to the pair and bowed down with his face to the ground. He looked up with an anguished expression. "I do remember my fault this day," he cried.

"What do you mean?" Pharaoh demanded.

"You remember that Pharaoh was angry with his servants and put me and the chief baker into the prison. While we were there we each dreamed a dream. There was a young man in the prison, a Hebrew, who was in high repute among the prisoners and with the officials. We told him our dream, and he interpreted to us. His interpretation was that I would be freed and returned to His Majesty's service and that the baker would be executed. And so it was. I had forgotten it until this day, miserable man that I am!"

The pharaoh immediately sent for Joseph and refused to eat until he was brought to him.

"When this Hebrew seer comes, do not expect too much, my lord," Isiri said. "Egypt is full of dream makers and those who interpret their dreams."

"No!" the pharaoh cried. "I know somehow that this is the man!"

He had no sooner spoken than the butler came in, his face glowing. He bowed deeply and said, "He is here, O Divine One."

"Bring him into our presence," Pharaoh commanded. "We will hear him at once."

Joseph arrived in the city filthy, exactly as he had come from working in his garden. He was promptly handed over to the servants of Pharaoh, who took him to the palace, washed him, treated his hair, and clothed him in rich garments. They brought him out into the gaily-colored vestibule with its tall ornamental columns wound with ribbons. There was a guard of armed men in front of the throne-room door, and as Joseph entered the room, he saw many people there, presumably waiting for an audience with the pharaoh. He could tell by their dress and jewelry that they were all wealthy, and he assumed they were the influential members of Pharaoh's court. He had no time to study them carefully, however, for Belsunu kept urging him, "We must make haste, Joseph. Pharaoh awaits."

Joseph had gone halfway across the room when a woman suddenly stepped in front of him and he halted. Shock ran along his nerves as he saw that it was Asenath. She was dressed in a gown of shimmering white, and her hair was tied back now. For a moment her lips were drawn together, but then she said clearly, "So, it is the assaulter of women."

Joseph did not speak, but everyone around gasped, for they had all heard of Joseph's history. They also knew the reason that Pharaoh had sent for Joseph. There were no secrets in Pharaoh's court. Asenath's father, the priest of On, stepped forward. "Say no more, daughter," he said.

"You think I am afraid?" Asenath lifted her voice to Joseph again. "When I first saw you, you were a slave. The next time you were a prisoner. So now you've come to Pharaoh, but you are still a slave and a prisoner."

Joseph bowed and said, "It is as you say, my lady."

The quiet answer stunned Asenath. She had thought much about Joseph since the two times she had encountered him during his prison sentence, and she had tried to belittle him as much as possible. She had even made one of her influential friends investigate how it was that Joseph had risen to such prominence and power in the prison, and she was disturbed to hear the good report that came back to her. Her friend had said, "He is apparently a man of great ability, and the governor trusts him implicitly."

Asenath had never really forgiven Joseph for his attack on her friend Lady Kesi. But when she spoke harshly to him, she saw no look of anger or bitterness in his eyes. This bothered her, for it proved that he was superior to her in this way.

"We must go! Come, Joseph!"

"Excuse me, my lady," Joseph said quietly. "I am, as you say, only a prisoner and must obey." He bowed and followed the butler out of the room.

Asenath was aware that her father was still gripping her arm and that his voice was filled with anger.

"Are you so foolish?" he snapped. "Who knows what will become of that man? If Pharaoh likes him, he will favor him. And he is no man to have as an enemy."

Asenath could not answer. Joseph's quietness, the softness of his eyes, and his calm expression had stunned her. She had also been aware that he was dressed in expensive garments, that his strong form was more like a soldier's than that of a servant or slave. He was tall and strong and, she had to admit, one of the most handsome men she had ever seen.

"Let us leave this place," she said to her father.

"No, we will stay. We must know what will come of this." The priest's face was lined with worry. "The pharaoh is susceptible to so many things. This fellow is good-looking and seems to have some power. We will wait for the outcome."

Asenath longed to leave, but her father was insistent. Reluctantly, she went to sit with the crowds of people who were waiting to see the pharaoh that day.

─────────

As Joseph was led into the throne room, he had difficulty taking it all in. It was really a garden house, for there were flowers and plants everywhere. Sunlight streamed through high, arched windows. The room was supported by columns painted with exquisite scenes. Sparkling gems and stones were set in them, making them glitter in the light of the many burning lamps.

The pharaoh sat on a cushioned throne richly set with gems. Joseph saw right away that he was an excitable man—small and unimpressive and in truth rather homely. But there was intelligence in his eyes.

Pharaoh said, "Come nearer. I am Pharaoh, but do not let it make you fearful."

Joseph advanced, and the pharaoh studied him carefully. "You are not afraid, I see. That is good." He turned to his wife and said, "Is he not a good-looking person, my dear?"

"Very much," Isiri said, "but it is not his attractiveness that has brought him here."

"That is true," the pharaoh agreed. "I have had a dream, and I wish to learn the truth of it. They say that when you hear a dream, you can give the interpretation. Is that so?"

Joseph found himself to be extraordinarily calm under the circumstances. It was as if God were protecting him with an invisible wall. He could see right away that Isiri had no faith at all in the interpretation of dreams and that the pharaoh was anxious but doubtful.

"It is not in me, O Pharaoh, but God Almighty who will give Pharaoh an answer of peace."

The words pleased Pharaoh, and he said, "I will tell you my dream."

Pharaoh began speaking eagerly, the words tumbling out of his mouth. "In my dream I stood on a riverbank, and seven very fat and well-favored cows came up out of the water. Then seven other cows came up, but these were skinny and starving. I've never seen such pitiful cattle in all my life! And then the seven lean cows ate up the seven fat cows. But when they had eaten them, they were still skinny and lean. Then I awoke. Do you understand, Joseph?"

"Yes, I understand, Your Majesty," Joseph said quietly. "But there is more, is there not?"

"Yes. I then dreamed of a field in which seven plump and good ears were growing on one stalk, and seven others that were thin and wasted sprouted after them. The thin ears devoured the seven good ears." Pharaoh broke off and stared at Joseph, then added, "I told this to my scholars, but none of them could interpret these dreams for me."

Joseph bowed his head, and Pharaoh watched, knowing that the man was praying. Finally he asked in a thin, anxious voice, "Is your god able to tell you the meaning of my dreams?"

Joseph lifted his head and smiled. "It is not two dreams, O Pharaoh, but one. They are the same."

"But the meaning? I have heard nothing but wild, fantastic interpretations. I want no more of them!"

"I think, O Pharaoh, that you yourself could interpret your dream."

Pharaoh looked blank. "I. . . ? I'm no interpreter."

"But think, Your Majesty, what is it that comes? The seven starving cows followed right after the seven fat ones in succession. What is it that comes out of eternity one after another, not together but in succession, with no break between them?"

"The years!" Pharaoh cried. "Of course! It's years!"

"Your Majesty is right, and the seven bad ears of corn that sprouted right after the seven good ones—they are the same number."

"Of course. They are years too."

"Now, that is the meaning of your dream. The seven good cattle are seven good years, and the seven good ears are seven good years. The dream is one."

"But what of the other, the thin cattle and the blighted ears?"

"These are years also. There will be seven years of great plenty throughout all the land of Egypt, and then after them will come seven years of famine. All the plenty will be forgotten, and the famine shall consume the land. It will be terrible."

Pharaoh's face had turned pale and he turned to Isiri. "It is good news and bad, my lady. It is good that there will be seven plentiful years of harvest but then a terrible famine." He stared at Joseph, then asked, "What must we do?"

"You must be very wise, O Pharaoh, as you surely are. Pharaoh must find a man who is discreet and wise to set over the land of Egypt." Joseph's voice rang with certainty, and Pharaoh stared at him without even blinking. "Then Pharaoh must appoint officers over the land to gather up a fifth of the good harvest to store during the seven plenteous years. They must store enough food in the cities to use during the seven years of famine. It is the only way to prevent starvation throughout the land. If Pharaoh does these things, he will be remembered throughout all eternity as a wise pharaoh indeed."

Pharaoh stared at Joseph, then declared, "You must brace yourself, for what I am about to pronounce will shock you greatly."

"I await your pleasure, O Pharaoh," Joseph said calmly.

"Are you prepared? Then hear this: There is none so wise and discreet as you, Joseph. You are the man who must lead throughout these years of plenty and the years of famine! You shall be over my house, and according to your word shall all my people be ruled. Only in the throne will I be greater than you. Now see that I have set you over the land of Egypt."

With great solemnity, he removed his signet ring from his hand and put it on Joseph's hand. Then he took the gold chain from around his neck and put it around Joseph's neck. "Come," he said, "we must tell the people."

Isiri watched in stunned silence. She knew she had lost some of her own royal power and influence through this decision. Once her husband gave himself to a cause, he would have his mind on nothing else. *What will come of it?* she thought with dismay. *This . . . this* slave *will now be ruler over Egypt!* She had no choice but to hurry along with them as Pharaoh led Joseph out of the throne room into the larger room where the court was awaiting. She took her stand beside Pharaoh as everyone bowed low.

Joseph too was stunned by what had happened. He stood beside Pharaoh and listened, but his eyes were fixed on Asenath, who was directly across from him. *She has never looked more beautiful,* he thought.

The pharaoh lifted his voice and said to all the people gathered, "Hear you all this word from the god of Egypt. I place this man Joseph as overseer of the entire land of Egypt. His word shall be my word. Anyone who insults this man insults their king. Bow your knees, for I am Pharaoh, and without you, O Joseph, no man shall lift up his hand or his foot in all the land of Egypt. Bow down all and give him obedience!"

Asenath stared at Joseph, her eyes locked with his. He neither spoke nor moved, but she was aware that people all over the room were falling on their faces before Joseph. For one moment she thought of staying on her feet and defying him. If she had seen one sign of arrogant triumph in Joseph's eyes, she would have done so, no matter what the cost.

But Joseph's eyes were soft. He was not looking at another soul in the room and did not appear conscious that he was standing beside Pharaoh. His gaze was only for her. He bowed to her slightly, and there was a gentleness in the gesture that Asenath could not understand. She felt a fullness in her heart that seemed to swell until it reached her throat. To her surprise she felt tears rise in her eyes. She felt herself kneel and then bow down, and she heard the voice of Pharaoh saying, "This is the Provider! All in this kingdom will bow down and obey him!"

PART FOUR

THE PROVIDER

CHAPTER

18

Except for those times when a new pharaoh was crowned, Egypt had never seen such a splendid introduction as Joseph received. The second day after Pharaoh's command that Joseph would be second in the land, the investiture began with a ceremonial procession in which Joseph drove in Pharaoh's second chariot directly behind the monarch. He was surrounded by troops of Syrian bodyguards and Nubian fan bearers, and the crowd hailed him by one of his new titles, "The Provider! The Provider! Hail to the Provider!" The women were entranced with him, for he was young and handsome, but all hailed him as Pharaoh had commanded.

Everything was a sea of color and pomp and fervent ecstasy as the intense Egyptian sunshine sparkled on the gilded columns of the magnificent city. The populace were decked out in their best dress, bowing and paying homage to Joseph as he passed, with cheers and dancing in the streets, the women jangling tambourines.

Joseph was taken to his spacious new quarters, introduced to his servants, and showered with gold necklaces, armbands, and vases. It took two slaves to gather all the treasures that Pharaoh heaped upon him.

Pharaoh could not do enough for his new favorite official, his second-in-command. He gave orders for the construction of an eternal dwelling place and conferred on him many exalted names: Great Provider, Friend of the Harvest of God, Nourisher of Egypt, Chief Mouthpiece, Prince of Mediation, and Good Shepherd of the People. There had not been such a thing before in the history of Egypt, and the people reveled in it as they will over any new thing.

Joseph kept a calm presence amid all of this, and that was one of his many charms. Most men would be puffed up with pride by such an elevation to power, but this did not happen, and it endeared him even more to the people. As soon as Joseph could persuade Pharaoh to cease having celebrations in his honor and giving him new names, he set about doing the job Pharaoh had assigned him. He became a great lord at court and in the entire country. All other favorites were demoted, and only Joseph's presence could make the king happy. Joseph never overstepped the bounds of his authority, but he promptly set in motion the plans necessary to save Egypt from starvation.

His first task was to undertake a journey of inspection throughout the country. He gathered a staff of young men who were brilliant and capable but had not been permitted to rise in government because of the older men who were firmly established in the positions of power. He quickly attained a thorough knowledge of the land and the laws concerning property. He discovered that, although theoretically everything belonged to Pharaoh, the actual estates of Pharaoh were not quite so spacious. The land was mostly divided up among small farmers and large landowners, all of whom paid taxes to Pharaoh but who owned the land themselves.

After his tour, Joseph established his staff in a large building and at once proclaimed the new law of the land. Without respect to persons, it fixed the produce tax at one-fifth, to be delivered to the royal storehouses at harvest. He gave orders for the construction of many new storehouses to hold one-fifth of the harvest of the land for the next seven years. A traveler in Egypt after this time would never be far from the sight of a cone-shaped corn bin, many of them standing in close rows or grouped in squares around a courtyard. They opened on top to receive the corn and had stout doors below to empty it out.

Joseph set all the machinery in motion to manage this new system of taxation. From the first day of Joseph's administration, the reins were tightened on the one hand and loosened on the other. It was a masterful stroke that put the emphasis of government on collecting the corn rent while looking leniently on other debts. Thus Joseph managed to achieve the goodwill of the nobles as well as of the common people of Egypt—and most of all of Pharaoh.

Ever since she had bowed low to Joseph in the outer throne room, Asenath had lived in a constant state of agitation. She, like all others in the land, was fascinated by the elevation of an ex-slave to the position of second in the land. She had followed his career with an intensity she had never given to any political situation, and she was shocked and amazed, yet pleased, at how rapidly Joseph took over the reins of government.

At the same time she was troubled by the situation. It was not Joseph's political prowess that bothered her, however. Instead she was caught up in a deep inner struggle. At Joseph's coronation, she had been shocked by the splendor and beauty of the man. She had always been aware of his intensely masculine good looks, but in his royal attire, he appeared to be a different individual altogether. She went over and over in her mind her first memories of him—how she had seen him garbed in a slave's apron, his back bruised and bleeding from the beating Ufa had given him. Every time she thought of it, her face burned, for although she had been only a girl at the time, she was ashamed of her behavior toward a helpless slave. She remembered clearly every encounter she'd had with him since then, and she began to see herself as far less admirable than Joseph. He had never shown her anything but quiet humility, while she herself had acted like a spiteful child.

Another thing was very obvious. Her father was badly shaken by the political changes signaled by Joseph's rise. She had been aware of this long before he came to her and spoke in a nervous, high-pitched voice with hands not quite steady.

"There's never been anything like it in all of Egypt!" Potiphera paced the floor for some time before speaking of his own position. "The pharaoh is so easily swayed. He may decide to close all the temples of all the gods."

"He won't do that, Father," Asenath assured him. "He knows there would be a revolution."

"Who knows what that child will do? For that's exactly what Pharaoh is—a child. And this man Joseph has his ear." He turned to her with a look of panic. "Why, I might be thrown out. We would lose everything!"

Asenath put her hand on his arm. She was fond of her father, yet they had never been very close. "It will be all right."

"You've met the man. You told me about him years ago when he was a slave in Potiphar's house."

"Yes, that's true."

"Well, what did he appear to be then? Did he seem like a man who could rise to such a position?"

"He was only a slave."

"Did you ever speak to him? Did you hear him say anything?"

Asenath was not anxious to repeat to her father the account of her first meeting with the Joseph who was now the "Provider of All Egypt." Her cheeks reddened, and she said, "He was only a slave, Father."

"But we saw him later when he was sent to prison. You remember that day?"

"Of course I remember it."

"And we condemned him strongly for his crime, did we not? He'll remember our part in that, Asenath. We're in grave danger."

"If he had any plans to seek vengeance against us, he would have done so already."

"Not necessarily. He may be waiting to expose us publicly. He's been busy with all these new programs, but you wait and see. We'll pay for the way we treated him!"

Asenath shook her head. "There's no point in worrying about what may never happen. I'm going over to see Kesi."

"And there's another one that's probably going to feel the wrath of the Great Provider. After all, there was gossip around that Joseph was not guilty of the crime he was accused of. I've heard rumors that it was Kesi herself who tried to seduce him and he refused."

"Where did you hear such a thing?"

"I have my spies out. Servants always talk."

"It's foolishness, and I wish you wouldn't speak of it again! I'm going now."

Leaving the room at once, she made her way toward Potiphar's house. "It *can't* be true! People always tell lies," she muttered as the bearers swiftly carried her litter along the roadway. "But I need to find out if there's anything to it. Kesi can be such a foolish woman. She might have done anything."

"Well, your days are numbered, Ufa."

Ufa was pale and unsteady, as he had been since Joseph's elevation to second in the land. "Please don't say that, master," he whimpered. "It wasn't my fault."

Potiphar, who had been sitting alone in the room where he liked to read, put his papyrus scroll down and stared at Ufa. He shook his head but could feel no pity for the man. "You were the one who had Joseph beaten."

"But Lady Kesi commanded it."

Potiphar had thought of that and had no answer, but he kept his bright eyes fixed on Ufa. "I would say that when Joseph has time to think of it, he will go through his past and pull out all of us that have hurt him. And, of course, I'll be one of them just as you are."

"You . . . you mustn't talk like that, sir! He was always a kind man, as you well know. All the servants loved him."

Potiphar grinned wolfishly. "All except *you*," he said with a rather fierce delight. "You were cruel to him from the time he arrived as a poor, skinny Hebrew slave. He's an intelligent man and has an excellent memory. I think he's letting us simmer a bit in our own juices. You'd better enjoy yourself, Ufa. That's what I intend to do." He picked up a glass of wine and sipped it, then looked up and said, "Now, be off with you. I might suggest that you run away. Very far away. Maybe you can find a place to hide. Just leave me alone."

Ufa scurried away, and even as he did, he encountered one of the servants, who told him, "Asenath is here. She wants to see the mistress."

"Well, take her to her, then."

The servant escorted Asenath to Kesi's room. Kesi was crouched in a chair, but when she saw Asenath, she jumped up and ran to her. Her eyes were swollen with weeping, and she threw her arms around her as if she were her mother. "Oh, Asenath . . . Asenath, you've got to help me!"

"Now, now, don't cry. What's the matter?" Although Kesi was several years older than Asenath, the two had changed positions socially and emotionally some time ago. It was now Kesi who was the child and Asenath the mother figure. "Come and sit down," she said. "Tell me what's wrong."

"You know what's wrong," Kesi sobbed. "It's Joseph. He's going to kill me! I know he will!"

"Don't be foolish. He'll do no such thing."

"Potiphar says he will. He'll have us all killed, everybody in the house."

Asenath saw that calming Kesi down was going to take more time than she thought. Privately she was not certain that Kesi's fears were unfounded. As she listened she became even more convinced of this.

Finally her sobbing friend said, "Joseph didn't try to rape me. *I* was the one who tried to seduce him."

"Oh, Kesi, is that the truth?"

"Would I lie about such a thing? I wanted him so badly! I thought I loved him. I just couldn't help myself, Asenath. I couldn't help myself!"

For the rest of the morning and on until the afternoon, Asenath stayed with Kesi. She gave her an herbal concoction, furnished by Masud, to help her sleep. While Kesi slept, Asenath thought of speaking to Potiphar but decided there was no point in that. She did hunt up Masud again and found that he was the calmest one in the house. "Masud, aren't you afraid of Joseph's wrath?" she asked curiously.

"No, I'm not. I treated him well. All of the servants loved him, except Ufa."

"Your mistress is terribly afraid."

"So is Potiphar, although he tries not to show it." Masud shrugged. "I think they have reason to be fearful."

"But Joseph doesn't seem like a cruel man."

"That's the old Joseph—Joseph the slave, Joseph the prisoner. What would you do, my lady, if you had been whipped unmercifully and thrown into prison and forced to do odious tasks? How would you feel toward those who did such things to you?"

Since Asenath had done some of those things to Joseph herself, she did not care to answer and merely shook her head. "I'm worried about the mistress."

"I think you should be. Joseph will come, and justice will be done."

Justice did come the next day in the form of the Great Provider of Egypt—Joseph himself. Asenath had stayed all night to try to keep Kesi's nerves settled, but during the morning of the next day, she heard a frightened shout and went to the front vestibule. She stayed out of sight while she watched Masud answer the door; then she ran to Kesi's room.

When Kesi saw her face, she sat up and asked, "What is it, Asenath?"

"We have a visitor."

"A visitor! Who is it?"

"It's Joseph."

Kesi let out a loud, piercing scream and fell backward onto her couch, covering her face. "He's come to kill me! I know it!"

"I don't think so. Come. We must wash your face."

"I can't go to meet him!"

"You must. He's the royal representative of the pharaoh. We must all go meet him and bow down low. You know that, Kesi. Now, come on."

Asenath managed to get Kesi presentable and took her to the largest room of the house, where Potiphar was standing flanked by servants on all sides. He was pale, but his face was calm. "I was about to send for you, my lady," he said to Kesi.

"Husband, save me! Don't let him kill me!"

"I have no power in this case, as you well know."

Asenath took one glimpse around and saw that the servants were not nervous, except Ufa, who was gray with fear, and his knees were clearly trembling. She had not time to look at him for more than a moment when the outer doors opened, and two royal guards stepped inside, then took their places beside the doors. Joseph entered grandly, and as he did so, Asenath could not help thinking, *He may kill us all, but he's a fine-looking executioner!*

Indeed Joseph was looking strong and healthy. His journeys throughout the land had brightened his cheeks and his eyes. His hair was black and sleek, and the muscles of his arms and chest were exposed by the short-sleeved garment he wore. The gold necklace around his neck flashed, as did the gold rings on his muscular arms.

"Welcome to my house." Potiphar fell onto his face, as did everyone else in the room.

As Asenath touched her face to the floor, she heard Joseph's strong baritone voice saying, "Rise, please, all of you." She got to her feet at once and saw that Joseph was looking around the room. His eyes touched on the servants and then on her, where they paused for a moment. He bowed slightly and smiled. "Mistress Asenath."

"Great Provider," she managed to whisper, for her heart was pounding.

Joseph turned to face Potiphar, but before he could speak, Potiphar said, "I know you are here to take your revenge, master. I only ask that you spare my wife. Do with me as you will."

Asenath had never particularly admired Potiphar, but she did at that moment. It was the voice of a man who knew his wife's faults but was doing all he could to save her.

A small cry came, and Asenath turned quickly to see that Kesi had collapsed. She was crouched over, with her forehead on the floor, making small, pleading noises.

Joseph said immediately, "Asenath, help your friend. Comfort her, for she need not be afraid."

Asenath stared at Joseph uncomprehendingly. There was no hint of anger in his expression—only compassion. She then went quickly to Kesi and put her arms around her. "Come, Kesi. It's all right. You're safe." She helped the trembling woman to a couch and then turned around to watch the drama that was unfolding.

Joseph was staring at Ufa, who could not endure his glare. He fell down and cried out, "Mercy, master, mercy!"

Joseph's voice was even but cold. "You are a cruel man, Ufa, and a man in your position should be kind." Turning to Potiphar, he said, "For the sake of your own house, Lord Potiphar, I advise you to remove this man from his position. Let him serve as one of your lesser servants until he has learned compassion."

Potiphar could not believe what he was hearing. He had expected to hear Ufa's doom pronounced, and now facing Joseph, memories came flooding back of how he had liked the man but had been responsible for his imprisonment. "What is your pleasure—about me, sir?"

The room was as still as a tomb. Asenath was staring at the two men, who seemed locked in some sort of struggle. Finally Joseph nodded. "You have great ability, sir, and you have had great sorrows. But I remember that you could have had me executed. You showed mercy, and so I show mercy to you."

Asenath saw Potiphar's shocked expression and knew he had expected anything but this.

"The pharaoh needs loyal servants," Joseph said and smiled, "and I will expect good things from you in times to come."

"Is that all my punishment, master?"

"Not all," he said, turning to Masud.

Masud's eyes were bright, and he smiled as Joseph came toward him and embraced him. "I have missed you, my friend."

"And I you, sir."

Joseph turned back to Potiphar. "Lord Potiphar, I would have your servant Masud raised to the position of chief overseer over all your house in the place of Ufa."

"It shall be done. It is done now," Potiphar said with relief. Ufa gave a desperate glance at Masud, then backed up and leaned against the wall.

Joseph looked around and said, "May God bless your house." He bowed to Potiphar, who bowed back. Then he turned and walked toward the door.

He was halted there, however, for Asenath could not bear it any longer. She rushed to stand before him and said, "O Mighty Provider of Egypt—" She tried to control her trembling hands but could not. "In the name of my friends, I thank you for your mercy, O Mighty One."

Joseph turned to face her, but she could not bear to look into his eyes. She had no idea of what he would say, but finally he said quietly, "If I have any qualities in me that are good, my lady, they were placed there by the God of my fathers. I bid you farewell."

Asenath bowed deeply along with all the others as Joseph left the room. As soon as he was gone, Potiphar expelled his breath in an explosion. He sat down as if his knees had lost their strength and gazed around the room, saying in a shaky voice, "I have never believed in miracles, but now I am forced to, since I have seen one in my own house." He got to his feet and said, "Masud, you are my right hand from this moment. Do as you will in my house." A murmur of joy went around among the servants, and then Potiphar went over to Kesi. "Come, my dear," he said, lifting her up. "We have been given life. Let us not waste it." Kesi clung to him as the two left the room, and the servants began to talk among themselves in a high-pitched babble.

Asenath left the house, filled with wonder, and the question burned in her, *What sort of man is this Joseph? And how could I have been so wrong about him?*

Rashidi looked up when Yafeu burst into his quarters with a stunned expression on his face. "It's Joseph—he's come!"

Rashidi got to his feet just as Joseph entered. Rashidi bowed and went to his knees, but Joseph came and lifted him up. Rashidi saw that, except for the expensive clothing and his additional weight, it was the same Joseph.

"How's the poem going, my friend?"

Rashidi laughed. It was indeed the same man. "It is going well, master."

"You will have to bring it with you."

"Where am I going?"

"I am going to make you my first lieutenant. I cannot do without you. You need my help to finish your poem."

"Well, I see, then, there is some justice in the world," Rashidi said, swelling up. "A man of my ability should be recognized."

"You are impossible!" Joseph laughed. He put his hand on Rashidi's shoulders and said, "What would you do if you were in my place?"

"That's easy. I would kill everyone who offended me while I was a slave or prisoner. It's what anyone would do."

Joseph did not speak for a moment, then answered soberly, "No, my friend, it was what I might have done at one time, but I have changed since I was thrown into the pit by my brothers. And since I came through your prison, I have no need for revenge. Now, you must come with me at once, for I need you by my side."

CHAPTER

19

The task of building enough granaries to hold seven years' worth of grain was monumental. Joseph put all of Pharaoh's prisoners on the project, as well as every man throughout the land who was not otherwise employed. The work progressed rapidly, drawing Pharaoh's intense interest as granaries sprouted like mushrooms all over the land. When the project was well under way, Joseph took him on a tour of the land, to Pharaoh's great delight.

When they returned to the palace, Pharaoh turned to Joseph, his froglike face filled with pleasure. "You have done more than I expected, my friend. You are the friend of Pharaoh indeed, as well as his servant."

"I trust I will always be both, Your Majesty."

"I have been thinking of what I could do for you," Pharaoh said, and a pixyish expression crossed his homely face. "And I have decided to do a great thing in your life."

Joseph smiled, for Pharaoh always thought that everything he did was a great thing. "You must not do me any more honor, Your Majesty. You have already done too much."

"Nonsense," Pharaoh replied. "I'm not speaking of gold or titles or offices. I want to give you something better, something warm and soft and pleasurable. In short," he laughed aloud and clapped Joseph on the shoulder, "I have decided to give you a wife."

Joseph was not easily surprised, for the pharaoh was not a difficult man to figure out. In fact, he was barely a man, being very immature for his years, but Joseph was careful to keep the dignity of their relationship in place. The pharaoh might skip around and punch Joseph in the ribs and slap him on the shoulder, but Joseph always treated Pharaoh with the greatest respect.

"I am grateful for your thoughts," Joseph said, "but marriage is out of the question for a time. You know how little time I am at home."

"That's right. You're always out building things and talking to people, but a man can be busy and have a wife. *I* do."

Joseph had to restrain a smile, for Pharaoh's business was mostly ceremonial. His own was serious and was for the purpose of saving the empire. "I beg you do nothing hastily, Your Majesty."

"Well," Pharaoh said, somewhat disappointed, "we'll wait ... for a time, but it's something you must have."

"The time will come, I am sure."

"There's something else," Pharaoh said, looking up into Joseph's face quizzically. "You've taxed everybody in the land except the priesthood. Will you tax them?"

"No, I think not, Majesty. You don't need any enemies among the priesthood. They are very powerful."

Pharaoh seemed disappointed, but, as usual, he accepted Joseph's decision. "Well, that may be so, but we're going to have to control them ... starting today."

"Today, Majesty?"

"Yes. We'll start at the top with the priest of On. Do you know him?"

"Slightly, sir."

"He and his daughter are coming to the palace today. You may not think it's wise to tax them, but I want you to scare them a bit."

"And why is that, Your Majesty?"

"Oh, it's good to keep the people afraid of you. As a matter of fact, I've often thought it would be a good thing to execute a priest every once in a while—you know, just as an *example* to the rest."

Joseph was not often outwardly amused at the pharaoh, but he suddenly could not contain his laughter. "I hardly think that would be a satisfactory solution, Your Majesty, not for the priest of On."

"I suppose not." Pharaoh seemed disappointed. "But together we will keep him in his place, eh?"

"I am sure you can do that without my help, Your Majesty."

———

The priest of On was rarely frightened, but as he approached the throne room with his daughter, he turned to Asenath and said, "Why would the pharaoh send for me?"

"There could be many reasons, Father." She had been surprised when her father had asked that she accompany him to meet with the pharaoh, but since she was considered a priestess herself, he felt it would be proper. Besides the duty she owed to her father, Asenath was intensely curious, for she understood from her father's words that Joseph would be present. *I've got to get that man out of my mind!* she had thought—and then had set about making herself as attractive as possible.

As the two made their way into the palace and went through the usual ceremonial rites required to go before the god of Egypt, Asenath grew more and more tense. When they were shown into the throne room, she saw Pharaoh seated on his throne with Joseph standing to one side. She and her father bowed, then Pharaoh said sternly, "Rise up! Come closer!"

"O Mighty Pharaoh, we have come at your command," Potiphera said, his voice shaking. Asenath listened as the two exchanged preliminary remarks, but her eyes were fixed on Joseph. He was wearing simple clothing, despite the riches that were now his, and wore a single gold ring on his right bicep. His eyes were clear, and he had a ruddy complexion as he stood respectfully back at the pharaoh's right hand.

"Potiphera, I have called you here to insist upon something."

"Anything, Your Majesty!"

"I do not believe you have recognized the state of my Great Provider. You have not shown him honor. I am displeased."

"Oh, please, Majesty, do not say such a thing! I and all the priests are delighted at the wonderful work that the Provider is doing in Egypt! I am second to none in my admiration of the Great Provider of Egypt!"

Asenath was totally disgusted. At home her father had done nothing but complain about Joseph's rise to power, and now he was groveling before Pharaoh like a whipped dog. She could hardly bear to glance at Joseph, but when she did she saw that he remained expressionless.

"Come. I must talk further with you," the pharaoh said, "but first I must have refreshment. Joseph, entertain Asenath."

"Of course, Your Majesty."

Joseph bowed slightly, then turned to Asenath, who stiffened as he approached. "I welcome you to the palace, my lady. Perhaps you would like to see some of the plans for the future."

Asenath could only nod and murmur, "Of course, Provider."

Joseph escorted her out of the palace and proceeded to show her the works that were under way. Many of them were still in the planning stages, drawn on papyrus sheets, but finally he said, "It is warm in here. Shall we go out to the garden? There are fountains there, and it is much cooler."

"I have no choice," Asenath said stiffly. "Pharaoh has made it plain that you can command everyone in Egypt."

Joseph's eyes opened with surprise, and he shook his head at once. "I will not command you, my lady, but I will . . . invite you. You would do me honor."

Asenath stared at him, hardly believing what she was hearing. She followed him to the lush garden, with its soothing greenery and sparkling fountains. A servant brought them cool, refreshing drinks, and she listened as Joseph spoke of the plans for storing up grain in preparation for the famine.

Suddenly Asenath could stand it no longer. "You must hate me, Provider."

Joseph stared at her, incredulous. "Hate you? Why, certainly not!"

"But you *must*," Asenath insisted, touching her hair self-consciously. "I don't know how to talk to you."

"Why, just as you would to any other man."

"You're not any other man. You are the Great Provider of Egypt."

"I don't feel any different," he said with a smile. "It's only a title. I am still the same man I've always been."

"You don't feel any different," Asenath asked with astonishment, "now that you're second-in-command of the land of Egypt?"

"No. I still feel like a servant."

"But that's impossible! How could you not feel different?"

Joseph was quiet for a moment, then said, "Would you allow me to tell you a little of my life history, my lady?"

"I would like very much to hear it." Asenath sat quietly as Joseph told her about his childhood. He was a fine storyteller with a vivid imagination and was able to re-create for her the story of how he had been a talebearer and earned the hatred of his brothers.

She was shocked when he told her how he had been thrown into a pit, and she interrupted him to exclaim, "How you must hate them!"

"No indeed. I love them, my lady. They were not entirely to blame."

"You have a far more generous nature than I."

Joseph smiled. "You are different than when I first met you."

Asenath's cheeks flamed. "I'd hoped you had forgotten that, but how could you?" She swallowed hard. "I must do something I should have done years ago. I must ask your pardon for my unpardonable behavior."

"You already have my pardon. You had no need to ask for it."

Asenath could not speak, she was so overcome by his generosity. "Will you be so generous to all your enemies?"

"I have no enemies."

"What about Lady Kesi?" When she saw him hesitate, she added, "She told me the truth—that you were innocent of all the charges."

"What do you think I should do?"

"Most men in your position would have her executed."

"Would you, my lady?"

"No, no. She's only a foolish woman. She deserves to be pitied."

They continued to talk, and to her amazement Asenath found herself feeling comfortable with this man with whom she'd had such a strange relationship. When her father came in to tell her that the pharaoh required their presence, she nodded. "We'll be there in a moment, Father." She arose, and Joseph rose with her. "I must thank you for my friend Kesi, and for the whole house of Potiphar."

"You've already done so, my lady. There's no need to repeat it."

Asenath hesitated, then put out her hand. Joseph took it, enclosing her small, fragile hand with his large, strong one. His hand was warm and his eyes gentle as he gazed down at her.

"I thank you for your forgiveness," she said, "and I . . . I hope you are right when you say I am no longer the foolish girl I once was."

"You are not a foolish girl," Joseph said. He started to say something else but changed his mind. Instead he leaned over, kissed her hand, and said, "Come, my lady, the pharaoh demands our attendance."

CHAPTER

20

The palm-frond fans that two servants waved stirred the air in a gentle sweeping sound. The breeze brushed across the faces of Joseph and Rashidi, who were playing their never-ending game of Hounds and Jackals. The contest had begun when Joseph was in prison and had scarcely been interrupted by Joseph's rise to the position of Great Provider of Egypt.

Rashidi was leaning back, his arms folded, studying Joseph carefully. The younger man had his eyes fixed on the board and appeared lost in a reverie. Finally Rashidi said, "It's your move, Great Provider, or have you forgotten?"

With a start, Joseph shook his head, looked at the board, and then made a wry gesture with his lips. "It appears that you have won, Rashidi."

"Of course I have. Anyone could beat you the way you've been playing lately."

"Well, I've had many things on my mind." Joseph leaned back, stretched, and yawned. "It's late. Let's go to bed."

"One more game. I'll win enough off of you to buy that vineyard I've been coveting."

Joseph shook his head. "No, not tonight."

Rashidi picked up one of the carved pieces with a jackal's head and stared at it for a moment, then looked up. "Your mind is on something else, eh?"

"As I told you, I've got many things on my mind. You know that."

"That never troubled you before. There's only one thing that could make a man like you be careless."

"And what's that?"

"A woman!"

Joseph blinked with surprised. "No!" he denied vehemently.

"Why so great a *no*? If it weren't so, a simple, soft-spoken *no* would have been enough." When Joseph did not respond, Rashidi went on, "You can have any woman in Egypt you want. All these society women are drooling over you as a dog drools over a piece of meat it can't have!"

Joseph laughed. "For a poet you make absurd similes." He rose to his feet. "You are wrong this time."

But Rashidi had studied Joseph carefully and now remarked casually, "I hear that the daughter of the priest of On has a suitor."

"Why do you bother me with these trifles?" Joseph said loudly. "I don't care anything about these society matches!"

Rashidi smiled gently. "Why do you protest so loudly? You know, it's a proven fact that when you throw a rock at a pack of dogs, the only one that yelps is the one you hit."

"You're getting senile, Rashidi! I'm going to bed." Joseph turned and hurried out of the room.

Rashidi toyed with the jackal's head and murmured softly, "Well, so you're human after all, Joseph, the Great Provider of all Egypt . . . but you won't admit it."

———————

Rashidi had been right about Asenath. A young man had appeared on her horizon named Lostris. He was considered quite a catch among the unmarried society women of Egypt. Many a mother had unceremoniously shoved her daughter in his direction, for he had position, his family had plenty of money, and he was a handsome fellow. He also was witty and could sing fairly well—although not as well as he supposed! He dressed stylishly, giving rather too much attention to his personal attractiveness. It was often said of him, "Whatever time Lostris can steal away from doing nothing, he will devote to primping his hair."

But such character weaknesses were no impediment to the mothers and young women who saw in him a possible fortuitous marriage. When he had started calling upon Asenath, her father had been overjoyed. Since her mother was dead, he himself had to see to her future marriage prospects. He realized that at the age of twenty-seven, she was beginning to be eliminated as a possible mate by eligible young men. Several much older men had sought her hand, but Asenath had coldly refused them.

"I would sooner be entombed with the Pharaoh than to marry such decrepit old men," she had told her father. She had, as a matter of fact, shown no interest in any of her suitors—even the young ones—but now Potiphera insisted it was time for his daughter to marry.

"Asenath, you must think of the future. You are not getting any younger, and Lostris is a very good prospect for you. I'm sure he would be willing too if you showed him some interest."

Her father's words did cause Asenath some concern. All of her friends were married by now, and most of them had babies. She alone remained single, and although she vehemently denied that it bothered her, the subject caused her much irritation. "There's not a lot of depth in him, is there, Father?"

"When a man has money, position, and looks, he doesn't *need* depth. You can hire a philosopher to talk to you about deep things if you're interested."

Asenath came over and put her arms around her father. "Don't worry, Father. I think he's attracted to me."

"Well, it wouldn't hurt if you would give him a little help."

"What sort of help?"

"Oh, the things women do to attract men."

"What sort of things?"

"You know what I mean," he said, red-faced.

"You mean flutter my eyes at him and lean against him from time to time?"

"Don't be impertinent, young woman!"

"I won't, Father. I'm really flattered that Lord Lostris is interested in me."

"Well, see that it bears fruit. That's all I have to say."

———————

About six weeks later Pharaoh Abadmon and Isiri discussed the courtship of young Lostris and Asenath. During that time Lostris had pressed his suit, and Isiri mentioned this to her husband. "I really feel quite good about this match between Lostris and Asenath."

"It would be a good match"—the pharaoh shrugged—"but it's not certain yet. She's turned down a great many suitors."

"But I've been talking to her, and I think I have changed her mind," Isiri said with a smile. She was an inveterate matchmaker, and if she had a hobby, this might be considered it.

While the pharaoh and his wife were talking, Joseph was sitting at a table in the same room working on tax proposals for the coming year. He could not help overhearing their conversation, but he did not let on that he could hear them. He did look up, however, when Pharaoh addressed him.

"You never take any interest in these things, do you, Joseph?"

"Very little, Your Majesty."

"You remember I told you once that I was going to find you a wife? I think you claimed you were too busy."

"I am still very busy, Your Majesty, as you well know."

Pharaoh laughed and turned to Isiri. "My dear wife, you will have to seek out a wife for Joseph. He's too busy to do such unimportant things himself."

Isiri sniffed. "Unimportant indeed! There's nothing more important than a man's finding a bride!"

"You're right, of course, my dear. I merely spoke in jest. Now put your talents to it."

"Please do not bother, Your Majesty," Joseph said quickly. "It is much more important that we fill the granaries of Egypt than that we find me a wife."

"Perhaps it would be possible to do both." Isiri smiled. "I shall put my mind to it."

———————

A few days later Isiri held a banquet, inviting the most important members of Pharaoh's inner circle. She decided to keep the number down to thirty guests, which left out several hundred who would have given their eyeteeth to have been invited.

Joseph sat at Pharaoh's right hand, enduring what to him were boring ceremonies with a smile. He was not unaware of the women at the banquet who vied for his attentions. He recognized all of their tricks—giving him coy looks, reaching out to touch his hand, leaning against him as if unintentionally. None of them that night impressed him, however, and as he sat eating the roast fowl that was before him, he could not keep his eyes off Asenath and her escort, Lord Lostris. He had been in their company twice before, and each time he had found Lostris an obnoxious bore.

As the meal progressed, he saw that Asenath was embarrassed by Lostris's loud boasting about how he would fight Egypt's enemies. Joseph happened to know that the young lord had no military experience at all, but aristocrats enjoying playing soldier by dressing up in uniform, armed with a spear and bow, and riding around in a war chariot. It was Joseph's opinion that the first sight of a Nubian warrior would send young Lostris off in full flight.

Though Joseph found Lostris a bore, several of the young women at the table found him amusing and hung on his every word. While Lostris continued to entertain them, Joseph noticed Asenath getting up to leave. When she stepped out of the banquet hall into the adjoining atrium outside, he excused himself and followed her.

He stepped outside and saw Asenath standing beside a stone banister. The air was fragrant with the scent of flowers, and for a moment he stood quietly in the shadows and watched her. The moonlight bathed her in its beams, and he admired her profile. Her skin seemed like alabaster, and her delicate gown floated on the breeze.

Joseph approached, and she turned suddenly, her eyes wide.

"Are you well, Asenath?" he asked.

"Very well, my lord."

"When you left the hall I thought perhaps you might be ill."

"No, I'm very well, thank you."

She seemed stiff in his presence, and he tried to put her at ease by remarking casually, "The sky is glorious tonight, isn't it?" He looked up and gestured with his hand at the heavens. A broad band of light encircled the moon, and the luster of the stars scattered across the sky was brilliant. "There's my favorite star," he murmured.

"Which one?" Asenath asked.

"There. It's called Sirius. If a man could have a ring made with such beauty, it would be priceless, wouldn't it? Clear, living, blue-white fire with dark rays of brilliance."

"You know the stars, Your Grace?"

"I know a little."

"What is that one over there?" She gestured to a star glittering brightly on the southern horizon.

"That is not a star but the planet Anum. And look. You see that one up there?" Joseph pointed upward. "That is Quibilah. What a splendid red fellow he is! He's like a huntsman, girded and armed with a bow and arrow."

"I have heard people talk about such things, but I can never see them."

"Look. Let me show you." He moved closer to her and said, "Look upward. You see those bright stars in a straight line?"

"Yes, I see them."

"Well, imagine that they are a belt, and then up over the belt those stars to the right and left mark his shoulders." Joseph went on explaining the constellations to her, very much aware that her perfume was more intoxicating to him than the heady fragrance of all the flowers that filled the atrium. He showed her the great lion constellation and then the great bear, and finally he noticed that she had relaxed. "You're really interested in the stars, aren't you?" he asked.

"I know a little about them." She hesitated, then said, "Some say they determine our fate."

"I don't believe that."

"You don't?"

"Not at all."

"Do you believe that they have anything to do with love? I have friends who claim they chart the stars to find out the man they're going to marry."

"They would be much wiser to simply find a man who treats his mother well."

Asenath laughed. "I believe you're right, Provider."

"You don't intend, then, to chart the stars to find whom to marry?"

"No, I shall probably marry Lord Lostris."

Joseph hesitated, then spoke boldly from his heart. "But you don't love him," he said bluntly.

His words startled Asenath, and her eyes flew open. "Yes, I do!" she said angrily. "Why would you say such a thing?"

"You couldn't love such a boorish man."

She faced Joseph squarely, her eyes aflame, her lips stern. "How can you say that? You don't know anything about me!"

"I know a great deal about you, Asenath." Joseph moved closer so that she was forced to look up at him. "I can prove that you don't love him," he said.

"You cannot!"

"Would you like to see the proof?"

Asenath was rather frightened by his bold confidence, but she refused to be intimidated. "Yes, I would certainly like to see it!" she snapped.

Despite Asenath's attempts to provoke him, Joseph leaned closer toward her with a boldness that surprised even him. He wanted to touch her face, to hold her close, to confess his feelings for her that he had so long kept hidden. Her beauty in the moonlight was too much for him to resist any longer. She was to him like beautiful music that makes a man feel strong enough to conquer the world. The softness of her lips, the lovely turnings of her body, and the melody of her voice stirred him so much he pulled her into his arms and pressed his lips to hers. He felt her shudder with the shock of this intimacy, but she did not resist. Rather she returned his kiss with eagerness, and to Joseph it was like falling into a wave of softness that washed over him with a power he had never experienced before.

Joseph's embrace took Asenath completely by surprise. She had given up all hope of love ever happening to her, yet in this wild, unexpected moment, she surrendered to her desire to give of herself fully to this man—even to be possessed by him. When she felt she could no longer breathe, she finally pulled back and took a quick intake of air. Joseph gazed into her eyes, and she stared at him, utterly unable to speak.

He took a deep breath and smiled at her. "That's why you can't marry that fool."

Asenath was caught in a whirl of emotions, but suddenly it all seemed wrong to her. Her unexpected longing for him began to turn to anger—anger with herself for giving in to such a passionate kiss. She threw her shoulders back and stared up at him, then said the cruelest thing she could think of. "I suppose now you'll *command* me to marry you."

Joseph felt as if he'd been slapped, and it took him a moment to respond. He quietly dropped his arms and stepped back, answering her snub very deliberately. "No, my dear Asenath, love can't be commanded or ordered. It must be freely given. But I know this—somewhere underneath all that pride of yours is a wonderful, beautiful woman. I just hope that someday you will allow yourself to love and be loved."

Joseph did not wait for her to respond but turned and walked away abruptly. She wanted to call out to him, to take back her harsh words, but her pride would not let her. When he had disappeared, she turned and grasped the stone banister. Leaning against it for support, tears came unbidden to her eyes, and she began to weep. The greatest tragedy was that she did not understand why she wept.

CHAPTER

21

For two days after the banquet, Joseph slept fitfully. He could think of nothing but the kiss he had shared with Asenath in the cool of the night. He grew so quiet during those days that Rashidi knew something was troubling him, and he strongly suspected it was Asenath.

When Joseph arose on the morning of the third day, it was to the sound of joyous cries. Rising from his bed quickly, he went to the window and called down to one of the watchmen. "What is the rejoicing about, watchman?"

"Sir, it is the Nile. It's begun the annual flood."

Joseph dressed quickly and hurried to the river. He found the Nile ominously swollen. During the night it had crept up far over the stone pylons of the harbor, and soon it would force its way into the irrigation canals that had been dry since the last flood. The water would follow the canals until it flooded the fields.

He returned to the palace to find it humming with excitement, for the annual flooding of the Nile was the lifeblood of Egypt. Except for the narrow green band that followed the banks of the Nile, Egypt was a barren land. But the black alluvial soil brought down the river each year, some from the far inner regions of Africa, deposited itself on the low banks and made the soil there incredibly rich, producing as many as three harvests a year.

The pharaoh was excited, and he greeted Joseph with a punch on the arm and a smile of delight. "It is time for the great celebration. It must be the best year we've ever had, Joseph."

"You are right, Your Majesty," Joseph said. "It is a time to give thanks."

The ceremony of the waters in which Joseph would play a prominent part was indeed one of the most joyous times of the year for the royal court and the populace alike. Joseph dressed himself in his finest, placed his gold chain around his neck, and then joined the entire household in a spontaneous procession toward the river. Pharaoh led the way in his best chariot, and Joseph followed immediately behind.

As they passed the temples, the priests—their heads shaven and shining with oil—followed along, chanting odes to their gods. It was a day for sacrifice, and Joseph knew that after all the celebrations he would be sequestered with his engineers and mathematicians to begin their observations and calculations.

Joseph soon found himself in the midst of a throng that was keeping him from moving. He got out of his chariot, commanding his servant to take it back to the palace. "I'll just walk," he said.

The servant was shocked that the Great Provider would walk like a common mortal but obeyed without question. Joseph murmured, "All this ceremony for an annual rise in the river! What folly men will let themselves in for." He made his way through the pressing crowds, unable to avoid the shows of homage the people made to him. He got weary of all the adulation and stopped a man with a gray cloak. "Your Provider needs your cloak."

The man was delighted and handed it to him. "Take it, O Great One, with my blessing!"

"I do not mean to take it from you on this day of celebration. I will pay for it." Joseph handed the man a gold coin ten times the value of the cloak. He ignored the man's screeches of delight, draped the cloak over his shoulders, covering his royal attire, and moved along. Thus disguised, at least partially, he made his way along toward the Nile.

As he approached the river, he noticed Asenath being carried in a chair with Lord Lostris walking beside her. Joseph drew near to better study the face of the young lord just as one of the slaves carrying the chair stumbled. The chair lurched, and Lostris managed to grab it and hold it upright. Another slave immediately took the place of the fallen man, and Lostris, his face pale with rage, snatched a whip from an overseer and began lashing the slave who had lost his hold. The poor slave curled in a fetal position and cried out as the whip struck his bare chest and legs, drawing blood. It was a brutal beating, and Joseph found the rage of Lord Lostris shocking.

Joseph did not move to stop him, however. The crowd around them was watching the beating, and finally Asenath got out of her chair and rushed over. "Stop, Lostris!"

Lostris turned to her, his lips tight. "They're animals!" he snapped. "You have to keep them in their place."

At this instant Asenath glanced up and saw Joseph. He had his cloak drawn about him, but she saw his face. She flushed and could not help thinking of the first time she and Kesi had met Joseph the Hebrew slave and had him whipped just as this slave had been whipped. A wave of shame rose in her, and she turned and walked away quickly, telling the bearers, "Take the chair home. I will walk." Lostris threw the whip down and ran after her.

Joseph was sickened by the incident, but he was not too surprised. He followed along with the crowd until they reached a temporary walkway that had been provided for the procession to pass over the flat, muddy banks of the Nile. The main channel of the river was still a quarter of a mile away, and it was there that the priests and the pharaoh would hold their special ceremony on a specially built platform. Others would have to stand on the walkway.

Joseph was moved by a sudden impulse. His lips twisted in a smile, and he murmured, "Well, Lord Lostris, you're pretty handy with that whip." He quickened his pace until he was right behind the pair. The street was crowded, and Lostris was on the outside edge, leaving more room for Asenath on the inside. There were no handholds or barriers, and Joseph moved up alongside him. He caught Lostris in midstride and gave him a strong nudge with his shoulder.

Lostris gave a shrill cry of alarm, and his arms began to wheel. But he was too far gone. He flipped over the side of the bank, turned a complete somersault, and landed facedown in the thick, reeking mud!

Although Asenath had not seen what he had done, she turned, and her eyes met his. Over the sounds of singing and laughter, as well as the enraged screams of Lord Lostris, who was trying to climb back up the slippery riverbank, the two seemed to be alone on the walkway.

Joseph winked at her and smiled. Her mouth dropped open, and she realized with a shock that he had been responsible for the mishap. Joseph looked anything but guilty, and Asenath whirled to watch Lostris trying to pull himself up the muddy slope. He was covered with the black mud from head to toe, hawking and spitting and trying to wipe the awful mess from his eyes. Servants pulled him back up onto the roadway and attempted to wipe some of the mud from his face while he was screaming, "Someone bumped me! Which one of you caused me to fall in?"

The surrounding crowd fell silent, and Asenath turned quickly to look at Joseph. He winked at her again, then came to stand directly before the poor muddy figure who looked like anything but a lord. "I'm afraid I am the guilty one, my lord."

A murmur went over the crowd, and Lostris stared at Joseph in silence. A servant handed him a cloth, and he partially cleaned his face. "You did it, Your Grace?"

"Yes. I am the guilty one." Joseph let the silence grow deeper; then he inquired, "Will you chastise me with your whip as you did the man who slipped while carrying Asenath's chair?"

Many had witnessed the whipping, and they saw that Lostris was absolutely stunned. No one in Egypt could lay hands on the Great Provider of Egypt, for Pharaoh would have him stripped bare of flesh down to the bone! Making a small cry, Lostris turned and plunged his way back down the roadway, shoving people to one side. The crowd began to laugh at the mud-covered man as he ran, and the people shouted rude things. When Lostris was out of sight, Joseph walked over to stand beside Asenath.

"You did that on purpose," Asenath whispered.

"Yes, I believe I did."

"But . . . why?"

"I wanted to see what he would do." Joseph laughed. "And we saw, didn't we?"

Asenath stared at him, unable to believe what he had done. "You did it to see what he would do?"

"That, and I wanted to see what you would do."

"I can't believe you'd do such a thing! I despise you."

"No you don't," Joseph said calmly. He then smiled and reached out to put his hand on her shoulder, well aware that people were looking. "When a woman kisses a man as you kissed me, Asenath, she does not despise him." He waited for her to answer, and when she stood absolutely silent, he said cheerfully, "Well, I must be going to perform my part in the ceremony. Be careful and don't fall in that mud."

Asenath watched him make his way toward the river, wanting more than anything else to turn and flee home. But she did not. She lifted her chin and thought, *I will not let him have his way. I will go to the ceremony!* She made her way with the crowd toward the platform that had been built, and when Joseph stood to make his speech as the second man of all of Egypt, he looked directly at her and winked. She flushed and turned away, unable to meet his gaze and strongly aware of a strange stirring in her breast.

CHAPTER

22

Lostris avoided Asenath for several weeks, and she assumed it was because he had been so humiliated by his fall into the mud of the Nile. Actually, his absence came as a relief to her. She had thought much about the events of that day and had seen a side of Joseph she had never been exposed to. She kept remembering how he had winked at her after deliberately shoving Lostris into the mud. It uncovered a sense of humor in him she had never dreamed existed.

Not only the sense of humor, but his last words to her kept coming to her mind. *"When a woman kisses a man as you kissed me, Asenath, she does not despise him."* She thought of those words constantly and spent a great deal of time denying them on the one hand and feeling intrigued on the other.

In all truth Asenath was deeply discontented with her life. Despite all of the luxury she had known and the fortune of being born into the upper levels of Egyptian society, something was missing. For some time she had denied this lack of satisfaction in herself, but now that she was a fully developed and mature woman, the sight of one of her old girl friends cuddling a baby to her breast caused a strong sensation in her heart. None of her friends had remained unmarried, and she longed for the fulfillment that she assumed a fully developed relationship between a man and a woman would bring. She was also aware that she was stirred by Joseph in a way no other man had ever stirred her. This caused her some shame—yet at the same time a strange sense of pride that she had within her the desires that a man would demand from a wife.

During these days her father watched her carefully and more than once attempted to pressure her to accept Lostris as a husband. She put him off by saying, "He hasn't come back since he took that dive into the mud. I believe he's too embarrassed to let me see him again."

But her prediction proved untrue, for early one morning Lostris came to her door, dressed in his finest and making no mention whatsoever of his inglorious dive into the mud. When she invited him in, he said in an excited tone, "You must come with me today, Asenath."

"Come where?"

"The pharaoh and his court are going out on a wildfowl hunt. You must come."

Asenath had been on several of these hunts—as a witness, not as a hunter—for wildfowling was one of the most ardent pursuits of Egyptian nobility. She was not interested in going on one today.

"Oh, I don't think so," she said offhandedly.

But Lostris was insistent. "You must come! Everybody's going to be there. The pharaoh and his queen, of course. . . ." He named off several members of the nobility, and finally his eyes lost their glow and he shrugged. "Of course the Great Provider will be there. I'm sure he'll be heroic."

Asenath noticed a bitterness in his tone, and it was all she could do to keep from smiling and asking, *Do you intend to take another dive into the mud?* Instead she said quickly, "Well, perhaps I will come. It should be entertaining."

"Of course it will be. We'll have to hurry, though. They're leaving within an hour."

"I'll get dressed as quickly as I can," Asenath said.

She ran to her room and picked out one of her most exotic costumes. The ladies of the court, even on wildfowling expeditions, spent great time and money preparing themselves. They were transported on the larger boats, which could draw close enough to watch the young men of the court as they shot down the wildfowl with arrows. As she dressed, she thought sardonically, *Well, why are you so excited? It's just another wildfowl hunt.* She tried to ignore the fact that she really wanted to go because Joseph would be there. *He probably won't even notice me, not with all the beautiful young women there.*

———

The air was filled with the cries of the birds that inhabited the Nile, and from where Asenath sat in the prow of the boat, she was aware of the thunder of wings as the air was filled with a vast cloud of waterfowl rising into the sky. She always delighted in this part of the hunt more than the actual killing of the birds. There were many varieties, including white ibises, with their vulturelike heads, sacred to the goddess of the river. The geese in their reddish brown plumage, each with a ruby drop-let in the center of their chest, flew over by the hundreds, maybe even thousands. She saw the herons as they made their way along the banks of the Nile, beautiful in their greenish blue or midnight black. She liked the way they had bills like swords and stabbed at the fish, then tossed them into the air and caught them expertly. It was fun to watch the fish go down their throats, making a lumpy progress. Lostris had chosen to sit beside her in the boat, and when she questioned him, he explained loftily, "There are so many bad hunters. They're going to frighten all the birds. We'll wait until later, and I'll show you how it should be done."

The hunt went on for some time, and finally Asenath said to the steersman, "Let's get closer. It's too far away to see from here."

"Yes, my lady."

The oarsmen picked up the beat, and as they seemed to glide across the surface of the Nile, Asenath suddenly saw Joseph. He was dressed in a snow-white apron, and his upper body glowed in the sun. The tone of his skin was different from that of most Egyptians, which had a slatelike, dull color. Joseph had a golden torso, and she caught her breath as she had once before when she saw his smooth muscles rippling under the skin. He was laughing, and she saw that his teeth were white against his tanned complexion. She heard him speaking to his boatsman, and once again marveled at what a touch he had with the common people. *But then, of course, he's been one himself,* she thought.

"Steer away from that boat," Lostris said with irritation, motioning toward Joseph's craft.

"Yes, sir."

The boat started to turn, but even as it did, a cry of alarm arose from Joseph. "A hippo!" he cried out in a shrill warning.

Asenath glanced at the waters ahead and saw that the glassy surface was disturbed. Then she saw something weighty and massive as the water roiled.

Lostris began screaming, "Turn around—turn around! It's a river beast!"

Indeed it was a massive bull hippopotamus! He surfaced, and Asen-ath was terrified by one glimpse of the enormous animal. He seemed larger to her than the boat she was on, and when he raised his head, puffs of steam seemed to blow into the air.

"Pull—pull!" Lostris was screaming. But the boat turned ever so slowly.

"He's gone!" Asenath cried, for the bull had disappeared beneath the surface. She glanced over to see Joseph in the front of his boat with a massive spear in his hand. He was poised to throw, urging his boatsmen on.

Asenath had no time to think of anything else, for suddenly the monster broke through the surface and blew a great cloud of steam from his lungs. For a moment his back formed what almost seemed to be an island in the river, and then he made straight for the boat in which Asenath and Lostris were sitting.

Asenath could not take her eyes off of the beast. His enormous mouth was open with his jaws gaped wide apart. It seemed to Asenath a tunnel of bright red flesh, and the jaws were lined with teeth such as she had never seen—huge ivory tusks designed to bite through the tough and sinewy stalks of papyrus. Such jaws, Asenath knew, could shear through a person as cleanly as if slashed with a razor.

She heard the cries of the spectators in the other boats, but she could not take her eyes off the monster. It was right there before her, and as she scrambled out of her seat, she noted that Lostris had already gone to the rear of the boat. His eyes were so wide she could see the whites of them, and he could not speak he was so terrified.

The beast struck the boat with his snout, knocking it sideways so that the craft almost capsized. Asenath had nothing to hold on to, and she was thrown clear of the boat. She hit the water and sank. Frantically she fought her way back to the surface. The weight of her clothing dragged her down, however, and she was not a swimmer. She had paddled a few times in the swimming pools created by craftsmen, but this was different. The brown water of the Nile choked her, but above all fear ran through her as she thought of the mighty jaws of the hippo.

A cry drew her around as she struggled to keep her head above water, and she suddenly saw Joseph in the prow, his body tense and corded, ready to strike with his spear. His boat struck the body of the hippo and nearly capsized, but Joseph drove the spear down with all of his force right into the back of the hippo's thick neck. There was a terrible roar, and the monster thrashed around. Joseph clung to the spear, which was imbedded deeply, and Asenath could not believe it when she saw he had left the boat and now straddled the monster's neck. He was forcing the spear ever deeper and deeper when the monster suddenly rolled over. Joseph disappeared, and the water was red with a bloody froth.

It was all she could do to keep her head above the water, and as she paddled frantically against the water, she cast one glance at her boat and saw that Lostris was urging the boatsmen to get away. She cried out, "Lostris!" He gave her one wild look, his face pale, then turned and began cursing the boatsmen for greater speed.

Once again Asenath sank, and water went into her nose. She held her breath and fought her way to the surface again, choking and gagging. The water was red with blood, and not ten feet away, the monster had risen. She could see down the red channel of his throat, but she also saw Joseph clinging to his back, forcing the spear ever deeper. The hippo was roaring with rage, and his red eyes seemed to focus on her. The beast started toward her, and Asenath knew that she was a dead woman.

But then the spearhead of Joseph found the joint of the vertebrae in the beast's neck, and miraculously the light in the reddish eyes went dim. The beast stiffened, fell silent, and began to sink.

Exhausted by her struggle, Asenath sank again, and this time she was too weak to fight her way to the surface. The water entered her lungs, and she had one thought: *This is death.*

A redness floated before her eyes, and then she was immersed in an unbearable white light. But even then she felt strong arms go around her. She felt herself being pulled upward, and then her head broke the surface. She gagged and choked and began to vomit.

"You're all right, Asenath. Don't fight me."

Asenath had no intention of fighting. She was too weak for that. She felt herself turned over on her back, and her savior's arm went around her chest, supporting her. She found his body was beneath her, buoying her up, and as she cleared the last of the water with a series of short, choking coughs, she was able to gasp, "Is the thing dead?"

"Yes." Joseph's voice was right in her ear. "It's all right. You're safe."

Never in her life had Asenath felt such security. His arm lay across her breast, holding her tightly, and all the fear left her. As he lifted her close, she whispered, "You saved my life."

His lips were so close she could feel them move against her ear. "I hope saving your life becomes a habit."

Asenath was conscious that the boats were coming. There were cries from rescuers now that the monster was dead, and she remembered how Lostris had deserted her and knew that he was out of her life forever.

"Why did you come for me, Joseph?" she whispered.

His arm tightened around her, and she felt his lips pressing a kiss onto her wet cheek. "Because," he whispered, "I couldn't afford to lose anything so precious."

CHAPTER
23

As time progressed Joseph worked night and day to complete the storage of the harvest. There were complaints from many that the Great Provider was overdoing the work, that to stake so much upon one dream was foolish. Joseph ignored all these complaints, and when even the pharaoh questioned the need for such excessive stockpiling, he said, "It was your dream, and I believe it was sent from God, Your Majesty. We must be faithful to the dream."

Pharaoh gave in, as he always did when Joseph put something before him in such a way.

Joseph worked long hours each day, traveling from fields to granaries, checking the storage units, and at night going over the accounts, an enormous task in itself. He even forced Rashidi to put aside his epic poem to help him, and Rashidi complained that the world would be robbed of a masterpiece.

"If we don't get the grain into the storage units, there'll be no one left to read your poem!" Joseph snapped. He was irritable now from lack of sleep, but he knew better than anyone in Egypt the urgency of the task.

During this period Jacob heard reports that Asenath had been transformed by her brush with death in the river, and if he had not been so busy he would have pressed his case. However, he determined that as soon as the harvest was in the granaries, he would court her in a manner that was proper.

Asenath was disappointed when Joseph did not insist on courting her immediately. She disposed of Lostris with a gesture of contempt, and he slumped away, knowing that he had proven himself a coward in her sight. Asenath had other suitors, but she waited for Joseph to come share his heart with her. When he did not, she became depressed, and she often thought, *He doesn't really care for me after all. He said a lovely thing when he was holding me in the river, and I still remember his arms around me, keeping me from death. But if I am so precious to him, why doesn't he come?*

Two months after Asenath nearly died in the jaws of the hippopotamus, Pharaoh visited Joseph and gleefully slapped him on the back. "The time has come, my dear Joseph."

"The time for what, sire?"

"The time for you to get married." When Pharaoh saw Joseph open his mouth, he raised his hand. "Say no more. I found *just* the wife for you."

"Who is she?" Joseph asked wearily, for he had been through this before.

"She is of the finest Egyptian stock. Royal blood is in her veins. She is rich beyond compare." The pharaoh cast a sideways glance at Joseph. "Of course she's a little older than you are, but what does that matter?"

"What's the lady's name?"

"Lady Taiga."

Joseph stared at the pharaoh in consternation. "You can't be serious, Majesty!" he exclaimed.

"I am serious. She's exactly what you need."

"Why, she's fifteen years older than I am!"

"What does that matter? She's rich and attractive."

"Attractive! She's as fat as a hippopotamus!"

Pharaoh looked shocked. "My boy, you mustn't say that about the lady. I've already begun negotiations."

"Well, then, Majesty, you must *un*-negotiate," Joseph retorted.

Pharaoh's face darkened with anger. "All right, I've tried to be patient with you. Now you've gotten proud and puffed up. I am therefore going to insist on this matter of your marriage."

Joseph saw that the pharaoh was in one of his stubborn moods and knew he would be doomed to be married to the hippopotamus if he didn't think quickly. "Majesty, as always, you are right about all things."

"Ah," the pharaoh said with a smile. "I'm glad to hear you are so reasonable."

"But," Joseph continued quickly, "if I may make a suggestion, there is another woman I would have as my wife."

Pharaoh's eyes brightened. "You haven't said a word about this. Who is she?"

"She is far above me. She is pure Egyptian, and I think even you will admit her status is good."

"Name the lady and you shall have her."

Joseph plunged right in. "Asenath, sire, the daughter of the priest of On."

"Excellent!" Pharaoh laughed. "Why didn't you make this decision a long time ago? Her father is rich. He will be a good connection for the throne."

"I'm not sure the lady will have me."

Pharaoh stared at him. "You still have a slave's mentality, I'm afraid, Joseph. The girl will have whomever her father and I *say* she will have." Angered by Joseph's suggestion, he ranted for some time.

Finally Joseph interjected, "Please, Your Majesty, let me speak with her."

"No, you will stay out of it! This will be my affair." He beamed then and said, "Say not one word to her. She will be yours as certainly as I am god of Egypt!"

Joseph felt the pangs of apprehension, for whatever good qualities the pharaoh might have, tact and gentleness were not among them. "He's worse than a bear rushing at someone," Joseph said in despair. "I could have handled this if he had kept himself out of it!"

Pharaoh did *not* keep himself out of it. As always when he got an idea in his head, all other things became unimportant. The first hint Asenath had of the matter was when her father came in to see her with a strange look on his face. When she asked, "What's the matter?" he hesitated. "What is it?" she pressed. "Is someone ill?"

"No, it's not that," he said. "But I . . . I have some news from the court of Pharaoh."

"Oh, what is it?" she asked, now only half-interested. Her father was always getting news from the court, and most of the time it did not matter to her in the least. "A messenger from Pharaoh has come, and he has news . . . concerning you, Asenath."

"Concerning me? What news?"

Potiphera licked his lips, reluctant to speak for fear of how his strong-willed daughter was going to react. However, there was nothing he could do but spit it out.

"Well, it's good news, if you'll choose to look at it like that."

Asenath stared at him. "Just tell me what it is, and I'll decide whether it's good news."

"Yes, of course! Well, the fact of the matter is, Pharaoh has favored you with his attention."

"He favors criminals with his attention, having them hung by their heels from the wall to be eaten by the crocodiles."

"Don't be foolish! This is *good* news."

"So you keep saying, but you won't tell me what it is."

Potiphera cleared his throat, then blurted out, "He has decided you are to be married!"

Asenath stared at her father in utter consternation, and her jaw dropped open. "Married! Married to whom?"

"He . . . he hasn't said yet."

"It's another one of those political marriages!" Asenath's voice rose with anger. "He probably wants to marry me off to some seventy-year-old Nubian who's wrinkled like a mummy."

"No, maybe not."

"You don't think he's interested in my well-being, do you? It's always about cementing political alliances. That's what these court marriages are. You can't let him do this to me, Father."

"Asenath, be reasonable! He's the pharaoh!"

"I don't care who he is!"

Potiphera stared at his daughter in frustration. "Please don't say that, Asenath! What if someone hears?"

"Well, *he's* going to hear if he tries to force me to marry some mummy!"

Potiphera did not know what to do. If his wife were alive, she could have better handled emotional things like this. But he knew something had to be done. He walked over and took her hand, and when he lifted her face, he saw that she was crying. He put his arms around her and comforted her, then kissed her cheek, something he did not do very often.

"I can't do it, Father—I just *can't!*"

At that moment Potiphera, the high priest of On, wished he were in some other profession, far removed from the court of Pharaoh Abadmon. But he had been in politics a long time, and he knew that the situation was unavoidable. "You must do it, my dear. I'm so sorry. If I could do anything to stop it, you know I would."

Asenath wiped away her tears. She shivered slightly and said, "When will this happen?"

"The . . . pharaoh is waiting right now. He wants to see us both."

Asenath straightened her back. Her face was pale, and the tears had left streaks on her face. "Let me wash and anoint myself, and then we will go."

"Maybe it won't be so bad, my dear."

"Oh no, Father, it *will* be bad!"

Pharaoh greeted the high priest and his daughter with a broad smile. "Welcome to you both."

Potiphera wanted to protest the Pharaoh's decision and defend his daughter's right not to marry a man of Pharaoh's choosing, but he saw that the king was jumping with delight over his decision. *The pharaoh is always happy,* he thought grimly, *when he's meddling in someone's business or making life miserable for others.*

The pharaoh mistook Potiphera's silence for approval and said with a broad smile, "I assume your father has told you of my decision, Asenath."

"He has told me, Your Majesty."

"It is the will of the god that you marry, and I know you are an obedient daughter."

All the way to the palace Asenath had struggled with the thought of marrying some old mummy, and now she burst out, "O Majesty, Lord of Egypt, please do not force me to go through with a marriage!"

Pharaoh stared at her in astonishment. "Do you not understand? I have already commanded it shall be so."

"Please, do not force me to marry a man I do not love."

Pharaoh suddenly laughed. "Oh, is that it? I would have thought you had gotten rid of those romantic notions when you were fifteen or sixteen. But don't fret yourself, my dear. Marriage is a contract like any other. I'm sure you will find my selection suitable."

Asenath pleaded again, "Please, Your Majesty, do not force me to marry."

"You *must* marry," Pharaoh said with irritation. "You are wasted as a woman. Surely you can see that."

"I agree, O Great One, that I have waited too long to marry. But I beg of you to let me make my own choice."

Pharaoh was astonished that this woman was challenging his decision! "No, I have decided," he said sternly. "You must love the man I choose for you."

"But, Your Majesty, I can't make myself love a man!"

"Enough!" Pharaoh shouted. "I *command* you to love him! I am displeased! You have spoiled my surprise!" He turned toward the door and called out, "Joseph, enter!"

Asenath watched Joseph enter, and she puzzled over the strange look on his face.

"*This* is the man I am commanding you to marry, Asenath," Pharaoh bellowed. "There are thousands of women who would be overjoyed at such an opportunity. He is far above you. He is the second in the land of Egypt. I *command* you to love him!" The Pharaoh turned and said, "Joseph, come here."

Asenath stood stunned as Joseph approached the throne. Pharaoh took his hand and then hers. "Hold her hand, Joseph. I command you to love her."

Joseph smiled. "I willingly obey my king, and I will love you, Asenath."

Asenath whispered, "The king must be obeyed." Joseph's hand was warm, and she remembered how thrilled she was before when he had held her hand. She looked up at him and saw that he was smiling at her. He winked, as he had winked after shoving Lostris into the mud, and Asenath felt a sudden gladness that somehow Joseph was behind this! She knew it with all her heart, and as he held her hand, neither of them listened to what the pharaoh was saying. Finally they heard him declare, "Your marriage is arranged by a god, so it will be good. Go and love each other. I have commanded it."

Asenath felt herself led out of the throne room into the outdoor atrium. As soon as they were outside, Joseph turned her around and said, "I must tell you something, Asenath."

"What is it, Joseph?"

"I must tell you that I loved you long before the king commanded me. Perhaps you don't love me, and I know you cannot love simply because Pharaoh commands it, but I will make you love me."

Asenath was no longer crying when he put his arms around her and kissed her. She slipped her arms around his neck and kissed him back with an emotion so strong she could hardly contain it. It was the feeling she'd had as a child when she had run to her father and he had put his arms around her. But now she knew she had found far more than a father. In their embrace they entered into the same mystery other men and women face when they marry. None can ever know for sure what good or tragedy will come of it. As he held her tightly, she said, "I am looking forward, Joseph, to your art of making me love you."

Joseph laughed and lifted her completely off the stone floor. He made several turns while she squealed and clung to him. Finally he put her down and put his hand on her cheek, which was smooth as silk. "I believe the pharaoh was right."

"About what, my beloved?"

Her words struck deep in Joseph. "Your beloved! That's what I am, and you are mine. I believe the pharaoh spoke truly when he said a god arranged our love—but it is not the god-king of Egypt. It is the true God, El Shaddai, the Lord of all the earth." He kissed her again and held her close, and she clung to him. "He made the first marriage, and I believe he will bless this one."

CHAPTER

24

Joseph reached out and took the red-faced screaming baby from the midwife. He held him up to the light and smiled as he studied the face. Then he knelt beside Asenath, who was weak and pale after her ordeal.

"You have given me another son, and he is as beautiful as his brother, Ephraim."

"Let me see him," Asenath whispered. She took the squalling infant and cuddled him next to her breast. "He is beautiful, isn't he?"

"Yes, he's red and wrinkled and hasn't got a tooth in his head," Joseph said with a smile. He stroked her hair, which was damp with sweat. "And he is as beautiful as you, my dear."

Joseph turned and said, "Come, Ephraim, and see your brother, Manasseh."

The three-year-old came quickly. He was a strong boy and already had the look of Joseph about him. He stared at his new brother and wrinkled his nose. "He's so red!"

"So were you the first time I held you in my arms."

Joseph reached out and put his arm around Asenath. He leaned forward and kissed her cheek. "You fill my life, my dear, and you've given me two fine sons."

"And you have been my true husband." Even after the pain of her labor, a light danced faintly in her eyes. "The pharaoh commanded you to love me, and you promised to practice the art of making me love you."

It is a matter they had teased each other about throughout the early years of their marriage.

"And have I made you love me?"

Asenath reached up and laid her hand on his cheek. "You are my true love," she whispered.

They looked at the infant and then Joseph said, "The good years are gone, and we will now have the lean, terrible years of famine."

"I know," Asenath said, "but you have labored so hard, and you, my dear, will save Egypt."

PART FIVE

THE BLESSING

CHAPTER

25

The smoke rising from the small fire drifted into Tamar's face, blinding her for a moment and causing her to turn away and cough violently. Her eyes watered, and she wiped them with the sleeve of her dress; then she turned back to look down into the pot. "I've boiled you for half a day and you're still tough as a sandal," she muttered. Tamar picked up a knife and probed the meat, muttering, "Soften up, you stupid bird! I don't know what things are coming to when the master has to eat a thing like this."

Tamar had killed the bird earlier with a stick and had wrung its neck, plucked it, and dressed it. The animal had been weak and starving and was therefore an easy target, but it did not promise to make an appetizing meal. She sighed heavily as she poked the boiling fowl again with her knife.

Tamar had made a place for herself in the camp and had become closer to Jacob than any of his many daughters-in-law. She had pitched her tent close to his, where she could attend to the old man's needs, and he had become quite fond of her and her twin boys. Judah stayed as far away from her and his two sons as possible. Tamar knew he was still ashamed of himself for having sired two sons with his own daughter-in-law, and she expected no attention from him. It was not a husband in her bed she wanted—only Judah's seed to carry on the line of the Redeemer.

She glanced around the camp and noticed how lackadaisical everyone seemed. There was really no danger of them starving in the near future, for they had goats, sheep, and cattle, but they had lost a great many of them during the long drought. Many of the animals had died for lack of water and others were so skinny they were hardly worth dressing. The crops they had planted had failed, and the grass had dried out to dusty strands that the herds and flocks could barely subsist on.

The sound of laughter and children's voices floated by, and Tamar looked up to see her boys, Perez and Zerah, playing a game. They already bore signs of looking like their father, Judah, with the same dark curly hair and soulful eyes—though, thankfully, they had not inherited the red-rimmed lids passed down from Leah.

Tamar tended the bird for another half an hour before it was soft enough to eat. She took it out of the water, cut the meat from the bone, put it on a plate, then rose and took it to Jacob's tent. The sides of the tent were tied up to catch every bit of the breeze, and she found Jacob sitting on the thick carpet, staring out into space. "I've got you a nice dinner here, master." She smiled and put the plate down before him. "And I've saved some sour goat milk that you like so much."

Jacob looked up, and although the hard times had further aged his lean, leathery face, he still had a smile for the woman. "What is it, daughter?" he asked.

"It's a bird I knocked down. I'm not sure what kind it is, but it will be a change for you." Tamar smiled and knelt down beside him. She opened the leather bag of sour goat's milk and poured some into a cup for him. "Eat up, now. You need to gain some weight."

Jacob picked up a morsel of the meat and tasted it. "It's good," he said. "You always know how to cook different things."

"I know you get tired of the same foods all the time."

"I think we all do," Jacob said. He took a sip of the sour milk, smacked his lips, and wiped his mustache with the back of his hand. Wistfully he said, "What I wouldn't give for some fresh green onions or leeks."

"Maybe the rains will come soon, and then you'll see the kind of meals I can cook for you."

"You've done wonderfully well, daughter," Jacob murmured. He continued to eat, and as he did, the two boys came running by. Perez was chasing Zerah and shouting at the top of his lungs. Jacob had lifted a bit of meat to his mouth, but he paused, and Tamar saw his eyes go to the boys. She had become adept at reading the old man's moods, for he made little attempt to hide his emotions. She watched him as he kept his eyes on the two youngsters, and she thought, *He hasn't accepted my boys as his own blood yet, but he will one day.*

"How are things with the people?" Jacob asked as he slowly chewed with his weak teeth.

"Hungry." She shrugged. "We were all hoping for a harvest of grain this year, but there was no rain at all. Most of the grain didn't even come up, and that which did was taken by the wild things."

"I just don't know what we're going to do. How much longer can this drought last?" Jacob whispered.

Tamar glanced up into his old, wrinkled face. She knew as much of the history of this man as anyone did, for it was to her that he spoke most often of his youth. The others may have been there for part of his life, but Tamar know how to elicit his many memories, even those from his childhood. Others were too busy or didn't care. His sons were always out trying to find food, but Tamar was always there by his side, and now she reached over and put her hand on his. "You must not worry."

"How can I help it? Still, we're better off than some. Those who don't have flocks are starving."

"God isn't going to let us starve."

Jacob blinked his eyes and stared at her strong face. Tamar had large, well-shaped eyes, a strong mouth, and a determined chin. The desert had dried out her complexion, but there was a strength in her that most women lacked. "You have more faith than most," Jacob murmured.

Tamar squeezed his hand and smiled. "God will not let us die."

"Why are you so sure of that?"

"Because of you, master."

"Because of me?"

"Yes, of course. You've been telling me for years now about how El Shaddai met you and actually spoke with you."

"You've always loved my stories." Jacob smiled and put his hand on her head. "You've been a blessing to me, Tamar."

"I trust I will always be your handmaiden."

As usual, she was able to cheer Jacob up, and finally he sighed and shook his head. "You have more family feelings than any of my sons."

"I have learned of your family from you. It's a wonderful story, master," Tamar said with enthusiasm. "Tell me some more."

Jacob laughed and sipped the last of his milk. He smacked his lips, and she refilled the cup. "I think I've told you everything that's ever happened to me."

"But there must be more about your father or your grandfather or about the beginnings of your people. Tell me about that."

As always, Jacob was impressed with this woman. He was not sure how much the rest of his family knew about the hope that was in his own heart. Somehow Jacob had received from his father and his grandfather the absolute certainty that their people, above all others in the world, had been favored by El Shaddai. His face grew sober and his eyes dreamy as he spoke, and Tamar leaned forward to catch every word.

"Back in the beginning there was only Adam and Eve, the first man and the first woman, and they had two sons. One was Cain and one was Abel. . . ." He went on to relate the story of how Cain killed Abel, and he shook his head. "Cain became a vagabond, and his children and his grandchildren forgot about the God who had made them."

"What about the other sons?" Tamar asked when he paused. "Not Abel, but the other children."

"God gave them another son whose name was Seth. He was a man who loved God, and his children loved God. That was the beginning of two lines of people in the world—those of Seth and of Cain, those who love God and those who do not. But the sons of Cain far outnumber the sons of Seth, I'm afraid."

"And who was Seth's son?"

The two sat there in the tent, the woman kneeling and listening intently, and Jacob going over the traditions that were burned into his memory. He did not know everything about the dark, cloudy past, but he spoke words he had learned from others. Finally he stared at her and laughed shortly. "You've heard this from me a hundred times, daughter. Why do you want to hear it again?"

"Because," Tamar said, her voice steely and determined, "out of all the peoples in the earth, all of the tribes in the nation, God is doing a great thing with you, master. From you will come Shiloh."

Jacob was always amazed at the strength and power and intensity that flowed out of Tamar as she spoke about this. He stared at her now and shook his head in wonder. "You are right, but I do not even know which one of my sons will be in the line."

Tamar smiled slightly. Her lips curved upward, and she wanted to say, *I know.* But she felt it would not be wise. "Eat some more," she said. "And tell me about meeting God. What does He look like?"

Jacob was slightly amused. "I've told you many times, He doesn't look like *anything,* daughter. God is not a man, and He does not look like a man. All I saw when God spoke to me was a light of some kind. God somehow is light."

Tamar tried to get him to speak more, but the old man got to his feet, picked up his staff, and walked outside. Tamar followed him, and Jacob said, "You boys, come here!"

Perez and Zerah had been rolling in the dust wrestling. They came at once but went to their mother and tried to hide behind her.

"Come out from behind your mother there. I want to look at you."

Reluctantly the two boys came out with a little help from Tamar, and Jacob stared at them. "What were you boys doing? Fighting?"

"No, sir, playing," Perez said, looking up at his grandfather.

The boy smiled, and Jacob realized that the child had more of Judah in him than the other. He looked at Zerah and saw his mother's features in the lad's face. "Why don't you walk with me, and I'll tell you a story."

Zerah looked up at his mother and clung to her. Perez's eyes danced. "Yes, Grandfather!"

Tamar watched as the three went off, Perez holding to Jacob's hand, and Zerah keeping his distance. "That's right," she whispered. "Get to know those boys, for one of them is in the line of Shiloh!"

None of the four Sons of the Maids were happy as they sat cross-legged on the ground, gnawing the meat off the bones of the sheep they had butchered that morning. "This meat is so tough I can't chew it," Gad complained.

Asher, his brother, was still heavyset, despite the scarcity of food. He licked the bone, trying to suck the marrow out of it, then shook his head as he tossed the bone over his shoulder. "At least we've got something to eat."

"We won't have if this keeps up."

Dan and Naphtali, Bilhah's sons, were seated across from Gad and Asher. Naphtali's face was badly scarred from being attacked by a wolf as a small child, and his twisted visage made him look constantly angry. Dan had a lean, intelligent face and was crafty, though he was no longer as wild and headstrong as when he was young. Now he stared with disdain at the remnants of the bones and exclaimed, "We're all going to starve to death if something's not done! Naphtali, what did you find when you went to the tribe over to the west?"

"I didn't find anything good," he said. He took a drink of tepid water from a leather bottle and spat it out. "They're as hungry as we are. I talked to the head of the clan. He said they're going to move south."

"I was there last week and things weren't any better," Gad said with a shrug.

The four sat there, drawn together by the circumstances of their births. They were merely the sons of Jacob's concubines, not the sons of one of his wives. This had set them apart all their lives and given them feelings of inferiority. No one spelled it out, but it was understood that the sons of Leah and the sons of Rachel somehow had a higher status. This had not sweetened the disposition of the Sons of the Maids, and they sat there complaining.

Finally Naphtali said, "There's always Egypt. Plenty of grain there."

Staring at his brother sourly, Dan shook his head. "A lot of good that does us."

"We could go there and buy some," Naphtali replied.

"No, we'll never be able to do that. Anyway, things are going to get better."

Asher had picked up another bone and was trying to nibble a morsel of meat that still clung to it. He was always hungry, and it was a mystery how he could stay fat while the rest of them were gaunt with hunger. "We're going to have to do something," he said. "The animals are going to starve. We're *all* going to starve if something isn't done!"

––––––––––

At the same time the sons of Leah were having their meal in their own part of the camp. The six of them were as discontented as the Sons of the Maids. Simeon, the second-born, was a lean man and had, perhaps, the hottest temper of any of the brothers. He cursed now and stared at the small portion of stew in his bowl. "Is this all I get?"

Levi, the third in order, was as short and muscular as Simeon was lean. He had black hair, dark eyes, and his temper was a match for Simeon's. "I'm sick of hearing you complain!" he shouted. "Shut your mouth or I'll shut it for you!"

Simeon came right back, and the two leaped to their feet and faced each other, ready for a fight. They were both good fighters, having spent much of their youth learning those skills.

Issachar and his brother Zebulun were the youngest of Leah's son's. Reuben, Simeon, Levi, and Judah had all been born in a brief period; then their mother had stopped bearing children. That was when she had given her handmaiden to Jacob to produce more children. But later Leah's womb had opened to bear Issachar and Zebulun. They were younger and did not have the fiery tempers of their older brothers.

Issachar stood up to get a drink of water but stopped and stepped up to Simeon and Levi. "Don't fight. It's too hot." He hated to see his brothers fighting. "Doesn't do any good to quarrel," he said with a sigh of frustration.

Simeon and Levi glared at each other, then plopped themselves down on the ground again.

Simeon flexed his arms and said, "My children are hungry all the time."

"So are mine," Levi muttered. "Everybody's hungry."

Zebulun was different from all his siblings in one respect. He had, from his earliest days of childhood, longed for the sea. This was rather strange, for he had seen the sea only once on a trip he had made with his older brother Reuben. The sight of it had burned itself into his brain. Everyone knew it would take very little to send him away from home to learn the trade of a sailor. He picked up a dried-out date, popped it into his mouth, and chewed on it. "What about going to Egypt? They've got plenty to eat there, if what I hear is true."

"Those are just rumors," Judah said. He shook his head and added, "I don't think there's as much food there as people say."

Reuben had been silent to this point, and his face was lean and drawn from lack of nourishment. "Everybody's talking about it."

"Talking about what?" Judah asked.

"Talking about all the food in Egypt."

"Do you believe it's there?" Judah asked with a little hope in his voice. "I've always thought it was just people boasting."

"No, I've seen some of the grain they've brought back. Old Menesee took a whole herd of donkeys there and brought them back fully laden."

"How much did it cost?" Simeon demanded.

"They didn't give it away," Reuben said with a shrug, "but at least they got enough grain to make bread and perhaps have some left over for seeding a new crop."

"I don't see what good it does to have seed," Judah said. "You put it in the ground and without water it dies."

Zebulun piped up, "I think we ought to go."

"Go where?" Issachar said. "To Egypt?"

"Yes, to Egypt!"

The brothers discussed this idea, and finally Reuben said, "I don't think we have any choice. We've got to go to Egypt."

"Ha!" Simeon sneered. "I can picture Father letting us go there!"

Reuben got to his feet and towered over them. His body was starting to shrink, but he was still a powerful man. "We've got to go. I think even he will see that. Judah, why don't you go talk to him?"

"You're the firstborn," Judah retorted. "I think it should be you."

Reuben looked down at the ground. "That doesn't mean anything anymore."

"Yes, it does," Zebulun said quickly. He got to his feet and came over to stand beside Reuben. He was very attached to his oldest brother and put his hand on his arm. "Go tell him that we have to go. And make sure you tell him *I* want to go. I never get to go anywhere."

Reuben tried to convince the others that he was not the one to talk to Jacob, but the other brothers insisted. Reuben sighed heavily, then shrugged. "All right, but I don't think it will do any good."

———

Jacob had been dozing at twilight when suddenly his eyes flew open. His hearing was still surprisingly good for one his age, and besides, Reuben made a lot of noise when he walked. "Is everything all right, son?"

Reuben came and sat down in front of his father. "No, things aren't all right."

"What's the matter? Any new problems?"

"The same old problem," Reuben said. "We've got to do something, Father."

"What can we do? We're not God. He's the one who controls the rain. Until it rains, it's going to be like this."

"Yes, that's right, of course." Reuben hesitated. He knew well how much his father hated the very idea of Egypt, but there was no way around it. "The only choice we have is to go to Egypt and buy grain there."

"No, I won't have it!" Jacob declared.

"But, Father—"

"Don't even talk to me about it, Reuben! It's an evil place filled with evil people."

"I can't understand why you hate Egypt and the Egyptians so much. You've never even been there."

"I don't have to go there to know what it's like."

"They're men just like all other men, some good and some bad."

"No, you're wrong about that, son. There's something wrong. They're an evil people."

"Evil in what way?"

"Why, they worship gods made out of mud." ·

"So do some of our neighbors, but we get along with them."

"There's something perverted about them," Jacob insisted, "and they don't dress modestly. Women wear dresses so thin you can see right through them."

"I'm not suggesting we go down to Egypt and look at their women!" Reuben said, somewhat irritated. But then he made himself calm down, for he knew Jacob could be persuaded only by tact. "Tell me why you hate Egypt so much."

Jacob closed his eyes for what seemed like a very long time before he began to speak. "A long time ago, right after I got the birthright from my brother, Esau, there was a famine in the land, son, just like this one."

"You never told me about that."

"It was terrible, just like it is now."

"Did it last a long time?"

"It seemed like forever. I was afraid we were all going to die."

"Some of us are afraid of that today."

Jacob did not appear to have heard. "I went to my father, and I told him we were going to have to go there to seek food. Even in those days the famine wasn't as hard in Egypt. That's because of the Nile, you know. The river always rises unless there's a world drought, and they always have food when the rest of us don't."

Reuben listened as Jacob meandered on. The old man liked to ornament his stories with side issues, and it took him forever to get to the point.

Finally Jacob seemed to recall himself. He shook his shoulders and brushed his hand across his face, adding, "I was very much afraid, but I gathered my courage to present my case to my father."

"What did he say?"

"He didn't say anything other than he'd think about it."

"Did he go? Did all of you go?"

"No. It was only a little while later that he came to me, and I still remember it clearly. We were out in the field. It was as dry as dust, and animals were dying everywhere. I was ready to go to Egypt then, but my father said on that day, 'We're not going to Egypt.'"

"Why did he say that?"

Jacob hesitated, then said, "He told me that God Almighty had appeared to him in a dream the night before, and He had said: *Do not go down to Egypt. Live in the land where I tell you to live. Stay in this land for a while, and I will be with you and will bless you.*"

Jacob told Reuben the rest of the story as he had heard it from his father, then said, "God knows best. If He didn't want my father to go down to Egypt, He doesn't want us to go."

Reuben was silent for a long time, and finally he said, "I believe you ought to think about it, Father. I don't see any other way."

"I can't imagine why God would want us to go to that place," Jacob said and closed his eyes.

Reuben sighed. He knew the conversation was over. He got to his feet, and without another word, he went back to give his brothers the bad news.

———————

No one ever really knew for sure what changed Jacob's mind about sending his sons to Egypt, but he called all eleven of his sons together and said, "We must have food. I have considered, Reuben, what you have said. If it must be so, then it must be. It saddens me, for I think no good can come of it."

"So we can go?" Reuben said quickly.

"Yes, you can go."

"Shall we all go?" Zebulun asked.

"All except Benjamin."

"Oh, Father, let me go too!" Benjamin cried.

"No, my son, you must stay here with me. Your brothers can go get the food without you."

Benjamin bit his lip, but he had little hope that his father would change his mind about the matter. He waited his chance, however, and when the others were gone, he said, "Please, Father, let me go with my brothers."

Jacob reached up and put his hand on his son's head. "You are all that's left of the True Wife. I cannot spare you, my son. Speak no more of this."

———————

The donkeys were all ready, and Benjamin had come to see them off. "I wish I could go with you," he said woefully to his brothers.

"We all know that," Reuben said. "I didn't expect Father would let you go."

"You'll have it easier here than we will. It's a long, hard journey," Judah said, trying to be comforting.

"I don't care, Judah. I want to go! I don't know why Father has to treat me like a child."

Benjamin helped the men with last-minute tasks, and finally when they were ready, he went to Reuben and said, "You're the firstborn. You can convince Father."

Reuben stared at him. "I won't get the blessing from Father. I don't deserve anything. You will probably get it," he said.

"Me! But I'm the youngest!"

Then Reuben said in an uncharacteristically sharp tone, "Our father has a way of manipulating people and events. If he wants the youngest to have the birthright and the blessing, you may be sure he'll have his own way." He put his hand on his brother's shoulder and squeezed it. "I'll bring you back something special, Benjamin."

"I wish I were going."

Reuben merely shook his head and turned to mount his donkey. Jacob had come out to see them off, as well as Leah, Tamar, Bilhah, and Zilpah. Jacob gave his blessing to them, and then the brothers all headed south. Jacob held on to Benjamin's arm, and Leah, who was standing on his other side, said, "You can't keep him forever under your hand."

Jacob could not answer, for he knew his feelings were irrational. He let go of Benjamin, took Leah's arm, and walked away with her. When they were beyond hearing distance of the others, he said, "I know I haven't been fair to you. I'm not a good man, Leah. I'm very selfish. You've given me six sons and a daughter, and I'm most thankful for them. I thank you now."

Leah was not accustomed to soft words or any expression of affection from her husband, and his words brought tears to her eyes.

When Jacob saw them, he put his arm around her shoulders and said, "Don't cry, now. It's going to be all right." He watched his sons disappearing over the horizon, his heart heavy as they faded from view.

CHAPTER

26

The drought had narrowed the width of the mighty Nile significantly. As the river wound down from its source in the hills of Africa, it picked up some rain, but nothing like in the years preceding the drought when the torrents had poured out of the heavens, filling it to a mighty flood that rushed all the way down to the delta of Egypt. The wildlife had suffered greatly, for with all their watering holes dried up, thirst drove the animals toward the muddy banks of the shrunken river in large numbers, allowing them to be easily trapped by the predators.

The sun burned white-hot, seeming to scorch the very air. The intense blue, cloudless sky appeared as hard as Egypt's dried-out ground.

Asenath sat in a chair that had been brought down to the river for her, enjoying the shade of the umbrella a servant had fixed overhead. The hot wind still brushed her face, but at least she was shielded from the sun itself.

The playful cries of Joseph and her two sons rent the afternoon air, and Asenath looked with pride at the two sturdy boys as they frolicked in the dirt with their father. Joseph was down on his hands and knees, and Manasseh was straddling his back and yelling at the top of his lungs. Ephraim was no less vocal and was pulling at Joseph's hair, his dark eyes flashing as he struggled to pull Joseph down to the ground. A quick spurt of pride ran through Asenath as she watched the three. The boys had some of her characteristics and some of Joseph's. Around the eyes and the mouth they resembled her, but the dark, rebelliously curly hair and the nose were Joseph's. It was already obvious that they were going to be tall and strong like their father.

Joseph suddenly collapsed, and the two boys swarmed all over him, pummeling him and yelling for all they were worth.

Asenath finally called out, "Well, Great Provider, no one would mistake you for the second most important man in Egypt right now."

Joseph grabbed Ephraim and roughed up the boy's hair, ignoring the boy's screams while Manasseh yanked at him. Like his sons, Joseph was dirty, coated with the dust of the dry ground adjacent to the riverbank, and wore only an apron, leaving his upper body and most of his legs bare.

"The second most important person in Egypt?" Joseph tried to look surprised and grabbed a boy under each arm, holding them there while they squirmed. "Why, I'm not even lord over my own house!"

Asenath laughed. "You are certainly a persecuted fellow. I don't see how a man like you can be such a great man in everyone's eyes. I wish they could see you now!"

"I'm glad they don't see me when you run over me like these boys are trying to do."

Asenath laughed aloud. Indeed, she did run over Joseph at times, as he put it, but their marriage had been wonderful beyond her expectations. She thought back to the time before she was married, when she was so unhappy and unfulfilled. But then Joseph had come into her life in the strangest and most dramatic way, and now she glowed with health and pride and love for her husband and her two sons.

Joseph rose up, released Ephraim, and grabbed Manasseh. "It's time for you to wash that dirt off," he said, and without further ado, he waded into the shallow, muddy water and tossed him out into the only slightly deeper water. The river was no more than two feet deep near the bank, and Manasseh turned a complete somersault and landed on his feet, screaming and laughing.

"Now you, Ephraim."

"No!" Ephraim yelled and started to run. Joseph caught him easily, carried him out until he was knee-deep, and then tossed him out beside his brother. The two boys at once began splashing and continued their shrill cries.

"Joseph, be careful!"

When Joseph turned to look at Asenath, she saw an expression come onto his face she had learned to recognize. "Why are you looking at me like that?" she cried.

Joseph turned back to his sons and said, "Boys, would you like for your mother to join us in the river?"

"Yes! Yes!" both boys shouted together.

Asenath saw Joseph come for her, and with a cry she jumped up and started to run. She was a fleet runner, but Joseph overtook her easily. "Put me down, Joseph!" He picked her up as easily as if she were a child and started back toward the river. "Don't you dare throw me in that water, you beast!"

"Mothers are supposed to join their children in their playtime," Joseph said, laughing. "It's what all good mothers do."

Asenath was screaming, but Joseph simply waded out into the river. "Enjoy the Nile," he said with a grin and dumped her in.

Asenath splashed noisily as her boys pulled at her. She was drenched and sputtering as she wiped the water off her face. She saw that Joseph was laughing so hard his eyes were squeezed shut. She started laughing too, and gathering what water she could in her hands, she threw it toward him, catching him in the face. "You are *awful!*" she cried.

"Pull him down, Mother!" Manasseh cried. He ran at his father, tugging at his legs, and Ephraim did the same with his other leg. Asenath caught Joseph in the stomach with her whole body and made a grab for his neck. The force of her leap overturned Joseph. With a boy hanging on each leg and his wife around his neck, he went down flat into the river, and the water closed about his face. He struggled and came up spouting water and grabbed Asenath. The four of them laughed and splashed under the sun as the servants, who stood nearby, tried to keep the smiles off their faces.

"Isn't this fun, Mother?" Ephraim said.

"Yes, it is."

"You've never come to the river to bathe with us."

"No, I haven't, but one time I was in this very river when a huge hippopotamus came to eat me alive."

It was a favorite story and the two boys begged to hear it again. There in the muddy waters of the Nile, Asenath told them the familiar tale of how she had almost been eaten alive by a hippo.

"But he didn't eat you, did he, Mother?" Ephraim said.

"No, he didn't because your father saved me. He took a big spear and killed that old beast, and then he picked me up, just like he picks you up, and saved me from drowning."

Joseph was stooped down in the water, allowing it to flow over his chest, enjoying the story. It was moments like these that made his life endurable. The pressures of being the second-in-command in Egypt were great indeed, and rare were the moments when he could get away to be with Asenath and his two sons. He listened as she spoke and thought again of how strange it was that God had put the two of them together. He often thought about life in this way, marveling over a God who would take such interest in puny human beings.

Finally Asenath said, "All right, boys. Come along. Try to wash off as much mud as you can." She sent them in toward the shore and called out to the servants, "Dry them off and get them dressed!"

Joseph waded toward her, put his arms around her, and drew her close. He leaned forward, kissed her, and then put his lips next to her ear. "You know what?"

"What?"

"You have been a good wife today."

"I have? But I'm always a good wife."

"Especially good today, so tonight ... I'm going to give you a *very* special reward." He leaned back and saw that she was blushing, as she always did when he spoke like this.

"Well, you haven't been all that good, Joseph Great Provider, so no reward for you!"

They stood there for a moment in the Nile, forgetful of the boys and everything else. "I remember when I pulled you out of the Nile so long ago. I told you then you were the most precious thing in the world, and you are today. You're more beautiful than you were when I married you."

Asenath tilted her head back, and Joseph kissed her. She was aware that the servants were watching and probably giggling, but they were used to this. As he kissed her, she was so thankful that he was a man who was not afraid to show his affection. He was the only man she knew who was like this, and she wondered if it was the Hebrew blood in his veins.

Finally she drew back and said, "Maybe I *will* give you a reward tonight, but first let's get this mud cleaned off."

———————

Joseph was irritated, for the pressures of work had piled up on him. "Where is Rashidi?" he yelled.

"I don't know, sir," said the clerk, a tiny fellow with a wrinkled monkey face.

"Well, when I find him, I'm going to have him whipped!"

"Yes, sir," the clerk said, unimpressed. "I think he might have gone to the market."

"To the market! He's got servants to go to the market."

Joseph wheeled and started toward the door, but Asenath caught him. "Where are you going?"

"I'm going to find Rashidi," Joseph said loudly, "and when I do, I'm going to have him whipped!"

Asenath smiled. "When was the last time you had someone whipped? You didn't even have Ufa whipped after the evil he did to you."

"Well, things are changing. I put that man in a position of responsibility, and all he does is spout his idiotic poetry!"

"You won't whip him," Asenath said quietly. "It's not your way."

"Maybe I'll change."

"No, you never will."

"Where have you been?" Joseph said to his wife.

"I went to visit Kesi."

Joseph's expression darkened. He had no hard feelings toward the poor woman, but he still felt that Kesi was not the best companion for his wife. Asenath had a compassionate nature now, something she had not had when she was younger. "How is Lady Kesi?" he said.

"Oh, she's unhappy, but then she always will be."

"I suppose if she had children, it might be different," Joseph said. He seemed to have forgotten Rashidi for the moment. "I feel sorry for her."

"Joseph, can I ask you something?"

Surprised, Joseph looked at his wife. "Why, of course. What is it?"

"How did you resist her? She was a very beautiful woman."

"I don't know. I've forgotten."

"No you haven't. You never forget anything. Was it difficult? Tell me. I've always wondered."

"Why, of course it was difficult."

"Oh."

"What do you mean 'oh'?"

"I mean—oh!" she said sharply.

Joseph looked at her, turning his head to one side, studying her face. "Are you angry about something?"

"I didn't know it was difficult for you to refuse a woman who was trying to seduce you."

Joseph looked puzzled. "Well, of course it was difficult. It's like poking food under the face of a starving man! It would be hard for any man to refuse."

"Well, I'm glad to find this out about you, Great Provider!" Asenath turned and whirled away.

But before she made it out of the room, Joseph caught her and turned her around. "What's wrong with you?"

"Nothing!" she sniffed. "Only, I suppose you still think about her pawing you!"

"Asenath, that's ancient history."

Asenath's lower lip trembled. "I'm sorry," she said. "I'm just jealous of you, that's all. I don't want any other woman to ever have any part of you, and I'm jealous of all the women in your past."

"Well, that's a short list," Joseph said. "And you don't have to be worried about anybody else. Why should I go to another woman when I've got the most beautiful woman in the world right here in my own house?"

"Do you really think so, Joseph?"

Joseph could never understand why Asenath felt so insecure. He told her often how he loved her and bought her gifts and was quick with his caresses, but somehow she seemed to feel a basic insecurity. "If you don't stop speaking like that—"

When he broke off, Asenath looked up at him. "What are you going to do if I don't?" she challenged.

"I'm going to throw you in the Nile again." He leaned over, kissed her, and then said, "I'm going out right now to find some beautiful woman and make mad, passionate love to her. Good-bye!"

Asenath laughed. She waved and said, "Come home early." As she did, she turned to find the scribe standing there patiently. "Do you think we're foolish, Benni?"

"Very foolish, my lady. People in love always are."

"You're right. You're a wise man, Benni, and I hope my husband and I are always this foolish."

———————

Joseph finally located Rashidi. He had sent servants out to look for him, and finally one of them returned and said slyly, "I have found Rashidi, O Great Provider."

"Well, where is he?"

"I don't want to say." The servant had a smirk on his face, and when he saw Joseph lift one eyebrow, he added hastily, "He is in the house of a woman whose reputation is not at all that good."

"Show me!" Joseph demanded. Rising from his seat, he followed the servant out of the house. The servant led him through the labyrinthine streets of the city until he finally stopped and said, "There. That's the house right there."

"Who lives there?"

"A man named Jehunni."

"Who is he?"

"He's a minor official, sir, but according to all reports he's a very jealous man. Lord Rashidi is not wise to tarry there."

"All right. Go back to your work. I'll take care of this."

Joseph marched to the door and, without even pausing, went right in. The house was large and comfortable for the house of a minor official, and hearing voices, he walked down a hallway until he stepped out into a much larger room. He saw Rashidi lying on a couch with a woman bending over him.

"Lord Rashidi, I am here," Joseph said loudly.

The woman whirled around, coming off of the couch, her eyes wide. She recognized Joseph and fell to her knees, bowing before him. She had a wealth of reddish hair and was attractive enough to tempt most men, Joseph thought.

"Get out of here, woman!" Joseph said.

"But . . . but, master, this is *my* house."

"Then find another part of it!"

Rashidi was not alarmed. He got up, stretched, and said lazily, "Well, I'm surprised to see you here."

"You're a fool, Rashidi."

Rashidi blinked. "Why do you come to that conclusion?"

"This woman's husband is jealous. He'll gut you like a fish if he catches you with his wife."

"Oh, he won't catch me. I had him sent all the way to Memphis on business."

Joseph shook his head. It was not the first time he had had to enter into the romantic life of his first lieutenant. "You ought to have better sense."

Rashidi stood to his feet, walked over to a table, and picked up a jug of wine. He poured two cups to the brim with the sparkling red liquid, picked them up, and came over to Joseph. Offering one of them, he said, "Come. Don't be angry."

Joseph took the wine and drank it down. He was not angry so much as puzzled. Rashidi had as much ability as any man he knew, but he floated through life fiddling with his interminable poem that Joseph suspected would never be finished, taking love where he found it, and sleeping. In between these three things, he did a little work for Joseph.

Rashidi finished his wine, then put the cup down. "You hurt me greatly, Joseph. You certainly do."

"Hurt you! I couldn't hurt you with a club."

"You don't understand why I do these things."

"Yes I do. You're a glutton, a drunkard, and a womanizer."

"But all that's only so I can experience life." Rashidi sighed heavily and tried to look repentant. "It's all for art, my dear Provider. I must experience everything so I can weave it into my poetry."

"Nonsense! You're a drunkard because you like to drink, and you chase after women because you enjoy them. Don't try to tell me there's anything noble about that."

Rashidi laughed. "You are right, O noble Provider of Egypt—but then you always are." He had been drinking a great deal and had to form his words rather carefully. "Tell me, Joseph, is there any hope for me in the hereafter?"

"You don't even believe in the life hereafter."

"But *you* do, and that worries me sometimes. If a wise fellow like you believes a thing, there's always a chance it might be true."

Joseph considered Rashidi carefully. He knew that beneath that bland face lurked one of the most penetrating minds he had ever seen. He made fun of Rashidi's poetry, but he actually was highly impressed with the epic that Rashidi had been working on for so long. He was convinced it would last long after the pyramids crumbled. "Are you serious, Rashidi?" he finally asked.

"Well, I think the Egyptians have the wrong idea about it."

"How is that?"

"All this trouble to preserve the bodies. That's all nonsense, I think."

"I think you're correct, Rashidi."

"I went through the House of the Dead once," Rashidi said. "I wanted to see what all the embalmers did, and it was a fascinating sort of thing but a gruesome affair."

"I've never seen that myself."

"Oh, it is quite a messy thing. The embalmers make an incision from a man's gullet down to his groin, and all his viscera are lifted out. The embalmer divides them into liver, lungs, stomach, and entrails, but they always leave the heart in place and the kidneys too."

"Why the kidneys?"

"Oh, they're associated with water and thus with the Nile, which is the source of life."

"What do they do, then?"

"Well, they put the viscera in beautiful jars made of milky alabaster. The more expensive ones also have stoppers in the shape of one of the animal-headed gods."

"What do they think all that does?" Joseph asked.

"Oh, they'll guard Pharaoh's divine parts until he wakes into eternal life. It is a grisly business, isn't it?"

"Yes, it is."

"Somehow I can't get it out of my mind. They have bronze scalpels which they use to disembowel the pharaoh, and they have a long, pointed spoon, which they push up into the nostrils and scoop out the contents of the skull. And then, of course, they soak him in their special formula and wrap him until he's shrunken like a monkey."

Joseph said soberly, "Well, I can't fault them too much. I have a superstition myself about this thing."

"About disposing of the dead?"

"Yes. My grandfather bought a burial ground. It's really the only piece of ground he owned. God told him he was going to own the whole land, but that was all he ever owned legally. He made a grave there for his wife, and he's there now too, along with Isaac, my grandfather. My mother isn't buried there, though."

"Why not?"

"She died on a journey, and my father buried her there rather than take her back. I'd like to be buried in the family tomb myself."

"Why? What difference does it make after you're dead?"

"Oh, I don't know, Rashidi." It was quiet in the house, but he heard the voices of servants speaking and laughing somewhere else. "Somehow I think God is caught up with people, and not just on this earth. He made the whole universe, all the stars and the sky. But I think He's more interested in us than He is in them."

"Do you really think that, Joseph?"

"I really do. I don't think God makes us just for the brief span of years we have here on earth, but I think when we die we go to be with those we love, with God's people and with God himself."

Rashidi did not answer but went over and sat down on the couch. He bent over and held his forehead in his hands. Joseph was surprised. It was not like the man to show emotion. He went over and sat down beside him and put his arm around Rashidi's shoulders. He found that to his amazement Rashidi was trembling. "What's wrong, my dear friend?"

"I make a joke of it, but . . . but I'm afraid of death." He straightened up and turned to look into Joseph's eyes. Joseph saw the fear there and was shocked at the intensity of it. "Are you afraid to die, Joseph?"

Joseph considered for a moment, then shook his head. "I'm not afraid now, but then I'm not dying now. When I come to that moment, I will probably be . . . what's the right word? Maybe frightened in a way that you're frightened when an experience lies before you you've never had."

"No more than that?"

"I hope not."

The two men sat there, and Rashidi became very still. Joseph sought for words that would comfort him, and he said, "There are some people eager to leave this life, people who are in pain. I had a teacher once who was old and in bad health. He suffered all the time from terrible pain in his joints. It took him some time to die, and he cried out many times, 'O great God, take me to yourself.' And when he finally did die, I was there. We all gathered around, and he told us good-bye, and then he smiled and said, 'I'm going to God.'" Joseph shifted his shoulders slightly and said, "Those were his last words before he went out into eternity. I've thought about him often."

Rashidi had grown very still as Joseph related the story of the dying man. He sighed and straightened up. "I'd like to feel like that when I die, but it seems so complicated."

"It does seem that way. But it is much easier if we can think of God not as someone who is stern and harsh but more like a father who loves his son. The son goes on a long journey and comes back tired and washed out. And there's the father waiting for him. The father gets up and runs to meet the boy, who is absolutely exhausted. That would be a good thing to have a father like that, wouldn't it?"

"I didn't have one like that myself."

"But there are some, aren't there?"

"I suppose so."

"I think my father looks on death like that," Joseph said. "He talks about God a lot."

"And you say he met God one time?"

"Yes, he did. More than once actually. He loved his family, but he never stopped talking about the times he met God. And his father, Isaac, met God. And most of all, my grandfather Abraham knew God well. I've always thought of one thing that makes me sure that when we leave this earth we go to God."

"What's that?" Rashidi asked eagerly.

"When God appeared to my own father, He identified himself. He said 'I am the God of Abraham and of Isaac.' You see what that means?"

"I'm afraid I don't."

"Abraham and Isaac, my great-grandfather and my grandfather, have been dead for a long time. But God still said He was their God. I don't think He's the God of dead people but of living people. So somehow I think, Rashidi, that He's the God of the living."

"How in the world can a man know a God like this?" Rashidi whispered. "I've been such a bad man I could never do enough good to make up the balance. You know what the Egyptians say. They think that when a man goes to the underworld, one of the gods puts their good deeds on one side of a scale and their bad deeds on the other."

"Yes, that's what they believe, and if a man's good deeds outweigh his bad deeds, he doesn't have to suffer torment."

"Do you believe that? It makes sense to me."

"No, I don't believe it," Joseph said. "From listening to my father and grandfather talk about El Shaddai, I think He's different from the gods of Egypt. I think that none of us could ever be good enough for God. I think of Him as being so good that a human can't even enter His presence. A man would die if he did. I think God's merciful, Rashidi. I think He forgives us because He loves us, just as we forgive our children because we love them."

Rashidi's eyes brightened. "A God that loves people! Now there's a new thought!"

"My father used to say, 'There will be a man who will come.' He always gave him the name Shiloh, which means *peace* in our language. When he comes, this great redeemer will teach us enough about God so that we can really know Him."

"When will he come?" Rashidi demanded.

Joseph stood up, and Rashidi rose with him. "Nobody knows that exactly, but my people believe that he will come."

"I'd like to see that day."

"So would I," Joseph said. "Perhaps we will. No man knows. Now come. We must leave here, and I need you, Rashidi."

Rashidi followed Joseph out, and when they stepped into the bright sunlight, he glanced up at the sun, squinting his eyes. "People here worship the sun."

"Yes, they do, but my people worship the God who made the sun," Joseph said. "Come now. We must get back."

The two men worked steadily at the business affairs that demanded their attention, and Rashidi was in one part of the house working with the scribe when he heard Joseph shouting. He left at once and ran to where Joseph was standing before a messenger. "What's wrong, Provider?"

"It's my brothers! They're here! They've come to Egypt!"

"Where are they? How do you know this?"

"At all of the stations where foreigners enter I have left a description of my brothers, their tribes, their language. I've been waiting all this time, for I knew that sooner or later they would be caught by the terror of the famine and would come to Egypt to buy food, and now, Rashidi"—Joseph's eyes glowed in a way Rashidi had never seen—"they're here in Egypt!"

Rashidi stared at Joseph dumbfounded. Joseph had a great natural dignity, but he lost that now as he skipped around the room lifting his hands. Tears were running down his face, and the messenger was staring at the Great Provider in astonishment. Rashidi whispered to the messenger, "Leave the room."

"Yes, sir."

Rashidi did not watch the messenger go but turned to watch the second-most powerful man in the world crying like a baby. *Well*, he thought to himself, *I've often wondered what it would take to shake Joseph up— and now I know!*

CHAPTER
27

The journey from Canaan to Egypt had been difficult, for although the ten sons of Jacob were naturally hearty men, they'd been severely weakened by the famine. Day after day they trudged southward, following the trade route that ran through the arid southland of Canaan all the way to Egypt. At first there were settlements, some large and some no more than a few huts, but as the journey wore on, they passed through long stretches where they saw almost no life.

From time to time they would arrive at a protected desert spring, precious oases in the desert where they actually had to buy their water and store up all they could carry in water bags. The journey to the borders of Egypt took twenty days, and they were all exhausted and not a little apprehensive.

On the night after they crossed the place that one traveler told them was the border of Egypt, they made camp. Their fire was a solitary source of light in the utter darkness, and they huddled around it as if trying to find some comfort in its cheerful blaze. Earlier they had supped on the last of the dried meat they had brought with them, but it had done little to satisfy their hunger.

Levi stared out into the darkness and shook his head. "This is a troubled land," he said. "I don't like it." He looked around the circle at the bearded faces of his brothers, their eyes caught by the flickering flames of the fire. "I wish we hadn't come."

"Hadn't come!" Simeon said heatedly. "We *had* to come. We had no other choice."

"That's right," Dan said. "There's no point in talking like that, Simeon."

A murmur went around the campfire, and Reuben, who was sitting back from the fire, his arms wrapped around his knees, studied the faces of his brothers. They all had a strange, pinched look, as if they had come almost to the end of their strength. As strong as he was, Reuben too felt weakened by the journey, and he could understand what Simeon had said. This place already seemed to be a strange land, and they were only on the border of it. He listened as they spoke in whispers, as if spies and robbers were gathering in around them. Indeed, such a thing was possible!

"One of these days I'm going to be out of the cursed desert." Zebulun picked up a piece of wood, stuck it into the fire, waited until the tip of it caught, then held it up and stared into the flame. "I'm going to be on a ship," he said dreamily, "with water all about."

"And when the ship goes down, you drown!" Issachar snapped. "No, no ships for me."

Always the practical one, Levi said thoughtfully, "I wonder where we go to buy the food."

"Why, Egypt, of course!" Naphtali retorted. "That's why we're here!"

"No," Levi answered crossly, "I mean the exact place! There's got to be a central food supply somewhere. We don't know a soul in Egypt."

"There'll be someone to help us, I'm sure," Judah said. He had been silent day after day, and now he stretched and said, "I'm going to sleep. We might still have a long journey ahead of us."

They all lay down, except for Reuben, who sat up for another hour, keeping the fire going. He stared into the flames blankly, then finally sighed, crawled into his blanket, and fell into a fitful sleep.

"Look," Issachar said, "there comes a train of donkeys."

Judah had already seen them. "It looks like they're loaded down with bags of grain. Maybe they will tell us where they bought it."

The train was a group of fierce-looking dark-faced tribesmen. When Judah asked them where they had bought their food, the leader, a tall man with a wicked scar running down his face, said, "You'd better have money. They're not giving anything away."

Judah smiled. "I didn't think they would, but tell us, do we buy grain from the pharaoh?"

"The pharaoh?" The tribesman laughed loudly. "You'll never see him, not the likes of you. You have to buy it from the Great Provider."

"I've heard of him," Judah said. "Where do we find him?" He listened as the man gave instructions, and then the tribesman said, "Watch out for the Provider. He's the one who runs everything."

"That doesn't sound too promising, does it?" Judah said to Reuben, who had listened to the conversation.

"I guess we don't have any choice," Reuben said. "Come on and let's get this over with. I'm anxious to get away from this place. I agree with Simeon. I don't like it here at all."

"Maybe Father was right," Judah said doubtfully. "It does feel like an evil place."

"Evil or not, they've got the food. So let's get started."

Two days later the brothers were stopped by an official wearing an emblem on a cord around his neck. He was a short, muscular man with slate-colored skin and an irate manner. "Where do you come from?" he demanded.

"We are of the tribe of Jacob. Hebrews from Canaan," Reuben said, staring down at the man.

The official peppered them with questions, then ordered, "Wait here until further notice."

"Why can't we just buy the food and leave?" Judah said almost desperately. He was quite anxious now to get back to his homeland as quickly as possible.

"If you want food, you'll do as you are told!" the official snapped. "Now, I'll get to you as soon as I can. Get your animals out of the way. There are others coming."

The delay brought a sense of despondency to the brothers, and it did not help that it lasted for two whole days. The brothers began to complain among themselves, and Zebulun said, "Let's forget it and go home. There's something wrong."

"We can't go home again without any food," Reuben said firmly. "We have to humble ourselves, so just make the best of it."

The official, whose name was Hyrim, had an odd look in his eyes as he scurried into the room where the brothers had been told to wait. "All right. I have some orders for you men."

"Are you going to sell us food?" Judah asked quickly.

"That's not up to me. It's up to the Provider. You must go to the central authority."

Simeon said quickly, "But there have been others who have gone right over to the storage facility to get their food. We talked with them."

"Well, you're not going there," Hyrim snapped. "You're going to the central authority, or you'll get nothing."

"But why?" Judah pleaded. "Give us some word."

"I have my orders. You can go to the central authority or not. That's up to you."

Reuben sighed heavily. "All right, sir. Tell us where it is, and we will go there."

Hyrim ran off a series of instructions, and soon the weary travelers were on their way. There was grumbling and not a little fear in the faces of the men as they moved along.

"There's something wrong with all this," Issachar said, stroking the head of his donkey that plodded along beside him. "I don't like it."

"We've got to do it." Zebulun shrugged. He looked ahead and said, "I wish we could go as far as the sea. I don't think I'd ever come back here if I could just get on a ship."

Rashidi had never seen Joseph in such a state. The two of them were in Joseph's favorite room. It had a gold-colored ceiling, green malachite lintels over the doors, and colorful friezes along the walls. It served Joseph as a library and lay between his sleeping chamber and the great reception hall. All around were the finest of Egyptian treasures, including lion-footed chairs with rush seats and backs of stamped and gilded leather. Plant stands bore potted flowers that had been carefully grown with precious water brought from the Nile, and there was an inlaid day-bed covered with skins and cushions, as well as carved chests on curved legs inlaid with mother-of-pearl and inscribed in gold leaf.

Joseph was walking back and forth in constant motion, his eyes bright. "They're here. They've passed the fortress. I knew it! I knew it! I'm so happy I don't know what to say."

"My dear friend, you must calm yourself," Rashidi said. "I've never seen you like this before."

"I've never had such an opportunity. They're my brothers, Rashidi, my own brothers!"

"Yes, I understand that, but I can't understand why you're so happy to see them."

"What do you mean? Of course I'm glad to see my brothers!"

Rashidi stared at Joseph, cocking his head. "And these are the same men who beat you and threw you in a pit to die and finally sold you into slavery? I don't think I'd be quite so anxious to see them."

"Yes, but look how it's turned out. God has been in all of it. Don't you see, Rashidi?" Joseph cried. "If I hadn't been thrown into the pit and sold into slavery, I would never have been here. I would never have had the glory I've found in Egypt. I owe everything to my brothers!"

Rashidi laughed, his eyes almost hidden as his face crinkled. "That's the most fantastic thing I've ever heard, sir."

"No, it's true!" Joseph insisted. He could not be still but snapped his fingers nervously and paced back and forth, looking frequently toward the door. "It's all been God's doing. I'm convinced of it. All the years I've been in Egypt have been at His direction, for His purpose. When I was a servant in Potiphar's house, and when I was in your prison, I thought about my family. And now they're here to buy grain. . . . But there's ten of them. That bothers me a little."

"Why is that?"

"Because I had eleven brothers. What if one of them is dead? I don't think I could bear it."

"Life is uncertain, Joseph, but perhaps they are all well."

Joseph finally calmed down under Rashidi's pleading and began to dress himself for the meeting. "I don't want them to recognize me," he said. "I don't think much of the men who paint their faces, but this time I'm making an exception." Indeed, it was the habit of many Egyptian men to wear makeup, especially around the eyes to make them look larger. Joseph called in a servant to apply his makeup and sat quietly while the servant prepared him. Finally he dressed and dismissed the servant. "Do you think they'll recognize me?" he asked Rashidi.

"After all this time? No, not possible. You were a mere stripling then. Seventeen, weren't you? Now you're a full-grown man, and they no doubt think you're dead."

"Well, I must tell you that I'm nervous, my friend. I don't want them to know who I am. It must come gradually. I don't know how I will do it, but somehow I will. Oh, Rashidi, I'm a perfect muddle of joy and dread and suspense! I've never felt like this in my whole life!"

"What do you mean to do with them?"

"I don't know at this point, but God will give me instructions. Come. We must go meet them."

"Why did you want to have them go to your office and not to your house?"

"I thought it would be better that way. More official. Come, we must go!"

The sons of Jacob either stood still with fear or moved about nervously. All of them felt that something was dreadfully wrong, and it was Dan who voiced their fear. "We're in trouble," he whispered so that the guard would not hear. "Have you noticed the guards from the reception station haven't left us? We're more like prisoners than buyers of grain."

"Maybe it's the way they treat everybody," Gad said. He was one to hope for the best, but now he looked as glum as his brothers. They were waiting in an outer hall of an enormous building, bigger than any they had ever seen, and the guards, with their spears and swords and knives, were very much in evidence. If there had been none, it was entirely possible all ten of them would have rushed back to their animals and made a wild ride to get away from the place.

After what seemed like a long wait, a tall, broad-shouldered man entered, and by his stern manner they knew he was a man of authority.

"You are from the land of Canaan?"

"Yes, master," Reuben said, bowing humbly. "We have come to buy grain, sir."

Rashidi stared at them. He had heard much of Joseph's brothers, and he studied each one carefully. There was little family resemblance between Joseph and his brothers, but Rashidi knew Joseph's mother had been a beauty, while the other wife and concubines had not been. "Come this way and bow down low when you come before the Provider."

As Judah marched beside Reuben, he looked quickly around the magnificent room to which they had been brought. Two double lines of orange columns covered with ornamental inscriptions on white bases ran the length of the room. There were tables with wild flowers and slender water jugs, and the gods of the Egyptians were painted on the walls in flowing lines and bright colors. Some of the scenes were of sowing and threshing, and all was beautiful, but it was the man seated on a raised dais that drew every eye. Over him were white ostrich feather fans thrust into gold shields held by pages with bobbed hair. About him were scribes and ministrants and lance bearers of his household guards all in a row.

The man seated on the raised platform was tall and powerful. He wore a gold chain signifying his office. He also wore a breast piece with falcons, sun beetles, and life crosses arranged with beautiful art. He sat with a ceremonial hatchet in his belt, his headcloth wound in the manner of the country with stiff lappets falling on his shoulders.

As Joseph looked out over his brothers, it was all he could do to keep his face still. He focused on one of the men who was as tall as a tower. Another had a leonine head, while another was solid and marrowy. His eyes went over all of them, and he said, "Do you men understand Egyptian?"

One of them spoke up, a man with a narrow face. "Very little, master. You will forgive your servants for their ignorance."

As Joseph listened to this translated through an interpreter, for such was what he had proposed to keep them from knowing he spoke their language, he had no trouble eventually identifying each of his brothers. His eyes went from man to man, and he could not help thinking about how they had dragged him to the pit, shouting and cursing him, and had sold him as a criminal to the Midianites. There were the red-eyed ones, all six of them, and the four Sons of the Maids. He felt tense, for his brother Benjamin was not there. He would have known him at once, and his father—what about his father, Jacob? Was he yet alive?

"We have come to buy grain, O Mighty Provider," the one who spoke a little Egyptian said.

Joseph forced himself to frown sternly. "To buy grain? That is what you claim?" His voice intimated that he believed not a word of it.

"There are ten of you. Who are you? Tell me about yourselves."

This time it was Dan who spoke. "We come from the land of Canaan to buy food in Egypt."

Joseph's eyes scanned the brothers and paused on Reuben. "You there, tall one, why can you not speak for these other men? Tell me who you are."

For all his size, Reuben was not the best speaker. Judah would be the appropriate spokesman, but he had been commanded, and so he said, "We are the ten sons of one man—"

"Stop!" Joseph commanded sternly. "That cannot be. You look nothing alike."

"That, Majesty, is because we do not have the same mothers. We are six from one, two from another and two from a third. But we are the sons of one man named Jacob, who has sent us here to buy food."

"I am surprised at your words. You do not look like people whose father is still alive."

"Oh, Lord, our father is really not so old for our tribe. Our ancestor was one hundred years old when he begot the true and right son, our father's father."

Joseph's voice seemed to break as he attempted to speak. "How was your journey?" he said, and he listened as Reuben described the journey, but his heart was rejoicing and singing. *My father is alive! He lives! Praise to the God of Abraham, Isaac, and Jacob—my father lives!*

Joseph stared at the men, making his face as fierce as possible. "And now. How do you like Egypt?"

The question troubled all of the men. None of them in truth liked it in the least! Judah said, "It is a land of marvels, O Great Provider. It is splendid indeed . . . that which our eyes have seen."

"I am sure you watched it well, for that is why you came to this place."

Judah stared at the man on the throne. "We came to buy grain, O Provider."

"That is your excuse, but do you not think I know why you have really come? You are spies!" Joseph cried out.

The ten brothers were shocked into silence for a moment as the interpreter repeated what Joseph had said. "Spies you are!" Joseph repeated, allowing anger to run through his speech. "You have come to search out the land so that you may bring an army back here to invade us. If this is not true, I pray you refute it!"

Judah was speechless. "My lord, your suspicion is false. We are honest men. We came to buy food. We must have food for our women and children. Please, Your Majesty, your servants have never been spies."

"Spies, I say!" Joseph answered roughly. "The kings of the east have hired you to search out the land, and merely to say it isn't so will not satisfy me. Am I to take your bare word that you are not spies when I know full well you are?"

Judah desperately looked around and caught Reuben's eyes. Reuben was utterly speechless, and Judah knew it was up to him. "Please, if you will allow me to speak. We are honest men, O Mighty Provider. Your servants are twelve brothers, the sons of one father—"

Joseph jumped up and pointed his hand at Judah. "So now you are *twelve* men! Then you were lying when you said you were ten!"

Judah listened to the interpretation, then said, "We tell the truth, lord. My father, Jacob, is the father of twelve sons. We never said that all of us were here. One of my brothers has been dead for many years, and the other is at home with our father."

Joseph stared at Judah and said, "So . . . your father is alive."

"Yes. You have asked that before. What do you want from us?"

"Don't question me!" Joseph snapped. "I will ask the questions here."

"Yes, my lord," Judah answered meekly.

Joseph stared hard at Judah. "Well, lion head," he said, "go on. Convince me that you are not spies."

Judah shrugged his shoulders slightly. "I know not how to convince you, sir. There are more than seventy in our tribe. All of us are married."

"The youngest, he is married too?"

"Yes. And he has many children."

Joseph was shocked. He was still thinking, he discovered, of Benjamin as a little fellow with the ruddy face and curly hair, as he had seen him before he left on his ill-fated trip to Shechem. Now he had to adjust to the idea that Benjamin was grown and married with children even as he himself was.

Judah made the best plea he could, but it all amounted to his word alone that they were not spies. Finally Joseph said, "You cannot deceive a man like me. As for your innocence, we will see about that. You say you are honest. Good! Bring your youngest brother of whom you speak here. If you will bring him and put him before my face, then I will believe what you have said."

"You mean," Judah whispered, "that we have to make the long trip home and then come back again with our youngest brother?"

Joseph said, "Not all of you. You are prisoners. I will keep you here. Choose one among you to go back to your home. Let him bring the youngest brother you speak of back, and then we will see."

Reuben spoke up. "My lord, my father will never let our youngest brother come to Egypt."

"And why not?" Joseph demanded.

"Our youngest brother is the last remaining son of our father's True Wife, the one he loved above all else. He loved our dead brother, and his youngest son is all he has left."

Joseph's throat seemed suddenly full when he heard this, but he concealed it by saying, "Nonsense! He would not let you ten die before he would send the other."

"Yes, my lord, he would," Reuben said simply and offered no more.

"Take them away!" Joseph shouted as if terribly angry. "I will deal with this matter later."

For the next three days the sons of Jacob were kept in a separate part of the palace. It was a fine room with benches running around it and grated apertures to allow in the sunlight. But for shepherds used to the open hills and the sky overhead, it was a prison indeed!

When they talked at all it was about which one of them should go back, but none of them were ready to undertake that. They were well fed and given pads to sleep on, but as the hours passed, they grew more and more despondent.

"We will all die in this place," Levi said in despair.

"I'm afraid you are right," Simeon agreed. "This Provider is a hard man."

Judah said nothing at all while the others were arguing about who should go back. Finally late one night when the argument had died down, he said, "This calamity has come upon us because of our sin." A deathly silence fell on the room, and he said, "God does not forget, and He has not forgotten what we did to our brother. We are guilty. We heard his cries, and we refused to have mercy."

Reuben lifted his head. "Yes, you are right, Judah. I told you so, and I begged you all not to lay your hands on the boy. Now his blood is on our heads!"

The time passed until finally the man called Rashidi came to summon them before the Provider. When they stood before the Ruler of Egypt, ten hearts were trembling and everyone expected the worst.

"I have considered what you have said, and I have decided to show myself a merciful man," the Great Provider told them.

Judah felt a rush of relief flow through him. It weakened his knees, but he stiffened them and listened to the words of the Provider.

Joseph stared at them for a moment, then said, "One of you will remain here as a hostage. That one there." He pointed at Simeon, and immediately two guards came forward, took Simeon by the arm, and pulled him out. "He will live until you prove faithful or unfaithful. The other nine of you return to your home. The food you came to buy will be provided."

Judah spoke for them all when he said, "We are grateful to you, O Mighty Provider."

"Do not be so grateful yet. If you do not return, I will know that you are spies indeed, and your brother's life will be forfeit. Go now."

The brothers stared at him, and Reuben could not help saying, "Did I not tell you how it would be when our brother cried to us? But you would not listen. Therefore his blood is on our head." His voice was broken, and tears ran down his cheeks.

Joseph quickly rose and left the room, for he could not contain himself. As soon as he was alone behind the closed doors, he began to weep. "Good Reuben! He still remembers and grieves! He still loves his little brother Joseph!"

CHAPTER
28

Joseph seemed to be walking on air as he entered the inner room of his office.

Rashidi smiled and said, "You put on a good act, Joseph. They're convinced that you hate them."

"I did do a good job, didn't I?" Joseph's eyes were sparkling, and he came over and gave Rashidi such a hard hug it made the other man gasp. "I can barely contain my joy! My father is still alive. And my brother Benjamin is alive too. Oh, how I thank God for His blessing!"

"Well, you don't have to squeeze the life out of me!"

"Oh, I'm sorry, Rashidi," he said, dropping his arms. "It's just that I'm so happy."

"You're the only man in the world who can be happy greeting a bunch of men who tried to kill you."

"That was a long time ago, and as I've tried to explain to you, God is in it all."

"If you say so." Rashidi shrugged his shoulders. "You still have a problem."

"What problem?"

"According to what they all say, your father will never let your younger brother come to Egypt."

Joseph stared at Rashidi and seemed to lose some of his exuberance. He paced back and forth, stroking his chin, then said, "God has worked so far. He will do the rest of it."

"So we're to release them all except the one hostage?"

"Yes, but I have a scheme I want you to arrange."

"You're a scheming man, Provider. What shall I do?"

"I want you to take their money they brought for the food, but before they leave, I want you to put that money back in their sacks."

"Give them their money back?"

"Exactly!" Joseph's eyes gleamed. He had learned to be somewhat of an actor during his years of administrating the land. He'd had to deal with people on many levels, and if truth be told, there was a little of his father in him. Sometimes he was mischievous, playing jokes on his wife or on Rashidi. Now his eyes gleamed as he said, "Yes, I want you to do this. It will confuse them. They may guess I've arranged it, but they won't know exactly what I'm up to. I'll leave it to you to accomplish."

"It will be as you say, master."

"Oh," Joseph added, "put the money in the top of their sacks so they'll see it when they open them on their journey away from here."

"It'll scare the wits out of them," Rashidi said with a shrug. "They won't know what in the world is happening."

"Just do as I say, and I want to have one more meeting with them before they leave."

———

The meeting took place as Joseph had demanded, and once again the brothers stood in front of the Great Provider. They were frightened half to death of the man, and all of them fell on their faces and pressed their foreheads to the floor.

"You may rise," Joseph said in a grand fashion. He had disguised himself once again, and now his eyes went from one to the other. He said harshly, "I have spoken, and you know what you are to do."

"Yes, O Great Provider," Judah said. His voice was clear, but his face was pale, as were the faces of the others. "We will do our best, but I must tell you again our father has never allowed our younger brother to leave his side."

"That may be a lie you are making up."

"No, Excellency, it is not a lie! It is the exact truth."

"Do not think you can deceive a man like me. I can see into men's hearts." Joseph stared straight at Judah and saw the man quail before him. "I have spoken! Now, as to the arrangements. You will be given food according to the prices that are now fixed. I will deal with you in an honest way as far as business is concerned. The nine of you will go back, and the arrival of your youngest brother will redeem this brother's life." He indicated Simeon, who by this time was reconciled to his fate.

He stared back at Joseph without saying a word. Joseph got up and left the room. The nine brothers gathered around Simeon, encouraging him.

"Don't be afraid, Simeon," Reuben said, patting him on the shoulder. "Somehow we'll persuade Father."

"I don't think so," Simeon said bluntly. "You know how he is about Benjamin."

"Never fear, brother. We will not let you down."

Simeon then said something that none of them ever forgot. He had been one of the most violent against Joseph back in the day of their dark hearts, but now he looked straight at Reuben and said, "We had another brother once, and we all failed him, and he was more righteous than I."

A silence fell over the group, and then the guards came and said, "Come, fellow," and all the brothers managed to touch Simeon, shaking his hand or patting him on the shoulder, as he was led away.

When the brothers had passed outside, Judah said, "Simeon is right. All I can think about is how Joseph cried to us and wept, and we hardened our hearts."

"Come, we must go," Reuben said loudly. "The quicker we get back to Father, the quicker we can start persuading him to let Benjamin return with us."

By midmorning the animals were loaded, and the purchase price was weighed out. It was paid mostly in silver rings, which they had brought for that express purpose. The sacks were loaded—huge sacks bulging out over the flanks of the heavily laden beasts. They were ready to leave, but to their surprise the lord named Rashidi provided a meal for them. It was a good meal of lentil soup, sugar-covered raisins, and goat meat that had been cooked to a tender goodness. Despite their troubles, they ate heartily. They were also given food for the first days of their journey.

"This is the custom in Egypt," Rashidi told them. "I would advise you to pay close attention to what the Great Provider has told you. He is not a man you can deceive."

Dan snapped at him, "We are not deceitful men! We are honest and have told the exact truth!"

"Ah, I trust that is so, for you may rest assured you will not get anything out of the Lord of the Nile except you bring your brother as he has commanded. And now I counsel you to hurry, for your brother will wait here with some impatience."

Reuben walked away toward the lead animal and led the group out of the city. They were all depressed about Simeon, and all were thinking about having to break the news to their father. It was a daunting thought, for Jacob was not a man to change his mind easily.

They traveled at a fast pace, and there was no talk among them except for the brief break they took at noon when they ate the food that had been provided. All of them seemed to avoid the glances of the others, and all were lost in their own thoughts. It should have been a time of gladness, for the beasts were loaded down with grain, which would be welcome at home, but Reuben said as they were eating, "This food won't last long shared among seventy people."

"No," Naphtali agreed, "and it won't do any good to come back again without Benjamin."

All afternoon they traveled, and finally at dark they chose a camping ground, a pleasant spot between lime cliffs on one side and rolling plains on the other. There was a well there, and other people had camped before. Quickly they built up a fire, and some of them prepared their evening meal while the others unloaded the donkeys and put the packs together. Others drew water and piled branches for the fire. It was Issachar who fed the animals. Of all the brothers, he had the greatest concern for the beasts—indeed, he even seemed to like them.

They were just preparing to eat when Issachar went to the feed bag and pulled something out. He stared at it and then shouted, "Reuben, come here quickly!"

"What is it?" Reuben said. He was bending over the fire, and the smoke was in his eyes. He rubbed them and said, "What do you want?"

"Look what was in my sack!"

Reuben tossed another piece of wood on the fire and then walked over to where Issachar was standing. "Look," he said. "What does it mean, brother?"

Reuben stared at the ten silver rings Issachar had brought to buy grain. He reached into the bag and picked up the rings, staring at them in his hand.

"What is it?" Judah asked, coming up beside Reuben.

Reuben turned and opened his hand. "It's . . . it's some of the money we brought to pay for the food."

"What's it doing in there?" Judah demanded. He turned and said, "Issachar, what have you done?"

"I haven't done anything! I just opened the bag and there it was."

"Didn't you give your money to the official?" Reuben demanded.

"Of course I did! You saw me do it, didn't you, Gad?"

All the brothers had gathered around now and were taking a good look at the rings. For a moment they all babbled, firing questions at Issachar, who denied any knowledge of how the rings got into his sack.

"What in the world could this mean?" Judah whispered.

"There's something terribly wrong about this," Levi said.

"Yes, there is," Judah said. Then a thought came to him, and he whirled and ran to his own beast. Jerking the feed bag off of the pommel, he opened it and stared down. "My money is here too," he said, astonished.

All of them rushed to open the feed bags, and all of them had the same story. Reuben stood staring down at the money in his own bag, and his mind seemed to be working slowly. "This is insane," he whispered hoarsely.

For a moment no one spoke, and then Dan said, "We'll have to go take this money back."

"No, we can't do that," Judah said.

"But they'll think we stole it."

An argument began then, some wanting to go back and some wanting to get away as quickly as possible. Finally Reuben said heavily, "I have no idea what it means, but we can't go back."

"We'll go to our father," Judah said. "We'll convince him that we have to go back and take Benjamin, and when we go back, we'll give this money back to the Provider."

It was not an answer that gave them any comfort, but they saw no other solution. Finally they ate a little, although their appetites were gone, then laid down in their bedrolls. In fact, none of them slept well that night.

Tamar had served Jacob his noon meal, a soup made from whatever she could throw together. She had made enough for Benjamin, and father and son had eaten together—the old man silent and Benjamin speaking about his brothers, wondering when they would come back. Tamar waited until they were finished, got their bowls, then retired, but not so far away that she could not hear what they were saying.

Benjamin had been moody during the absence of his brothers. He still was grieved that he had not been permitted to go, but he had stopped complaining to his father, for that was useless. The two had been talking about the history of his people, and Benjamin, after a long silence, decided to ask about something that had been troubling him for a long time.

"Father, may I ask you a question that may cause you a little grief?"

Jacob laughed and reached out and took the young man's hand and squeezed it. "Of course you can. I'm used to people asking me hard questions."

"I've wondered about it so long, and no one seems to have any answers."

"Just ask the question, my son."

"How was it that you got the birthright instead of your brother, Esau?"

Jacob looked at Benjamin in surprise. He would have resented it if any of his other sons had asked such a question, but with Benjamin he could not be angry. "It is not a pleasant story, my son."

"But it's always better to know the truth, isn't it, Father?"

"Yes, I think it is." Jacob picked up a cup that was half filled with the sour milk he liked so well, took a swallow, then put it down. "People do not really understand what happened at that time. What have you heard?"

Benjamin hesitated, then said, "Well, sir, what I have heard is that my grandmother wanted you to have the blessing instead of Esau, and because your father was old and blind, she disguised you, and you pretended to be Esau, and that's how you got the blessing."

"And what do you think of that, Benjamin?"

"Well, it doesn't seem—"

When Benjamin broke off, Jacob said quietly, "It doesn't sound honest, does it?"

"Well, I'm sure the story has been twisted. It's probably very different. I can't believe that Grandmother would do such a thing, or that you would, sir."

"But we did." Jacob saw the young man flinch and said quietly, "We did exactly what you said. I remember it so well. Indeed, how could I ever forget it? It changed my whole life. You must remember, my son, that most of life is just one boring day after another, but then there will come one moment when everything changes. It's like a man bends over to pick up something, and when he straightens up, the whole world around him has changed."

"I don't understand you, Father."

"Then listen." Jacob took another sip of the soured milk and began to speak. Behind him, but staying hidden, Tamar was listening intently.

"My brother, Esau, was older than I. He was the firstborn, and he deserved the birthright. It was his according to all the traditions of our fathers. There's no question about that—but there's one thing that nobody really knows."

"What is that, Father?"

"Before Esau and I were conceived, my mother, Rebekah, was barren for many years. She had no children, and, of course, it was a grief to her and to my father also. So my father entreated the Lord for his wife, because she was barren, and the Lord heard his prayer and my mother conceived."

"You and your brother were conceived at the same time."

"That is true, but you know our tradition. The one who is born first, even if only by minutes, is the firstborn." Jacob's eyes were dreamy, and his voice fell so low that Tamar had to lean forward to catch his words. "But my mother felt strange about this birth. She knew she was carrying twins, and at times as she told me, it seemed that my brother and I were fighting in her womb."

"That must have been strange."

"Indeed it was. So strange that my mother went to inquire of the Lord. She told me she prayed, 'Why is this thing happening to me? Why is there such struggling in my womb?'"

"And did the Lord hear her?"

"The Lord always hears, but sometimes He does not answer." Jacob smiled faintly. "But this time He did. She told me the exact words that the Lord said to her, and I have kept them all the years that have passed since then, for it was the most important thing God ever said to any of our people since he first spoke to Abraham."

"What were the words, sir?"

Jacob remembered the words exactly: "'Two nations are in your womb, and two peoples from within you will be separated; one people will be stronger than the other, and the older will serve the younger.'"

Benjamin stared at his father. "The older will serve the younger? That's what God told Grandmother?"

"It is, and that, my son, is why my mother was determined to see me get the blessing—because God told her that was the way it would be."

Tamar put her hand over her mouth and rocked back and forth. Here was a woman after her own heart! The wife of Isaac, Rebekah, had done exactly what she would have done! She had seen to it that her son would receive the birthright. It was what she herself, in effect, had done when she had interfered with the natural, traditional laws of the tribe in order to produce sons by Judah's seed. She leaned forward once again to listen to the two men as they spoke.

"Do you understand, my son, what my mother felt?"

"It must have been hard for her, Father."

"I don't think it was. She was a strong woman, and she decided that when God speaks, one must obey. That is why she explained to me that it was absolutely necessary I receive the birthright and the blessing of the firstborn and not my brother, Esau."

"I have heard you were your mother's favorite while Esau was your father's favorite."

"Yes. Esau was a man of the field, and Isaac loved the meat that he would bring in. I stayed closer to my mother."

Jacob fell silent, and finally Benjamin asked, "Is something wrong?"

"One thing I haven't told you. When my mother told me to disguise my arm with a fleece so I would seem to be hairy like my brother, I told her I didn't think I could do it. I thought it would bring a curse on me, not a blessing. And I have never forgotten to this day what my mother said: 'My son, let the curse fall on me.'"

Benjamin looked up, for his father's voice was trembling, and he saw tears in his eyes. He reached over and took his father's hand. "What's wrong, Father?"

"After my father died, my brother threatened to kill me, and my mother sent me away. I remember the day I left. My mother clung to me and said, 'Go to Laban, my son, and stay with him a few days.' Those were the last words from her I ever heard—it was the last time I ever saw my precious mother on this earth!"

Jacob was weeping in earnest now, and Benjamin could do no more than put his arm around the old man. Jacob said between his sobs, "I don't know to this day if the curse of God came upon my mother because of what we did or not, but I like to believe that she thought she was doing the will of God when we deceived my father."

Benjamin stayed with his father for a time, but the old man wanted to be alone, so he got up and left.

A short ways away he encountered Tamar, who said, "Be kind to your father, Benjamin."

"Of course," he said, surprised. "Why would you say that, Tamar?"

"Because he's an old man and he needs his people."

Two days after Benjamin had listened to his father's tale, he was crossing the camp when he heard a shout. He looked up and saw a caravan coming into view. He ran to his father's tent, shouting, "Father, they're back!"

Jacob rose as quickly as he could and grabbed his staff. He limped outside and shielded his eyes with his hand. Despite his age, his eyesight was fairly good, and the first thing he said was, "There are only nine of them."

Benjamin had not thought to count, but now he did. "You're right, Father! One of them is gone. Who is it?"

The caravan approached until they were only a few yards away, and Benjamin's eyes went to every face. "Simeon's not with them."

The two stood there waiting while the returning brothers were greeted by their wives and children. There was laughter and shouting about the food, and the women started unloading the animals.

Judah and Reuben left the group to greet their father. Before they could speak, Jacob said in a stern voice, "Where is my son Simeon?"

"We will tell you everything," Judah said quickly, "but we're back safely and with food."

"But all of you are not back. Where is my son?"

"He is not with us for the moment because of the way the business turned out," Reuben said, looking awkward and guilty.

Jacob demanded, "Where is he?"

"He's . . . he's still in Egypt, Father," Judah said.

"*Why* is he in Egypt?"

Judah cleared his throat. "We ran into a problem while we were there, and Simeon had to stay until it was cleared up." The other brothers had now gathered around and listened as Judah tried to explain the missing member of their group. They all sat down in a circle, and Benjamin looked at their faces while Judah spoke.

"It's necessary, Father, for you to hear whole the story of what happened to us in order to understand why Simeon had to remain behind. We arrived safely, and we went before the lord of the land called the Great Provider. He is a rather strange man, given to fits of some sort."

"What sort of fits? Physically, you mean?"

"Oh no, but he was often friendly and grim at the same time. He wanted to know everything about us."

Jacob listened as Judah explained, leaving out no detail. He heard how the Provider had accused them of being spies and how they had told him they were the ten sons of one man. Then later, when they had said there were twelve, he had accused them of lying.

Finally when Judah ended the story, Jacob said, "I have heard you through, Judah, but you have not answered my one question. Why is Simeon still in Egypt?"

"The man thought we were spies," Judah said in despair. "He said he would not believe us until we brought the younger son we spoke of."

"That will never happen!" Jacob cried out.

"But he said he would keep Simeon until we came back with our younger brother. We have to go back for Simeon's sake."

Benjamin sat straight up, his face aglow and his eyes dancing. "I would very much like to see this strange man. I must go with them, Father."

"Be still!" Jacob snapped. He stared at the others and said, "Now I know why I did not want you to go to Egypt. Did I not tell you it was an evil place, and have not my words come to pass? You have left the very best of you as a prisoner."

Reuben said impulsively, "You did not always speak so well of Simeon."

Jacob's face grew red. "You dare talk to me like that! You who defiled your own father's bed!"

Judah saw Reuben collapse and said, "Father, you're not being fair. If all eleven of us had gone, this would never have come up. You should have let Benjamin go with us in the first place."

"Oh, so it's my fault now!"

"We've got to go back!" Judah said defiantly.

The brothers fell to arguing with their father, all nine of them speaking up in defense of Judah's explanation.

"We have no choice, Father," Levi said. "We must go back."

"You shall not go back!" Jacob insisted.

"Listen to me," Reuben interjected. "Let the boy go. If we don't come back, then you may kill my own sons."

"What wild talk is this, Reuben? I reject you and all that you say. Benjamin's brother is dead, and he alone remains to me."

The brothers fell silent then until Zebulun asked, "But, Father, what about Simeon?"

"I will mourn for him. Now leave me."

Jacob turned and limped off to his tent, and Benjamin spoke up, "Don't be bitter with him, brothers, and don't think this makes me happy to be treated in this way by Father. I wanted to go with you from the start."

Reuben put his arm on Benjamin's shoulder. "I know that's true, little brother, but he will have to be brought to reason. We cannot leave our brother Simeon to die."

"That's true. And besides that, the food we brought won't last all that long. When he gets hungry enough and sees the family starving, he'll have to listen to us."

CHAPTER
29

Weeks passed, and the family of Jacob kept time not by the passage of the sun or the shadows that began to lengthen, but by the diminishing food the brothers had brought back from Egypt. Day by day the supplies shrank, but it was as if Jacob had put the whole affair out of his mind.

"He's ignoring the problem," Levi said one day to Reuben. Levi had lost weight, and even his quick temper seemed to have been extinguished. He had lost all hope of going back to Egypt. "Father's ignoring the fact that we're all going to starve to death."

"I'm sure he thinks about it," Reuben said hopefully. "We'll just have to wait until things get worse."

Indeed, things did get worse, for as the weeks rolled by, the food diminished until the women were scraping bottom again.

One evening while the brothers were sitting around their fire, Jacob suddenly appeared. It was so unusual they were all startled. They got to their feet, and Reuben said, "Good evening, Father. Are you out for a walk?"

"No, I have come to talk to you about our people. Sit down."

They all sat back down, but Jacob remained standing. "None of you is blind or deaf. You see that there is no food and our children are crying for bread."

"Yes, we have seen this, Father," Reuben said quietly. His eyes were on his father, and hope began to rise in his heart.

"Are you all just going to sit there and let us starve?" Jacob demanded.

The brothers looked at one another in surprise.

"What do you want us to do, Father?" Judah asked.

"Why, you must go back to Egypt, of course. They are the only ones with food."

"That would be very wise," Reuben said. "I think we should leave at once, but, of course," he added, seemingly as an afterthought, "we must take Benjamin with us."

Jacob had evidently been prepared for this. "No, you will not take him."

"Then there's no point in going back!" Levi snapped. "We told you all about that, Father."

Judah stepped forward. "Father, we must go, and Benjamin must go with us, or we will all die. Put Benjamin in my care. If he does not return to you ... hold me responsible. If I do not bring him back, I will bear the blame before you all my life."

Jacob stared blankly at Judah for a few moments, but then he blinked, shook his head as if to clear his thoughts, and continued as if Judah had not spoken. "You will take double money and that will satisfy the man. I'll hear no more about it. Leave tomorrow."

Jacob turned and limped back into the darkness.

"There's no point in going back with double or even triple money," Naphtali said, the flickering light of the flames making his scarred face look sinister. "I'm not going anywhere without Benjamin."

"I told you Father would never change his mind. Benjamin is dearer to him than the rest of us put together," Asher said. "That's the end of it."

———

Tamar had followed Jacob out and listened to his speech and his command to go back to Egypt. She went back inside and found Leah pounding corn into meal in a stone vessel. "Jacob has just told the men to go back to Egypt."

"He should have told them that weeks ago," Leah said bitterly. "There's no other place to get food."

"I think he'll have to let Benjamin go."

"Did he say he would?" Leah demanded, her eyes lifting to meet Tamar's.

"No, he didn't. As a matter of fact, he said he'd send double money but not Benjamin."

"Then they won't get the food. My sons have all told me about this strange man they call the Great Provider. They say he has no mercy in him, and unless they bring their youngest brother back, they'll get nothing."

Tamar said no more but went about her work. After seeing her two boys down for the night, she left her tent and moved through the darkness, glancing at the stars overhead. They were always a miracle to her— how many there were and how bright they seemed. It was that way on this night, and as she made her way toward Judah's tent she wished she knew their names.

"Judah?" she whispered as she came to the front of the tent. She heard movement inside and then Judah stepped out. "What is it, Tamar?"

"I heard what your father told you."

Judah stared at her face in the bright moonlight. "It won't do any good to return without Benjamin," he said.

"You must convince him."

"It's all over. I'm tired of everything," Judah said. "I wish I'd never been born—or that I was dead."

"Judah, you must never, never say that!"

"But it's true. There's no hope."

"God is a God of hope. He will not let us perish."

"I don't really believe that."

Tamar stepped closer. "Don't you remember the medallion your father wears around his neck?"

"Of course I remember it."

"You know the story of it. It's come down from the ancient past. Why, it may have come straight from Seth."

"I know the story," Judah said, "but it means nothing to me."

"Why do you say that?"

"Whichever one of my brothers gets the blessing and the medallion, it won't be me."

"Oh, Judah, don't give up! You don't know what God is going to do."

"Tamar, I'm a sinful man." Judah stared at her, then said bitterly, "*You* of all people should know that."

"All men are sinful, Judah, yet God still uses them. Sometimes," she whispered, "he can use a crooked stick to get the job done."

Judah stared at her and shook his head. "I wish I were a better man, but I'm not." He turned abruptly and disappeared into his tent.

Tamar stood there uncertainly, then walked swiftly to Jacob's tent. She was usually the last one to minister to him in the evening. She saw to it that his bed was made and then went to where he was sitting beside a lamp that cast its yellow beams over his wrinkled face and sparse white hair. She sat down beside him and did not speak.

Finally he sighed heavily. "These are hard times, daughter."

"Very hard."

"I don't know what's to become of us."

"Master, I've often wanted to ask you why you think Egypt is such a bad place."

"I've always thought that ever since my father told me something about it."

"What did he tell you about Egypt?"

"There was a famine in the land, daughter, just like there is now."

"There are always famines. There always will be."

"I suppose that's so, but anyway, my father wanted to go down to Egypt, just as my sons pestered me."

"Did he go?"

"No, he didn't. God appeared to him and commanded him not to go. My father told me this many times."

"Was that all God told him?" Tamar asked.

"No, he also made him a wonderful promise that I think about all the time."

"What was that?"

"He said, 'I will make your descendants as numerous as the stars of heaven and will give them all these lands, and through your offspring all nations on earth will be blessed.'" He turned and stared at Tamar. "Isn't that a wonderful promise? But I don't understand how it can happen. We're just a small band of people. How could all people be blessed because of us?"

"Don't you see, master?" Tamar whispered. "Indeed, we are small, but a river is small in its beginning. Why, I suppose the great Nile River at one point is so small a man could leap across it. Like the source of a river, your people are only a few dozen now, but they are the people God has chosen above all other nations. The Hittites may be stronger and the Amorites more numerous, but they are not the ones God has chosen." Tamar's voice grew stronger, and she lifted her hands. "He has chosen Abraham and Isaac and now Jacob, and from you, master, will come One that will be in the line of Shiloh, for the Redeemer will come, and He will save His people."

Jacob stared at Tamar, speechless. He had been greatly puzzled by this woman, and her history was a mystery to him. "So, what are you saying to me, Tamar?"

"I think this is a very different thing from what your father encountered. True, there was a famine and true, God did tell him not to go to Egypt at that time, but has He told *you* not to go?"

"Well . . . no, He hasn't, but . . ."

"He has not told you. Therefore, I think you should use every means to save your people—for what would happen if our people all perished? Would Shiloh ever come if the river were suddenly cut off?"

"God would have to choose another man, another Abraham."

"No, that cannot happen. You yourself have said that God promised Abraham that *he* would be the father of a great nation. Now he's told it to your own father and to you too. But, master, we are going to die here if we don't get food."

"What would you have me do, Tamar?"

Tamar had her answer ready. "I think you should seek God and pray about it."

"What if I get no answer?"

"Then that might be the answer."

"What do you mean?"

"If God doesn't say no, then you have freedom to move." She paused. She knew that Jacob had a huge store of wisdom and would not be pushed. She rose and said, "Come now. Sleep, and maybe God will give you a dream. If He does, then you must obey. But if there is no word from God, you must do what a man can do."

Jacob was too tired to argue any further, and he couldn't avoid the truth that some of what Tamar had said made sense. He lay down on the cot, and she put a light covering over him.

"Good night, master," she whispered and left the tent.

Jacob lay in the darkness and thought about the problem for a long time. He was weary of life, but he began to pray, "O God of my fathers, speak to me that I might have your wisdom. I do not know which way to turn, but your hand is on all men. Let me know what to do!"

———

For three days Jacob fasted. Tamar watched him constantly and saw that he had plenty of water to drink, although he touched no food. She did not speak to him much, for he was caught up with a great inner struggle. When Judah came once and asked about his father, she said, "He's praying for wisdom, and I think he will send you all to Egypt."

The whole camp knew that their fate lay in the balance. Starvation was like a pack of lean, hungry wolves that surrounded them on every side, so Jacob was certainly not the only one praying for wisdom.

Early one morning Jacob said, "Tamar, I will eat now."

Tamar quickly fixed him a meal. It was merely a thin soup with a few bits of meat floating in it, but it brightened the old man's eyes. He said, "Go find my sons and tell them to come."

"Yes, master!" Tamar went at once, and within thirty minutes all of the sons of Jacob were there, including Benjamin.

Jacob tried to hold himself in an upright position as he spoke to his sons. He looked weak and frail, but his voice was strong. "I have asked God, and I have no answer." He heard a groan go up and said quickly, "But I consent. Take double money and take many gifts. Take the very best of the food we have and take back the money that was found in your sacks."

Everyone was listening breathlessly, and finally Jacob forced himself to continue. "And take Benjamin." An uproar went up from the brothers, and Benjamin made a glad cry of joy. Jacob allowed them to talk for a while and then finally said, "I give my consent, and may El Shaddai keep you all safe."

Benjamin was beside himself. He was a grown man with a family of his own, yet he had still been kept under his father's hand. Now he was elated to be going on a journey, and he threw himself into the preparations along with the others.

––––––––

The preparations did not take long, and on the second day after Jacob gave his permission, once again the animals were in line, and the brothers were ready for their departure.

Jacob, supported by his staff, came out and blessed their journey. He prayed for them fervently, and finally Jacob embraced Benjamin, unable to speak.

The brothers all watched this with anxiety. Dan whispered, "He may change his mind even now."

But Jacob did not waver. He came to Judah and said, "Judah, you have given your bond for this child, but you are released from your bond. I do not build my trust on you. I will trust El Shaddai alone that He will bring all of you back. Now go in the name of the Almighty." He turned and walked away sadly, limping worse than ever.

The brothers all watched him go, and then Judah said, "Come, brothers, it is time."

The small caravan wound its way out of the camp, and as they disappeared from sight, Tamar said, "God will watch over them!"

CHAPTER

30

Time passed slowly for Simeon during his imprisonment in Egypt. He knew it would take at least twenty days for his brothers to make the trip back to Canaan. He counted what he assumed would be the time needed to persuade Jacob to allow Benjamin to go, and then added the time for the return journey to Egypt. But that time quickly passed, and no matter how he figured it, the one element he could not change was the heart of his father. No one knew better than Simeon how Jacob had protected Benjamin all of his life, and he couldn't be certain that his father would ever let him leave home. As the months passed and Simeon pondered these things, he gradually fell into a dark depression.

Joseph got regular reports about Simeon from Rashidi, and he commanded his lieutenant to see to it that his brother got special attention. "Go sit with him. Try to encourage him all you can," Joseph had told him. "He must be feeling low, but I cannot go myself."

Rashidi was curious about Joseph's brothers and took the command as an opportunity to find out more. He had made several visits, and late one afternoon after his work was done, he went to the room where Simeon was kept, taking Joseph's Hebrew interpreter with him. There was only one door, and a guard was posted outside.

As Rashidi and the interpreter stepped in, he saw Simeon standing at the window gazing out. The window was barred, and the sunlight flowed in, throwing a pale golden beam on Simeon's face. The Hebrew, Rashidi saw at once, was miserable. For the first few visits that had not been the case, and Rashidi had reported to Joseph that his brother was doing all right. Now, however, Simeon's mouth was drawn down in a scowl, his eyes were hooded, and his shoulders slumped in a posture of utter dejection.

"Well, my friend, I have just been to the kitchen. I commanded them to bring you a delicacy. What would you say to some fine beer soup with raisins and a joint of mutton?"

Simeon turned at the familiar voice and waited for the interpreter to translate. Then he nodded. "Thank you, sir. That sounds very good."

"I think you will enjoy the soup," Rashidi went on. "It's very fine. I also gave orders for them to bring some very special wine," he said, plumping himself down on a bench against the wall. "It was intended for one of the lower magistrates of the courts, but he got so drunk he wouldn't have appreciated it, so I gave him some cheap stuff. I thought it might be a treat for you."

Simeon nodded briefly and murmured in a listless voice, "Thank you very much." Then he turned back to stare silently out the window.

"Well, now. You seem a little out of sorts this morning. I can understand that."

"Can you? I very much doubt it."

"You don't think I've ever had any problems? All men have problems."

"I suppose that's true."

"You *suppose* it's true? Of course it's true! Surely as the smoke flies upward, each of us has to eat our peck of dirt."

A momentary smile touched Simeon's broad lips as the interpreter tried to translate this idiom. "Well, I have more than a peck of dirt to eat, sir."

"We all think that when we're in the middle of trouble, but even the darkest day will produce some sunshine sooner or later."

"Perhaps."

"In addition to the wine, I have another very special treat for you," Rashidi said expansively. "Something not every man will get."

Simeon turned with a faint flicker of interest in his eyes. "And what is that, sir?"

"I am a poet, and I have brought you a portion of my epic poem. I would be glad to read it to you."

Again Simeon smiled faintly. "I'm not sure that poetry can help me."

"Nonsense! Poetry can help everyone."

"I'm afraid I'm not very poetic. I don't understand poetry very well."

"It's not necessary to understand it to appreciate it," Rashidi said. "Just the sound of the words as they roll—the exact word in the exact spot—it's like an arrow driving home into the very center of the target.

Ah, that's the glory of poetry. Shall I read you a bit of it?"

"I suppose it can't do any harm."

Rashidi began to read from the papyrus scroll he had brought in. He loved to read his own poetry, and his voice rolled sonorously. His stentorian tones drifted out through the window and past the door so that the guard outside rolled his eyes and said, "O you gods, more of that abominable poem of his!"

Simeon listened for a time to the sounds of the poem as Rashidi recited and could sense the artistic rhythm and flow of the Egyptian language, but of course he could not understand a word of it. The interpreter could only tell him in general what the poem was about but could not translate it word for word. It left Simeon puzzled by the meaning and purpose of it.

When Rashidi stopped, he smacked his lips and shook his head. "Oh, that's a glorious piece of work!"

Simeon, despite his gloom, was amused. "You don't mind praising your own work?"

"Mind? Of course not! I'm the one who appreciates it more than anyone else. Most people don't really know what a work of genius this is."

"I am sure it will bring you great fame," Simeon said dryly. "Is there money in being a poet?"

"Money? Money is the last thing I think of, Simeon!"

Simeon sat down on the bench next to Rashidi and looked into the man's eyes. "So you don't care about money."

"Not a bit! I could be happy with nothing but a ragged rug to sit on and a wooden bowl for my food as long as I can have my poetry."

Simeon looked at Rashidi's rich clothing, the gold rings on his biceps, and the rings glittering from his fingers. "Have you ever been poor?" he asked.

"Well, not really. My father was a wealthy man, and he took care of me. I went into government and became a governor of a prison, and now I am the third most important man in the country. Pharaoh's the king, the Provider tells him what to do, and I tell the Provider what to do!"

"If you've never been poor, how do you know you could bear it?"

The question seemed to puzzle Rashidi. He clawed at his hair, digging his fingernails into his scalp, his face twisted up in an expression of deep thought. "I just know it," he said finally. "My art's more important than my comfort."

"I'm afraid you'll have to help me with your poetry. I am a very simple fellow, just a herdsman. I had a brother once who was very much of a scholar. He could read and write all sorts of languages, and he liked poetry too. As a matter of fact, he even wrote some."

"Which one of your brothers was that?"

"Oh, none that came with me. We..." Simeon looked down at the ground, his face again assuming a gloomy cast. "We lost him many years ago."

"Oh . . . was it a sickness?"

"N-no, not exactly."

"Torn by wild beasts, perhaps."

"I really don't want to talk about it."

"Well, you should appreciate my poem, then, because there are many lines in it that talk about how to handle loss. A man must expect it and give himself up to the will of the gods without arguing."

Simeon turned and demanded, "Have you ever had a loss? A loved one? A wife? A child?"

"No, I can't say that I have."

"Then you don't know what you're talking about," Simeon said flatly. His anger was stirred by the richly dressed Egyptian who proposed to solve the problems of the world with a few lines written on papyrus. "One of these days you will, though. Someone you love will die, or you will get sick, or you will fall from favor. Something will happen. It always does."

Rashidi stared at Simeon. "Well," he said finally, "I can see that we don't need to talk about poetry."

Simeon looked directly at Rashidi. "Tell me. What kind of a man is the Provider?"

"What kind of a man? Why, you can see."

"I've only seen him briefly. You can't make a judgment about a man like that. Tell me about him."

"Well, he has a very strict sense of justice. He will not permit injustice of any kind."

"Does he believe in the Egyptian gods?"

"As a matter of fact, he seems to care very little for the gods of Egypt."

"What does he believe in?"

"I'm no theologian myself, so I can't really understand it. But he believes in a very peculiar concept of the gods."

Simeon continued to ask questions of Rashidi, who managed to avoid most of them with bland and evasive answers. Finally he changed the subject. "What will you do, my friend, if your brothers never come back?"

Simeon looked up, and his eyes were dull. "Then I will die here," he said simply.

"Well, let's hope for better things."

"I have no hope."

"But, man, you must have hope!" Rashidi exclaimed. "Without hope man cannot exist."

Simeon only shook his head and said, "It's no more than I deserve."

Rashidi studied the Hebrew for a long time. "Are you a murderer?" he asked finally.

Simeon was looking down at the floor, but at the question he lifted his head. His small eyes fastened on Rashidi, and his voice was raspy as he said, "A murderer? I am much worse than that!"

"What did he say, Rashidi?" Joseph demanded as soon as his lieutenant came into the room. "Tell me everything."

Rashidi had come directly to Joseph's quarters as soon as he had left Simeon's cell. He went over and picked up a bunch of grapes and plucked one and threw it into his mouth. He let the juice trickle down his throat, then picked another one, but Joseph came over and snatched the grapes away from him. "Never mind eating! Tell me what he said."

"Well, he's rather a strange fellow. What was he like when he was younger?"

"We weren't particularly close. As a matter of fact, he couldn't stand me."

"I can't understand that. A handsome, intelligent fellow like you." Rashidi grinned.

"I wasn't all that nice when I was younger. Not like I am now," Joseph said.

"Not nice? What did you do? Did you bully them? Beat them up, perhaps?"

"Of course not. I was too young for that. They were all grown men, and I was just a boy. As a matter of fact, Simeon pounded me a few times. He was very lean and quick and hot-tempered. He could be cruel at times."

"Well, that's been taken out of him."

"What did he say?"

"He's pretty much lost hope, Joseph," Rashidi said with a shrug. "I read him some of my poetry to cheer him up."

"Well, that was a fool thing to do!" Joseph exclaimed. "That interminable poem of yours would never cheer anybody up!"

Rashidi shot Joseph an insulted look. "You don't appreciate art."

"I don't appreciate boring poetry. Now tell me what my brother said."

Rashidi began to give a word-for-word account as far as he could remember it, and Joseph listened intently. When Rashidi came to the end and told how Simeon had proclaimed that he was worse than a murderer, Joseph started.

"His heart must have changed!" he exclaimed. "Simeon would never have admitted he was wrong in the old days. The only thing that could have brought him to this is a guilty conscience."

"He looks guilty, all right. As a matter of fact, we ought to take his razor away from him. He looked gloomy enough to slit his own throat."

"No, I don't think he would do that. It appears he's had a change of heart."

Rashidi went over and took the grapes from Joseph's hand. He sat down on a padded chair and began to eat them one after another. His voice was garbled as he asked, "Do you think a man's heart can change?"

"Why, certainly!"

"Have you ever seen it happen?"

"Of course I have. My own heart has changed."

"Do you think a man like me can have a change of heart?"

Joseph looked at Rashidi to see if he was teasing. Rashidi had no religion as far as Joseph could determine. He merely went through the pomp and circumstance demanded by the customs of the land, paying money to the priests, going through the sacrifices with a bored expression, trying to keep from yawning, but more than once Joseph had seen that beneath that careless and caustic exterior was a quite different vein.

This was not the first time Rashidi had asked him about the matters of the heart, and now Joseph said quietly, "A man's heart is in his own hands, my friend. In one sense I think we all do what we want to do. Those who want to get drunk, get drunk. Those who want to take another man's wife do it, and those who want to do better, finer things find a way to do that as well."

Rashidi listened as he munched the grapes, and there was a glow in his dark eyes. He was not a man who had many friends or who trusted many, but he had learned to trust this man. Now as Joseph spoke of such things as honor and truth and justice and kindness, he did not speak. But when Joseph finally ended, he tossed the stem of the grapes back on the table and said, "I've always thought it was too late for me."

"It's never too late for anyone who wants to find God."

Rashidi looked vulnerable for a moment, and then he quickly covered up what he considered a weakness by giving a short laugh. "Well," he said in a blustering tone, "if I find this god of yours, I might have to change a great many things."

"Yes, you would." Joseph went over and put his hands on the smaller man's shoulders. "You might have to change some things in your behavior—and you would even have to change some things in your poem."

"Change my poem?"

"Yes. There's a gloominess in it and an uncertainty. But a man who has God in his heart doesn't have those things. Now I must leave."

Rashidi watched as Joseph left the room. He paced nervously back and forth for a time, then lifted up his head and said softly, "Well, Joseph, Great Provider of Egypt, you've got me confused now. I was all happy in my godlessness before I met you. Now you've brought all sorts of troublesome thoughts to my mind." He laughed shortly and shook his head. "And now I'm talking to myself. That's a sure sign of a crazy man!"

Asenath sat beside Joseph, holding one of his hands in both of hers. He had come home in a strange mood. She knew at once that he was troubled, so she had listened carefully as he had repeated what Rashidi had told him of his visit with Simeon. He could not be still but twisted his shoulders back and forth and spoke more rapidly and in a less fluid manner than was usual for him.

"And so the poor fellow is there in prison. He's on the edge of despair, and he's pretty sure that my brothers will never come back."

"Why would he think that, Joseph?"

"Because my father has an obsession with Benjamin. He had it about me once, but now that he thinks I'm dead, it's Benjamin he protects. Simeon believes my father will never let Benjamin out of his sight, so all he can see is a slow, lingering imprisonment here for the rest of his life."

"He must think better of his brothers than that."

Joseph did not answer her directly, thinking about the dreadful treatment he received at the hands of his own brothers. "I wish I could do more to help Simeon, but I had to keep one of them here. I thought it was the only way I would ever get to see Benjamin again."

"He's very special to you, isn't he?"

"Yes. We were very close. I was almost like a father to him, holding his hand wherever we went. He was very trusting, and he loved me greatly."

"He's a man now, though. He might have changed."

"That's possible," Joseph admitted, "but I don't think so. There was a sweetness in Benjamin."

"If your brothers don't come back, what will you do to Simeon?"

Joseph shook his shoulders restlessly. "Oh, I'll let him go when it's obvious they're never coming back."

Asenath studied her husband's face. It was tight with emotions, and his lips were drawn into a thick line. There were shadows in his eyes, and she asked curiously, "What will you do if they come back? Will you take your revenge on them?"

"Of course not, Asenath! You don't understand at all. I'm doing all this so I can help my family."

"It seems a roundabout way of doing it."

"Maybe it is, but you know I've been thinking about the way God dealt with some of my ancestors. He seems to be a God who works in roundabout ways."

"Tell me about that." Asenath had become fascinated with Joseph's God. She herself still went through rituals for the Egyptian gods, but she had no heart in it. "Tell me about how he works in a roundabout way."

"Why, there's the matter of the Redeemer, the One that is to come and save us all. My father called him Shiloh. I think I have told you that."

"Yes, you have."

"If you or I were going to choose some man to save his people, we would go find the most powerful, strongest man alive to do it, wouldn't we?"

"I think we would."

"But God chose a simple man named Noah and told him that He

was going to flood the whole earth and destroy everything, except for Noah and his family."

"Why, we have a myth like that in our own history!" Asenath exclaimed.

"Yes, as a matter of fact, the Babylonians have one too. Most cultures do, but this is no myth. This is history."

"So what did Noah do?"

"Well, he probably didn't know much about boat building, but he built a boat large enough to carry a pair of every kind of animal. Then he and his family got on it, and the floods came, the waters fell from heaven, and every human being died on earth except for Noah and his family."

"How terrible!"

"But Noah was saved, and his three sons and their wives and all the people on the earth now are descendants from one of those three sons. I would say that's a pretty roundabout way of saving the earth."

"So, then, you think God would have you forgive your brothers?"

"He forgives me," Joseph said simply. "Therefore, I must forgive them."

As Asenath listened to Joseph speak, she remembered that he had never taken revenge on Lady Kesi or on Ufa—nor even on her. She held his hand tightly and listened as he continued to speak, and she tried hard to think of some way she might help him through this difficult time.

One day, just when Joseph was close to giving up all hope of his brothers' return, Rashidi burst into Joseph's quarters. "They're back!" he cried with excitement. "There are ten of them."

"Yes, I've already had word from the guards," Joseph said. His eyes were glowing, and he could barely contain himself. "My brother Benjamin must be with them."

"I think that's possible. You won't be able to fool them this time."

"What do you mean by that?"

"I mean you can disguise your face and talk gruffly, but I've heard you talk about this younger brother of yours. Your voice gets soft, and your eyes begin to mist over." Rashidi shook his head. "They will never believe that the Lord of Egypt would weep over a man he does not know—especially a Hebrew."

"Well, I must deceive them for a little while longer."

"Will you receive them in the hall of audience?"

"No, this time I want to have them here at my home for a meal. Go make provisions for it, and invite some people in."

"Which people?"

"Oh, it doesn't matter. Some of the hangers-on. They all want something from me. It doesn't matter which ones." Joseph paced the floor as he continued. "And another thing. I've made out a list here. I want you to seat my brothers in this order."

Rashidi took the list and asked, "What is this?"

"That's the age of my brothers. Big Reuben first and little Benjamin last." He suddenly laughed. "Little Benjamin. He may be larger than I am now, but I always think of him as a child."

"Very well, but won't they wonder how you would know such a thing?"

"Exactly! I want them to wonder."

"You're a fox, Provider!"

CHAPTER

31

Benjamin enjoyed the trip to Egypt immensely! He felt a freedom he had never experienced, and throughout the trip he sang and talked nonstop.

His joy, however, was not shared by the rest of the company. Most of them spent a great deal of time handling Benjamin as if he were made of glass. After all, the trip would be utterly meaningless without him. Fear drove the brothers, and a sense of gloom pervaded them.

Benjamin, however, seemed oblivious to all of this. He wore his best clothing—a fine, colorful robe with fringes—and his hair was anointed until it looked like a shiny helmet. He laughed and said to his brothers, "I make the rest of you look like paupers."

"You won't be so lighthearted when you stand in front of the Great Provider," Judah warned.

Benjamin only laughed again.

As soon as they arrived in the land, they faced difficulties. They were commanded to go to the Provider's private home. This shook all of them—except for Benjamin, of course, who said, "Well, that doesn't sound to me like a cruel man. Having us to his own home—that says something about him."

"It means something, but it's not good," Dan grunted, and the others nodded their assent.

"You're all worried about the money in your sacks," Benjamin said. "Don't worry about it. It was just a mistake of some kind, and we've brought it back, haven't we?"

When they reached the Great Provider's home, a gracious villa in the best section of town, and the brothers tied up their animals where they were directed in the courtyard, the Provider's lieutenant came to greet them, with the Hebrew interpreter close by his side.

"Welcome back," Rashidi said. "It is good to see you again."

Judah spoke up quickly. "Sir, we must tell you something at once. There has been a terrible mistake."

"A mistake? I cannot imagine what."

"We do not how it happened, but when we were on our way home with the grain we bought, we found the money we had used to pay for it in our sacks. Here—we have brought it all back again, along with money to buy more grain."

"That sounds serious. I cannot understand it," Rashidi said, keeping a straight face.

Suddenly they all began talking, and Rashidi held up his hand. "Be calm, my friends. I'm sure it will all be straightened out. Perhaps this god of yours was amusing himself by playing a joke on you."

"Certainly not!" Judah said indignantly. "Our God would never do such a thing."

"Well, come along. It will all be straightened out, I'm sure. Now I am sure you would like to see your brother, and then you will have a meal with the Great Provider."

They were led to a sumptuous meeting room, where Simeon waited for them, and they all gathered around him, talking at the same time. Simeon's face shone, and he asked them question after question, but his eyes lit up most when he saw Benjamin. "You're here, little Benjamin! Thank God for that."

"It's been a wonderful trip," Benjamin said. "You're looking fine, Simeon."

"Well, I wouldn't be looking fine if you hadn't come."

"Come along," Rashidi said to the brothers. "You must prepare yourselves for dinner. You can wash and put on a change of clothing."

When this was done, Rashidi led them into the elegant banquet hall. Benjamin could not take it all in at once. His eyes fell first on the long table filled with spiced delicacies and sugarcoated fruits and nuts, and then he studied the guests in their fine clothing and expensive jewelry.

A few moments after the brothers had entered, Benjamin looked up to see a man enter the room, and his heart gave a little lurch. This was the Great Provider, the second greatest man in all of Egypt! He had thought of little else but this man since his brothers had brought him the strange report that the Provider must see him before he would deal any further with the sons of Jacob.

Everyone fell down before the Great Provider, including Benjamin, but then Joseph commanded, "Greetings to all of you. Stand up and let me see your faces. You have had a long journey, but I am happy you are back." He smiled then and said, "You notice that I am speaking to you now in your own tongue. I see you are shocked and amazed, but a man like me can do things like this. I decided it was worth my while to learn your language. First tell me, is your old father still alive?"

Judah spoke up. "Yes, lord, he is alive and very well."

Joseph then turned and hesitated, his eyes fixed on Benjamin's face. "And is this the youngest brother you told me about?" His language was somewhat clumsy, for he had not used it in twenty years. He moved forward slowly until he stood directly in front of Benjamin. He took in the clear eyes, the sensitive features, and said quietly, "May God bless you. I wish—"

Suddenly the guests, including the brothers, were shocked when the Provider broke off with a cough, put his hand before his face, whirled, and left the room.

"What have we done?" Reuben asked in dismay.

"Nothing at all," Rashidi said quickly. "The Provider has had a slight illness. He will be back at once, I'm sure."

Indeed, Joseph did return shortly, with his back held straight. "Let me introduce these travelers to you," Joseph said in Egyptian to his guests. "This tall one here is Reuben. . . ." He named them all off, ending with the youngest. "And this is Benjamin." Then he addressed the brothers in Hebrew, telling them the names of each of his Egyptian guests. Finally he commanded the whole company to sit down.

The servants began to bring out the food on golden platters, and the guests ate. The brothers were amazed at the sumptuous spread. All of them sat in comfortable chairs with footstools at a large table, but each of them also had their own small table by their side. The servants continued to pile the tables high with rich foods, the likes of which the Hebrews had never seen. Benjamin was astonished at the variety and freshness of the fruits, cakes, vegetables, meats, and pastries.

From time to time Joseph would send special foods to various guests, a roast duck or perhaps a new type of jelly. He sent most of these to Benjamin's table, and soon Benjamin's place in front was full and so was the smaller table by his side. He laughed and said, "Sir, I could not eat all of this in a month."

Despite Benjamin's pleasant demeanor, in truth he was upset. Something about the presence of the Great Protector had done it. Time after time Benjamin would steal glances at the face of the man who sat at the head of the table. He would look into those black eyes that met his and seemed to sparkle with an inner joy but would then grow veiled as if they were concealing something.

An old peculiar feeling came to Benjamin he could not explain— something that went all the way back to his childhood. Even though it troubled him, it also gave him a strange and almost exotic sense of pleasure. During the meal Joseph spoke more to Benjamin than to anyone else. He asked him question after question about his life, his father, his wife and his children, and then he talked to him of his own sons, Ephraim and Manasseh.

Finally Benjamin said, "May I ask you a question, Most Exalted One?"

"Certainly."

"I cannot understand how you knew our ages. You introduced us in order and our places at the table are set in that way. How could you know such a thing?"

"A man such as I has many abilities," the Provider said, smiling slightly. He picked up the silver cup in front of him, drank from it, and said, "Do you see this cup?"

"Yes, sir, of course."

"There are times when I look into this cup, at the wine that's in it, and knowledge comes to me. I believe it is the way that I know things. It's a mere superstition, of course. We grow foolishly fond of certain items. Perhaps you are the same way."

"Yes, I am very fond of a garment I had when I was a small child. I still have it and take it out often to look at it, wondering where the small child is who wore it before me, for he is no more."

"What sort of a garment is it?"

"It's a simple blue tunic. Nothing fancy. It reminds me of..."

"Reminds you of what, my son?"

"Oh, it just reminds me of my childhood, and..." Benjamin stumbled over his words and looked down at the table. "And it reminds me of my brother."

"Which of your brothers?"

"Not one that's here. My brother Joseph, who is dead. I was wearing that small garment the last time I saw him, and when I learned he was dead, I cried myself to sleep. And I put the garment away and never wore it again."

Joseph could not speak. He took out his handkerchief and coughed and blew his nose. "I have this illness. It's destroying me," he said finally, getting control of himself.

"I am sorry, but you must have good physicians here in Egypt."

"None that are able to solve the particular ailment I have," Joseph said evasively.

Joseph continued to converse with Benjamin as the meal continued. Eventually the Egyptian guests grew bored, and one by one they made their excuses and left. Finally only the sons of Jacob were left, with Rashidi looking on as Joseph spoke almost exclusively to Benjamin.

Finally Joseph looked around and seemed startled. "Well, the guests have all left, but you gentlemen are still here." He stood to his feet. "You will probably be gone by the time I rise in the morning, for you must leave early. Rashidi, I would ask you to send back a double portion of grain. Provide animals if necessary." He turned to the men, who had also risen to their feet, and studied them carefully. "Perhaps you should consider coming to live in Egypt."

A startled cry leaped to the lips of Judah. "Leave our homes and come to Egypt?"

"It's a possibility you should consider," Joseph said quietly. "The famine may go on for many years. There are how many of you—seventy, I believe you said? I think grazing grounds could be found for your flocks, and, after all, you are a migrant people."

"Our father would never leave our home," Judah said firmly.

"That is unfortunate. Well, I must say good-bye now." He looked around, his eyes lingering on Benjamin, and then he turned and walked away without another word.

As soon as he was gone, Rashidi said, "Come, gentlemen, I will see that you have accommodations for the night. As the Provider says, you will want to get an early start."

"We have brought money for the grain."

"Certainly, we will take care of the business tonight, and you will leave at first light tomorrow."

"Are you certain this is what you want to do, Joseph?"

"I have thought it over carefully. Take my silver cup and put it in my brother Benjamin's sack."

"But why?"

Joseph seemed triumphant after the meal with his brothers. "The play is not yet over. There is still one more act."

"I do not understand you. You talk like a poet."

"No, the thing is clear to me, but I shall not explain it. Put the silver cup in Benjamin's feed sack. When they have been gone one day, come upon them after they have made camp."

"And what shall I do to the young man?"

"You must tell the others that they can go back, but Benjamin must remain here forever."

"That's a hard thing," Rashidi said slowly. "I'm surprised at you."

"You are a poet. Figure it out," Joseph said gruffly. "Now go!"

The brothers were in better spirits than they had been at any point of their journeys. They were carrying heavily loaded animals back with twice as much grain as they had paid for, and with a lightness of heart they laughed and joked—all except Benjamin. Though he had been the most lively and joyous on the trip to Egypt, he was now silent. Reuben noticed this, and as the sun was going down, he brought his animal close to the younger man and said, "Why are you so sad, Benjamin?"

"I can't say. It has just come over me."

"You should be happy. We've got everything we asked for."

After that the eldest and the youngest son of Jacob fell silent for a time, until Rueben asked a question he had been mulling over since the evening before. "What did the Provider speak with you about at the banquet? He talked to you more than anyone else."

"Oh, we talked about our children."

"You were laughing. I've never seen him laugh before."

"Well, he is charming. He knows how to talk to everybody."

"Yes, he knows how to be stern too."

Benjamin turned and asked, "What do you think about the last thing he said to us?"

"You mean about moving to Egypt?"

"Yes. What's your idea on that?"

"It will come to nothing. You know our father. He is tied to our homeland. He would never move to Egypt." He laughed suddenly and said, "The Provider doesn't know as much as he thinks. He doesn't know our father in the least." The two continued to speak of the strange visit they'd had until Reuben finally called a halt.

They stopped at the same spot they had stayed two nights before, and they had barely begun unpacking their animals when Gad stood straight up. "Somebody's coming," he said.

They all heard it then. They turned around to see a chariot approaching with several other chariots behind.

"It's the servant of the Provider," Reuben said. His heart grew cold, and he could not speak as Rashidi got out of his chariot and came toward them.

His face was stern, and there was none of the humor or lightness they were accustomed to. "So you thought you could get away," he challenged, a scowl on his face. "Do you think we're fools here in Egypt?"

"But, sir, what is it?" Judah cried out. "What's wrong?"

"I believe you know very well what's wrong."

"No indeed, sir," Judah said quickly, "we have no idea." The others all agreed, and Judah asked again, "What is the problem?"

"The problem is that someone has stolen the Provider's silver cup, the one he treasures so much. You were the last ones seen in that room, so the Provider has sent me to search your baggage."

Reuben said loudly, "Go ahead and search. You won't find anything. We are not thieves. We are honest men."

Rashidi gestured to the soldiers and commanded, "Surround these men!" Instantly the armed soldiers made a circle around the brothers. "Search their baggage—everything! It must be here," Rashidi cried out.

They all began to protest, but Rashidi cut them short. "Shut your mouths!" he shouted. "Open your sacks."

Eagerly the brothers ran to their animals and pulled off the sacks. Judah set his on the ground. "Here, search it."

"Indeed I will!" Rashidi smiled. He prowled through Judah's sack and then glanced around. He went straight to Benjamin's and said, "Open your sack!"

Benjamin obediently untied his sack. Rashidi thrust his hand in and let out a cry of triumph. "Oh ho!" he cried loudly. "The cup!"

Judah's heart turned to ice. He saw the silver cup in Rashidi's hand and uttered, "We are doomed!"

"Here it is!" Rashidi cried out to the officer who was with him.

"Found in the youngest brother's sack. So you are in a bad fix, young man."

Benjamin did not say a word.

Judah cried out, "Benjamin—tell them you didn't take it!"

But Benjamin's head was down and he remained silent.

Finally Issachar shouted, "You were a fool to take that cup!"

"He didn't take it," Judah said. "Our brother is not a thief."

But all the brothers except Reuben and Judah lost their tempers, crying out in agony and grief.

"Your mother was a thief!" Levi shouted. "She stole her father's gods, and you inherited her thieving ways. It's in your blood! Why have you disgraced us?"

"That's enough of that!" Rashidi said. "The rest of you are free. Go back to your home. Only he who took the cup will go with us."

Judah said at once, "We will all go back with you, sir. Not a one of us will go back to our father's house."

Judah glared around at his brothers, with Reuben standing by his side. All of the others dropped their eyes, ashamed at their accusations. "Come," Judah said heavily, "we must look to God in this matter."

"I think you'd better look to your god," Rashidi said. "This is serious business. All right, back to the Provider."

CHAPTER
32

Joseph could not remember a time when he was more tense. He had set the machinery in motion, and now that the final act of the drama was upon him, he found himself unable to sit still. He knew Rashidi would return with his brothers, and over and over he ran through his mind how he would react. He had not left his house but had prowled the rooms, speaking at times to his sons, but his mind was not on them.

Asenath had watched him and finally came to his side and said, "What's the matter, Joseph? You are beside yourself."

"I am worried about what's going to happen." He had told her of placing the cup in Benjamin's sack, and she had rebuked him for playing games. She did so now with a frown on her face.

"I don't understand all of this, Joseph. Why don't you just tell them who you are?"

"I want to see if they really have had a change of heart. It's impossible to tell. If I had told them at the very first that I was their brother Joseph, they would have put on faces of repentance. I want to see it happen before they know who I am. I think I will—"

At that moment a servant hurried in. "Master, Lord Rashidi has returned with your brothers."

"Where are they?"

"He has them in the banquet hall, sir."

"Shall I go with you?" Asenath asked.

"No, but if all goes well, you will meet them soon. Please do not leave the house."

"Very well."

Joseph walked into the room and saw that the face of every brother was drawn and filled with fear—except for Benjamin's. The youngest of the brothers was standing straight, a soldier beside him, and he was looking directly at Joseph. Something passed between the two men, and Joseph said loudly, "I am gravely disappointed in your behavior. You have said all along that you are honest men, and indeed you were truthful in the matter of your youngest brother. But I gave you my hospitality, and you repaid it by stealing something that was very precious to me. I assume that you know your guilt."

There was silence among the brothers, and then Judah stepped forward. "My lord, we are guilty in that your cup was found among us, but we are not thieves. How the cup came to be among us we do not know, but we can only tell you that we are innocent."

There was a simple nobility in Judah at that moment. He who had spent years under the burden of guilt and groaned over the treatment of their younger brother, and he who had so mismanaged his own life now stood straight as a tree and faced Joseph courageously.

Joseph was impressed, but he played his role to the hilt. "I am the right hand of Pharaoh, and I know many things. The one thing I do not know is whether all of you sinned or only your youngest. He sat beside me at the table, and I told him the cup was precious to me. The cup was found among his things, and therefore the rest of you are free to go, but the youngest stays with me."

Judah took a deep breath and moved closer. His voice rang out clearly. "My lord, I must tell you the truth. You cannot detain our youngest brother. You cannot keep him here with you."

"You say *cannot* to me?" Joseph demanded.

"I must, my lord. But I will make you an offer that I hope you will accept. May I speak from my heart?"

"Speak," Joseph replied.

"When we came before you at first, you were suspicious of us, master. You asked many questions about our family, and I finally told you that our father had a wife by which he had two sons. The name of one was Joseph, the other was Benjamin. Joseph is gone, and our father clings to Benjamin as a man clings to his dearest possession. To snatch him away would mean the death of our father."

The room was silent, and Judah gained more dignity as he spoke, holding his head high. "My lord, I believe in the God of my fathers, and I do not understand how the cup got into my younger brother's sack. It is a mystery, but you must remember that you are the one who insisted we bring our brother. It was almost impossible to get our father to consent to this. He spoke for days about his wife Rachel and how he might lose both the sons of his True Wife, but after much weeping, he finally consented. Now we are here, and I, Jacob's fourth son, speak to your heart, my lord. You are a father and have sons whom you love."

And then Judah, with his massive head and broad shoulders—very much like the lion for which he was named—lifted his voice. "I took the responsibility, and I vowed to my father that if I did not return Benjamin to him, I will answer for it with my own life. And now, O Great Provider, I beg of you—let me stay here instead of my brother. I will be your slave, my lord. Only let Benjamin go home with his brothers." Judah's voice broke, and he began to weep. "How could I possibly go to my father and not have him with me? He would die, and my heart would break."

Judah was shaking and his face was pale as he ended his speech, and Joseph rose from his seat, tears running down his cheeks. He cried out, "All of you who are of Egypt, go out at once!"

The guards and Rashidi left. As soon as the door had closed, Joseph stretched out his arms and cried, "I am your brother Joseph!"

The brothers stood stunned, not able to respond. Then Benjamin uttered a strange cry and rushed forward. "Joseph—Joseph!" he sobbed. He threw himself into Joseph's arms and looked up into his face. "You are my brother Joseph! You are not dead!"

Joseph held the trembling form of his brother in his arms, and tears ran freely down his cheeks. He stroked Benjamin's hair as he had done when he was a small child. The two stood locked in an embrace, and finally Joseph turned to the others, but kept his arm around Benjamin's shoulders. He faced the brothers, who were still standing in shocked silence. "Yes, I am your brother Joseph, whom you sold into slavery. But you did me no harm, for God has been with me. Now tell me. Is my father truly alive?" The brothers were still unable to speak, so Joseph continued, "Judah, that was a great speech you made, and I embrace you and congratulate you."

Judah was trembling and weeping, as were most of the other brothers. "Joseph," he whispered, "I . . . I can't believe it!"

And then Reuben said hoarsely, "How is it possible, my brother?"

"God did all this," he said with a sweep of his arm at the elegant surroundings. "It was El Shaddai, the all-powerful One, who planned it from the beginning. He knew the drought was coming, and He sent me to this place so that I would be able to help *you* when the famine came." And then the brothers gathered around, all talking at the same time. Several of them actually reached out and touched Joseph, and every one of them was suddenly aware of the lifting of a burden they had borne for years.

Finally Joseph said, "We must make many plans. Our father must be brought here, but it must be done gently."

"Yes," Benjamin said quickly. He reached up and took Joseph's hand and clung to it. "The shock would kill him. I cannot think how it must be done."

"We will talk about that later," Joseph said with a smile. "Now you must meet my wife and two boys. We will eat and drink, all twelve of us. The twelve sons of Jacob!"

There was talk, and the brothers were introduced to Joseph's family. And the next day all of the capital swarmed with the news, and Pharaoh himself was told that Joseph's brothers had come to Egypt.

Pharaoh was happy. He turned to Isiri and said, "We must make them welcome, my dear. After all, we owe everything to Joseph!"

CHAPTER

33

Ephraim and Manasseh were somewhat overwhelmed by their father's eleven brothers. They stared into the bearded faces but were unable to absorb the Hebrew names, for they were so far different from Egyptian ones. Benjamin smiled and knelt down so that he was on the level of the two boys. "Don't be confused by how strange we look," he said. "We are your uncles, and I hope to become better acquainted with you."

Ephraim, the more talkative and bolder of the two, said, "Do you have any little boys?"

"Yes, I do, and I hope one day you will be able to play with them and that I can take you all fishing."

"Do you have any little girls?"

"I have two."

"I don't like to play with girls," Ephraim said staunchly.

"I didn't like to play with girls either when I was your age," Benjamin replied. He got to his feet and turned around and saw that Joseph was watching him with a smile. "You have two fine boys here, brother. I'm sure you must be very proud."

"I am," Joseph said, "but it is my wife who deserves the most credit. All of their good qualities come from her."

Asenath had been only slightly less overwhelmed than her sons by the invasion of Joseph's eleven brothers. But she was a woman of some sophistication and was able to ignore their rather wild and woolly looks as she greeted each of them with an extended hand. Having a good memory, she quickly mastered all of their names.

Issachar and Zebulun were both enchanted by Lady Asenath.

Zebulun in particular was so impressed he could not take his eyes off of her. When she found out he wanted to be a sailor, she endeared herself to him forever by saying, "You must let me persuade you to come on a voyage. Your brother and I love ships very much."

Zebulun was captivated and later said to Joseph, "You have married the most wonderful woman in the world. I love her dearly."

"So do I, Zebulun," Joseph laughed, "and indeed we will take you on many voyages as soon as you return with our father."

Zebulun looked troubled. "Do you think we can persuade him? You know how he is about his homeland."

"I know, and although he owns only a graveyard there where our fathers are buried, he still thinks of all of that territory as his because God promised Abraham that one day it would be."

They all sat down to a meal, and the brothers relaxed considerably. They were all listening to Joseph, especially Reuben, who could not take his eyes off of him.

Joseph was aware that there was some awkwardness, and he talked a great deal to Reuben during the meal. "One of my fondest memories is of the time you made my first bow and taught me how to shoot it."

"That was a long time ago," Reuben said.

"Yes, it was, but I still remember it. It was a fine bow. I wish I still had it as a keepsake." When Reuben responded with just a nod, Joseph continued. "I'm anxious to meet your family. Tell me about them."

Reuben was pleased that Joseph was showing him such attention. At one point he saw that the others were listening to Lady Asenath, and he lowered his voice to confess, "Brother, I failed you."

"Failed me, Reuben?"

"Yes, you know I did."

"Why, I know no such thing."

"I should have stopped my brothers from throwing you into that pit."

"I think there was very little you could do, Reuben. Please don't torment yourself over something that happened so long ago."

Reuben looked down at his big hands. He clasped them together and shook his head. Joseph could barely hear his words. "Not a day has gone by since that awful time that I haven't thought about it and hated myself for failing you."

Joseph was touched by Reuben's words. He had always liked the big man who had been so kind to him when he was a boy. He put his hand on Reuben's shoulder and said, "It was all in God's plan, and it's turned out well. Promise me you won't grieve anymore."

Reuben turned to face Joseph and managed a small smile. "You're too kind, brother. I can't promise, but I'll do the best I can."

After the meal was over Joseph took time to speak personally to as many of the brothers as he could. He tried not to pay too much attention to Benjamin, but he did have a few moments before the brothers left for the rooms he had provided for them. "I am looking forward to meeting all of your families but especially yours, Benjamin."

"I think you'll like my wife." Benjamin smiled shyly. "She's the sweetest woman I ever met."

"What a fine thing to say!" Joseph exclaimed.

"It's true. You have a fine wife, but mine's even finer, I think."

"A man should say that. And what about your children? Tell me some more about them." They had talked about Benjamin's children before, but the subject fascinated Joseph. In the back of his mind he still pictured Benjamin as a small boy with black hair like a helmet as it clung to his round head. He could not imagine that boy having children. "I'm looking forward, brother, to having you here close by me in this country. It would be like a dream. I've missed you more than I can ever say."

"I cried myself to sleep every night for weeks after you disappeared, Joseph," Benjamin said, and indeed there were tears in his eyes now. He had been emotional from a young age, and Joseph loved him for it. "But I fear it will never be."

"You speak of our father and his ties to the land."

"Yes. I love my father, but he's very stubborn."

"Yes, he is. But somehow we will have to convince him. This famine will go on for a long time, and he can't keep sending you here to buy food. You would wear out the animals."

"I would love to come here. My father hates Egypt, but I don't."

"It has its charms," Joseph said, "but it has its dangers also."

"I haven't seen any of those."

"I live in the midst of idolaters, Benjamin. So would you if you came here. Egypt has thousands of gods. Every town can make its own god and build a little temple for it. It might be made of mud, but they will bow down and worship it. It breaks your heart."

"But we're surrounded by idolaters where we are also. I don't think any of our neighbors believe in El Shaddai."

"Some of them may believe but not know His name. I've always felt that. If God spoke to Abraham, what would prevent Him from speaking to other people?"

Joseph had provided special lodging for his brothers, and as they left, he greeted each one of them personally, looking into their eyes and smiling. He saw that they were all still conscious of the wrong they had done him, and after they left he spoke to Asenath about this. "They all feel terribly guilty, wife. I saw it in their eyes."

"They should feel guilty."

"No, they shouldn't. I've forgiven them, and that's all there is to it."

"You think things like that can be wiped out in an instant!" Asenath exclaimed. "I grieved for years over the way I treated you the first time I saw you."

"Yes, you did," Joseph said. He put his arm around her and drew her close. Smiling down at her, he murmured, "And I told you it was foolish."

Asenath reached up and put her hand on Joseph's cheek and left it there. "You are different from any man I have ever known, or any woman, for that matter."

"Well, I hope I'm different from the women." Joseph winked.

"Don't be foolish!" she laughed shortly. "Everybody I know holds a grudge against someone, but you never seem to notice when people hurt you."

"I'm sure you're wrong about that, but I've had to struggle with it, Asenath. It just does no good to hold a grudge. Who do you hurt? Not the one you hold the grudge against. He probably doesn't even know it. You hurt yourself."

Asenath sighed and put her cheek against his chest. She had her arms around him, and he held her tightly. "I love you, husband. You're a good man."

"I'm glad you think so, but I still wish my brothers would forget about the past."

The next morning Joseph singled out Judah and took him for a drive around the countryside. He intended to do this with each of his brothers to have some time alone with them, but especially with Judah. Judah was interested in everything, but there was an innate gloom in him that was only interrupted briefly by slight smiles. Finally they came to stand beside some herds that belonged to Pharaoh, and Joseph pointed out that to the Egyptians, shepherds were an abomination.

"That doesn't bode well for us," Judah said, shaking his head.

"On the contrary, it may be a good thing."

"How is that?"

"I have a plan. I'll tell you about it later."

The two walked around the herds for a time, and when Judah did not speak of his personal affairs, Joseph said, "I am sorry about the death of your two sons, Judah."

Judah struggled for words and then said quietly, "They were not good men, either of them." He looked up and said, "I assume that you have heard about my sons by my daughter-in-law."

Joseph was suddenly uncomfortable. He had heard it from Reuben. Reuben had not volunteered the information, but Joseph, having heard part of the story, wanted to know it all, and now he said, "We all make mistakes."

"This was more than a *mistake*," Judah said. "It was wrong, a sinful thing, and I will never cease to be ashamed of it."

"But what about the two boys that Tamar bore you?"

Judah looked up, and a odd expression crossed his face. "That's a strange thing, brother. I love those two boys more than I loved my sons by my wife. Of course I can't understand it."

"I have heard that Tamar is very attached to our father."

"She is very much. From the time she came to us, she absorbed the stories of our family, and she cannot hear enough about Shiloh, who is to come."

The two walked along, and Joseph finally put his hand on Judah's shoulder. Judah had always been a handsome man, and he had grown even more so as he had gotten older. There was a majestic aspect to him with his leonine head and eyes that were less afflicted with the redness of Leah's other sons. His eyes were a strange, smoky gray color and seemed to have a depth behind them. Joseph studied him and said, "Judah, there are only three things you can do about something in your life that was wrong."

"What three things?"

"You can repent, and I know you have done that. You can do every-thing possible to make it right, and from what I hear you have taken care of Tamar, though not as a wife, and you have provided for those boys in a very real way."

Joseph paused, and Judah said, "And what's the third thing?"

"Don't grieve over it."

"How can I not?"

"I can't tell you that. You know I had the same problem."

Judah was shocked. "What did you ever do? Was it a sin with a woman?"

"No! It was a sin against my brothers." Joseph saw surprise wash across Judah's face, and he said, "I wronged you, Judah, you and the others, all except Benjamin. I carried stories of you to my father. I was nothing but a talebearer."

Judah knew this was true, but he was surprised to hear Joseph say it. "You feel it that deeply?"

"I felt it when I was in the pit and thought I was going to die. I saw then what an abominable thing it was to carry tales to my father about my brothers. I repented of it in that pit, and now," he said, "I'm going to try to make it right with you. And then I'm going to forget it. Let me urge you, brother, don't grieve over this business. You have two fine sons. Throw yourself into helping them. Be all the help you can to Tamar and her children, and God will bless you for it."

Judah's eyes brightened, and he swallowed hard. "Brother, if I could do that ... if you could help me ..."

"Who knows?" Joseph smiled. "It didn't seem that there was any meaning to my experience, but looking back I see that there is. Who knows, Judah, God may have some great thing to do with one of those two boys. You hang on to that."

"I will," Judah said. He stood straighter and took a deep breath. "I feel ... I feel that a load's been lifted."

"That's what brothers are for—to lift loads. Come. Let's go back and see what the others are doing."

The brothers stayed two more weeks, but finally it was time for them to go back to Canaan. Their departure was instigated by the pharaoh himself. He called Joseph into his presence and inquired into the minute details of their reunion, and then he said, "I want to be generous to my friend Joseph, the Provider. Do this, then. Send your brothers back to the land of Canaan and have them bring your father and everything they own back to Egypt. I will give them the good of the land of Egypt."

"You are most generous, Your Majesty."

"Not at all. Now, have them take wagons back with them to transport their little ones, their wives, and their father. Tell them not to bother bringing much back with them, for all their needs will be provided when they get here. See to it at once."

───────

The pharaoh's command was exactly what Joseph was hoping for. He immediately called his brothers together to give them the message. "I will have the wagons ready. You will take them almost empty, for there's no need to take a great deal of food this time. Only enough to make the return journey."

Judah said doubtfully, "But our father ... I am not sure he will come."

"You must persuade him, Judah. All of you must persuade him."

Reuben was troubled. "We will do our best, brother."

"That is all a man can do." Joseph smiled. "You will leave tomorrow at first light."

───────

The next morning the caravan was ready by dawn. Joseph embraced each of his brothers, but he held on to Benjamin a little longer and whispered, "You can do more than anyone to convince our father, Benjamin."

"I? What can I do?"

"You are the son of the True Wife. Tell him about me. Tell him about my children and my family here. Be gentle with him, and I believe all will be well."

The wagons pulled out at once, each of the brothers driving one. They all looked back and saw Joseph and his family watching them. Indeed, Joseph kept his eyes on them until they were out of sight. Then he turned and said to Asenath, "I think all will be well. God is in it."

CHAPTER
34

Jacob sat in the shade of a tree staring toward the southern entrance to the valley. The sheep were white dots that moved slowly across the pasture, but he paid little heed to them. Overhead, not too far off, three vultures were making their deadly circle, spiraling down toward the earth, eying some gruesome feast. The sight depressed him, and brushing a pesky fly away from his face, he leaned his head back against the tree. A voice roused him, and he looked up to see Tamar bringing him a cup.

"Master, you must be thirsty. Please have some of this wine."

"That would be very good, Tamar." Jacob took the cup, sipped it, and licked his lips, staring down into the purple surface of the wine. "They have been gone a long time, it seems," he murmured.

Tamar moved closer and knelt down before him as was her custom. "It's a long journey, and the heat is very bad."

"I suppose you're right."

Tamar studied Jacob critically. The old man had lost so much weight his robe hung on him, and his hands seemed shrunken. His eyes were set deep in their sockets, and the vertical lines around his lips were much more pronounced.

"I wish you would not grieve so much," Tamar said. "All will be well."

Jacob smiled faintly. "You are always a comfort, Tamar. You have great faith that things are going to work out well." He sighed and shook his head. "I hope you always feel that way."

"Master, only think of how El Shaddai has worked in your life and in the life of your father and grandfather."

Jacob watched Tamar as she sat down beside him. Despite the lack of food, she was still a strongly built woman and attractive in her own way. She had turned down several husbands since her sons had been born, and he wanted to ask her about it but somehow felt strangely inhibited. She had been a comfort to him in many ways, not just physically but spiritually—in a way he could not quite understand. She had seemed content with life since the birth of her sons, throwing herself into their upbringing and devoting much time to caring for Jacob as well. "I think they will be home very soon. El Shaddai has surely watched over them."

"I worry about Benjamin."

Tamar touched his hand lightly. "He will be fine, master. Do not worry." A thought passed through her mind, and she looked off in the distance where her boys were playing and said, "Why don't you tell the boys some more stories about the family? It will occupy you, and they love it. Especially Perez."

"All right. I will," Jacob said and smiled. "You always find a way to divert me. Go get the boys."

———

Even as Jacob began telling Tamar's two sons the stories of his youth, the caravan of wagons was drawing nearer to Hebron. They had brought plenty of feed for the animals and had stopped at the now familiar wells and water holes along the route. They had hurried as much they could by day, but the nights had seemed long. All of them had two things on their mind: How would they tell their father that Joseph was alive? And how could they convince him to go to Egypt? All of them were convinced that this was the thing to do.

On the last night of their journey, they had sat around the fire and discussed ways to tell their father the good news. Levi had begun the conversation by saying, "I can't imagine any way to break the news to him. Good news can be more unsettling to an old man than bad news."

"I've thought about that." Simeon nodded. He was sitting close to Levi, their faces illuminated by the fire. "I think maybe the best way is to come right out with it. Just tell him."

"No," Reuben objected at once. "The shock would be fatal. We've got to figure out another way."

Judah sat and listened as the brothers argued back and forth. He had changed since having his talk with Joseph. There was more life in him, and he seemed to have lost the deep-seated gloom that was never far beneath the surface of his personality.

Finally, when silence fell across the group, he said, "I agree that it's going to be a difficult thing. If we don't do it exactly right, it could go very badly with our father." He poked at the fire with a stick and then shook his head. "A man doesn't take hold of a joy straight off when he's been in sorrow for so many years. It's brought a great bitterness into our father's life, and I fear some of it has been directed toward us."

"You are right about that," Asher said. He had grown fatter with the good food they had enjoyed in Egypt and even now was eating honey-soaked raisins. He popped them into his mouth, chewed on them, sucked the goodness out of them, and finally said, "I don't think all of us can rush in. That would be too much."

"No," Gad said, brushing back his black hair, which hung down in his eyes. He was, perhaps, the most honest and forthright of the Sons of the Maids, and he had thought deeply about this. "One of us must tell him, but not I. I was never able to speak well."

Issachar spoke up at once. "I think it should be you, Reuben. After all, you're the firstborn."

"I don't speak well either," Reuben mumbled. He did not say that the relationship between him and Jacob was any worse than that of the other brothers. They all knew that. He turned suddenly and said, "Judah, it must be you."

"Yes, it must be you!" Dan yelped. He had a wild, headlong nature and fixed upon the idea at once. "The way you stood up to Joseph when we thought he was our enemy was wonderful. You're getting to be quite an orator."

Judah blinked in surprise. "No, I don't think I could do it."

"I really think you must," Issachar said. "You can do it better than any of the rest of us."

The argument went on for some time, and finally in desperation Judah said, "I will do it, if I have to, but we must all agree to say absolutely nothing to anyone about Joseph being alive until Father knows, not even to our families. You know how gossip travels among our people. We must think much more about this. Since I was the one who pledged my own life, I will greet him initially, but then we will just have to see."

A murmur of agreement went around the circle, and then they went to bed. Judah lay back, staring at the stars from the bed he had made in his wagon. They glittered and sparkled, and he saw a sudden line of silver trace itself across the sky—a falling star. He watched it until it disappeared, then sighed and rolled over and tried to sleep.

"They're here! They've come back!" Jacob had been dozing, and he was startled awake. He got up, reached for his staff, and hobbled out of his tent. Many of the family were already there, talking excitedly, and he heard Leah say, "Look, Bilhah, wagons! They've come back in wagons!"

Bilhah was staring wildly at the caravan from which rose columns of dust high into the air. "So many of them. Look."

Zilpah was standing beside the other concubine. "There's a wagon for each of them," she said. "I wonder if they're full of food."

The wives and the children could wait no longer. They ran forward to meet the returning husbands and fathers. Jacob stood still, with Tamar beside him. "You see," she said, smiling at him. "I told you it would be all right."

"Yes, you were right, but what are all these wagons for? I hope they're full of food."

But as the wagons drew closer, Jacob saw that they were not heavily loaded. The animals, fine healthy ones that he had never seen before, were pulling them easily across the ground. Jacob stood there waiting until the brothers drew the wagons up at the edge of camp. His sons all dismounted and were surrounded by their wives and children. Jacob did not move until Judah finally separated himself from Tamar's boys, who were clinging to him. He came straight over to Jacob and said, "Father, we are back."

"So I see, but not in a way that I expected."

"Eleven wagons," Tamar said. "What's in them, Judah?"

"There's some food in there," Judah replied. "I'll tell you more about the wagons later. You look thin, Father. You've lost weight."

"I'm fine now that you're back." His eyes lit up when he saw Benjamin, who was hugging his children and laughing, his white teeth flashing against his dark complexion. "You've brought my son back."

"Yes, we're all back." Judah was holding Perez and Zerah, and the boys were pulling at him, asking question after question.

"Let your father alone," Tamar said. "Here, Judah, let me have them."

"No, I'll hold them," Judah said. "They look fine." He looked at her and smiled. "You look fine also. You've taken good care of everyone."

It was the kindest remark he had ever made to Tamar, and she flushed slightly. "They are easy boys to care for. Now, I must go get started helping with the food. We'll have a feast tonight."

"We brought many special things back from Egypt, so it will be a real feast."

"And you'll tell us all about your journey?" she asked.

"Yes, I will."

The rest of Jacob's sons began to gather, and Judah stood off to one side, holding his two boys, one in each arm. "Were you good boys when I was gone?"

"No," said Perez, "I was very naughty."

Judah laughed. "Than I will have to punish you. What about you, Zerah?"

"I was a very good boy. I always am."

"Well, I'll punish you later, Perez. In the meantime, I've got gifts for both of you. Come along. We'll find them."

Judah and Jacob found time to talk before the feast began. The old man had sent for him, and the two sat down a distance off, watching the women as they cooked. There was much laughing and singing, and Jacob said, "I haven't seen our people so happy in a long time." He turned then and said, "Tell me about your journey. I want to hear it."

Judah had planned his speech well. He knew he must not tell too much, and yet he had to somehow prepare his father for the news that Joseph was alive. He began to tell him about Joseph as ruler but always called him simply the Provider. He told about their welcome but left out the unpleasant part about the silver cup for the moment. Jacob listened intently, and finally he began to ask questions about the man who was second to Pharaoh. "He is not an Egyptian?"

"No, he is not," Judah said.

"That is strange that the pharaoh would not choose one of his own people to be in such a responsible position."

"The man has a marvelous story," Judah said carefully.

"I would like to hear it."

"Well, you will a little later, but it's almost time for the feast now."

Jacob sat very still, then looked up and smiled at Judah. "You did well, my son. I'm proud of you."

Judah was touched. His father was not given to compliments, and he knew that the door was open to at least begin the campaign of persuasion. "We have a surprise for you, my brothers and I, but it must wait till tomorrow."

Jacob laughed. "You play games with me, but I tell you, it cannot be better news than that you have all come back safely."

Judah shook his head and smiled. "When you sleep tonight, do me a favor. Think of the most wonderful thing in all the world."

"I cannot think of anything better than having you all back, but I will try."

Judah waited until after the feast was over, and then he called all his brothers together and told them what had happened.

"We will have to tell him right away. We can't let this thing go on," Reuben said with a worried look.

"I know," Judah replied. He took a deep breath and looked around at the brothers. "Are you certain that I should be the one to tell him?" He saw them all nod, and then shook his own head. "I do not feel capable."

"I will tell our father."

Everyone twisted around to stare at Benjamin. Being the youngest, he had never once, as far as any of them could remember, attempted to make a decision that involved all of them. But now there was a strength and a calmness in his features. His eyes were steady as he met their glances, and he said, "Joseph and I talked this over before we left Egypt. It was his feeling that I should be the one to tell Father."

"That is an excellent idea!" Judah cried at once, relieved to be freed from the burden. "You are his favorite son."

"Yes, and besides that," Dan said, "you have a gentleness about you that the rest of us lack. I think you are exactly right."

The rest of the brothers all agreed, and Benjamin left to go home to his family. As they watched him go, Judah said, "I pray that it will not be too much for Father. I do not see how even Benjamin can break this to him in a way that will not do him some harm by the shock of it."

"We must have faith in our younger brother," Reuben said. "Come now. Let's all go to bed."

Jacob found Benjamin waiting for him immediately after his breakfast. He had slept well, and now he embraced his youngest son heartily. "It is so good to see you back, my son."

"You see? All your fears were for nothing. The things that we worry the most about sometimes don't happen."

"Sit down, my son. Judah has told me some of what occurred, but I want to hear more."

"First I want us to pray together, Father."

Jacob stared at Benjamin in surprise. "It is always a good idea, my son, but about what?"

"I want us to pray for you—that you will not be overcome."

"Overcome by what?"

"By the good news we bring and the future that lies ahead of us."

"Good new concerning you and your brothers?"

"It concerns all of us, but mostly you. Come, let us pray."

Jacob bowed his head and listened as his youngest son prayed a beautiful prayer. It was short but filled with joy, such joy that Jacob could not understand it. When Benjamin was finished, Jacob lifted his head, and his eyes glistened with tears. "That was a fine prayer, my son."

"Good. Then I know that El Shaddai will not allow you to be overcome."

"I was not overcome by the angel when I wrestled with him."

"But you are older now," Benjamin said with a smile, "and good news can be very overwhelming."

Jacob sobered and stared at him. "Does this have anything to do with what Judah mentioned last night?"

"What did he say?"

"He only said that you all had a surprise for me, but he wouldn't tell me what it was."

"That's right. Now, take my hands and be very calm."

Bewildered, Jacob reached out his hands, and Benjamin, who knelt before him, took them firmly in his. "What would be the one thing you would rather have in all the world if you could have a wish?" Benjamin asked.

Jacob stared at him. "Well, I would like for my family to be safe and well."

"That is a good wish, and it is part of the very good news that we have brought back from Egypt."

"I would not have thought anything good could come from Egypt."

"You will have to rearrange your thinking about Egypt, Father. But for now, I want you to think of something that you would love to be true but that you think is impossible."

Jacob was very puzzled. He thought hard and made several false starts; then he shrugged. "Well, of course, my first wish would be that we had your brother back again, but that can never be."

"We're very close now," Benjamin said. "Keep that in your mind. The thing you would like most if you could would be to have your son Joseph back. Now, suppose a stranger came in here, Father, and said, 'I am going to give you your son Joseph back to you alive.'"

"Only God could do that. Why are you saying these things to me? It disturbs me greatly. I don't like to talk about them."

"Father," Benjamin said, holding the old man's hands tightly, "I have to tell you plainly now." He hesitated and saw that Jacob's eyes were fixed upon him and said, "Your son Joseph did not die as we thought. He was not slain by an animal."

Jacob started and began to tremble, then swayed back and forth.

Benjamin grabbed him and said, "You must be strong, Father. Just breathe deeply and listen. Sometimes good news is hard to take. You have met with God and endured, and now you must endure the good news. The best news that you could possibly imagine."

Jacob's lips trembled, and his eyes were wide. He was breathing hard, and he whispered hoarsely, "Benjamin . . . is Joseph . . . is Joseph truly alive?"

"He is alive, Father. He did not die all those years ago."

Jacob closed his eyes, and Benjamin changed positions. He moved to his father's side and put his arm around his shoulders, supporting him. "This is something that God has done, and you must accept it as such."

"He is alive and you saw him in Egypt?"

"We could not help but see him, Father. Your son Joseph is the one whom they call the Great Provider. He is second in Egypt only to Pharaoh."

"How can this be?" Jacob whispered.

"It could be because God has done it. El Shaddai used a terrible way to send Joseph to Egypt. You will hear all about it. But there he rose to power, and now he wants to see you."

Jacob began to weep, and Benjamin held the old man for a long time. Finally, to his relief, Jacob took a deep breath. He wiped the tears from his eyes with his sleeve and said almost fiercely, "I will see my son. Now tell me everything, Benjamin!"

CHAPTER
35

Benjamin was ecstatic as the brothers gathered, and he explained what had happened. "I told him everything! I told him that Joseph was alive, and he is well!" he exclaimed.

Judah gave an exultant cry. "Wonderful—wonderful! I'm proud of you, brother. You've done well."

"However did you do it?" Reuben asked, shaking his head in wonder.

"I think God was with me. Father is so excited now, and he wants to see us all."

"Did you tell him everything?" Dan asked, a worried tone in his voice.

"No. I didn't tell him about the cup in my sack. I left that out, but I told him everything else."

"Did you tell him about the pharaoh's insistence we move to Egypt?" Simeon demanded.

"No, I didn't tell him that either. I was so worried about telling him the really big news, I didn't mention the other yet. But I suppose we need to tell him soon."

"It ought to be easier to break that to him now," Simeon said, nodding. "He'll be anxious to see Joseph."

"Yes, he will," Judah agreed. "I'm certainly ready to leave this land with its endless heat and drought. Those green fields along the Nile look mighty good, and the pharaoh promised we could put our flocks in the rich land of Goshen. Surely Father can see the wisdom in that."

"There's only one way to find out," Benjamin said cheerfully. "Let's go meet with him."

The brothers went to their father's tent to talk with him. Judah was glad to see that Jacob looked much better than when they first arrived. He was standing straight, and there was a glow in his eyes as he greeted them all. "Come in, my sons. I want to hear more about this wonderful news!"

"It would take a long time to tell it all, Father," Judah said. "It's still hard to believe."

They sat for a time, each sharing their thoughts, and finally Benjamin looked around and saw that his brothers were all watching him. He knew they were expecting him to bring up the subject of the move to Egypt.

"Father," he said, "there's one more thing. One more bit of good news. Do you think you can take it?"

Jacob laughed heartily. "I can always take good news, but it could not be as good as that which you have already given me."

"No, nothing could be better than that, but Joseph and the pharaoh have issued an invitation."

"An invitation? To whom?"

"To you and to all of us and our families."

Jacob blinked with surprise. "An invitation to visit?"

"No, it's even better than that," Benjamin said with excitement. "You have seen our flocks and herds dying off, and this drought seems to be getting worse. Another year and we'll have nothing left."

"I fear that's true," Jacob said sadly.

"Yes, it is true, Father," Benjamin said. "But the pharaoh has made us a wonderful offer. Tell him about it, Judah."

Judah was surprised, but he had seen more of the fields of Goshen than any of the others. He began to tell his father about the richness of the land of Goshen, then said, "The pharaoh wants us to come live there."

"You mean ... permanently?"

"The ground is rich there," Judah explained, "and the Egyptians don't care for shepherds. They'll be happy to have us take care of the pharaoh's flocks while we raise our own. Joseph's talked to me about it."

"But this will mean leaving our home for good."

"Yes, it will. There's no denying that," Reuben put in. "But think of the advantages. We're going to starve if we stay here. There we'll have good ground, and we can increase our flocks."

"I hate to think of leaving my home. It's where my people are buried. *Our* people, I should say."

"We can always come back when the drought is over," Dan said eagerly. "It's a marvelous opportunity."

But Jacob was hard to convince, as they had all known he would be. After a long argument Benjamin finally found the key.

"You haven't thought of the best thing in of all this, Father."

"What's that, my son?"

"If we lived in the land of Goshen, you could see Joseph anytime you wanted to. You could see his children and meet his wife. We would all be together, all twelve of us, a family again, and you know how wonderful it would be to have Joseph with us!"

Something changed in Jacob's face, and Benjamin instantly pursued his advantage. "I think God has put Joseph there as *our* provider, not just for the Egyptians."

A silence reined over the group, and Jacob said, "I will have to think about it."

"Of course you will," Benjamin said at once. "There's no hurry."

Actually, there was a need to hurry, for Joseph had urged them to move quickly, but the brothers waited for several days, allowing Jacob to mull over the idea. He was obviously troubled, and none of them dared mention it to him.

"We can't pressure him," Reuben muttered. "He'll have to make up his own mind."

It was Tamar who applied the final pressure. When she saw that he was resisting what seemed to her the wise thing to do, she came to him late one afternoon and sat with him for a long time. She began to talk about his family and how they needed his help. "You've always been able to provide for them," she said.

"Well, I hope so. That's what I'm most interested in, of course."

"Well, I know that you don't like the idea of moving to Egypt, but we can keep our people apart from the Egyptians, just as we have kept apart from the Hittites and other idolaters around here. And we can always come back," she argued skillfully. Slowly she saw the old man begin to change his mind, and she ended up with Benjamin's argument. "I'm so anxious to meet Joseph. I've never met him, you know, and he seems like such a dear man."

"You would love him, Tamar. Everybody did." This was not precisely true, but in Jacob's memory it seemed to have been that way.

From that moment on Jacob began to speak about the journey,

asking how long it would take, and interrogating Judah about the fields and the grazing for the flocks. They were all careful not to get too excited, at least in front of him, but Judah summed it up when he said, "I think it's going to be all right. He's going to make the sacrifice."

Two days after Judah pronounced this, Jacob called his sons together and smiled at them. "Well, you're going to have your way. We will go to Egypt."

Cries of joy went up from the brothers, and they all rushed to press into their father and tell him how wonderful it was going to be. He put his hands up and said, "Egypt will be for us what we make it. If we join in with the Egyptians and their awful idolatry, we will not survive. But we will be together, and all twelve of my sons will be alive."

"It won't take long to get ready to leave," Judah said eagerly.

"I must visit the family grave first, for I may never see it again."

"I will take you there myself," Judah said softly. "We will go tomorrow."

The journey to Egypt began in the spring when all of their affairs were wound up. The long caravan left from Hebron, heading toward Beersheba. This was where Jacob and his father were born and where Rebekah had once obtained the birthright for Jacob by devious means.

They made an impressive sight as they moved along with their flocks and possessions and all the family members, young and old. There were at least seventy of Jacob's own family, but in addition there were shepherds, drovers, drivers, baggage men, and slaves, making over a hundred people in all. The train was like a noisy, slow-moving caterpillar, enveloped by clouds of dust raised by the flocks and the herds.

The members made the journey any way they could, some of them walking, some in the wagons, some of them riding. In addition to the wagons, there were two-wheeled oxcarts, which carried not only household goods but some of the women and children as well. The people themselves made a colorful sight in their woven garments dyed in various hues. The women had black braids hanging over their shoulders and wore silver and bronze bracelets on their wrists. Their foreheads were hung with headbands of gold coins, and their nails were reddened with henna.

Along the way they feasted on the rich foods the brothers had brought back from Egypt—roasted onions, sour bread and olives, honey-covered dates, and dried meats. They ate so well on their journey that by the time they reached Egypt, they were much healthier than when had they left.

They took the ridge road going down from the heights of Hebron to the deeper southland of the Negev. Jacob led the procession in the first wagon, staying well in front of the dust raised by the flocks. He made a dignified sight. The fine wool of his head-covering was fringed unevenly across his forehead and lay about his neck and shoulders, falling softly on his dark red tunic, which he wore open in the front to reveal the medallion he always wore on top of his embroidered undergarment. The breezes touched the strands of silver beads he also wore around his neck, and his eyes studied the land as they went.

Each night they stopped in plenty of time to set up a comfortable camp. This journey would not be completed as quickly as when the brothers had traveled, because Jacob's comfort was now their chief concern, along with the needs of the women and children.

Each afternoon the women prepared a feast, and at night before the blazing campfires, the people sang and danced.

When they were midway to their destination, Jacob sat with Tamar and her two boys. Benjamin had joined them, and he and his father had been talking for some time.

Finally Benjamin said, "You're not sorry about this, are you, Father?"

Jacob, the patriarch, looked at his youngest son. "No, I'm not. I feel almost young again at the thought of seeing the beloved child of my True Wife after all these years. It is God's miracle. I just regret that it takes so long to get there."

Tamar stroked Perez's hair as he lay beside her deep in sleep. Zerah was also asleep with his head in her lap. Her eyes were dreamy as she said, "El Shaddai is working things out in His own way. One day out of this little band of people, Shiloh will come."

Jacob smiled at her, reached out, and touched Perez's hair. "Yes, we must wait patiently until that great day comes," he agreed.

Benjamin looked at the old man and thought ahead to the time when Joseph and he would meet. *That will be the greatest thing of all, and God has done it.*

Tamar saw that the old man was tired, and she hustled him off to bed like a mother putting her child to sleep.

Jacob awoke suddenly in the middle of the night. Seeing that the others were still asleep, he rose quietly and walked away from the camp into the darkness to look at the night sky. Something was unusual about this awakening. As he stared in wonder at the majesty of the starry sky, he had the strangest feeling that someone was watching him, but he knew that could not be.

They had camped that night at Beersheba, the very place that his grandfather Abraham had settled after God had rescued Isaac from being sacrificed. Jacob felt a strong connection to this place and sensed an urgency to offer a sacrifice here to God, thanking Him for His wonderful protection and provision for him and his entire family.

He gathered stones for an altar and wood for a fire. So as not to wake the others, he crept back into camp and quietly gathered a young lamb and a knife for the sacrifice, and made a torch to carry fire to the altar.

With tears of joy, he offered his lamb to the God of his fathers and lit the fire to consume the unblemished animal in thankfulness for God's great goodness.

And then he heard his name. He turned suddenly in all directions but saw no one.

The voice spoke again: *"Jacob! Jacob!"*

And then Jacob knew. *It is the Lord!* he thought. Great joy flooded his soul, and he felt like the young man he had been when he had seen the ladder going all the way up to heaven. *Here I am, Lord,* he whispered in his spirit.

The voice spoke again, strong but gentle, seeming to be nowhere but everywhere. *"I am God, the God of your father. Do not be afraid to go down to Egypt, for I will make you into a great nation there. I will go down to Egypt with you, and I will surely bring you back again. And Joseph's own hand will close your eyes."*

The voice faded, and Joseph fell to the ground and wept, calling out, "Thank you, Almighty One. Mighty Creator of all things. Thank you for your promise. I will never doubt you again!"

CHAPTER
36

The tribe of Jacob left Beersheba and continued south toward Egypt, following the well-traveled trade route. On the earlier part of their journey from Hebron, they had frequently passed settlements, some of them large and some small. But now as they made their way through the southland, the desert here was virtually empty. They finally reached the border of Egypt, coming first to a fortress where strangers were stopped and interrogated. Jacob called Judah to him and said, "Son, go before us. Find your brother Joseph and tell him that we have arrived."

Judah nodded eagerly. "I am sure he will come at once to see you, for he longs for that more than for anything else in the world."

Judah quickly mounted the swiftest of the beasts and rode at full speed until he reached the palace in the capital. He got off the animal and was stopped at the front gate by a guard, but when Judah identified himself and the guard had gone back inside, it was Rashidi who came out smiling.

"Well, my friend," he said. "You are back. The Provider will be happy."

"Can I see him, sir?"

"Certainly. Come in. He has been waiting anxiously for your return."

Judah followed Rashidi into the building, and when they went into the room where Joseph conducted most of his affairs, he found his brother smiling and happy indeed to greet him. When he came forward, Judah dropped to his knees, but Joseph took his arm and lifted him up. "We'll have none of that!" He embraced his brother and said, "I trust you had a safe journey. Where is the caravan?"

"It is at the border. Our father requests that you come and see him."

"I will go at once. Come—you shall be my guide."

The spot where Jacob waited was not close to the guard house, but a short distance away at a small oasis. The caravan had come to a halt, and they had unhitched the animals, allowing them to drink, but no one unpacked anything. Children were playing and shouting, and women were sitting in groups, caring for the younger ones and speaking among themselves.

Jacob was seated in the shade of a cluster of palm trees beside a small pool. His sons surrounded him, and for a while the old man half closed his eyes, enjoying the hum of their voices. From where he sat he could see white ibises, which fascinated him, but time and again his eyes went back to the road where they expected Joseph and Judah to appear.

Benjamin sat close to his father and said little. He was studying his father's face and wondering what was going on in his mind. Finally he asked, "Are you anxious, Father?"

Jacob turned and faced his youngest son. "I feel as if I am in a dream," he said in a soft voice. "All the years I thought my son was gone forever, and now to see him—it's more than I can take in."

"He's changed, of course. I had remembered Joseph the way we last saw in Hebron, seventeen years old and slender with a fresh, glowing face."

"He is changed much, my son?"

"As a man should, he has grown up. But you will know him. He is the same Joseph, although taller and heavier than we remember him." He looked up and squinted into the distance. He did not speak for a moment, then jumped up and shouted, "It's him! It's Joseph!"

All the brothers rose to their feet and began looking at the road. A cloud of dust was coming, and as Jacob got painfully to his feet, he watched until he saw the glittering and flashing of the sun on metal. The chariot that bore the two men was pulled by two magnificent black horses. There were runners in front and Egyptian soldiers in the rear carrying long spears. As Jacob shaded his eyes, he said, "Is it my son, Benjamin? Is that Joseph?"

Benjamin put his arm around his father to support him. "Yes, Father, it is Joseph."

Jacob watched as the tall, broad-shouldered man got out of the basket of the chariot, wearing beautifully colored clothes, a heavy gold chain around his neck, flashing in the sunlight.

"I will go to meet him," Jacob said.

Jacob moved forward, his vision focusing on the son he had given up to the grave so many years earlier. He forgot his limp and forgot his age, and everything around him seemed to blur and disappear except for the sight of that face he had dreamed of and mourned over for so many years. He saw the clear eyes, the smooth face of a mature man accustomed to command, and as he moved forward, he saw the smiling lips form the words, "Father."

As Joseph came close, he opened his arms, and Jacob moved forward, his arms extended. As the two men clung to each other, all of the brothers stood back. It was a scene in which none of them had any part. Benjamin watched as Joseph, towering over his father, enfolded him in his arms, but then he saw Joseph look down into the face of his father with tears in his eyes.

Jacob reached up and put his hand tentatively on Joseph's cheeks. He was looking into his face as if searching for something long lost. At first he saw an Egyptian face, but then as tears filled the big man's eyes, he realized—they were Rachel's eyes! Yes, they were the eyes of his beloved, his True Wife, long buried beside the road but here again in the eyes of the big man who held him. Jacob's own eyes filled with tears, and he let his head fall on the shoulder of his long-lost son, and he wept, his body quivering.

As for Joseph, it was not surprising that his own tears flowed. He had lived through terrible things, but always in the back of his mind or hidden deep in his heart was the hope that one day he would hold his aged father in his arms. The memories flowed back and forth through his mind, and suddenly, still clinging to Joseph, Jacob lifted his head. "You are my son. I see you again after all the years of sorrow."

"We will put those years behind us, Father," Joseph whispered. "Now we have found each other. We will never again be separated."

"It is the great and almighty El Shaddai who has done this," Jacob whispered. He touched Joseph's face again and said, "It is almost as if I were seeing my beloved Rachel again. I see her in Benjamin too, but more so in your dear face."

As the two stood there for a moment longer, Joseph realized that Jacob was trembling with either emotion or fatigue. "Come, let us sit down," he said to his father, pointing in the direction of the shady spot by the pool.

"No," Jacob said, standing away. "Let me first look at you." His eyes took in Joseph's green-striped costume, his yellow headdress with its gleaming ornaments, the costly gold chain, and finally the gold buckles on his sandals. "Joseph," he said, "I have always feared the land of Egypt, and I fear it now."

"Why do you fear it, my father?" Joseph said quietly. "I have brought you here for nothing but good."

"I am afraid of the world outside of El Shaddai."

"But El Shaddai owns the whole world. He made everything!" Joseph smiled. "I know what you fear—the idols of Egypt, the sins of the people—but it need not be that way with us."

"I will depend on you, my son, to keep our people pure, as I am sure that you have kept yourself."

"We will do that together. Come now. It has been a long journey, and I have prepared a place for you."

Joseph looked up and led his father back to where his brothers were waiting and greeted them with great joy. "You have done a marvelous thing! Now we will go into the city and have a great feast and rejoice this night."

———————

After the arrival of Jacob and his band to the capital city, the days passed quickly. Joseph spent much time with his father, and the old man seemed to feed on Joseph as a starving man will feed on food. He touched him often, putting both of his hands on Joseph's cheeks, staring into his face and smiling, a smile that came from deep inside his heart.

Joseph settled the entire band in the land of Goshen, the most beautiful pastureland in all of Egypt, and he met with his father and brothers to give them strict instructions as to how they should act when they went before the pharaoh. "We must be wise," he said, looking around the group. His father sat to his right, his eyes filled with pride as Joseph spoke. Joseph turned to him. "I have asked the pharaoh for an audience, and some of you will go with me to see him, including you, of course, Father."

Simeon, who had spent more time in Egypt than the rest, said, "It is a fact, brother, that the Egyptians do not admire shepherds."

"No, they do not, but for what reason I cannot tell. I will put it to Pharaoh that it would be well if he would appoint our tribe as overseers over his own flocks."

"What is he like—this pharaoh?" Judah asked curiously.

"He is a winsome man, and he will welcome my family. I will take you, Judah, and you, Benjamin." His eyes went over the rest of his brothers, and he chose Reuben and Zebulun to go as well.

Jacob sat and listened as Joseph gave instructions, and finally he said, "You have told him about our God?"

"He is very interested in God. Yes, I have told him everything, Father. He is a charming man, as charming as one can be with all that power."

"Power usually corrupts a man," Jacob said, "but it has not in this case, I suppose."

"Not as much as usual," Joseph said with a smile. "Come, now. We will go in three days."

———

Pharaoh looked down at the brothers and father of Joseph from his throne and smiled. "I welcome you to Egypt, family of Joseph."

The sons bowed low, and Jacob bowed as much as his aged back would allow.

Pharaoh studied them carefully. He was surrounded by a ring of palace officials and was adorned in glorious attire. He finally asked, "What is your occupation?"

Judah spoke up. "We are shepherds, Your Majesty. We have been brought up from our youth to tend animals."

Pharaoh turned and declared, "The land of Egypt is before you. Take the very best of the land and make your home now in the rich land of Goshen."

Joseph then nodded to his father, and Jacob moved forward slowly. He stood before the pharaoh, and the two men made a dramatic contrast—Jacob, the man who had spoken to the true God, and the young pharaoh who was so confused about God he could hardly frame his own thoughts.

Joseph watched closely and saw that there was a contest of wills between these two. He knew his own father could be stubborn beyond belief, and the pharaoh was accustomed to having the world bow down to him. But Joseph realized that Pharaoh Abadmon was surprised by Jacob's response. He was accustomed to people being stunned in his presence, and Jacob obviously was not.

Pharaoh finally said, "And how old might you be, father of the Provider?"

"The years of my pilgrimage on this earth," Jacob said strongly, "are a hundred and thirty, sire."

"And you are a servant of God, I am told."

"I serve the almighty God, the supreme One who created all things."

Pharaoh was overwhelmed by this old man, but he could not have said why. He stared at him briefly, searching for an appropriate blessing to confer on him, then finally said, "May your god give you many more years of life."

Jacob studied Pharaoh, then lifted his hand and blessed him in return. He turned and walked away with a sort of majestic formality that left Pharaoh staring after him.

When the brothers had all bowed their way out of the throne room, escorting their father, who simply walked away with his back to the great god-king of Egypt, Pharaoh turned to Joseph and said, "Your father is not like other men."

Joseph bowed slightly. "When a man has wrestled with God face-to-face, he cannot remain unchanged."

"You have told me that story," Pharaoh said with sadness in his eyes. "That old man has seen your god, and I, who long to see this god you speak of more than I long for anything else, cannot find him." He turned quickly and walked away.

Joseph stared after the pharaoh and shook his head. "The most powerful man in the world and yet in some ways the saddest." He hurried out of the throne room to join his father and brothers.

CHAPTER
37

"Have you sent for my son Joseph?" Jacob's voice was thin, and he blinked at the face that hovered over him.

"Yes, master. He will be here soon." Tamar looked down into the aged face of Jacob and asked, "Will you sit up and take nourishment now?"

"Yes, I believe I could eat a little."

Tamar helped Jacob to a sitting position and fed him a little gruel. As the old man ate, his mind seemed to be far back in the past, and once he looked up at Tamar and asked, "Daughter, do you ever think of our home back in Hebron?"

"That was a long time ago—seventeen years," Tamar said. She wiped away some of the gruel that had fallen into Jacob's beard and said, "God has blessed us here in Egypt."

Jacob nodded. "I have been content here, but my heart, now as I approach death, goes back to the place of my birth and of my manhood." He fell silent and sat very still. He had sent for his son Joseph, for he knew the time had come when he must leave this earth. Sitting beside him, Tamar said, "I hear animals approaching." She got up and looked out the window of Jacob's house and came back at once.

"It is Joseph," she said, "and his two sons are with him."

"Yes," Jacob replied. "I told him to bring them."

Tamar stood back as the three men entered the house. Joseph spoke to her pleasantly, and then he went at once to his father's bed. While he spoke to his father, Tamar studied the two sons of Joseph, Ephraim and Manasseh. They were in their twenties now, dressed in the colorful and expensive garments of the court, with gold bands on their arms. Both of them stood back respectfully as Joseph embraced his father.

"Did you bring your two sons?" Jacob asked.

"Yes, they are right here. Are you ill, Father?"

"Not ill. Just old." Something came into Jacob's face, and he asked, "Do you remember the promise you made to me, my son, about after I die?"

"Yes, I remember it well. I am to take you back to the tomb of your fathers."

"Yes, I wish to lie with my fathers. Carry me out of Egypt and bury me with them."

"I will do as you have asked, Father."

The promise seemed to relieve Jacob, and he said, "Bring your sons forward."

Joseph gestured and the two young men approached the bed.

Jacob could no longer see well, but he embraced his grandsons and kissed them. He looked at the two young men and was silent for so long that Ephraim and Manasseh grew nervous. Then Jacob said, "And now these two sons who were born in the land of Egypt are mine just as Reuben and Simeon are mine, and their children shall be called mine." Jacob studied the three men, and tears came into his dim eyes. "I never expected to see your face again, Joseph, and here God has let me see your children also. Blessed be the God of our fathers! Come forward."

Joseph had prepared for this moment. He placed Ephraim toward Jacob's left hand and Manasseh toward Jacob's right hand so that Manasseh, the firstborn, would receive the blessing.

But Jacob suddenly reached out his right hand and laid it on Ephraim's head, and he crossed his arms so that his left hand rested upon Manasseh's head. Then, before Joseph could move, he said to them, "May the God before whom my fathers Abraham and Isaac walked, the God who has been my shepherd all my life to this day, the Angel who has delivered me from all harm—may he bless the boys. May they be called by my name and the names of my fathers Abraham and Isaac, and may they increase greatly upon the earth."

Joseph was disturbed. "Father, this is the firstborn." He put his hand on Manasseh. "Put your right hand on his head."

But Jacob, with his characteristic stubbornness, shook his head. "I know it, my son, I know it. From him shall also come a great people. But his younger brother will be greater, and his children will become a multitude of nations."

Joseph was disappointed, but there was nothing he could do when his father was in a mood like this. He could only accept the old man's blessing as it was given, and then he took his leave.

As soon as the three were gone, Tamar, who had heard all of this, came and saw that Jacob was very tired. "You must lie down, Father," she said. "You must rest."

"Joseph is disappointed, but God is always right. He has chosen Ephraim over Manasseh, the firstborn."

Tamar put the old man to bed and stood staring down into his face. She knew his time on earth was short, and she also knew that before he died, he would call all his sons together, and at last he would identify which of his twelve sons would receive the blessing and through whom would flow the stream that would culminate in Shiloh, the One who would redeem His people. She covered the old man up and turned away, her thoughts deep within her.

———

A month had passed since Jacob had given his blessing to Ephraim and Manasseh, and Judah came one day to see Joseph. "My brother, you must come at once. Father is very ill."

"Are the rest of our brothers there?" Joseph asked.

"Yes, we must hurry. He is slipping away quickly."

Back in Goshen, the rest of their brothers were outside of Jacob's house waiting for the arrival Joseph and Judah. Though his years on the earth were starting to take their toll, Reuben was still a tower of strength. He stood alone, leaning against the wall of the house, and Benjamin caught a glimpse of unhappiness on his older brother's face. He moved forward and said, "It is sad that we are going to lose our father, but such things must be." Benjamin knew that Reuben had never forgotten his bad behavior with Bilhah.

The two were talking when Simeon and Levi came up to them.

"It's a sad day," Simeon said, shaking his head.

Levi said grimly, "It will be even sadder for us in a while."

"What do you mean?" Benjamin asked.

"I mean that I am expecting nothing pleasant to come from our father's last words."

"That is a wrong thing to say," Benjamin protested.

"You do not know him, Benjamin. You have always been one of his favorites, you and Joseph, but the rest of us know how he can speak harshly."

The other brothers murmured their agreement, and Benjamin was shocked to see that most of them believed that Jacob's last words would not be kind. He could not think like that, since he had known only kindness from his father.

Finally Jacob announced, "Look, it is Joseph and Judah."

The two dismounted from the chariot, and Joseph's face was grave. "Is he still alive?"

"Yes," Reuben said heavily. "He is waiting for us."

The brothers went into the house and gathered about Jacob's bed. The sun was setting, and two oil lamps on high stands sent their golden light over the dying man. Beside him, her gray hair covered with a veil, was Tamar with her two sons. Jacob lay propped up on cushions, and his skin was pale, tinged by the glow from the lamps. He wore a white band around his forehead, the one he usually wore when making sacrifices to God, and his gaze went from one son to another as they surrounded his bed. His lips moved, and it was only with great effort that he said, "Gather around so I can tell you what will happen to you in days to come."

The sons took a step closer and looked down on the face of their father as he said, "Reuben!"

Reuben came to the edge of his father's bed and knelt down. "Reuben, you are my firstborn, my might, the first sign of my strength, excelling in honor, excelling in power." Suddenly Jacob's voice changed, and he said, "Turbulent as the waters, you will no longer excel, for you went up onto your father's bed, onto my couch and defiled it."

A shock ran around the group, for he was speaking the truth, but it was a harsh truth that all of them would rather not have heard.

Jacob stared at the tall form of Reuben and said, "The right of the firstborn is taken away from you. You are not worthy of leadership. Your deeds are weak. You are not worthy to receive the blessing of the firstborn, because you have wasted your strength."

Reuben straightened up, and his face was fixed in a stare. There were no tears, for he had expected nothing less.

Joseph, however, felt a sudden compassion for the big man. He'd always had a special affection for him despite his weaknesses, and now he was grieved at the sight of Jacob's firstborn receiving not the blessing but a curse.

"Simeon and Levi, come before me," Jacob commanded. The two came at once, both braced for what they knew their father would say.

"Simeon and Levi are brothers—their swords are weapons of violence. Let me not enter their council, let me not join their assembly, for they have killed men in their anger and hamstrung oxen as they pleased. Cursed be their anger, so fierce, and their fury, so cruel! I will scatter them in Jacob and disperse them in Israel."

Simeon and Levi flinched before the stinging words, which Jacob used like a whip. But they had expected nothing better. Their father had never forgiven them for having avenged the rape of their sister, Dinah, by killing the men of Shechem, and now they moved back and took their place in the back of the crowd.

"Judah," Jacob said, and his voice lifted with a new sense of power.

Judah moved forward. He had been a man of sorrow for many years, and the shame of some of his past deeds still clung to him. He glanced at Tamar and her two sons, the fruit of his sin.

As the crowd remained silent, Judah stood there awaiting the words that would cut to the bone, as they had Reuben, Simeon, and Levi.

But to everyone's shock, Jacob cried out, "Judah—you are the one!" Jacob's eyes were glowing, and his voice exultant. "Yes, Judah, you are the one! Your brothers will praise you; your hand will be on the neck of your enemies; your father's sons will bow down to you!"

Joseph stared at Judah's stunned face. He himself was shocked, for he had somehow expected that he might be the chosen one—or if not him, then Benjamin. It would seem that one of the children of the True Wife would get the blessing of the firstborn, but it was not to be. As he watched, Joseph realized that this could only be of God. In his own human power, his father would surely have chosen one of his favorite sons, but it was clearly God who had chosen Judah to be in the place of the firstborn.

Joseph listened intently now as the words of God flowed through Jacob, and he spoke of Judah as a lion. "You are a lion's cub, O Judah; you return from the prey, my son. Like a lion he crouches and lies down, like a lioness—who dares to rouse him?"

Judah began to tremble, and he fell on his knees beside his father. Jacob placed his hands on Judah's cheeks, and the son looked into his father's eyes. And then Jacob cried out with the voice of a young man, a strong voice that none of his family had heard for many years. "The scepter will not depart from Judah, nor the ruler's staff from between his feet, until Shiloh comes!"

Everyone who heard Jacob's voice knew what this meant. Shiloh had long been Jacob's name for the One who would come to redeem all the earth, and now he had plainly said that it was through Judah that the stream would flow.

Jacob pulled the gold medallion off from around his neck and thrust it into Judah's hands. Everyone there knew that God had chosen Judah to be the carrier of the seed which would produce the Redeemer!

Startled by these events, Joseph turned and looked directly at Tamar. Her two sons were beside her, and Joseph stared at Perez and Zerah and knew with a thrill of certainty that one of them would be in the line of the Redeemer.

With the giving of the medallion, Jacob seemed to have expended his strength. But after a few moments of rest, he began to speak of his other sons, of Zebulun, of Issachar, of Dan and Gad and Asher and Naphtali, prophesying of their futures as well.

Finally he turned to Joseph and said, "Joseph is a fruitful vine, a fruitful vine near a spring, whose branches climb over a wall. With bitterness archers attacked him; they shot at him with hostility. But his bow remained steady, his strong arms stayed limber, because of the hand of the Mighty One of Jacob, because of the Shepherd, the Rock of Israel, because of your father's God, who helps you, because of the Almighty, who blesses you with blessings of the heavens above, blessings of the deep that lies below, blessings of the breast and womb."

Jacob's final words were to his youngest son, and they too shocked the assembly at what appeared to be a contradiction of the man they knew. "Benjamin is a ravenous wolf; in the morning he devours the prey, in the evening he divides the plunder."

None was more surprised by these words than Benjamin himself, who wondered at his father's terrible words and what they might foretell about his own future.

With those last words, Jacob's voice failed, and he grew silent. He struggled for breath, then whispered in a voice they all had to strain to hear, "I am about to be gathered to my people. Bury me with my fathers in the cave in the field of Ephron the Hittite, the cave in the field of Machpelah, near Mamre in Canaan, which Abraham bought as a burial place. . . ." As soon as he had spoken of his burial, he closed his eyes and took two rapid breaths and lay still.

They all stood looking down on Jacob, the son of Isaac, the grandson of the great Abraham, and each of them felt a terrible sadness and grief that a great man had passed from the earth.

While Joseph wept over his father, the others began slowly to file away from the room. Eventually Joseph rose and went his way as well, leaving only Judah behind with Tamar and her two sons. He came over and stood before the three, putting his hands on the heads of Perez and Zerah.

No one said a word, but Tamar knew that her mission in life had been accomplished. Shiloh, the Redeemer of the world, would come through the blood of her sons!

CHAPTER
38

After their father's death, Joseph and Judah worked together to make the arrangements to transport Jacob's body back to Canaan for burial. First Joseph ordered his embalmers to prepare the body, a process that would take forty days. Had the brothers known the gruesome details of Egyptian embalming methods, they would have been horrified. But Joseph was by now used to them, and he knew it would enable them to transport the body safely on the long journey. During the weeks it took to accomplish the embalming, Joseph grew very close to Judah.

The two men spoke often of the years that had passed in Egypt, and finally Joseph broached the subject of the future. The occasion arose when Judah seemed apologetic for taking authority over Joseph, who, after all, was the mightiest man in Egypt next to Pharaoh himself.

"Brother, you are the firstborn in our father's eyes, not I. Through your blood will come the Redeemer."

Judah had received new strength from his father's blessing. It had infused him with authority, so now he stood straighter and no longer slumped. His voice rang when he gave commands, but now he was troubled. "I am totally unworthy," he murmured.

But Joseph said, "Our God does not make mistakes. You are the one He has chosen. Our father's words made that clear. You are the Lion of Judah, and through your blood flows the stream. One of your sons will be the next to wear the lion medallion, I have no doubt. But which one?"

"I do not know, but God will reveal it to me when it is time."

"Yes, you must pray that God will show you."

———

The funeral procession that made its way from Egypt back to the burial site of Jacob was nothing less than spectacular. It was preceded by a host of soldiers, trumpeters, and drummers. After this came Nubian bowmen. Then there were fan bearers, keepers of the pharaoh's wardrobe, and members of the court.

After them came the coffin of Jacob, shaped like a man and sparkling with gems, with a gold mask and beard on the outside. It was resting in a cart drawn by twelve white oxen.

Joseph, along with his sons, his eleven brothers, and their sons and grandsons—all who bore male names in Israel—followed Jacob's coffin.

As they passed through the countryside, crowds appeared from the towns and settlements along the way to stand and gawk at the long caravan of splendid horses decorated with bright feathers and glittering weapons. When they reached their own country, Joseph's eyes grew dim with tears as he relived scenes of his childhood.

"This brings back old memories, doesn't it, brother?" Benjamin said quietly.

"Yes. Time is like a river, and much has flowed since that day."

"It was the saddest day of my life when they told me you were dead."

"But now it is all right. God has worked in all of us."

The two stood outside the cave where the bodies of Abraham, Isaac, and now their father, Jacob, were buried. They had a long journey back to Egypt but would rest a few days before they began.

―――――――

Before their departure the next day, Joseph was sitting enjoying a spot of shade one afternoon when three of his brothers—Simeon, Levi, and Dan—came to him. He rose to greet them and said, "Are you ready for the journey tomorrow?"

Dan glanced at his brothers, and Joseph saw fear on their faces. Suddenly the three bowed down before him, and Joseph was astonished. "What is this, my brothers! Do not kneel to me. Rise."

But they did not rise. They said, "Forgive us for our terrible sins against you, Joseph. We grieve over what we did so many years ago."

Joseph stood there amazed. He had thought the matter was settled. He immediately pulled them up to their feet, one at a time, then embraced them and said, "Do not be afraid. Am I in the place of God? You intended to harm me, but God intended it for good to accomplish what is now being done, the saving of many lives. So then, don't be afraid. I will provide for you and your children."

Then Joseph called all of his brothers together and once again spoke warmly of his love, encouraging them all to put away the things of the past that troubled them.

After a time the brothers were consoled and went their way, while Benjamin and Judah remained with Joseph. He looked at the two and said, "I hope they can forget. It is not good for men to remember the past in such a way."

Judah put his hand on Joseph's shoulder. "You indeed are a fruitful vine, just as our father said of you."

"And you are truly the Lion of Judah."

Benjamin watched his two brothers silently, knowing that he was standing in the presence of great men.

Asenath had not been able to accompany her husband on the funeral procession to Canaan, but as soon as Joseph was back, she embraced him and pampered him outrageously. For two days she fed him every good dish she could concoct and was constantly seeking to find something to please him.

Finally, late one evening, they were walking in the garden. Overhead the stars were glittering in all their glory, and Joseph was quiet, as he had been all evening.

Asenath put her hand on his arm, and when he turned around, she put her arms behind his neck and studied his face. A question had been on her mind ever since Jacob's death, and now she took courage and spoke. "Husband, may I ask you a question?"

"You always do." Joseph smiled, leaned down, and kissed her. "What's your question?"

"Are you disappointed that it was Judah and not you who was chosen by your father to take the place of the firstborn?"

"It was not Jacob who chose Judah. It was the Lord—and it is well."

"Then you are not troubled by it?"

"I rejoice that God is bringing One to the world called Shiloh. That may not be the name men will know him by, but he will come one day, and when he does, the whole world will be changed."

"You have told me about the medallion that Jacob passed on to Judah—with the lion on one side and a lamb on the other. What does it all mean?"

"I am not sure," Joseph said quietly. "It somehow speaks of the Redeemer to come, but how can a man be like a lion and a lamb both? It is a great mystery that one could be as strong as the king of beasts and yet gentle as a lamb. But Shiloh will be like that when he comes."

"And you truly don't mind that you are not the chosen one?"

"No, I do not mind," Joseph said, smiling. "Judah can never have the one thing I have, even though he has received the blessing."

"And what is that, my husband?"

"He can never have the fairest wife in all the world."

Asenath smiled and put her head on his chest. The silver moonlight flooded them as they held each other, both thinking of the One who would come through Judah to redeem the earth.

Then looking up at the stars that dotted the heavens in a fiery display, Joseph's voice rang out clearly into the night: "O Creator of the Universe, who made all things . . . watch over us until Shiloh comes!"

A GRAND SERIES
OF FAITH AND HISTORY!

Epic in scope, Gilbert Morris's HOUSE OF WINSLOW series is nothing less than the compelling story of the forces and people that shaped American history. Each book has a plot that takes you away to another time with characters whose lives are examples of heroism, courage, faith, and love.

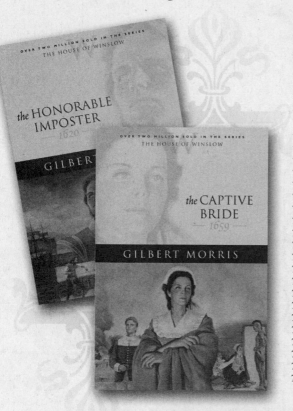

*"It's hard to sustain momentum in a series, but...
Gilbert Morris delivers everything his fans have come to expect:
romance, mystery, exotic locations, and spiritual epiphanies,
all infused with strong moral messages."*
—AMAZON.COM

◆ BETHANYHOUSE

LYNN AUSTIN

GODS & KINGS

A NOVEL

From the
Three-time Winner
of the
CHRISTY AWARD
for Historical Fiction

BIBLICAL DRAMA,
Historical Insight, Powerful Faith!

Acclaimed historical novelist Lynn Austin offers
riveting biblical fiction with this retelling of the life
of King Hezekiah. In her CHRONICLES OF THE KINGS
series, Austin wraps historical realism, grand drama,
and faith into a memorable story readers will love.

BETHANY HOUSE